WARPHAN

Aunt Carol,
I hope you enjoy the story.

WARPHAN

The Anavarza Archive
Book One

JD MULCEY

Artwork by Gonzalo Kenny

A Tome
forged
in the

Fayden Fantasy Works

© 2015 JD Mulcey

All rights reserved.

This is a work of fiction. Names, characters, magical creatures, places, events and incidents are the products of the author's overactive imagination. Any resemblance to actual persons; living, dead, or undead; or actual events is purely coincidental.

Forged in the
Fayden Fantasy Works,
an imprint of Compass Hill Press

ISBN 978-1-944114-00-8

Artwork by Gonzalo Kenny
Anavara Emblem by Martin Buchan
Author photo by C. Rodriguez

Acknowledgements

The author wishes to thank the people who made this book possible and contributed to the final product. The workshopers on scrib, but especially Stella and John, thank you for pointing out that new chapter needed to be nuked. Jean for the excellent critique that led to me having to write six new chapters, which of course, made the whole story better by a large margin. Gonzalo for the awesome artwork, I have it on my phone too. Floyd Largent for wirebrushing the prose until they cried uncle and then polishing them until they sang. Edith Jones for picking through the words and finding all those little errors. And of course my family who endured countless hours of me sitting before the computer screens trying to make this whole thing a reality.

- For Clare & Lia

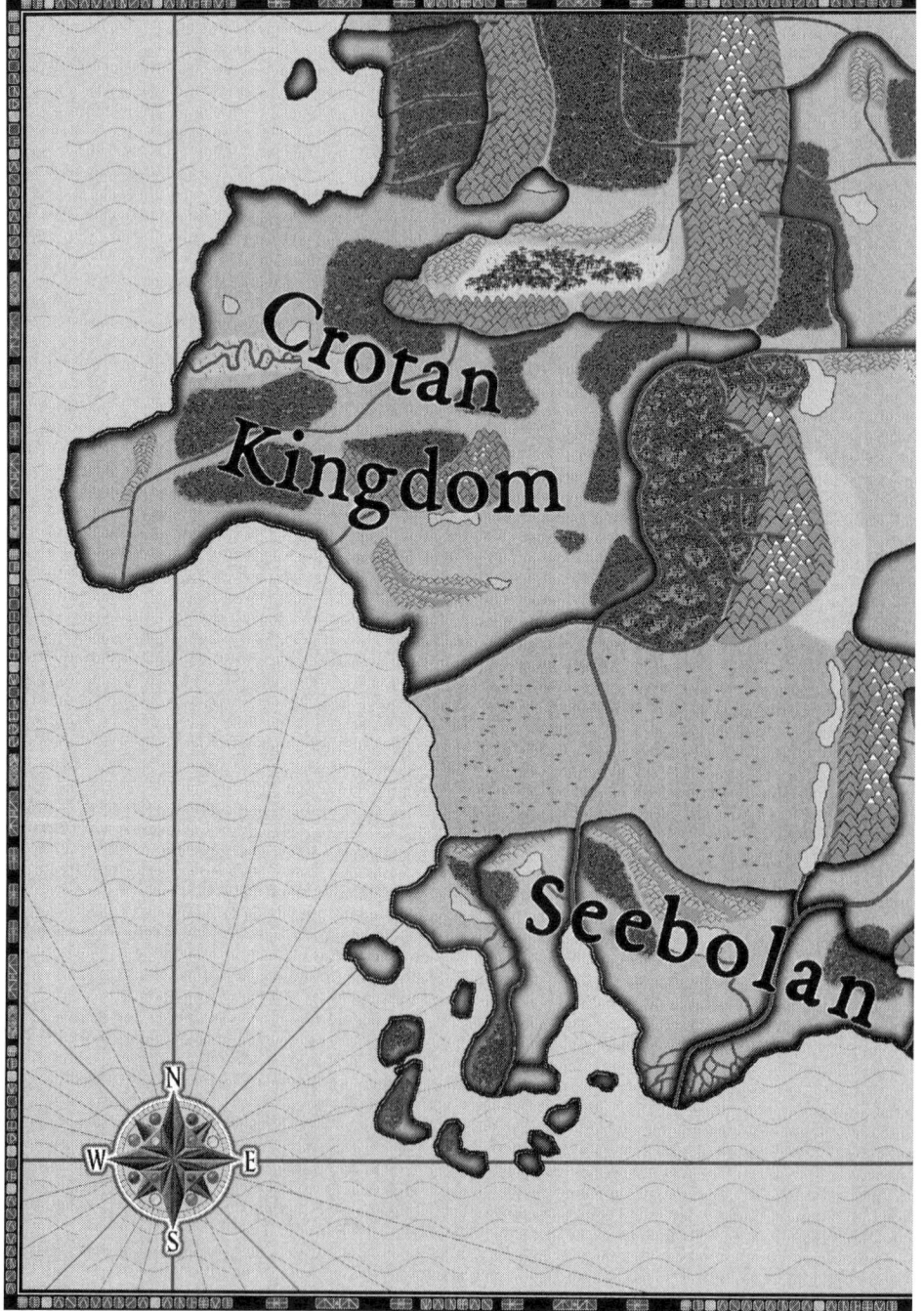

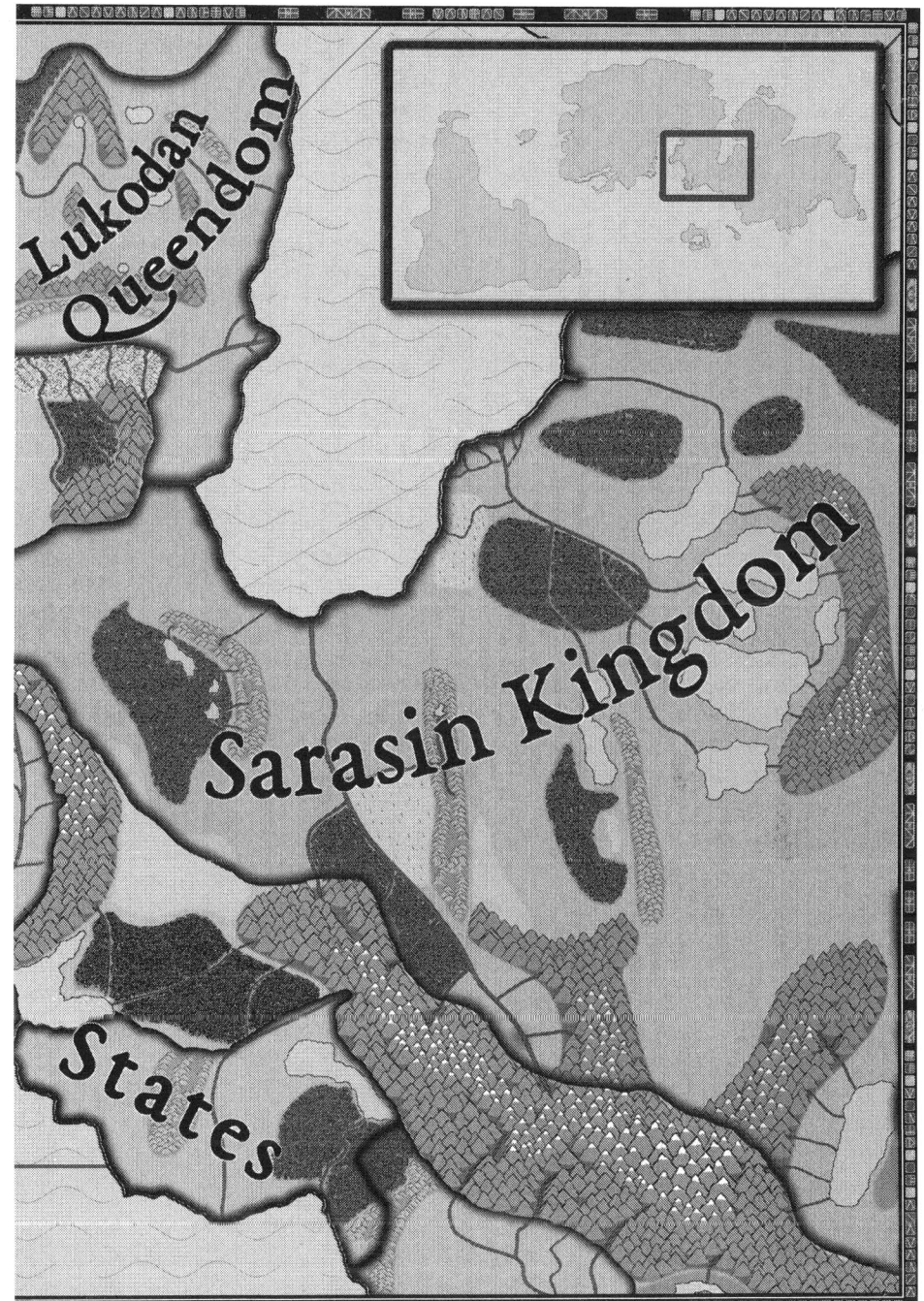

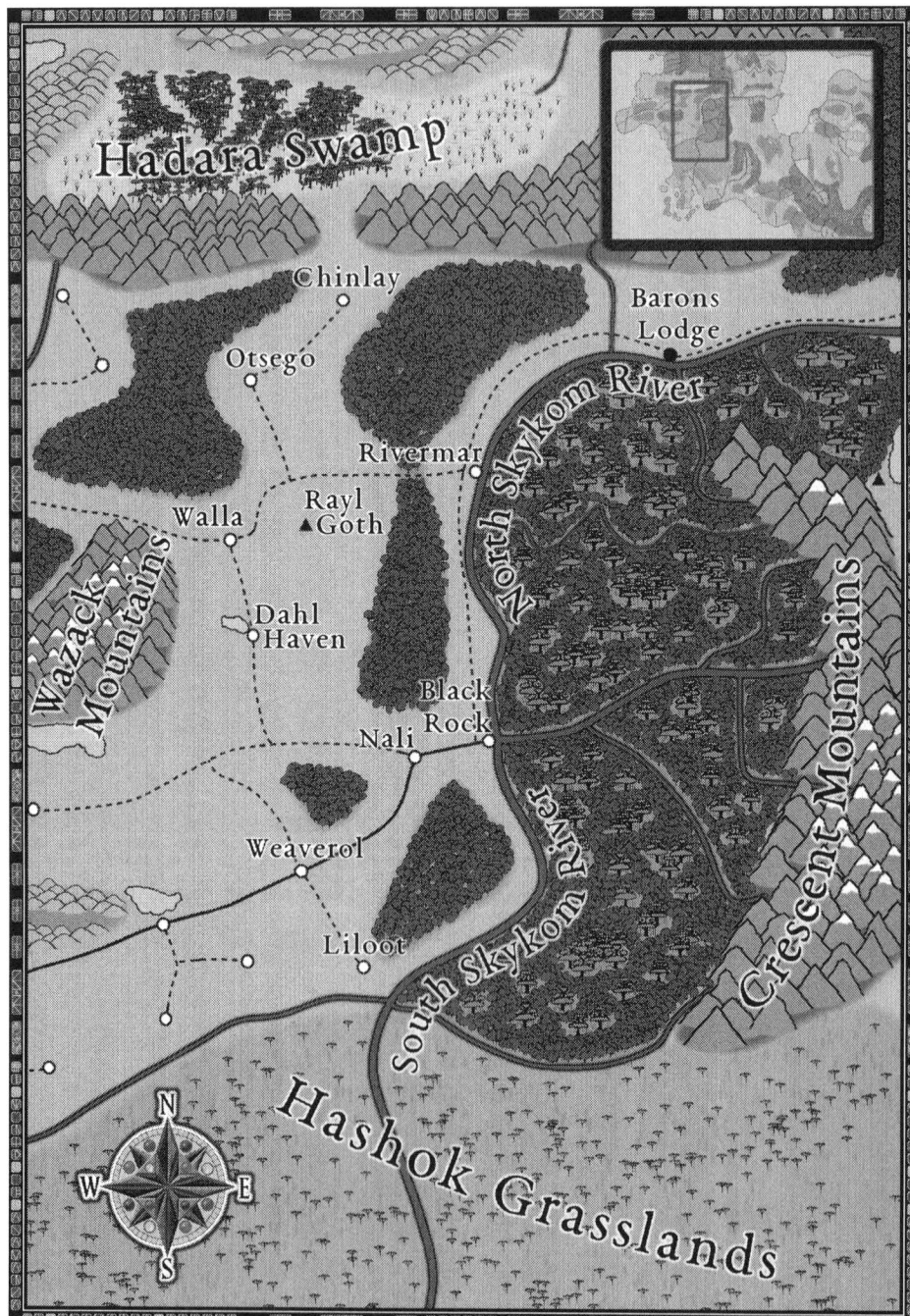

WARPHAN

Chapter One

This little plant was going to change Cayne's life forever.

It stood knee-high, with several tender branches reaching out from a delicate central stalk. He looked at the ghostly white leaves and shuddered, a tingling sensation spreading across his body, as if the plant were calling to him on a primal level.

He'd heard stories of plants like this, but never thought he would actually see one. The midday sun baked his exposed arms, but the sweat in his palms wasn't from the heat. This plant could be the biggest thing that had ever happened to the village of Dahl Haven.

Cayne heard a faint song at the very edge of audibility, like a forest of crystals chiming together in harmony. The tone shifted abruptly, becoming harsher, provoking a sense of alarm in him. He stood up and swiveled. He saw nothing but wheat, still green in the early summer sun, spreading out to the horizon. A gentle breeze swirled and curled the stalks, bringing the scent of dry dirt and green growth to his nose. He let the warm rush of air wash across his face for a moment before dropping back down to stare at the plant.

Cayne had brutish-looking hands, but they were far more graceful than most assumed. He loved the land, and often cradled struggling seedlings as he stripped the weeds away from them. Though he knew many people thought of him as a lumbering oaf, it never bothered him.

Passing a hand behind a shimmering pale leaf, he saw the fuzzy outline of his fingers right through it. Normal plants caught the sun in their green leaves, but the angelia plant didn't need sunlight to grow: it soaked up the White magic flow instead. Cayne didn't know of an angelia plant being born in his lifetime, and he was certain something like that would have been the talk of Dahl Haven for years. He tried to remember more about the plant, but the stories were too distant. In school, there had been lessons about the magic flows, but that was long ago; and even when he attended, he'd paid scant attention to the subject. What would a farmer need to know about magic? His logic had seemed sound at the time, but now he wished he'd listened a little more. No matter; his father would know more about it. He stroked the silky leaves, glad to hear the angelia's singing turn to a purr.

Its song stopped in mid-stroke, and Cayne got the distinct feeling they weren't alone anymore. He jumped to his feet, and turned to find a figure looming over him. Cayne froze, staring into shimmering eyes framed by a tattered brown hood. The hood cast the old man's face in shadow, except for those sparkling eyes, which shifted colors as he watched.

The lilting voice of the angelia changed again, and Cayne sensed that the plant detested this man.

"My apologies, Cayne," the man said. "I didn't mean to sneak up on you again."

"Again? I don't know you." Cayne stepped away from the man, careful not to trample the angelia. "Who are you?"

"Markas." He removed the hood to reveal a deeply lined face. "You can call me Markas."

Cayne looked away from the man's mesmerizing eyes. Markas' black hair was streaked with gray, and he wore a simple white tunic and leather moccasins. There was a youthfulness about him, but he still would have been the oldest man in Dahl Haven. Though his smile seemed genuine, and Cayne felt an instant affinity for him, the shrieking of the angelia plant kept him on guard.

"I plan to see you again, but I think this is the last time we will speak," Markas said gently.

"We've never talked before," Cayne assured him.

"I'm truly sorry for what will soon come to pass."

"Sir..." Cayne said hesitantly, unsure who this man might be, and how much respect to pay him. "I'm not sure who you think I am, but I've never met you before."

Markas smiled. "You will."

Then he disappeared. Cayne whirled around, looking in every direction, but there was no one in sight. He eyed the angelia plant. *Was he real, or did the plant cause a waking dream?* he wondered. After all, it was magical, and he had no idea what it could do. He needed to find out more about this plant.

He ran home through ripening fields of wheat, then the maize and bean fields. Now seventeen, Cayne had run through these fields every day of his life, and he knew every knoll, hole, and bush. They grew herbs close to the house, and the fragrance always reminded him of home. He smelled lavender, basil, salt weed, and dozens of others. At night, he could find his way home by scent alone. In the colder times, the smell of the fields was what he missed most.

Their home was a modest farmhouse, always a welcome sight after a long day in the fields. His thoughts turned back to the angelia and the riches it would bring. With that much wealth, they could surely fix up the house, and wouldn't need to cut back on meals during the winter. By the time he landed on the front porch, he wore an irrepressible grin. He flew through the front doorway and skidded to a stop. His father sat at the table, flanked by Cayne's two younger brothers.

His brothers never sat at the table like that except to eat or receive a lecture, and there wasn't any food on the table. It was against their nature to sit still, and neither was smiling. His father rarely smiled, but his scowl was unusually distant today. Cayne had seen the look before, but he couldn't remember doing anything bad—not lately, anyway.

"Cayne, where have you been? Sit down."

"Father, I found a—"

"It can wait," his father said. "I wanted you all to hear this together." He waited for Cayne to take a seat, then rubbed his rough hands together and sighed for far longer than was comfortable for anyone. "The king has requested another levy of warriors. One hundred men."

"A hundred men?" his mother said, entering the room. Her voice was sharp and quick. "He's already levied us for two hundred men! There aren't a hundred men left in Dahl Haven."

"No. There are not."

His father looked grimly at each of the boys, and his mother flew into a panic. "No," she said, "they're just boys! It's bad enough I had to send you off to war twice already. I won't send my boys!"

"The king has decreed it, and it must be done. King Alarak's army met the Sarasins east of the Crescent Mountains. He lost, and he needs more men."

"What of the men we already sent?"

"No word of them, but it cannot be good," his father said slowly. "Many died during the rout."

Two hundred men from a small village like Dahl Haven was almost every able-bodied man there was. Cayne had been surprised when they hadn't taken him in the last levy. He was old enough and ready for war; moreover, he had wanted to go.

He looked at his brothers, wondering what they were thinking. Burke was two years younger than Cayne, but nearly as tall. He was always quick to joke, but his face was a weathered rock today. Next to him, Rait—the youngest—was excited, which was typical for him. Rait always talked about leaving home to find his fortune, or for adventure, or to frighten their mother.

His mother glared so intently at his father, Cayne thought she might bore a hole in his face. "There's more, isn't there?"

"A hundred boys need a leader," his father said. "One who has experienced combat."

His mother shook her head. "You too? No, not all of you." She looked at Cayne and then to her husband. "Nate, you're too crippled to go to war."

She'd never called his father a cripple before, and Cayne felt the anger rise up from the older man and ripple across the table. His father stood up painfully. Cayne wanted to help him, as he often did, but he was nailed to his seat.

"I am no cripple!" Nate barked. "I *have* to go. I can't let these boys go off to war with no one to lead them." He didn't yell often, but when he did, no one dared speak until he signaled that his anger had passed. He rubbed his face, and when he spoke next, his words were even and calm again. "The council granted me a request. I go, Cayne stays."

"No! I want to go," Cayne blurted. "If everyone else in the village is going, then I can't be the only one left behind. Everyone else will bring home stories of adventure, and I'll be—"

"Cayne, you're not going. You're too rash. You'd get people killed. Besides, we're not going on some splendid adventure from a story. We're going to war, and some of your friends won't return. Maybe none of us will."

The words hung heavy in the room, drenching them like a cold winter rain. Burke and Rait traded dark glances with each other. Even Rait finally seemed to grasp the situation for what it was. The idea of war had always been exciting to Cayne and his brothers... until today.

Cayne was torn between his own fear of going to war and an even greater fear that his younger brothers would be going, and he wouldn't be able to look out for them. Rait was only thirteen. How could his father take him to war and leave Cayne behind? It made no sense. He'd always looked out for them, and now he'd be helpless to do anything but wait for them to return.

Nate gave Cayne a knowing grimace. "I know, Cayne, I know." He turned to the younger boys. "Burke, Rait, we muster on the village green at dawn, and I have many preparations to make, so I won't see you until then." His father nodded to the room the three boys shared, and they both understood that they were dismissed. Turning to Cayne, he said, "I need you to take me to the meeting hall. Go and prepare the wagon. We'll talk more on the way."

Cayne shuffled outside, staring at the uneven wooden floor as he went. He lingered at the door, hoping to hear what his parents might talk about, but they were waiting for him to leave before speaking.

He shut the door and walked out into the sunshine; the familiar heat felt distant now, like the winter sun that burns without warmth. He walked around the corner of the house, stopping under the open window. "Do something, Nate," his mother pleaded, her voice low but urgent.

"What would you have me do?" Nate asked, resignation in his voice.

"Something more than lead your sons to their deaths." Her voice was forceful now, not quavering at all. "You're going to war for a half-witted king who will lead you to your doom, assuming he can lead anything more than a horse on a circle mill's tether."

Cayne had never heard his mother speak ill of the king. She'd be flogged if anyone heard her.

"You may speak the truth, Silya, but still we must go," Nate said. "What else can we do? The king led his army to defeat, and now we need to defend our lands against the Sarasins."

"I care nothing for that," she said. "We'd be better off if he had died as well."

Cayne swallowed hard. His mother wished the king dead! Those words could end her life if the wrong ears heard them.

"Perhaps so," said Nate. "He certainly deserves it. But the Sarasins march on our lands now, and we must defend them regardless of who is king."

"This is the same king who ordered your death! Have you forgotten? He killed your brothers and your father—and we'd be dead too, if we hadn't come to this village on the edge of nowhere!"

"Is your life so bad, Silya?" Nate asked gently.

Her voice softened. "I love my life here with you and my boys. I don't want it to end with you taking them to die for some stupid quarrel among despots." His mother began to weep. Cayne felt embarrassed for listening to their conversation, and was about to walk away when he heard his name.

"Why Cayne?" Silya asked.

"He is too rash."

"Please don't insult me with that ruse," she said, her tone hardening once again. "You can tell it to the boys, but don't try to pass that story off on me."

Instead of answering, Nate sighed. Cayne knew the sound of his father hoping the topic would go away.

"It won't happen, Nate. It will never be." She paused, but Nate remained silent. "Take Cayne with you, and leave Rait."

"Cayne is the one," Nate said finally. "I've seen the boys in Dahl Haven. They follow him. He has something that makes people want to follow him. He can do it. Rait isn't the same."

"You're not listening," she said. "He can't go back. None of us can."

"There are shieldmen who would still answer our call," Nate said insistently.

"Any shieldmen who were loyal to our name died with your father. They're all gone. The only thing in doubt would be whether the Crotans or our own people would be the first to kill us."

"Cayne will do it," Nate said with certainty.

"You're delusional. Is that why you keep that stupid banner under our bed? Do you really think it will fly again one day?"

"It *will* come to pass," Nate said, though he sounded like he was talking to himself. "Our banner will fly again."

"What are you talking about?" she asked. "Have you gone mad?"

"It was no accident that I missed that murderous meeting all those years ago. I told you I fell from my horse on the way to the meeting, but in truth, it was stolen. I was too embarrassed to tell anyone. The man actually said he was sorry as he rode away."

"Why is that embarrassing? Theft happens. And don't change the subject."

"I would have been at that meeting," he said, ignoring her. "I would have died. I saw that same man again during our flight. He gave me back my horse and told me which route to take."

"What does all this have to do with anything?"

"I saw that same man again just a quarter-moon past. He told me a decision was coming and that if I took Cayne, he would die.

But if I left him behind, then the Falconstorm banner would fly again."

"Who is he, and why would you believe him?"

"I just do."

"Just like that?" she demanded. "You risk your family on the word of a stranger? I think he told you what you wanted to hear."

"He offers hope; and where I sense hope, I will cast my lot."

"You're not taking my boys."

"I wasn't asking for your permission, Silya."

She paused for a few moments. "Don't bring yourself home without those two boys."

A strained silence lingered until Cayne could listen no more. He drifted away from the house and wandered toward the barn, where he prepared the wagon, brought it around, and waited in front of the house.

"Cayne, help me onto the wagon."

His father hobbled out of the house, a clattering sword at his waist. Cayne hadn't seen that old sword in years, not since the time he'd decided to use it to slice ears of maize. His father had not been pleased, and had hidden the sword away.

Cayne felt sadder than ever, thinking on the chances of a cripple in combat. He was the only one of his brothers who remembered his father returning from the last war, ten years ago. He was seven then, but the sight of his father being carried through the front door was branded into his mind. He'd cried at the time, though he hadn't understood why. His father was in pain and his mother was crying, so it felt right. Years passed, and his father didn't get better. When Cayne asked him about it, he'd just say it was the price of war. *What will the price be this time?*

Nate kept a constant scowl on his face as the wagon lumbered down the dirt track. "Cayne, I understand what you're feeling," he said eventually.

Cayne had been gathering his thoughts, but his words spilled out in a flood in response to his father's statement. "I want to go. What will they think of me? I want to be with you and Burke and Rait and everyone else."

Nate nodded. "I'll make sure everyone knows the reasons." He hesitated for a long moment, his mouth open as if the speak further, then finally said: "I chose you to stay here for a reason. You worry me the most." He stopped on the verge of saying more, rubbing his hands. "You're too rash, running into trouble without a thought."

"Father, I can handle myself on the battlefield. I've beaten all the other boys at swords. I'm bigger and stronger than any man in the village."

His father held up a hand. "I don't doubt your strength or your bravery. If anything, you're *too* brave. Last year you jumped into a fight without even knowing what was happening."

"I knew what I was doing. They were picking on Tarken, and there were four of them. You were the one who asked me to look out for him."

"Yes, but at what cost?"

"I made them pay," Cayne said, smiling as he thought of how he'd beaten up the other boys. He looked to his father, but there was no trace of amusement on his face.

"Cayne, you almost killed two of those boys. All because they were saying mean things to Tarken. Do you know what it cost us to settle with their families?"

Cayne looked down to his moccasins. He knew those families were angry with him at the time, but it had all blown over. They got along now.

"Neither one of them was able to help with the harvest. It cost us a quarter of our own harvest. And all I heard from you were complaints about only two meals a day."

"You never told me we had to give away a quarter of our harvest."

"Yes, a quarter to them and another quarter to the king."

"I didn't think that would happen."

"That's my point, Cayne. You never think first. You just do, and then apologize if things go wrong." Nate took a breath and spoke again with a calmer demeanor. "There are no apologies on a battlefield. You're a natural leader, and I don't want the boys in this village following your example and getting themselves killed."

The words stung, but Cayne could offer no defense, not to his father. "I'll do better."

"I've heard that before, and I'll take no chances. Rash boys get beat up. Rash warriors get killed."

"I'll do as I'm told this time."

"Then I'm telling you to stay here."

Cayne fumed, refusing to look at his father. He gave the reins a sharp snap, and the wagon lurched forward. He felt his father's stare, but said nothing, gazing off in the distance. *My fault. I didn't think, and we all suffered.*

"Cayne, you have a big heart and even bigger arms. You would acquit yourself well on the battlefield. I just wish you could think more before you act."

"I can, father," Cayne pledged halfheartedly.

Nate shook his head. "If you believe that, then there may be another issue here. You are who you are. Don't deny it."

Cayne lowered his head. His father had the weight of history behind his words. Cayne was every bit as impulsive as his father claimed, and they both knew it. Cayne wasn't about to admit it though, so he remained silent.

His father picked up his sword and handed it to Cayne. "Take this. I can't use it, and you might need it. In some ways, your task may be more dangerous than ours."

"Why would I need your sword?"

They were nearing the village. His father spread his arms out as if holding up the entire village. "How many able-bodied men remain here? None. The men are gone, and soon even the boys will be gone. Only the women, the sick, and the old will remain."

"And me."

"Yes, and you. These are dangerous times. Brigands roam the land looking for easy prey." He used the sword to point to the houses ahead. "I've talked with Elder Paulos. He was a good swordsman, and will teach you how to use this sword properly. You may need to defend all of Dahl Haven with it."

How can I defend an entire village? His thoughts flashed to the angelia plant, and he wondered if it could somehow change things.

"Father, I found an angelia plant growing in the north tract today."

Cayne's father peered at him, trying to read the truth of it. "I... can't recall a plant like that being found in a hundred years." Nate scratched his cheek. "My grandfather spoke of one being born when he was a boy." He smiled for the first time. "A simpler and happy time. But that story did not end well. Are you sure it was an angelia?"

"It was pure white, I could see right through its leaves... and it sang to me. What else could it be?"

"An angelia plant portends good fortune. Maybe this war will end without further bloodshed."

Cayne was bubbling now, forgetting the former conversation. "Father, it will be worth at least two seasons of crops! I know it will. It's valuable."

Nate's eyes shifted to the sky, and he cupped his chin with his palm. "Yes. Maybe too valuable. Be wary of who you tell."

"I'll tell no one."

Nate's expression soured, and his brows gathered in the center of his forehead. Cayne knew this look well. His father often though out loud. "You couldn't sell such a thing here. You'd have to go to Black Rock to find someone with enough gold to buy it."

Gold? Most things in Dahl Haven were bought with copper or iron, and though Cayne had seen a few silver beads, he'd never seen gold.

"I know you only see riches, but I see danger." Nate slowly shook his head and rubbed the back of his neck. "Black Rock is not like Dahl Haven. Any number of foul merchants there would kill you for the plant as soon as pay you. And you'd have to leave your mother alone." Nate kept shaking his head. "Cayne, I want you to destroy the angelia plant. And do it quickly. They grow fast."

Cayne's mouth dropped open and his breath left him.

"Did you hear me?"

"I don't understand, father."

"I told you that the story I know about the last angelia plant didn't end well for the man who found it. Men came to take it from him." He made a fist and shook it. "He fought them off, but lost two of his sons in the melee. Two sons. A great loss for any father." He looked at Cayne, a flash of pride in his gaze. "He sold it for a great sum. Then he and his whole family were slaughtered in the night, and the gold was never found. The moral of the story—"

"I get the moral," Cayne snapped. He tightened the reins, and the cart slowed down.

"Kings would move whole armies to have that plant. They'd think nothing of slaughtering everyone in Dahl Haven if that's what it took."

"I can handle this," Cayne said. "All I need to do is get it to Black Rock, get the gold, and that will be the end of it."

"No, Cayne, that would be the end of *you*. It would be different if your brothers and I were not departing, though maybe not even then. Perhaps it's hubris to think I could defy the moral of the story any more than you could."

"How can you ask me to kill an angelia plant? It's magical, it's, it's—"

"It's mortally dangerous." Nate raised a silencing hand. "No more of this. Destroy the angelia plant before it destroys you."

Dahl Haven

Rann was the most important person in Dahl Haven, and he had no idea how anyone could think otherwise. As the High Fourpriest, he alone kept this wretched village in the good graces of the gods. He always wore full festival robes, brown flowing cloth adorned with red accents to honor Gol. In other villages, fourpriests reserved these for the festival days, but Rann wore them every day.

He was the keeper of the calendar, telling these people when Dyn's time would bring the winter, and then Gol the spring thaw; when Ahn's time would bring ripening days, and then Gia the harvest. He even tracked the trio of 28-day months leading up to the seven days of festival that marked the changing of the seasons. The denizens of this village would not even know what day it was if not for his efforts. Yes, it amazed even him how he accomplished so much in such squalor.

The summer festival would be upon him in a few more weeks. He was almost ready, lacking only a sack of burlwood power, but that was the most important scent of the festival.

He stood in the center of the fourshrine. The octagonal building was a single room with four great windows and four wide doorways that kept the building from becoming an oven in the summer. It also allowed each of the gods to enter through a doorway unsullied by any of the other gods. In the center of the room was an octagonal pedestal, blackened from countless burnt offerings. Rann had prepared a small stack of wood and charcoal, and all he needed was the burlwood powder.

He strolled out of the shrine and onto the road along the village green. On most days, he thought, placing the shrine next to the market was an affront to the gods; but today it was convenient. He ignored the inconsequential greetings and waves of the locals, making his way directly toward the market. There were more important things than meaningless small talk with the equally meaningless people of Dahl Haven.

Rann walked among the stalls of sweating merchants. They all seemed to sell fish or other foul-smelling goods. He found the dubious trader he was seeking near the western section of the market. He wasn't sure if this was the same trader who had sold him the burlwood powder last year or not. That powder had been low quality, and he intended to get a better product this year.

"My dear merchant, I require your best burlwood powder," Rann said, sharing his best smile to mask his contempt for this thief. *It's what these people are. Buy here, sell there, and take money for nothing.* There were three guards behind the merchant. They knelt over a set of dice, not interested in the affairs of their employer.

"Of course, my good fourpriest, I have one small sack of burlwood left."

"High Fourpriest," Rann corrected him, ignoring the fact that he was the only fourpriest in this little village. He flourished his long robe for good measure.

"Of course, *High* Fourpriest." The merchant searched an open trunk and produced a paltry sack.

Rann graciously ignored the way the man said 'High' and focused on the sack. It was too small. That much powder would barely last three days. "Is that all you have?"

"You're lucky I have this much. There's war in the Seebolan States."

"There's always war there," Rann scoffed.

"Yes, but this year one of the states at war is the sole producer of burlwood."

Rann sensed what the merchant-thief would say next. "How much for this meager sack of burlwood powder?"

"Three gold beads."

"Three golds! I paid six silvers last year for twice as much."

"That was last year, friend. This year, supplies are limited. It cost me more than six silvers to buy this," he said, putting the sack back down in the trunk. "You wouldn't want me to lose money, would you?"

Rann cared nothing for the toils of this thief. *He should offer it for free.* It was for an offering to the gods, and three golds was insulting. Rann turned and stormed away.

He still needed that powder, though. Rann collected tithes from the people, but that money not only paid for the offerings to the gods, it was also his only source of income. If he had to pay three golds, then it would come from his own cache of beads, and that was just another insult.

He shoved his way through the market crowd and back to the main street. His eyes focused on two boys playing on the green, and an idea formed in his mind. That merchant was trying to swindle him, so he would return the favor.

"Bale, Boon, come over here," he called. They were twins, and always in trouble. Without fail, one of them would get into some mischief and then claim it was the other. No one could tell them apart, so they often got away with such delinquencies.

The boys walked reluctantly to Rann. They looked like they would rather be talking to a raging tankadon.

"I need you two boys to perform a service for your gods." He explained their task three times to make sure they understood, gave them a copper bead, and then sent them on their way. He grinned at his resourcefulness, just another of his talents. He returned to the shrine and waited. It was so simple. One of them would distract the merchant, while the other would grab the burlwood powder.

He heard a commotion and walked to the green, his smile turning to a frown. That blasted merchant was at the center of a crowd, and he was holding Bale and Boon by their arms. Rann felt sweat break out along his spine. He rushed over to hear what the merchant was yelling.

"These boys tried to rob me," the merchant shouted to the crowd.

Elder Paulos made his way through the crowd and to the merchant. He was one of the council that managed the affairs of Dahl Haven.

"What's the matter here?" Paulos asked.

The merchant shoved the two boys forward, then motioned for two of his guards to take the boys. "These two pilferers tried to steal a sack of very valuable merchandise. I demand their hands."

Rann swallowed hard. His plan was sound, but these stupid boys could not accomplish even the most basic task. Still, he would be the one to pay the price. Clearly, they'd not spoken yet of his involvement in this matter, but they would certainly speak if threatened by a behanding.

"Wait," cried one of the two boys; he wasn't sure which one.

"What is this business?" Rann shouted, forcing himself to the center of the crowd. "My good merchant, I'm sure we can reach an accommodation. These are mere boys and I'm sure this is all a misunderstanding."

"They tried to steal from me and I want their hands. They tried to steal some—"

"Yes, I'm sure your goods are valuable," Rann interjected. "I will purchase this property on their behalf. Will that appease you?"

The merchant twisted his head from side to side, pondering excessively. "That will be acceptable."

"Good," Rann said, reaching grudgingly for the belt under his robes.

"That will be six gold beads," the merchant said with an easy smile. The crowd gasped.

Rann squeezed the gold beads in his hand so hard they almost bent. He wanted to scream. This thief was robbing him in full view of the entire village.

"I will tell you what, my good High Fourpriest," the merchant bellowed, like an actor addressing his audience. "Since you are in such a benevolent mood, I will accept the sum of only five golds."

The crowd murmured approval of the merchant's apparent generosity. Rann gritted his teeth, and counted out five golds. *These dolts are thanking him for robbing me.*

The merchant hefted the beads and then signaled to his guards to let the boys go. Bale and Boon tore away, vanishing into the crowd. The merchant laughed and tossed the sack of burlwood powder to Rann.

Rann turned his back on the crowd and walked back to the shrine. He was eager to put the whole matter behind him and get on with the more serious matters of the festival. His first request of the gods would be for this merchant-thief to die a horrible death. The gods would surely respond with great vengeance against someone who had so brazenly wronged their humble servant.

Chapter Two

Cayne drove the wagon in silence, refusing to even glance at his father. The road became hard-packed and the houses more frequent. He drove into Dahl Haven at least twice a week. It was familiar and unchanging, and to his mind, both were good things. Compared to the farm, he liked the smells in the village. More bread and less dung.

He saw Tarken from a good distance. He lived at the north end with his mother, and watched every cart that came that way. Cayne knew Tarken would be stalking him, and it was only a matter of time before he presented himself.

Cayne steered the wagon toward the town meeting hall, then helped his father down. When he tried to help him up the steps, his father put a hand on Cayne's shoulder and shook his head. "I can make it from here." Nate ascended one step and turned back to Cayne. "Promise me you'll take care of your mother while I'm gone, son. And I forgot; she asked me to have you get some eels. I think she wants to prepare a special dinner tonight."

"I'll get them for her. And I'll keep her safe and even try to watch over Dahl Haven." He tried to smile, but was sure he failed.

"And destroy that plant," Nate said firmly, before he continued into the hall and shut the door.

Cayne tied the horse to a post, reflecting on his promises. He'd promised to watch over his mother and the farm, but he hadn't actually promised to destroy the angelia plant. His father didn't understand, couldn't understand. He didn't see it. Destroying the plant, killing it, would be murder, not like pulling up a stalk of maize.

Covered in grass and devoid of trees or bushes, the village green was the main gathering spot for all of Dahl Haven. This was where they held festivals, and where Cayne and his friends strolled along with everyone else in the village. There weren't many other options. Few people strolled on the green today. He spied Tarken in the distance, but he was watching Cayne, making no move to greet him. That meant someone was around that Tarken didn't like.

Cayne swiveled to find Gliff marching right toward him. Gliff was the local rain-sayer. If not for his talent for predicting the weather, the village would have driven him away. The man could read the winds and sniff out the faintest scent of a wolf in the area, but he was also the oddest man in town, generally making no sense at all. Most disturbing of all, he was a Fayden Sight, and everyone knew it. Cayne had heard Fourpriest Rann speak out many times against the faydens, saying they mocked the gods by their very existence. He often tried to get the council to lash and banish Gliff, but poor farmers had to take whatever meager help came their way.

Gliff veered sharply and walked right past Cayne. "Young Cayne," he said, after he'd already passed. He twisted his head back to Cayne. Gliff wore a dirty tunic, and his shaved head contrasted with his mangy beard.

"Good day to you, Gliff." Cayne grew agitated just looking at him. Gliff moved in jerky spasms that were too frequent for Cayne's liking.

"There is something amiss. I can feel it." Gliff bent down and grabbed a handful of grass. "The green is bleeding. Yes, blood on the green." As usual, Gliff spoke in riddles.

Cayne shivered, not so much because of Gliff's words, but because of his tone. He spoke with certainty and fear. *What could scare a fayden who can foresee the future?*

Gliff stiffened, his movements calm now and his gaze distant. He looked right through Cayne. "It's too much, young Cayne. The weight of the suffering squeezes me. I'm certain of what will be."

"What suffering?" Cayne asked. Instead of answering, Gliff grabbed his hand. Cayne tried to pull his hand back, but the odd man's grip was surprisingly strong.

Gliff's eyes turned to Cayne. They widened, like he was reading Cayne. "There will be blood on your hands, young Cayne. Much blood on your hands." More shivers ran up and down Cayne's body.

"What did you mean by 'blood on the green'? Whose blood?"

"It doesn't work that way, young Cayne."

"Whose blood?"

"I see blood and feel sorrow. So much sorrow."

Cayne wrenched his hand free. "You should stick to guessing the weather."

Gliff's face flashed him a questioning look, and then he smiled as though he remembered nothing he had said. "Rainy—well, misting, but not today, tomorrow." He turned and hurried away, shouting, "Good day, young Cayne."

Cayne stared after the seer. *Blood on my hands? Blood on the green?* He was the only one not going to war. He was the least likely man in town to have blood on his hands, unless his father was right about brigands. *Whose blood? My blood?*

Gliff was a freak, and he was an outcast, but he was seldom wrong. Cayne smiled. *Father will take me with him.* That must be what it meant.

Tarken Ware sped at Cayne, stopping right before colliding with him. Tarken was more or less attached to Cayne whenever he was in Dahl Haven, but truth be told, Cayne enjoyed having a sidekick. Tarken was a head shorter than Cayne, more prone to letters than swords, and knew every moccasin in Dahl Haven, as he spent most of his time staring at them instead of their occupants. They were opposites, but Tarken was drawn to Cayne; or at least, that's how Cayne thought of it. Today, Cayne was the one who wanted to see Tarken. If anyone would know something about the angelia plant, Tarken would.

"I saw you coming in with your father," Tarken said. "What did Gliff want? You were talking to him, and I didn't want to intrude."

"Sure." Cayne understood what he meant. The truth was that Tarken feared Gliff, but then he was a fayden, so any gods-fearing person would be afraid of him.

"He said..." Cayne crooked his head. "It made little sense."

Tarken shrugged his shoulders and rubbed his hands. "Can you believe it, Cayne? We're all going off on a marvelous expedition! It'll be like a big, long-ranging adventure. We'll hunt and make camps and sleep under the stars."

"Tarken, you hate hunting."

Tarken put on a big smile. "I didn't mean *I* would be hunting. You can hunt, and I'll prepare the meals."

"I'm not going with you," Cayne said, looking away from Tarken. "My father is leading the group, and he's making me stay behind."

Tarken's mouth gaped; he was clearly at a loss for words, which was unusual for him. Cayne saw his thoughts turn inward and waited for something to plop out of his mouth. Tarken had good insights, but today he was silent, so Cayne moved the conversation to the topic he wanted to discuss. "What can you tell me about angelia plants?"

The turnaround in Tarken was instant, a smile spilling across his face. Tarken loved nothing more than giving lectures on almost any topic. Cayne prepared to receive an onslaught of information, though this time he was actually interested to hear it... well, some of it, at least. Tarken could talk.

"Right, angelia plants," Tarken said, rubbing his hands together. "The angelia plant is exceedingly rare and valuable. It's one of the many varieties of flora and fauna that can become sensitive to the magic flows, as you know."

"How valuable?" Cayne asked.

Tarken rubbed his chin for a moment. "I'm not sure. The fruit is valued for its medicinal properties, the leaves can soothe almost any ailment, and even the root is sought after, though I can't quite recall its exact purpose at this very moment."

"What about the White magic flow?" Cayne walked off the green, and Tarken followed him without asking where they were going.

"Yes, well, as you know, many things are sensitive to the four flows, and depending on the particular magic flow, the plant or animal will develop in different ways. The angelia plant was named after the Pure Ones known as the Anaga, as you know."

Tarken always seemed to think everyone else knew as much as he did, finishing most of his sentences with 'as you know.' Cayne seldom knew what Tarken was saying, and he'd come to expect the words. "That much I got from school," he responded. "How long before it bears fruit?" Cayne turned onto a narrow road leading out of town.

"I recall one book mentioning the angelia, but it talked about its uses, not its life cycle." Tarken put his fingers to his temple. "It was a book about merchants in the far north that traded with the Tainted Ones." Tarken's mother taught all the school classes and borrowed books from Black Rock. Tarken had read every one at least once. "It wasn't a long passage, sorry."

"That's all right," Cayne said. Tarken was his best chance for finding out more about it. It would have to be enough.

"Where are we going?" Tarken asked, a hint of concern in his voice.

"I need to pick up some eels," Cayne said as casually as he could.

"Right, got to go. I have a book to read." He tried to stop and turn around, but Cayne grabbed his shoulder.

"You're coming with me, friend."

Vale Maagen kept a large pool of water near the shore of Lake Haven. It teemed with eels, some wild from the lake and others raised from hatchlings. Nate and Vale were like brothers. They had grown up together in the north, moved here together, and even gone to war together. They'd been passed over during the last levy of troops, the town council deeming them too injured to be of much use in combat. How desperate had the war become that they would call on his father now?

Cayne hoped to see Vale or his wife tending the eels; unfortunately, he recognized the slim figure of their daughter. Lyssa Maagen turned to him, a hard look of distaste on her face, as usual. She had her dark hair pulled back so tight it looked like she was wearing a helmet. It stretched her face, like a doll overstuffed with wool, and made her sharp features even sharper.

"I understand you're the only coward not answering the king's call," Lyssa said, satisfaction in her voice.

The words stung, but Cayne put on a fake smile. "My father ordered me to stay here and protect the village."

Lyssa screwed her face up and, in between laughs, she said, "You, protect Dahl Haven? From what? A roving band of rabbits?"

Cayne hated talking to Lyssa now. They always argued and he always lost. It hadn't been like that before. Now it was unavoidable. Lyssa was a tall girl, normally with long braids, and Cayne called them eels when she wasn't within earshot. She was somewhat pretty, and he had liked her before, but over the past year her acrimony for him had burned away anything but contempt.

"I need some eels. Three will do."

Lyssa gave him a cold, hard stare and mused, "Maybe we'll be attacked by ants and you can stomp them. The first thief that comes this way will most likely run you through with his sword." A smile formed in her eyes and slowly traveled to her lips.

She'd like me out of the way. He could do nothing to her, and arguing with her was frustrating. He wanted to smack her in the face.

"Hello in there?" said Lyssa, getting annoyed with Cayne's disengagement. "A defender of the village needs to be a little more alert. It's no wonder you're not going with everyone else. The battle would be over before you realized it was happening." She packed in as much mocking as she could muster, but Cayne knew better than to engage her.

"You hate me, but I'll protect you the same as everyone else."

"No thanks," said Lyssa, not missing a beat. "I think I'd rather die than be in debt to you." She put a finger to her lips. "On second thought, go right ahead. You'll most likely die in the process, and that would be lovely."

"Can I just have the eels?" Cayne looked over to Tarken. He had backed away from the conversation, and was doing his best to stay out of Lyssa's peripheral vision. Cayne focused back on Lyssa, thinking perhaps just a small shake, instead of a slap, would do her some good, but he knew how it would end. She'd tell her father, who'd tell his father, and then Cayne would get the real beating. It might be worth it, though.

Lyssa waited for a reaction, but Cayne kept his face expressionless. She grabbed a wooden pole with a net on the end. She dredged the pond, her net coming up with a few slithering eels. With no hesitation, she snatched one by the tail and slung it across a boulder. She took a small club leaning against the rock and smashed the eel in the head, all the while looking at Cayne. She killed two more and then handed him the limp bodies. Vale never charged them for the eels.

"Well, such a wonderful conversationalist you are, as usual." She turned and walked away with a snort.

"And such a bitter hag you are... as usual," Cayne muttered. He spun around and caught up to Tarken, who was already back on the road.

Tarken turned back to Cayne. "She abhors you."

Cayne didn't know what that word meant, and he didn't want to ask. Just being around Tarken had grown his vocabulary with a harvest of words, but Tarken always managed to pull out a new one.

Tarken gave up on waiting for the question and looked up with a thoughtful gaze. "Mother says girls sometimes act like that when they really like you."

"No, she hates me," Cayne muttered with a sigh, "but it's not my fault. It wasn't my idea."

Tarken shook his head. "I can't believe you have to marry her."

Interlude

Walla

Shari slipped into the fourshrine and headed directly for an altar covered with candles. She didn't notice the other people in the corner until she was placing her candle among the rest.

Fourpriest Gasho whispered to a familiar woman: her mother. *What is she doing here?* Shari couldn't hear any of what they said, but they hadn't seen her. Her hands shook as she tried to light her candle from the flame of a burning wick. It was no use. She abandoned the attempt and dropped the unlit candle, then tiptoed back the way she had come, not breathing until she was outside. If her mother saw her offering a candle to the gods, she would ask why, and Shari hadn't thought to invent an excuse. She banished the idea of lighting a candle, though she was going to need the gods' good favor for what she was about to do.

She strolled to the north end of Walla. The village was the hub of social and business activity for the many farms surrounding it, but Shari's family lived in the village itself. Her mother mended clothes and her father was a prospector who used Walla as a base. He usually ranged out into the Wazack Mountains, but sometimes he went into the vast forest to the north. Shari had thought prospecting was full of adventure until she went with him on one of his trips. She'd spent days riding in his cart, and still more days trudging up and down the peaks and valleys. She liked the forest even less. Though Walla was nestled among a small forest on the west side, most of the surrounding area was open plains. The northern forest felt suffocating, with little visibility, and the sense that the trees stretched on forever.

She kept her gait casual, waving to the friendly faces. Three big oak trees surrounded the hut on the extreme north end of Walla. She eyed the home as she passed it four times. Each time she felt ready to approach it, she'd spot a familiar face nearby and veer off. Finally, on the fifth pass, there was a clear path to the hut, and she didn't see anyone near her. She sped up and practically ran to the door. Rapping furiously, she looked over her shoulder to see if anyone had seen her. The door opened, and her knocking fist hit nothing but air.

Without waiting for an invitation, Shari charged inside. Meda's home was modest by village standards. A simple bed of straw and furs was tucked in the corner, away from the windows. Other than a few cabinets, the low table was the only furniture.

"What are you wanting, Shari?" Meda asked.

"My fortunes."

"Ah, yes," Meda said with a knowing smile. She shut the door and motioned to the table. Meda moved as if she was older than her thirty-something years. She sat cross-legged on the dirt floor, which was completely inappropriate given the shortness of her dress. Shari was mindful of her own dress. Her skirt fell to her knees and was adorned with frills and beads most of the way down her calves. She sat on her heels, knees together.

"Before we are starting, you are knowing the cost?" Meda asked.

Shari paused to make sure she understood what the seer had said. Meda was a Fayden Sight, a heretic with the ability to see the future. Something about that ability made her speak without a sense of time or tense, often making her hard to understand.

"I have beads." Shari reached inside the top of her blouse and put a string of metal beads on the table. She hoped it was enough. It was hard to find out how much Meda charged for her services without being able to ask anyone. All faydens were heretics, and though Walla tolerated some like Meda, no one wanted to be seen associating with them. Consequently, few admitted using her foretelling services. Shari had to guess at the cost based on rumors.

Meda perused the beads. She stuck out her hand and passed it back and forth over them, but didn't touch them. Satisfied, she leaned back and nodded. "This is sufficient." She looked Shari in the eyes and asked, "What are you knowing?"

Shari wasn't sure how many things she could ask, so she started with the most important. "My mother has been trying to promise me in marriage, but my father won't allow it. Eventually I will marry, though. Who will it be?"

In a small village like Walla, Shari knew every marrying-age boy. She had her preferences among them, but most had already been promised. Marriages happened at the summer solstice festival, and again this year she would not be a part of the ceremonies—though it was possible her mother might make an arrangement yet, since her father was off in the king's army. If she did, Shari wouldn't want to be around when that argument happened between her parents.

Meda grunted as though she'd expected Shari's request. Of course, she was a seer, so maybe she had. "A moment," the seer said, raising a hand. She closed her eyes for a few moments, then scowled. She held out her hand, palm up on the table. "Hand."

Shari put her hand on top of Meda's. Shari felt nothing unusual, but the seer mumbled to herself. She opened her eyes and pulled her arms together, crossing them in a tight motion. "New boys in your future."

Shari pulled in a sharp breath. No one new ever came to Walla. Travelers passed through and merchants stopped for a time to sell or buy, but no one stayed. Did that mean *she* would be leaving? The thought thrilled and frightened her. She leaned in to hear more.

"A small group of them. And danger is abounding. You are leaving Walla, or you are dying." Meda spoke the ominous words as though she were forecasting rain for tomorrow. "Well, not dying, but perhaps worse."

Worse? Panic filled Shari's chest as she tried to breath. She'd only wanted to know whom she'd marry. Now there were strangers and danger. *Why did I ever come here and ask her anything?* A fleeting urge to run gave way to curiosity. "You said I'm leaving. Am I leaving with them?"

"With who? Oh, the boys." The seer put her finger to her lips. "Yes and no."

"Yes and no? Can you explain that?"

"Yes, and no."

Shari wasn't sure if Meda was repeating herself or actually answering her question. A wave of questions washed into her mouth. "When will these boys come to Walla? Who are they? And where am I going?"

Meda considered the questions, crooking her head to one side. Her eyes stared past Shari. She started to mumble again.

"Only seeing boys, nothing else." She crinkled and flared her nose as if she was sniffing something. "The place is a farming village."

"Walla is a farming village," Shari pointed out.

"No, not Walla. Not enough trees." Meda gave her an annoyed glance, as though she'd seen a vision of the place too and was asking an obvious question.

Frustrated, Shari asked, "When? When will these things happen?"

Meda looked up to her thatched roof for several moments before answering. "Soon."

Shari bit back a groan, but she was reaching the limits of her patience. If she didn't find out more, she'd be living in fear of her life indefinitely.

"When is soon? A week? A month?"

Meda stared at her intently and said, "Don't fear the wolf."

"What wolf?" She asked, her mind spinning at the new revelation.

The seer flashed a queer look at her and shrugged. "I am not knowing. A wolf. Nothing more."

Shari felt tears in her eyes, and her fists were so tightly balled her fingernails were digging into her palms. She stood up, leaving the beads on the table. "Thank you for your time."

"Take your beads, Shari." Meda smiled at her like nothing had happened. "You're a nice girl and I don't think you heard what you wanted to hear."

"No, I didn't." She jerked the string of beads from the table. She took a breath and settled herself. "What you saw, will it come true?"

Meda frowned and said, "I'm not every time seeing what is happening and I am not always understanding what I'm seeing." She stood up and walked to Shari, giving her a hug that surprised them both. She patted her on the back and pushed her toward the door. "You are being safest if you are being who you are."

She could only chuckle at the advice. It made no sense at all.

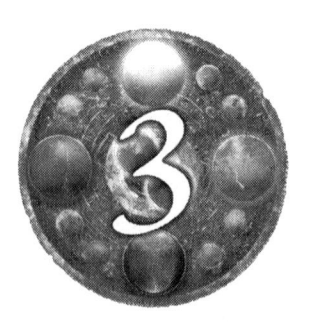

Chapter Three

Faylin stepped on the dirt road, eager to know what the town blacksmith wanted from her. The streets of Walla were soggy from a recent rain, and her moccasins left light footprints as she walked. She took a short cut behind the town hall and emerged on the main road across from the blacksmith.

Master Ganji was outside, wearing his long leather apron. Other than a scruff of hair around the sides of his head, he was bald, and his face bore the marks of long years toiling at his forge. He gave her a smile and waited for her. "Faylin, you look well today."

"Master Ganji, I came as soon as I heard you needed me."

"I haven't forged iron in years, but with my sons and grandsons away with the king, the town elders asked me to pick up the hammer." He motioned to his forge. "As you can see, my forge is cold. I need charcoal."

Faylin's father was the town charcoaler, but he was with the king's army too. The king's decree for warriors had taken every man who could wield a sword.

"I'm afraid we've sold all of it," Faylin said with a shrug.

The Ganji frowned thoughtfully and rubbed his white beard. "I really need charcoal. Are you sure there isn't any left?"

"No, there isn't," she said sullenly. Her frown turned to a smile suddenly. "But I can make more." Ganji's eyes lit up. "I've helped father make charcoal hundreds of times," she said. "It will be easy, but it will take a few days."

They agreed on a price and Faylin left, a growing sense of pride in her breast. The town needed the blacksmith and he needed charcoal, so he needed *her*. She went over every step of the charcoal-making process as she sped back home. The house was empty, and she wasn't about to look for her mother. *She might tell me not to go.* Faylin went to the cart at the back of their home. It held all the tools she'd need.

She pulled the cart, surprised at how hard it was to manage alone. He father pulled it easily enough, but he was clearly much stronger. She was eighteen and thickly built, but still she had great trouble pulling the four wheels over the rough ground.

Once she had it on the road, it traveled more easily. She stopped the cart in the road and ran back to the house. Faylin strapped on her father's hunting knife before grabbing her bow and a few arrows. Her father used the well-worn blade to skin hares and other small game while they were on the plains. It reminded her of those times spent sitting around a fire, eating and laughing with him. She wanted him to be home again soon.

Not wanting her mother to worry too much, she called her neighbor over to the road. Shari was the same age as Faylin, but they weren't friends anymore. When they were children, they were the best of friends, but now they didn't speak to each other, except on rare occasions. These days Shari had her equally pretty friends, and Faylin had none, but that was fine—or it would have been, if her father were here.

Shari got entirely too much attention from the boys, though she hadn't been promised to any of them. Faylin wasn't sure why. There certainly wasn't a lack of suitors for her. Faylin's parents hadn't even hinted at suitable boys for her either, but she suspected the issue was an acute lack of offers for her hand. It was just as well. Faylin had no mind to listen to a fool boy who thought he owned her.

Faylin pasted a smile on her face. "Shari, can you give my mother a message?"

Shari smiled so warmly it almost made Faylin regret her dislike of the girl.

"Tell her I went to make charcoal for Master Ganji, but wait a while before you tell her."

Shari seemed concerned, but then Faylin was on the road, pulling the cart before she could say anything in response.

She continued through the center of Walla and headed east, until the farms ended and she could find a good stand of trees near the road. Her father would have felled a wide hardwood and chopped it to pieces, but Faylin set her axe to a smaller tree. In time, her sweaty efforts dropped three trees, and she used a hand-saw cut them into arm-sized chunks.

With the rising sun reaching its zenith, she dragged her hands through her sweat-soaked hair, and dug a shallow hole with a shovel before building a fire nearby. While the fire burned, she carefully made a chimney of sturdy branches, and then stacked the wood around it. Finally, she covered the whole pile with wet dirt, leaving a hole at the bottom.

She stepped back and admired her work. The sun was setting now, but she had done it. She scooped the smoldering fire onto an iron plate. This was the most important part. She would need to move quickly, before the plate became too hot to handle. Faylin put the burning plate next to the hole she'd left, and used a long branch to push it into the center of the mound. With a few heaves of fresh dirt, she covered the hole, and the job was complete—for now. She knew freshly cut wood took longer to convert to charcoal than seasoned wood, but the hard work was over.

Faylin gathered the tools, thinking she might make it home before the twilight melted to darkness, when branch snapped nearby. The hairs tingled on the back of her neck. She peered into the brush, but saw nothing in the fading light. Reaching into the back of the cart, she grabbed her bow.

Faylin drew the bow and scanned the waist-high grass shifting in the light evening breeze. She'd been out here on the plains hundreds of times and was never fearful of a breaking branch, but her father had always been with her before.

She edged toward the road, eyes on the tall grass, ears straining. Sudden movement caught her eye, and she loosed the arrow without aiming. A gray wolf sprang out of the grass and slammed into her, knocking her to the ground and sending her bow flying from her hands. She saw the teeth coming toward her neck and put her arm out to block the bite. Its teeth sank deep into her arm, and it thrashed brutally from side to side.

Faylin yelled in pain and anger at the wolf, but she sensed growing bloodlust in its hot breath. The heavy wolf stood on her chest, keeping her down. She reached for the dagger with her free hand. Gripping the wooden handle, she slid it from the leather sheath.

Without hesitation, she thrust the dagger up and into the wolf's belly. The beast let out a powerful groan, but then lunged forward even stronger. She pulled the dagger upwards, slashing the wolf from pelvis to sternum. Warm entrails spilled on her, but still it lunged for her neck. She thrust the blade toward its heart.

Faylin felt something deep inside her stir and rise to the surface. It filled her with lust, the lust to kill. She shoved the dagger into the wolf again and again. As the life drained from the beast, her thrusts became stronger, more urgent.

The wolf was still, but Faylin continued to stab it. She felt the rush of something coming into her, something driving into her soul and filling her with power—as though she had taken something from the wolf, something terrifying and wonderful.

Her senses surged, and then she felt a strange serenity. She looked back at the meaningless mound of burning wood, wondering why she had wasted so much effort on such a worthless task.

Calmly, she stepped over to the road and looked to the west, knowing the miserable village was there beyond the low hills. *How had she ever thought that place was important? Why did I stay there for so long?* she wondered. With that, she jogged away from Walla and off the road. Freedom. An open range to roam. Her bleeding arm didn't even bother her. She ran like she had never run before: faster, more agile than ever. She ran like a wild beast, like a predator.

Like a wolf.

Chapter Four

Cayne sat on the porch and listened to the lilting tones of a flute rippling through the evening sky. Burke, never one for talking, spoke with his flute in ways that words couldn't express. Cayne had played the flute when he was young, but his melodies sounded like dying boars. He had no talent for music, but Burke could make the gods weep with his harmonic ballads. To Cayne, it was like the land itself was singing, with the chorus of insects accompanying Burke's tune.

The sun settled below the distant Wazack Mountains, and the orange glow on the maize fields made the music seem more haunting and beautiful. Even the meal bell seemed timed to the chorus, so much so that he ignored it until he heard it a second time.

Cayne's stomach grumbled, and though his mother had heavily spiced the eel, it still tasted bland to him. Burke was usually quiet, but Rait ranted through most dinners; however, even he was lost in thought tonight. Silya looked from Burke to Rait and then back again. She kept them long after dinner, but all she did was look at them. Finally, they returned to their room for the night.

"Are you going with us?" Rait asked.

Cayne shook his head. "I tried to talk father into letting me go, but he won't."

"I only meant, are you going with us to see us off?"

"Of course." *Typical Rait. He doesn't care if I go or not.*

Burke shoved Cayne. "Remember when we dug up half a field, because Cayne thought there was silver buried there?" Burke laughed before anyone could respond. "We would have dug up the whole field if father hadn't found out."

They all laughed, looking back and forth at each other. "I won't ever forget that." Cayne rubbed his backside. "At least there are *parts* of me that will never forget."

"You deserved it," Rait said, needling Cayne.

"Yeah, I know."

They talked through most of the night, reminiscing like old friends reuniting after a long absence. On most nights, their mother would have told them to settle down, but not this night.

The next morning, Silya prepared a plentiful breakfast and bid a long goodbye to Rait and Burke that left them all wiping their eyes. Then Cayne walked with them through the pre-dawn mist that obscured the road. The sun lightened the eastern sky, revealing a pasty bank of clouds. The talk was light, and ended as they neared Dahl Haven.

On the green, hundreds of villagers were milling around over the dew-covered grass, speaking in hushed tones. Nate was directing the throng of boys into a ragged line, five abreast. He was walking on his own, but his movements were strained. He gave little regard to Rait or Burke as they took their places at the end of the line.

Elder Paulos and Rann strode up to Nate. Paulos was doing his best to keep his back to the shouting Rann. "They cannot leave today!" Rann yelled.

Elder Paulos faced Rann. "There is no discussion on the matter. We cannot delay."

"To send our men away right before the festival would be insulting to both Gol and Ahn!"

"You want us to wait until after the festival?" Nate asked. He shook his head.

"To offend the gods so openly is to invite their wrath!" cried Rann.

"The king's orders were quite specific," Elder Paulos said. He turned to regard his wife as she joined the conversation; she was also an elder. The two had overseen village affairs for as long as

Cayne could remember. Gliff followed right behind her; and given her quick pace, he'd been badgering her about something.

"Elder Dineh," Rann said with a slight bow of his head. "You must talk sense into your husband. We cannot send these boys away to war on the eve of the festival. The gods would surely punish such insolence."

"Yes, yes, no one must leave," Gliff said, bobbing his head.

Rann recoiled, clearly not happy to see Gliff agreeing with him. Rann was a fourpriest, and faydens like Gliff were walking, talking blasphemies.

Dineh regarded the men in turn before she spoke. "If we delay, the gods will be pleased and the king will be displeased. However, if we send them, the king will be pleased and the gods displeased." She looked at the boys lined up on the green. "And I cannot remember the last time the gods beheaded someone for disobeying an order."

Nate and Paulos nodded in agreement.

"No, no," Gliff insisted, his gaze locked on the ground. "You must not leave! Blood on the green. Blood, blood, blood! How can you not see it? I told them!"

"Told who?" asked Paulos.

"What more can I do?" Gliff screamed to no one in particular. Then he spun on his heel and stalked off.

They all shook their heads and shrugged. Then Nate turned to Rann. "We understand your concerns, but how would we explain it if we missed the battle?"

"You are the greatest fourpriest we've ever had in Dahl Haven," Elder Dineh said soothingly. "If anyone can set this right with the gods, it is you. I am confident you can."

Cayne heard the obvious flattery in her voice. Rann, however, took the compliment as though she was simply pointing out the obvious. He nodded his head in long bobs. He seemed to consider the idea, a frown forming on his face.

"Or perhaps you agree with Gliff?" Elder Dineh said.

Cayne watched Rann with amusement. Rann would rather cut off his own hand than agree with Gliff.

"Yes, perhaps I can do this," Rann said. "With enough of the proper sacrifices, I do believe the gods will see our plight in a favorable light."

"I'm sure we can make a special collection for the shrine," Elder Dineh said.

Rann perked up and rubbed his hands greedily. "I wonder if that merchant is still here?"

"You mean the one you wanted me to put in the stocks?" Elder Paulos asked.

"He's a thief."

"You still haven't told me what he stole from you."

"Never mind. I have a use for him now, and I still haven't lost faith that the gods will punish him. I have work to do now." Rann nodded to each of them, then walked toward the shrine.

Cayne waited for the two elders to finish talking to Nate, and then stepped up for one last attempt. "Father, Rait and Burke are here now." Cayne lifted up his knapsack. "I'm ready to go, if you'll let me."

"We've talked about this," Nate said sharply. "Someone must remain."

"None of the other families get to leave anyone behind."

Nate stared at him for a moment, and then drew close. "Have you destroyed the plant?" Cayne looked down, avoiding his father's eyes. "That's what I thought."

"Father, you don't understand. It's *alive*."

"That's not the point I was making. I told you to do something and you didn't do it. You don't think or listen when you should." Nate's voice kept rising until he was almost yelling.

Cayne looked around, finding most eyes locked on him. "I can listen."

"Then listen to me now. These boys, they look up to you. They'd follow you no matter what folly you led them into. I can't have you leading them astray."

Cayne took stock of the other boys. He was one of the oldest, and certainly the biggest. "They were going to put me in charge. *That's* why you're going."

"You don't know what you're talking about."

"They didn't ask *you* to lead, you asked them."

"I have done what I have done. I needn't offer you any explanation. Now accept it and go home." His father took a quick breath and his voice softened. "You may understand one day." He turned his attention to the boys ambling into the line, leaving Cayne standing by himself.

He's afraid I'll get them all killed.

Cayne saw all his friends lined up to march away to war. They had no armor and few weapons, but Nate told them they would be marching to Black Rock first, where arms awaited them, along with transport on a pyreship. Waves of excitement filled the boys, and Cayne wished he could go with them even more now. He'd seen pyreships at the docks in Black Rock, but he never imagined he'd ever get to sail on one. Of course, since he wasn't going with them, perhaps he never would.

He waved to Tarken, but didn't bother to go and speak with him. Lyssa was there too, talking through flowing tears with Nodin. He was older than Cayne, and they had been friends until Lyssa was promised to Cayne. She loved Nodin, not him. It was hard to keep any relationship a secret in Dahl Haven, but they hadn't really tried very hard. Cayne's feelings for her were distant at best, but still they were to be married, and seeing her with Nodin stung.

He turned to leave, but paused, thinking about whether he would see any of them again. He walked back to the line and gave an arm grasp to everyone in the line, from his father to Nodin to Tarken.

"You take care of yourself, Tarken. Don't do anything stupid."

Tarken smiled and nodded his head. "I'll tell you all about it when we get back."

Cayne didn't wait for them to depart. He felt like a coward running from a battle. The sun was up now, trying to burn through the dense clouds, but the mist stuck stubbornly to the road. Walking past the farms, he felt they were already vacant, like he was alone listening to the gathering drone of farm animals.

Cayne found his mother sitting quietly in the kitchen. For once, nothing was cooking in the hearth. She looked up at him and offered a weak smile. "They've gone now?"

Cayne nodded and sat down across from her. The table, where they'd shared their every meal for as long as he could remember, seemed long empty already. Memories of laughter and arguments filled his mind.

"Mother, I overheard you and father yesterday." Cayne looked down at the table.

"I'm glad you did. I wasn't sure how to start the conversation." She lifted his chin and looked in his eyes. "Your father asked me to tell you the truth of our past, in case he can't do it himself." Her words trailed off, and she seemed on the brink of tears, but she took a deep breath and continued. "He wanted you to know about our family, to know where you came from."

"We are not from Corsel?"

She shook her head. "Not precisely. We're from Manteo, a place north of Corsel. Your father did grow up in Corsel, as the ward of Lord Niatha Wildbear, so he knew enough of the place. When we moved here, there were many questions, but his knowledge seemed to satisfy them, though I doubt anyone here had been to Corsel or even known anyone who had ever been there."

"Why did we leave?" Cayne asked.

She sighed, the words coming heavily. "Your grandfather was the lord of Manteo, a place where the Crotan king held little sway. They fought for a time, and King Alarak proposed a truce. Instead of a peace settlement, however, the king seized your grandfather and his most loyal supporters while under the white flag." Her eyes fixed him in place. "He killed them all. Your father was delayed, thank the gods, and he missed the truce meeting, or he would have been killed as well."

"We fled?" It was all he could manage to say. *My grandfather was a lord?* He knew they came from the Navataw lands in the north, but he'd thought they had been farmers there too.

"Your father did the right thing. Many of your grandfather's shieldmen dishonored their vows and sided with King Alarak."

Hatred grew in her voice. "Most of those who remained loyal were betrayed and tortured. Your father was alone with a baby and a pregnant wife. They were hunting us."

"Hunting?"

"King Alarak wanted our entire line extinguished. Only by the fortune of the gods did we escape with our lives. Your father grew up with Valewa Wildbear, Lord Niatha's son, and trusted him completely. Together, our families fled to the south, to here."

"Valewa Wildbear? Is that Vale Maagen's real name?"

She nodded. "Vale was the youngest of Lord Niatha's sons. They were inseparable as youths. Even now, they seem to be bound by some bond I cannot fully understand. We all took new names when we came here."

Cayne's mind swirled with a torrent of questions, but most were incoherent. He simply asked, "What is our real name?"

"Falconstorm. You are the grandson of Lord Baran Falconstorm of Manteo. His heir, actually."

"Why did you never tell me?" Cayne snapped, pushing back from the table.

"Your father didn't want you to do anything rash. He said he would tell you when he thought you were mature enough."

"I'm not a child." He slammed his fist on the table, and Silya flinched away. She was scared of him, his own mother, and he wanted to take back his hasty outburst.

Two years ago, she had raised her hand to slap him. He'd deserved it, too; but he grabbed her hand in midair and held it there. He was angry and he gripped her tightly. His father could swing a switch quite effectively despite his injuries, especially when he was mad, and Cayne recalled that time as the angriest his father had ever been with him. Though the welts from his father's switch had faded in a few weeks, the looks from his mother hurt him more than any lashing ever could. He'd apologized, but he could never take back his actions. Now whenever he yelled or lashed out at anything, she looked afraid of him.

"I'm sorry, mother," he said sincerely. "He always calls me rash and treats me like a child." He put his hand on the table. She hesitated, but then took his hand. He smiled and bowed his head. "I interrupted."

"Perhaps if you stopped acting like a child, you would be taken more seriously. We can never go back, but your father held to his stubborn wish to restore our name." She looked at him proudly. "Your father saw something in you. Yes, you're impulsive, but you have the spirit and the courage needed. I think he hoped *you* would return to Manteo and return our family to power."

"Then why didn't he take me with him? Why are we even fighting for the king? Why don't we leave this place?" It was a strange thought. He'd never known any other place.

"I don't know," Silya burst out. "I asked the same questions of your father, but he has some ridiculous idea about defending the realm. What honor is there in defending a realm that wants you dead?" She settled down, looking tired. "I don't know why we would help a king who wants us dead. Your father spoke some drivel about roots and honor."

Cayne paused for a few moments. "I'm sorry, mother. I should not have questioned your—"

"No, Cayne. I'm sorry. I shouldn't have yelled so loudly." She got up and walked to her room. "I'm tired. We will talk more of this tomorrow. Tell no one."

"He doesn't think they're coming back, does he?"

She turned back, locking her eyes on Cayne. "There are people who would kill you, if they knew your real name. Never speak it to another." She didn't wait for a response, closing the door behind her.

Cayne stayed a short time, alone with his thoughts, and then went outside on the wooden porch he had helped build. There was work to be done in the fields, but the darkening clouds told him rain would come soon. He sat on the porch for the rest of the day, as a steady drizzle blanketed the farm. It was just as Gliff had told him. *Misting rain. Blood on the green, blood on my hands.*

Cayne awoke, still lying on the porch, in the light of a new day. His mother had placed a blanket on him at some point, and he felt warm and comfortable. The rain had passed, and the sun was stretching into the morning sky. He wondered where Burke and Rait were now, and what they were seeing and doing. A melancholy took him, leaving him near-motionless, staring out into the sky until mid-morning. He got up, knowing he'd neglected his chores for an entire day.

In addition to the satchel he normally took with him, he wore his father's sword. It made him feel better to have it rattling against his side.

He found Silya in the yard, feeding dried corn to the chickens. She never did any tasks in the yard. That was his responsibility. He tried to take the feed bucket from her, but she pulled it away. "It's been a while since I've done this. Having you boys around has spoiled me."

"I'll do it, Mother." Cayne guessed she'd done it the previous day too, out in the rain. He stared at his feet, knowing she only did it because he had failed to.

"I don't mind. It takes my mind off of things." She threw a handful of corn to the pecking chickens surrounding her. "Go tend the fields."

He passed the plow that they used to prepare the fields. Two years ago, their ox had died during a harsh winter, and since then Cayne had pulled the plow each spring. Rait had taken to calling him the family ox, and though the name annoyed Cayne, he wished Rait was there to call him that again.

Cayne shuffled away and walked to the fields. He trudged past the root crops and herbs without looking up. He looked at the growing corn, and knew he needed to plant more beans now that the corn was strong enough to support the beanstalks.

He heard a faint singing, more shrill than before. *The angelia plant.* He ran by memory back to the north tract where he'd found it, ignoring two rabbits that were hungrily eating his crops. The urgency of its call compelled him to sprint the last distance. He slid down a small dune and saw the plant. It had doubled in size and was as high as his hips now, but there was something else...

He stopped before reaching the plant, and looked in horror at another plant growing next to it. With its black stalk and serrated leaves, and a black mist that seemed to dance around it, he knew what it was: a dynabane vine. It was as ugly as the angelia plant was beautiful. The thick, gnarled vine had dozens of tendrils, reaching like fingers desperate to strangle the angelia. Razor-sharp thorns glistening with black oil covered the vine. Cayne thought he could actually see the vine growing before his eyes.

Everywhere the dynabane vines touched the angelia plant, its delicate flesh was bloated, throbbing, and filled with dark puss. The berry-sized fruit of the angelia plant had already set, but the spines of the dynabane had lanced most of them, and they were withering. Near the top, three clusters of fruit remained untouched, but black vines were reaching for them.

Cayne drew a small knife. He carefully put the blade to the base of the dynabane and began to cut, but the skin at the bottom was tough, and he made little headway. The scratches he made in the dynabane oozed a black gel that stained his blade. That poison could kill with a scratch. As he sliced, he heard the cry of the angelia plant increase in pitch, so he stopped cutting, and the shrill cries subsided to a steady whimper. He sheathed his knife, careful not to touch the poison on the blade. The angelia continued to weakly sing its song of death; no, its song of *murder*.

He desperately wanted to help the angelia. His eyes darted around, but there was nothing to help him. Cayne grabbed one of the unspoiled berries and twisted it off. It came off easily, almost happy to be away from the reach of the dynabane. The angelia plant spoke in his mind, urging him to take the rest while there was still time. He took all of them that were still unspoiled.

He stepped backwards, unable to avert his eyes until he was a dozen paces distant. The cry of the angelia pitched higher as he walked away. Tears welled in Cayne's eyes, and waves of guilt rolled over him. The song became weaker, more distant, though he had not moved farther away; then mercifully, it ended. He sat down, knees to his chest, and wept.

Chapter Five

The night held little sleep for Cayne. Long after his mother had gone to sleep, he held the angelia fruit in front of his face. Even in the dark room, they glimmered faintly. Though unripened and firm to his touch, there was a warmth to them.

As soon as he heard his mother moving in the kitchen, he dressed and joined her. Silya sat sullenly at the table. She managed a small smile for him, but she looked tired despite the night's rest. A yellow banner lay across the table. At the thickest end, there was a falcon grasping two lightning bolts in its talons. The tapered end ruffled over the table and onto the floor. "Our family banner?" he asked. "I'll do you one better." He put a handful of the berries on the table in front of her. Silya shot forward, her tiredness retreating. She regarded them with wide eyes, then looked to Cayne questioningly.

"I found an angelia plant in our fields."

She stroked one, her eyes distant and pondering.

"I only just managed to take these before a dynabane vine killed the angelia."

She pulled her hand away from the fruit as though it was poison.

"It didn't taint these," he assured her.

"When did this happen?" she asked sharply.

"Yesterday. Well, a few days ago, it's—"

"Why am I just hearing of this now?" she demanded. She sighed and lowered her voice. "I'm sure you had your reasons. Tell me now."

Cayne lowered his head to avoid her eyes. It was always easier to talk with her than with his father. Nate would have lectured him for half a day before he let Cayne say a single word. He told her his story of finding the plant, leaving out that strange fellow, Markas.

"So Nate knew of the plant, but not the fruit?" she said, taking one of them and holding it in front of her face.

Cayne nodded. "I didn't know how fast they matured. The first time I saw it, it didn't have any fruit at all."

"He'd have taken these with him," she said, picking up a second berry. "He needs to have them."

"But they left."

"Then you need to catch them."

He looked up to her eyes, noting the determination on her face. His pulse quickened at the idea of joining the rest of the boys, but still he felt obligated to say, "Father told me to stay here and watch over the farm and Dahl Haven."

Her expression didn't flicker. "You tell your father that I sent you, and if he has a problem with that, then he can march his rump back here and take it up with me." She stood up and gathered the fruits. "Pack your things. I'll prepare you rations for the road."

He rushed to pack his satchel while Silya gathered enough food for several days. When he was fully loaded, the burden was nearly half his own weight. "They've quite a lead on you," Silya told him. "You'll need to move swiftly to catch them. Take the horse."

"But that would leave you without one."

"I'll get along just fine. Now go."

She touched his face the way she had when he was a child. It felt warm, and he smiled to her. He stepped out into the sun and took a deep breath.

"Cayne, you did the right thing by not destroying the angelia plant. You may have saved many of our boys."

He'd known it was the right thing to do, but it was good to hear her say it anyway. Cayne jogged to the barn and opened the well-worn door. Sola was a yellow stallion they'd purchased three years ago. They used him to pull wagons, but Cayne felt the horse wanted to run every time he hooked him up to the wagon. He patted Sola's neck. "You'll get your chance today."

He kept the pace to a slow trot until they passed Dahl Haven, not wanting to push Sola until he'd warmed up. Once past the village, though, he only had to loosen the reins and Sola gleefully accelerated to a gallop. The warm air rising over the fields rushed past Cayne as he waved to the occasional farmer. Some waved back, but most of them shook their heads. They were all old, and didn't like anything the younger generations did.

He pushed Sola harder, though he slowed on the steeper sections. Cayne slowed him to a trot as they moved up one such hill and, as they crested it, Cayne yanked hard on the reins. Splayed out in front of them was an army so massive he couldn't see the end of it. There were thousands of warriors. The army clogged the road, and off to the sides he saw lightly armored lines of men trotting far out to the flanks.

Sola sensed the danger first, and the big stallion reared. Cayne tried to hold on to the saddle, but fell to the ground, the breath knocked out of him. He rolled quickly to get out of the way before he got trampled, and watched helplessly as Sola galloped away.

Cayne ran after the horse, sprinting down the hill and gaining speed entirely too fast. His body got ahead of his feet and he tumbled to the bottom in a heap. Covered in scrapes, he looked to the hilltop and was glad to see that no one was chasing him yet. He got up and took a step. His ankle gave way under his weight, and he winced in pain. He hobbled several more steps and stopped to check his ankle. It wasn't broken, but it was a bad sprain. It would get worse if he ran on it, but there was little choice. Cayne stumbled, trying to keep his weight on his good ankle. He kept looking back, waiting for the warriors to get to the top of the hill.

It might be the king's army, in which case there was no reason to run; but something told him it wasn't a friendly army. He ran off the road toward a small copse of old oaks with thick undergrowth. It wasn't as far from the road as he would have liked, but there was no place else to hide. Cayne trudged through the tangled brush, cursing as the thorns scratched and stung him. He hopped to the largest tree and found a small hollow at its base. He dropped his pack and sat with his back to the tree, his father's sword unsheathed and lying next to him.

For an interminable time, he heard the sound of the approaching army. Eventually, he kept his head low and crept out to see it.

They wore armor painted a multitude of colors, with each contingent sporting a unique combination of hues. Swords dangled at their sides, and many carried spears, bows, or war hammers. At the end of each group, a score of wagons plodded after the soldiers. Draft horses drew a few of the wagons, but most had men toiling to keep them moving. The lead man in each group held a colored banner, though with no wind they hung limply, so he couldn't see how they were decorated.

Just as he'd hoped, the flankers went wide and around his hiding spot. He'd never even heard of an army in these parts, let alone seen one, and now one surrounded him. Cayne didn't know which army it was, but it marched toward Dahl Haven, toward the farm, toward his mother.

He kept his head low until the last of the army passed, along with most of the remaining daylight. Without a horse, he stood little chance of catching up with his father. Besides, he was more concerned about his mother. Cayne left the copse and shadowed the army from a safe distance.

As the light faded to twilight, he saw lights flickering to life. The army had stopped, and now a whole town of tents sprang up, with campfires dotting the horizon and filling the air with the smell of burning wood. He continued to walk toward the fires until he saw a gang of men walking toward him. They were backlit by the campfires and carried torches. Cayne saw them long before they could see his lone dark figure in the night. He turned, but saw strange lights on the road, coming at him from the other direction. He scrambled into the long grass alongside the road. Hunkering down, he peered through the patchy grass as the bobbing lights and men converged.

A pair of trotting horses closed on the warriors, who fanned out around the road like a fence. The horses slowed as the men raised their torches and spears in challenge. Their speech was fast, harsh, and angry to Cayne's ears. *Not a local accent.*

"Halt," called one of the men. He stuck out a long spear to emphasize his point.

The horses had lanterns fixed on poles that rested on a mount in the saddle. The riders stopped, and one jumped down in front of the spears. He patted his horse, then turned to address the men. "We're here for a war council," he said flatly, in the same rapid manner as the first man.

"What's your name?"

"Zane, steward to Lord Darwan," he said, motioning to the other rider.

The spearman changed to a respectful tone. "My apologies, Lord Darwan. You and your steward may pass." His fellow spearmen lowered their weapons, and the two riders continued toward Dahl Haven.

The soldiers set up a fire not twenty paces from Cayne. He started to squirm backwards, but his legs brushed the long grass, and it bent with a rustling sound that froze him in place. The men didn't take any notice, but to Cayne the sound was as loud as thunder. His heart was beating so hard he thought they might hear it too. He fought back the rising panic.

There was no place to go, and they would see him once daybreak came.

Chapter Six

Lord Darwan rode ahead of Zane as they approached the village. The small livery stable teemed with horses. Before they had crossed into these lands, the king had ordered all of the horsemen away to quell a rebellion; thus, the only horses left belonged to lords and messengers. Judging by the number of horses, nearly every lord was here.

The village was another disappointment. Somehow, it was actually smaller than the other villages he'd seen. It was perhaps fifty rickety hovels in the middle of nowhere. He wondered how miserable these people's lives must be.

Darwan had lost track of the days since they'd crossed the Skykom River, but he had yet to see anything even resembling a town. This kingdom was nothing more than one large farm. *And they had the gall to invade our lands.* It was not surprising that these farmers had performed so poorly in battle. These people were weak, more accustomed to wielding a hoe than a spear or sword.

He threw his reins to an attendant and waited for Zane to catch up. Large fires blazed on an open green, warriors drinking and eating in the flickering firelight.

"It's early for the war council to be starting," Zane said from behind him.

Darwan turn to look at his steward, noting that Zane's eyes were on the festivities around the fires, his nose flaring at the smoke of nearby pipes. Zane was young compared to Darwan, but had a well-worn face. He drank like a horse and smoked anything he could stuff into his pipe. His armor was brightly polished, and he wore a single sword at his waist. Left on his own, Zane wouldn't have cleaned his armor for weeks on end, but as Darwan's steward, his appearance was a reflection of his Lord, so Darwan demanded he maintain it in perfect condition. "Stay near here," Darwan said. "I'll send for you when the council starts." He probably wouldn't. What would be the point? By that time, Zane would be too drunk to stand, a total embarrassment.

Zane floated towards the fires, looking for a seat and an empty tankard. Darwan shook his head and looked around for a tavern. He spied a high building at the far end of the green with a high concentration of men milling around it. He walked between the fires, taking in the welcome smell of burning wood, meat, and smoking-weed.

The building was just a single story, though it had a high roof. Glancing around, he saw that it was the only tall building in the whole wretched place. There were guards posted on either side of the door. He straightened his posture and walked confidently past them. They regarded him with a nod, and made no move to stop him.

The tiny interior was packed tighter than the stable, but with lords instead of horses. A fire raged in the fireplace at the back of the single room, making it stiflingly hot, especially in full armor. He didn't need to wear it. He was safe here with the army, but appearances were everything at a war council. All the sweating lords in the room wore their armor, and the clinking of that armor was a constant background drone.

Pale green light flooded down from lanterns hung among the rafters, giving everyone a familiar green glow. The assembled lords sat and stood around dozens of mismatched tables. Ceramic goblets tinkled faintly, and Darwan smelled stale wine. It was a testament to the army's organization that they could have a proper drink after so many years in the field.

He adjusted his armor, surveying the crowd. He saw many familiar faces, but none friendly. His armor was made of banded iron strips painted with red and black enamel. It gleamed like it was freshly polished, which of course it was, though not by his own hands. Darwan believed in appearances, so he was clean-shaven, with his hair cropped close. He had a single sword at his waist, according to the current style for proper Sarasin lords. Ornate colored glass adorned the scabbard, and black and red braids covered the hilt below the cross-guard.

He milled through the crowd, angling toward an open chair near the fireplace. He extended his hand to grab the back of the chair and quickly sat down. A small table separated him from another man; he looked at Darwan, his brows narrowing to a hateful glare. "Lord Darwan," the man said, practically spitting out the title.

"Unlord Verak," Darwan said in his most pleasant tone. "It's good to see that you're still alive."

Verak snorted, then looked around the room. He wore the same armor as Darwan, with the same color scheme. The only real differences between the two men were Verak's bald head and about ten years. "Are you keeping yourself busy these days?" Darwan asked, trying to hide his discomfort.

"Yes, quite busy," Verak said, leaning in slightly toward Darwan. "Sucking up to the king, trolling around the royal court, and waiting for one of you bastards to die. I nearly thought you were going to oblige me in that last battle."

Darwan thought about finding another place to sit, but it was too late. Leaving now would make Verak feel he'd driven Darwan off. The last battle had not gone well for the lord, and he didn't want to discuss it. "It was a close matter," Darwan admitted.

Verak leaned back with a mighty laugh. "Close it was. I saw the whole thing. You should be dead. I don't know how you survived."

"I'm sure it was your pleas to the gods on my behalf that made the difference." Darwan smiled at him. "How many years has it been since the last Tekahtaman? The solstice is almost upon us, isn't it?"

Verak's smile vanished, replaced by a hard stare. He forced a breath between his gritted teeth. "Arta Nakis refused the traditionalists again." Verak leaned close to Darwan. "How can we accept this?"

"Surely you're not speaking against the rule of our king," Darwan said coyly. He faked a concerned look and stifled a chuckle. "Five years, hasn't it been?"

"Seven years," Verak said flatly. "Though I can understand how someone with a lordship could lose track of time. And how are my lands and my wives?"

"Prosperous and fertile," Darwan said without hesitation. In truth, he hadn't seen either of them in several years, and both men knew it. He'd only visited his estate three times in the last seven years, and he couldn't even remember what any of his wives looked like. They had not borne him any children, and both men knew that, too.

"Ah, yes," Verak said with a smile, leaning back in his chair. "I did hear that one of my former wives did bear a child this past winter. You must be very proud."

Darwan hadn't heard of any such child, but Verak was the former lord of Darwan's lands, and he might have sources for such information. More likely, he was making it up to aggravate Darwan. It worked.

"Your boys are weak," Darwan said, leaning in closer. "Much like their father. I doubt they'll amount to much. Like their father." Under the customs of Tekahta, Darwan inherited not only Verak's lands, but also the wives, servants, and children of the lordship.

Verak narrowed his eyes and forced a breath before he spoke, but hatred still dripped from his words. "You got lucky."

Darwan shrugged casually. "You were the lucky one. Lucky I didn't kill you. You should be thanking me for sparing your life. A shame the Tekahtaman hasn't been held since." At the last contest, Darwan had challenged and beaten Verak, taking his lordship and leaving him an unlord. Since then, the king had refused to hold another Tekahtaman. He'd kept the army, along with all of the lords, in the field the entire time. The king used the extended deployment as his primary excuse for not holding the contests.

Among the many games of the Tekahtaman, men of the lordly class could challenge standing lords. Victory meant taking the lordship and its associated possessions. The defeated lord, if he survived, became an unlord. Unlords were men of minimal stature. With no retinue or resources, most soon succumbed to an assassin's blade. Lords made enemies, and when they lost their lordships, scores got settled. Verak was a wily one to have survived this long. He could challenge a lower lord for his lordship, but that required the king to hold the Tekahtaman.

Darwan turned toward a disturbance at the door. Two new arrivals entered the crowded room, and lords parted in front of them. Side by side, Prince Pevane and Princess Ayasha strolled into the room. They were the youngest of the king's children, both in their late teen years. "The war council must be soon," Verak grumbled.

Pevane wore fine banded armor painted with rich purple enamel. He was the most diminutive of the four royal children, though probably the most dangerous. He had the face of a weasel, which was not softened by his mottled goatee. His armor bulged across his chest, and Darwan suspected he was wearing padding to augment his skinny frame.

The royals surveyed the room and then headed straight toward Darwan. He realized his table was the only one in the room with just two chairs at it. These two royal brats disliked company. "Lord Darwan, Unlord Verak," Pevane said, as he hovered over their table, offering nothing but a vapid smile.

Darwan turned a respectful glance up to Pevane. *He wants us to leave the table, but won't ask.* "Prince Pevane. Good to see you again."

Darwan looked around Pevane to his sister. Ayasha was dressed in a decorative green silk dress that was more suited to the royal court than a war council. It clung to her in a distracting way, and her eyes, though pretty, had a coldness to them. She was the most sought-after bride in the kingdom, since marrying her would give a man a direct connection to the king. She was also the least known of the eligible daughters in the kingdom. No lord had ever held a conversation with her for longer than it took to exchange the barest of pleasantries.

"Princess Ayasha, a rare pleasure to see you," Darwan said quietly.

She crooked her neck, her eyes refusing to make any contact with Darwan's gaze. She stared off to a vacant corner of the room.

Pevane stepped between them, his smile vanishing. "My sister is not in the mood for conversation with the likes of … you." He stood there staring at Darwan until the standoff quieted the conversations at nearby tables.

Darwan didn't want to give up his table to this spoiled brat, but inviting the ire of the king over such a simple matter would damage his stature in the court. Darwan smiled to Pevane and stood up, grabbing the back of his chair. "Princess Ayasha, please take my seat."

Pevane's eyes flashed hatred for the briefest moment, and then he was stepping around the table to take Verak's chair. Darwan held out his hand to help Ayasha take her seat, but she ignored it and seated herself. "Thank you for offering your seat," she said without looking at him. Her voice was fuller than he'd expected.

He waited for her to say more, but she leaned across the table and whispered to Pevane. The two started a quiet conversation, ignoring the two men standing by the table.

Verak sidled away, but Darwan remained, waiting for an acknowledgment. These two coddled children needed a lesson in respect, and Darwan yearned to be the one to give it to them. "These Crotan villages are pathetic," he said, trying to get a reaction from them. "Almost a shame to add them to our kingdom." They sat up from their whispering, but neither of them even glanced at him. "They're a weak people."

Pevane turned an annoyed eye to him. "My father was right about them, of course." Then he fixed his stare on Darwan, putting his fist under his chin. They stared at each other for a time.

Darwan nodded, breaking the contest of glares. He'd made his point, however minor. There was no point in making enemies. He bowed and turned to leave.

"You know I'm responsible for ... assessments," Pevane said. "I don't think your lands have been reassessed in some time. I shall have to look into that."

Darwan stiffened, and then looked back at the smug little turd. That conversation hadn't been very satisfying, and now it would cost him. He wanted to grab the boy by the throat and land a good punch to his face, but that might cost him his life. He hid his anger and shrugged to the prince.

"You're both wrong," Ayasha said loudly enough to be heard several tables over. Pevane turned to her, a look of surprise on his face. She didn't look at either of them, but she kept talking. "All three of you, actually. These villages aren't Crotan. These are Skykom lands. The Crotans conquered the Skykom people two generations ago." She swiveled her head around, giving Darwan the briefest of eye contacts before looking back down at the table. "You should both learn more about your adversaries."

Pevane balled his fists and glared at her, clearly enraged at her admonition. He surveyed the room full of lords. "Sister, you should know better than to offer your thoughts where they are not wanted." Pevane rose and pulled back an open palm; she winced, getting ready for the blow.

Darwan stepped forward and grabbed Pevane's hand before it could strike the princess. The boy reached for his sword at his belt, but froze as a booming voice thundered across the meeting hall. "Pevane!" King Arta Nakis stood in the doorway, arms crossed.

The king rammed his way into the room, his retinue close behind. He stood a head taller than any other man in the room, and his arms were like aged oak branches. He'd held the kingship for the longest period in recent memory. The Sarasin king was chosen in the same way as the lords; High Lords could challenge the king at the Tekahtaman and seize the throne. There was a certain decorum to the challenges. Only the loftiest lords could issue a challenge to the king.

Arta Nakis was a beast with a sword or a hammer. After brutally smashing his opponents well beyond death in his first few years as king, the challenges stopped coming. He'd held the last five

Tekahtamans without a single challenge. Then he'd refused to hold them in the past seven years, so there could *be* no challenges. Fifteen years without a new king. It was unSarasin-like to go so long without a change in leadership. Eventually the wars would end, though, and Arta Nakis would have to hold the Tekahtaman again.

His two older sons followed him. They wore the same purple armor as their father, and oozed arrogance like the stink after a garlicky meal. The older of the two was Varthan, the mirror image of the king. Tall and stout, he was known for his brutality on the practice field and his sadistic tendencies toward the peasants—which, for him, was almost everyone.

The other son fancied himself a military leader, trying to issue orders to everyone in the army. His name was Kaan, and despite his pompousness, he may have been the cream of the royal crop. All four were true children of the king, sired by Arta Nakis himself before he'd taken the kingdom. Normally he would have left his children and wife with his lands, but he broke with tradition, taking all of them with him to his kingship.

The young children of the previous king had simply disappeared.

The king strode up to Pevane, and without the slightest hesitation, slapped him with a vicious open hand to the face. Pevane's feet left the floor, and he sailed into a table of nearby lords.

"Is that what you intended to do to Ayasha?" the king demanded. "You need to learn. If you're going to hit a woman, you should do it in private." Arta Nakis bellowed a mighty laugh at his son.

Pevane wobbled to his feet, clutching his reddened face. He kept his head low, cowering before his father. *A much-practiced stance for the little brat,* Darwan thought smugly.

Men cleared the tables from the room, and a rough circle opened at the center. Arta Nakis stood there alone, waiting for quiet. He didn't wait long.

"It is as I told you," he said, splaying his arms out. "This land is ours. The weakling King Alarak has no power to resist us, or even slow our advance." He paced around his small circle. "His so-called *army* squats impotently behind walls far to the east of here, while we pillage his lands. His capital lies open to us."

Murmurs of approval and grunts of satisfaction rolled around the crowded room. It was much as he had said. They'd crossed the mighty Skykom River and invaded the southern regions of the Crotan Kingdom, but the river itself had proven to be the greatest obstacle.

Darwan watched the king, but felt the burning stare from the young prince. Pevane couldn't do anything to the king, but Darwan was another matter. The boy had influence with the king, and apparently on Darwan's taxes as well. *Nothing to be done for it now.*

"I trust all of you are now well north of this place," the king said.

Darwan cleared his throat and said, "No, sire. My command is just to the south of here."

The king regarded him questioningly. "Were my orders not clear? All forces were to move north with haste. Do you know what haste is, Darwan? When will your men arrive here?"

"We were held up in the last village," Darwan replied. In truth, he'd received no such orders, but the king had not been sympathetic the last time he'd used that excuse.

"When will they arrive?"

"Tomorrow at midday."

"How can they be that far away?" the king demanded.

"It will take some time to break camp and get them in marching order."

The king stared intently at Darwan for several seconds. "Are you telling me your men are camped for the night?"

Darwan tried to shrink away, but there was nowhere to go. He nodded and waited for the king's tantrum. If the king spoke to you, it was rarely ever praise. Darwan was well prepared for shouting, only it didn't come. The king looked thoughtfully around the room, but he seemed distant in his thoughts. He snapped back to the room and smiled to Darwan. "You are distant from the main body of my army. We will not wait for you. Your warband is depleted, so I doubt you'd be of much use in a battle." Arta Nakis stroked his long beard.

Depleted because of you. Darwan thought of the last battle. The king had deployed them on low ground right below a hill, knowing the Crotan army was headed toward them. They swarmed over that hill and descended on his warband. Though pressed hard, Darwan and his men stood firm against the charge, and that was his mistake.

"Just like last time, Darwan." The king sighed. "You failed to move when ordered then, and now you have failed to march when ordered."

I didn't receive either of those orders. Darwan gave a sigh of his own, and saw both Pevane and Verak smiling at him. Darwan adjusted his armor absently. There was nothing to say.

"Since you are at such an irrelevant distance, you might as well perform some useful duty," the king said to the assembled lords. He waited for the low snickering to subside, and then held out his hands. "We had to pass through this place with haste and were unable to give it a proper visitation. When your men arrive here, I want you to stay the night and give these farmers a taste of Sarasin culture."

Darwan knew what he meant. They had raped and pillaged their way through these lands for over a week now. He'd never minded putting the sword to their enemies, but the carnage in the last village weighed on him. The screaming and wailing still echoed in his ears. These people were weak; they offered no resistance. *They deserved it,* he told himself, but some part of him remained unconvinced.

"We are coming and they should get accustomed to our rule. You are sowing the seeds of our conquest." The king crooked his head. "Sowing the seeds. Literally." He laughed uncontrollably. His laughter spread across the room.

Darwan glanced to Ayasha, glad to see she wasn't laughing either. She stared at the floor, a look of disinterest on her face. Next to her, Pevane's laughing ended, and he glared at Darwan before stepping forward to block Darwan's view of his sister.

"Darwan, I think you can go now," Arta Nakis shouted between his guffaws. "You don't need to hear the rest of the war council. Just keep heading north until you come to a crossroads." He turned to his oldest son. "Varth, what was the name of that place?"

"Walla," Varthan said. "Father, perhaps I could remain and help Lord Darwan with his task." Varthan was well known for his cruelty. As a boy, he had tortured animals, but he'd graduated to people at some point, and he was reportedly quite good at it. Sarasins by nature enjoyed crushing enemies, but there was a limit, and Varthan was well beyond it.

The king stopped laughing and gave Varthan a disgusted look. "What if there was a battle? You would miss out on glory for the sake of tearing a few limbs off these peasants?" He shook his head. "No, you will ride with me. You'll have to satisfy yourself with our morning presents for the villagers here."

Chapter Seven

Darwan fumed, spitting curses under his breath. The king had treated him like a child in front of every other lord. He stamped his way across the green, looking for his steward. Zane was sitting by a fire boasting to a dozen other warriors. Darwan gestured for him to join him, and his steward reluctantly left the group.

"That's enough for tonight," Darwan said. Zane teetered to one side and Darwan had to grab a shoulder to keep him from falling over. "We're leaving."

"So soon?"

"We're breaking camp and marching north," Darwan said.

"The men won't be happy."

Darwan fixed him with a stare.

"You don't look happy either," Zane said. "Rough council?"

"Let's go."

"That's not good," Zane said, shaking his head. "But better you than me."

A man in armor was striding toward them, and Darwan instinctively shifted his hand to his sword. He wore purple armor with white bands, making him one of the king's men, but low ranking.

"Lord Darwan," the warrior said. His voice was high-pitched, and as he neared, Darwan saw that he was a mere boy.

Darwan shoved Zane toward the stables. "Try not to fall off your horse, fool. I'll be along to join you soon."

Zane twirled a finger in the air as he stumbled across the grass. Darwan watched him disappear in the darkness, then turned to the young warrior.

"The king orders you to wait for him. I can show you to the home he is using."

Darwan led him to the stable. He found Zane sleeping against a post, and slapped him to alertness. He shook his steward and shoved him toward his horse. "Get to the camp and have the men ready to march by the time I get back. I'll be along shortly."

Zane gave a weak salute, mounted, and kicked his horse into a sudden gallop. He whooped and disappeared down the road. Darwan shook his head. That idiot was going to get himself killed. "Probably time for a new steward anyway."

"My lord?"

Darwan had forgotten the small warrior trailing behind him. He motioned for the boy to lead the way, but kept his hand on his sword. They walked a short distance and entered a crude home just off the green. The boy saluted Darwan and then left, closing the door behind him.

The meager place was just four walls and a few windows. Darwan scoffed at what passed for a window in this land: a squarish hole through the wooden wall, with wooden shutters on the outside. He wondered if any in these lands even knew of glass windows. He cracked a shutter, noting the young guard posted just outside the front door.

While he waited, he withdrew a small tin box from a pouch inside his armor. It felt warm in his hands, and he slowly opened it. The pyrus shimmered with a faint red glow. It was neatly cut into small cubes with a grainy, sugary feel, and had the acrid odor of burnt metal. While his men might afford poppy or smoking weed, pyrus was far too expensive for any but a lord to afford. He'd purchased it many moons ago, but thus far, he'd only looked at and fondled it. He felt diminished just holding the tin, for no Sarasin lord worthy of the title needed such tonics, and yet he could not bear to discard it. *I'm weak for having it, and weaker still for not getting rid of it.*

The only furniture in the house was a single bed, and he had no desire to be sitting on it when the king entered. He sat on the dirt floor, legs crossed, and stared at the pyrus. *Maybe just one.*

He heard approaching armor and the guard shuffling outside the door. He quickly tucked the pyrus back into his armor, but remained seated. The king burst through the door and Darwan ignored his instinct to jump to his feet. If the king wanted to kill him, Darwan could not stop him. The king was a vicious fighter, and there was little doubt about who would be victorious.

Arta Nakis stood over Darwan, arms on his hips. "Please don't get up. I'm only your *king*."

Point made, Darwan got to his feet and bowed. "Your Majesty."

"I have a delicate matter to discuss," the king said, studying Darwan. "Can you be trusted?"

"You can trust me, but after what you said in the war council—"

"Bah!" he said with a wave of his hand. "Just words in a council, and it's better if the rest of the lords think that I distrust you."

Darwan wondered if the scene in the council was really just for show, but he kept the question to himself. "What can I do for Your Majesty?"

"Darwan, these new lands will yield many new lordships. Most will go to the burgeoning lordling population, but I'll need experienced lords as well."

Any child of a lord was part of the lordling class. They belonged to the land until they reached the age of fifteen; then they got a stipend and were spewed out into the world. In the past, they would have competed at the Tekahtaman for the lower lordships, but with no contest, most found service in the king's army. They were growing quite discontent with the lack of upward mobility. Darwan well recalled the endless complaints of the two lordlings assigned to his warband before they were killed in battle.

Darwan looked around the room and said, "I'm not sure a lordship here would be considered a step up for me. This place is more backward than the Toltan region."

"Most of their larger cities lie along the coast, west of here," the king said. He surveyed the room. "Could they not even find one chair for me?" Arta Nakis put his hands behind his back and paced around Darwan. "I was not talking about a lordship. I will need new High Lords to oversee these young lords."

Darwan perked up. A High Lordship? That *would* be a step up. "Which region would this High Lordship control?"

"I am not saying you would become a High Lord, Darwan," the king said coyly. "I am saying I will need new High Lords in these lands. High Lords I can *trust*." He stared at Darwan intently, but his meaning was plain enough without the heavy look. "I will place this new province under Varthan, and he will control the Crotan peninsula."

The king produced a rolled scroll from under his armor. He scowled around the room again. "No tables either." He shook his head. "Hold this end."

Darwan held the open end of the scroll with two hands, and Arta Nakis rolled out the rest of the scroll to reveal a map. He pointed to a peninsula. "Here. This will be Varthan's region." He stroked the map next to another coastal area. "This region is known as the Pikwa valley. I understand the city of Manraven is quite prosperous."

Darwan took a hand from the scroll and pointed to another city. "What of this city? Eventide."

"I believe it's considered part of the Skykom region, but that's a Crotan construct. I could include that city within your region. I mean, the region of the new High Lord."

Darwan restrained his smile. He'd become rather annoyed with the lack of the Tekahtaman himself. He had no ability to seek a larger lordship, but now he might get a High Lordship without even a competition.

"You are familiar with the Lady Margella?" the king asked.

Darwan nodded. Everyone in the army knew her, or at least knew of her. She'd come to the Sarasin court years ago, though her heritage was dubious. She didn't seem of Sarasin stock, but she still found an important patron in the king. Every time Darwan had seen her, she'd been wearing a veil that covered most of her face, but she covered little else.

"Have you seen the queen?" Arta Nakis asked. When Darwan shook his head, the king added, "This Gol-damned village is too small. Tabila is here somewhere, and so is Margella. It's getting too hard to keep them from finding each other. I need someone to safeguard the Lady Margella, but preferably far from the main body of my army."

He wants me to be a chaperone? Half-insulted, Darwan's anger ebbed immediately. It was a small task for such a great reward, if that was all he had to do. He rubbed his face thoughtfully, waiting to see if the king would say more, but he was waiting for a response. "I'm sure she would be safe within my camp."

"Excellent, Darwan. She's waiting at the stables. Leave immediately." Arta Nakis motioned to the door.

Darwan nodded and turned to the door. "I'll keep her safe."

"And unspoiled."

"Of course, Your Majesty," Darwan pledged, pausing at the door.

"When your warband gets to this village, make these oathbreakers howl. Margella will like that."

Darwan nodded and pushed out into the night. He found her ladyship waiting outside the stable on a black mare. She wore a dark cloak, making her hard to discern in the distant firelight. Darwan found his own mount and rode over to her.

"Lady Margella." He tried to make eye contact, but she wore a veil that covered most of her face. The rest of her hid behind a fur-lined cloak the color of night.

"Lord Darwan, I presume." Her voice was smooth and confident. She sounded older than he'd expected.

"We should ride slowly in the darkness," he said, setting his horse on the road.

"I can see just fine," she said, passing him. "Try to keep up." Her horse shifted into an easy trot, despite the darkness.

They passed the picket line and rode on into the night. Darwan kept behind her, his lantern barely lighting up the ground in front of him. He cursed her dark horse and even darker cloak as he tried to keep sight of her. She sped on in front of him, almost carelessly pushing her horse ever faster. Darwan clutched his reins, the sweat from his palms making the leather slippery. It was all he could do to keep her at the edge of his vision, and he lost sight of her at regular intervals. *How can she see in this darkness?*

He felt relief at the sight of his camp on the horizon, as the firelight outlined Margella's horse several lengths ahead of him. Her horse slowed unexpectedly. He had to pull hard on his reins to keep from running into it.

"Your camp, I presume," she said, a sense of disappointment in her voice. "It's small. And far from the rest of the army."

"I think that was the point," Darwan said, his hands relaxing, though his pulse still raced.

"Yes, we wouldn't want the queen to find me."

Darwan pondered the thought of Queen Tabila finding Margella. He'd pay a decent sum to watch that encounter... from a safe distance.

The camp was a hive of activity. When he'd left earlier in the day, it was settling into the nightly routine of soup and beer. Apparently, Zane had been successful in both making it back to the camp and getting it ready to move. Margella turned to Darwan. "This is not what I expected."

"We're breaking camp to march to that village," Darwan advised.

She stopped her horse and was quiet for too long. "Are you telling me that you dragged me all this way and now you want me to go right back to where I was?"

"I intend to have my warband in that village before midday."

"And what of my comforts?" Margella asked. "No sleep? An entire night in the saddle?"

"The king asked me to keep you safe, not comfortable." Darwan rode past her, not wanting to deal with her moaning. *The men will be griping enough without her adding her complaints.*

"I'm not going now," Margella said indignantly. "Leave a tent for me. I'll catch up with you tomorrow, assuming I survive a night alone."

Darwan halted his horse and raised his eyes to the sky. He exhaled loudly and then turned back to her. "You can't stay here alone."

"Then I guess you'll have to stay here with me," she said.

"We only have a handful of horses, but the ones who do have them will remain here." He pointed to the men milling around the camp. "The men on foot will march ahead. We can catch up with them in the morning."

"Acceptable," she said.

"Please stay here. I'll arrange for tents."

Darwan jumped from his horse, his thighs happy to be out of the saddle. He took only a few steps before a figure materialized from the shadows. Rogan was his First Sword, the leader of the men in Darwan's warband. Good at killing and intimidation, he had no other discernible skills. "Lord Darwan." Rogan wore the smug look of someone who'd just gotten away with something.

"Rogan, we need to keep a few tents. The Lady Margella doesn't want to march until she's rested." He doubted he'd managed to disguise his annoyance with the woman.

"Where did you find that rayth?" Rogan asked flatly. He rarely showed any emotion unless he was taunting someone.

"She's the king's adviser."

"Of course she is," Rogan said. He was armed in the classical Sarasin fashion, though it was out of favor now. He wore armor of banded iron strips painted with black and red enamel, twin daggers at his waist, and twin swords slung over his back. The armor was pockmarked with dents and scrapes, and some of the red on it wasn't actually enamel. It covered his shoulders, but only thick leather sleeves protected his arms. A leather kilt and leggings rounded out his garb. In combat, he wore a traditional Sarasin helmet, but at the moment his oily hair flowed around a haggard face.

"I need you to lead the men north along this road," Darwan said, pointing into the darkness. "Well, there's a road out there somewhere. I'm sure you can find it. I'll remain here with Zane and the messengers. We'll join you as soon as we can."

"The men aren't happy."

"Break out an extra ration of roca leaves. That should placate them."

Dried roca leaves were rehydrated with juice from the blood fruit. The men would place the leaves in their cheeks and let the euphoric juices leech into them. The habit was common in the army, though prolonged use stained the men's teeth a deep shade of red. They thought it was magical, that red teeth was the mark of Gol, the god of the Red.

Darwan knew better. He'd seen the leaves harvested in huge bales, and knew there was nothing magical about the roca leaves, except for the calming effect they had on the men. It allowed them to accept the most awful conditions, as long as the roca kept flowing.

Rogan nodded and walked away, giving a vague salute that could have been mistaken for a nervous tic. Darwan watched him corral the men into rough lines, torchbearers walking in front. The men were fully armed and prepared. They'd be safe unless they walked into the Crotan army, and that was unlikely. Their army was weeks away, if the reports were accurate.

Once the warband faded to flickering points of light, Darwan sensed the silence of the open plains. They had three tents and a small fire. The sense of safety he felt with the warband around him was gone, and threats abounded even here. In the quiet, he heard the distant calls of wolves. He hoped they'd remain distant.

Margella took one of the tents for herself, and didn't appear to want any company. Darwan looked at the fire, seeing just three men. Zane, his steward, and two messengers sat around the small fire, glancing nervously into the black night. Campfires were usually noisy, stoked by beer and bravado, but this fire was quiet. Beyond, five horses stood tied to a post.

Darwan kept his distance from the fire, not wanting to sit with his men, nor sleep in his tent. He paced around the edge of the firelight, searching for signs of danger and fingering the warm tin in his pocket.

Darwan had bought the pyrus several months ago, before they'd left the civilized borders of the Sarasin lands. It was expensive, even for the small number of cubes he had purchased. Pyrus was made from the magical pyrus weed that soaked up the Red magic flow. Only the heretic Fayden Forges could transmute the pyrus from mere weed into the drug. They called themselves alchemists, though everyone knew they were faydens, but their craft was so useful that most ignored their heresy.

He opened the tin and picked out a cube with his fingers. Bringing it to his nose, he blanched at the smell of burnt metal. *I guess I've tried worse*. He plunged the cube into his mouth. It kept its form for a moment before disintegrating into a thick liquid that seared his mouth and forced its way down his throat as though he'd just drunk from a crucible of molten lead.

The heat passed into his belly and radiated outward. A primal thumping in his ears accelerated, then settled into a deep throbbing. Feeling his own pulse, he discovered that the thumping in his head was not in time with his heartbeat. The realization came to him that the pounding was not the rush of blood through his ears; it was the pulse of the Red.

Chapter Eight

Cayne watched the last of the warriors depart from the checkpoint. He'd spent most of the night wiggling away from the road. Through the morning, he watched the warriors break camp and march north, toward his home. He hadn't slept at all, afraid they'd detect him at any moment. He had eaten his remaining supply of food after his stomach grumbled so loudly he feared the soldiers would hear it.

The smell of burning wood filled the air, and small plumes of smoke rose over the horizon. He turned toward home and broke into a steady run, keeping just beyond the sight of the Sarasin warriors. He passed farm after farm, some reduced to smoldering piles of wood, others just ransacked.

Flies and carrion birds swarmed over the carcasses of slaughtered livestock. The buzz of the flies and cries of the birds filled his ears. At three farms, he saw burned bodies nailed up on scorched trees. He swallowed back bile and forced himself to look away. He wanted to bring them down and give them a proper burial, but visions of his mother pushed him toward home. There would be time for burials later.

He neared Dahl Haven, hearing voices for the first time. The wailing shook him; his stomach clenched, as if gripped by an invisible hand. He left the road, crossing a field to where a small stand of trees bordered the houses on the south end of the village. The houses weren't burnt, but the doors were broken and the window shutters were strewn across the yards. He closed in on the voices, but there was no comfort in them. If sorrow and pain had a smell, he swore he smelled it.

Stealing across an empty street, he hustled through the abandoned market, catching his first glimpse of the green. Spears poked up through the crowd. *The Sarasins are not gone.* He placed his sword in the fishmonger's empty stall, hoping he could blend into the crowd.

Even at the height of the summer solstice celebrations, he'd never seen so many people on the green... but this was no festival. Most of the people were crying or sobbing on the ground, while others sat silently, staring into the distance. Cayne slipped into the crowd. If he stood upright, he could see over everyone, but he didn't want to stick out. He kept his head low, trying to blend in.

He saw little boys and girls crying hysterically and clinging to their mothers' skirts. Even the few remaining men, ancient and weathered, who never displayed emotions other than anger in public, were weeping. Cayne filtered through the people, the foreboding grip around his gut tightening further still.

He broke out of the crowd and got his first clear view of the green. Before he could mentally take in the scene, his body had already reacted. Warm, acid-soaked beef, still in bite-sized chunks, surged up through his mouth and splattered down on the grass. It was not the only pile of vomit on the green.

A circle of wooden pikes had been driven into the grass. On the top of each pike was a bloody, decomposing head, and in the center of the circle stood a very-much-alive Tarken Ware. The sight, the wailing, the smell, the flies were too much for Cayne. His stomach convulsed again, but only burning acid came up this time. *Who are, were these heads? What is Tarken doing here?*

Cayne shifted his eyes from head to head. They were disfigured, some branded with hot metal, some with clean cuts across the neck and others with jagged tears. They were young, no older than Cayne, and through the bruising and cuts, they were familiar.

One stood out to him, the vacant eyes searching past him. Burke. A circle of blackened skin around his nose and swollen cheeks couldn't disguise him from Cayne. He stared at Burke without a single thought in his head.

"Cayne," Tarken whispered.

Cayne barely noticed him, though Tarken was standing in front of him now. Slowly he shifted his gaze from Burke's head to his friend. Tarken was battered, his eyes swollen red and raw. Cayne could find no words. He managed only a questioning look.

"It was horrible," Tarken said. "They killed them all in front of me."

"W-w-what?" Cayne stammered. It was too much. In the back of his mind, he knew his brothers and father were dead; but in the front of his mind he refused to accept it. They'd eaten dinner together a few days ago. They couldn't be gone.

Tarken looked at the ground and then to the warriors standing disinterested at the other end of the green. "We were camping on the first night, and when we woke up, Sarasins were everywhere. They took us all."

"My father?"

Tarken looked down again, sweeping his foot on the grass. "The Sarasin king himself came to us the next morning. He screamed at us, calling us oath-breakers. He knew your father had two sons with him, and he made him choose one to live, to tell the story." Tarken cried, but no tears fell. "Your father refused to choose between Burke and Rait. I don't think he believed the king would really spare any of us. It was just to torture him. Your father turned to me and said he owed a blood debt to my father. He said my father died saving him. He chose me to live. I wish he hadn't."

"I don't understand."

Tarken sobbed, but still no tears came to him, as though he was pumping a dry well. "Cayne, they held every head up for me to see. They all looked at me. Their eyes were still moving. It was like they were still alive, but just a head. It was horrible. Some of them took more than one chop. They screamed and screamed." Tarken began to fall apart, screeching like a beast. "I was glad when they finally died. I was glad." Tarken stepped closer to Cayne and touched his arm apologetically.

"My father?" he asked, though he knew already.

"The Sarasin king took your father's head off himself. It was the worst of them." Tarken's eyes widened and he looked right through Cayne. "They put me in a wagon with all the heads and brought us here."

Cayne took Tarken's hand and started to lead him away from the green, but Tarken stood firm, pulling his hand away.

"They're making me stay here," he said, looking to the soldiers. "Making me tell my story to everyone. If I leave, they'll kill me."

"We need to get them down."

"Don't try. Lyssa's father tried." Tarken motioned over to a lifeless heap across the green. Lyssa stood over the body weeping, but not touching. "They wouldn't let anyone help him. He bled to death in front of us."

The villagers parted on the other side of the green, and Rann emerged from the crowd, followed by a detachment of Sarasin warriors. They dragged two hooded men to the center of the green amid the pikes and threw them to the ground. Both men were bound with their hands behind their backs. Rann stood over them with a solemn smile.

"Rann is in charge now," Tarken said.

"Rann? What about the elders?" Cayne asked.

Tarken shook his head slowly and grimaced. "King Arta Nakis blamed them for sending us to fight for King Alarak."

Rann flourished his robes and cleared his throat before addressing the villagers. "King Arta Nakis has instructed me to make all the necessary offerings to the gods in order to obtain their blessings for his campaign. Two among us have so blasphemed the gods that we must visit retribution upon them."

A cold and confused murmur spread across the crowd.

Rann turned to the Sarasins and said, "Do your job."

One of the Sarasins stepped forward and seemed about to attack Rann, though the fourpriest clearly didn't notice. The Sarasin's glare moved from Rann to the two men lying on the ground. He kicked them until they both lay face up. Then he reached down and tore off the hoods to reveal Gliff and another man, who was dressed like a merchant.

"He can't do that," Cayne said to Tarken.

"He's in charge."

The Sarasin pulled out a broad axe. He stood over Gliff and said, "Don't move. Trust me, you don't want me to miss." Gliff rolled over and struggled to pull away. The Sarasin shook his head and then swung his axe, cleaving Gliff's leg off at the knee.

Gliff let out an animal screech and rolled onto his back. He stared up at Rann and spat at him.

Rann wiped the spit from his face and yelled at the Sarasin to finish his work.

The executioner grabbed Gliff by his remaining foot and dragged him away from Rann. "I told you not to move." He swung the axe, but Gliff shifted and it struck grass. The Sarasin fell on Gliff, digging his knees into Gliff's chest. He took the axe and put the blade to Gliff's neck. Then he pushed while he slid the blade back and forth. Gliff cried out only once, but he thrashed wildly.

The crowd looked away in unison. Rann wore a satisfied smile on his face. Gliff had been a fixture of Dahl Haven, and despite his crazy rants, he was one of them. He attended every festival, was first to warn of an impending frost, always grinning with his demented smile. His crime was being a fayden. Cayne felt an inner rage building, but what could he do? Charge the Sarasin warriors and die with Gliff?

The Sarasin finished the cut and held out the severed head to Rann. Then he turned to the merchant and the axe went up high again. "I told him not to move." The second man tried to roll out of the way as well, but he wasn't as fast as Gliff. The blade missed his neck, but cleaved the top of his head off with a sickening scrape. The top half of his skull flopped over and his brain slid partially out.

"That should teach you to extort gold from the gods for your precious goods," Rann said to the second corpse.

Cayne turned from the two corpses and scanned the heads, still rotting on their pikes. Most wore masks of violent terror. One had graying hair. *Father.* This time he couldn't bear to look upon the face. He glanced quickly to the next head, but that face was familiar too. Rait. The agony on his youngest brother's face made Cayne feel burning fury and sorrow at the same time.

Tarken was saying something behind him, but Cayne heard only a faint mumbling. Cayne wiped his nose and stared blankly around the green, much like the other villagers. None of this seemed real. He blinked through blurring eyes.

They were all dead.

Three warriors ran toward the green, the crowd parting to let them pass. They ran up to the other warriors, the first shouting, "Lord Darwan's warband is in sight! They'll be here soon!"

The Sarasin executioner turned to Rann, smiling. Rann didn't return the smile. His face was uncertain with a flash of fear.

"You can't leave," Rann said.

But they did just that.

"The new guards will be here shortly," Rann yelled to the crowd.

"We have time to get them down," Cayne said and took a step forward. Rann intercepted him, placing a hand on his chest.

"The king, your king, King Arta Nakis ordered these to remain for seven days."

Cayne spoke a low growling voice. "I'm taking them. Get out of my way."

The villagers watched the standoff, no one moving.

"Cayne, I am in charge of Dahl Haven, and you will respect my orders." He motioned to the corpses. "Or there will be consequences."

The frustration and anger boiled over and Cayne could hold it back no longer. He grabbed Rann by the front of his robes and poured his fury into a vicious blow. Rann staggered back, clutching his face, and fell to his knees.

The crowd had seen enough. Like a migrating herd, after the first of them jumped into the river, they surged forward to claim their sons. Many were apparently off balance, for as they passed

Rann, they kicked him. Some were clearly staggering, because they kicked him several times.

Cayne stepped in front of his father's head, looking at it fully for the first time. Thinking of his father's last requests, he realized he had failed him in every one. He looked away and saw Lyssa trying to drag Vale's body away. Walking over to her, he gently took her trembling hands away from her father. Cayne took Vale's limp arm, pulled the body up, and raised it on his shoulders. He staggered back to Lyssa's home. There was a grave already dug behind their house, and a body rested at the bottom.

"Mother tried to help father," Lyssa said. She had a lifeless look in her eyes. This Lyssa was unfamiliar to him.

Cayne placed Vale's body as gently as he could into the grave. He stepped back and bowed his head. He turned to Lyssa and put his arms around her. She pushed her weight against him.

"Your father was a good man," Cayne said.

"Yours was to. They loved each other like brothers."

"Your mother was the nicest person I've ever known."

Cayne sighed and squeezed her harder. Lyssa dropped to a mound of dirt. She pushed heavy clumps into the grave. Cayne put a hand on her shoulder. He put his back into a shove with the other, moving a quarter of the pile into the grave.

After they filled the grave, she motioned for him to wait as she went into her house. She reemerged and handed him a large sack of rough cloth. "You'll need this."

He nodded to her and made his way back to the green.

"Cayne," she called after him. "Promise me you'll kill some Sarasins. For my father." Her voice was cold and angry.

He surprised himself with the hatred in his own voice. "I have many to avenge, and I'll add your father to my list. I'll kill them by the hundreds, if I can." It was a boastful and ridiculous statement, but he meant it. She flashed a weak smile at him.

Cayne could see more soldiers marching into Dahl Haven from the south, and he knew he had little time remaining. He recovered his sword and sprinted back to the green. Only three heads remained. Gliff and the merchant were gone, but Rann lay face down on the green. His flowing robes ruffled in the light breeze, but he didn't move. His back was covered with hatchet marks and blood.

Soldiers neared the green, and he knew he was out of time. Without the regard he wished he could give them, he ripped the last three heads from their pikes, ignoring the unnerving sloshing noises. He shoved them unceremoniously into the sack and headed for home.

He ran. Fear for his mother occupied his every thought. He felt disgusted at the way the heads bounced as he ran, but he kept up the pace.

From a distance, he could see the splintered front door of their house, and his stomach clenched again with dread. He sprinted the rest of the way, his vision closing on the open doorway. Bounding off the porch, he skidded to a stop, his eyes adjusting to the darkness within. He gently lowered his sack of heads to the floor.

Across the room, near the hearth, a slumped figure lay motionless in a pool of blood. Dropping his satchel from his back, he ran and knelt next to his mother. She had two deep gashes on her back. He spread his arms around her. Anger and sorrow rushed over Cayne, then guilt, and finally shame. He'd wanted to prove himself to everyone. He'd wanted to be rich, but wealth meant nothing anymore. He wanted his family back.

Cayne looked at his hands. They were covered in blood, some dried, some still wet. Gliff's words echoed in his head: *blood on his hands, blood on the green.*

He cried over his mother's body until the flies came in the afternoon. He swatted angrily at the first few, but soon there were more than he could keep at bay. He knew what he had to do. Cayne left them in the house, and went to dig a hole behind the house. He chose a spot under a sprawling white oak tree.

The recent rains had softened the surface, and he cut a square trench with the precious iron shovel. Cayne dug until he was chest deep in the ground, attacking the dirt as though it was responsible for all this. The few roots he encountered he took off with single sharp blows. Though he'd never seen the Sarasin king, a vague figure formed in his mind. He'd never wanted to kill anyone, but he wanted Arta Nakis to suffer and die, and he wanted to be the one to do it.

He finished the job with the barest sliver of sun remaining on the horizon. He then carried his mother to the hole and gingerly placed her at the bottom, stopping to fix her hair and dress several times, until they were just right. She wouldn't tolerate a messy dress. He took his father's head, and placed it next to his mother, ear to ear, so they'd touch forever. Burke he put at her left side, her arm gathered around him. He put Rait on her right. He stood back and adjusted them repeatedly. This was where they would remain forever. He felt some jealousy, for they would be together... and he was alone.

He stood above the hole, staring, trying to burn their faces into his mind, so he'd never forget. Staring at the dirt pile next to the hole, he shoveled without looking back into the hole until he was certain he'd see only dirt, so as not to ruin his last glimpse of them.

His somber task complete, he walked back to the house, and in the empty space that had been a home just yesterday, the weight of everything fell upon him. He sat on his parent's bed and waited to be scolded for it. He'd seldom even been in their room since he was a child. It was their space, sacrosanct. Then a thought stuck him, and he reached under the bed, finding dust-covered piles of old clothes. On top of them was the Falconstorm banner. He took it and carefully folded it before placing it in his satchel.

Cayne wanted to be away from this place, and yet he couldn't bear to leave. He walked through the dark house, confident in every stride. Opening the door, he took a last glace inside the house. There was only darkness.

He sat on the porch and hugged his knees. He allowed himself the illusion that it was an ordinary night, and that at any moment someone would poke a head out the door and tell him to come inside.

Reality rushed back at him and crushed him. He bawled like a child. He wished his mother would comfort his tears, or that his father would scold him for crying; but that would never happen again in this life.

He curled up on the porch and fell asleep, as he had many times before, but this time no one came to cover him with a blanket.

Chapter Nine

Faylin sprinted to the top of a grassy hill. She felt the long stalks of wild grass bend under her relentless steps. Dew made the grass slick, but she recovered from every slip until she reached the summit. The new morning sun shimmered over the mountains, warming her muzzle. Sitting back on her haunches, she howled toward the sky. Her stomach grumbled in answer. She'd been running aimlessly for more than a day, and though she remembered chasing gazelles and wild turkeys, she hadn't eaten anything.

She released something within her, and power swirled from her fayden. Yes, she had a fayden within her. She knew it as plainly as she knew she had eyes. The only mystery was how she'd not known sooner.

The fayden communicated with her with thoughts, visions, and intuition. At first, they were confusing, but it was getting easier. She looked at her human arms covered in mud and grass. Faylin wanted to cover her naked body, but there was nothing but grass as far as she could see.

Her stomach moaned again. She sensed that Walla lay to the west, so she turned away from the sunrise. Reaching for the fayden's power, she changed in an instant, her paws trampling the grass. She bounded down the hill and toward home.

Faylin reached the first farm by afternoon, but kept her distance. The choice was either to skulk in as a wolf and maybe get an arrow in the side, or traipse into town in the nude. She wasn't sure which would be worse. So she kept to her wolf form, but napped until dark. Then she loped through the night along the abandoned road toward Walla, and shifted to her human form on the outskirts of town. Knowing there might be people near the village center, she stayed on the side streets and sprinted once she was near her home.

Faylin breathed a relieved sigh when she saw her mother and sisters sleeping. She stepped gingerly across the wooden floor, but still it creaked.

"Faylin!" Her young brother hurtled across the single-room house and hugged her. He jumped back from her in surprise. "Eww, why are you naked?"

"Taiza, be quiet."

It was too late. Everyone in the house was stirring. She ran past her little brother and found an old dress. She didn't like wearing dresses, but liked being naked even less. The cotton dress was her mother's, and it fit poorly.

"Faylin, where have you been?" her mother demanded angrily before embracing her. "We went to look for you. We found a dead wolf and thought you were dead." Her ire faded, and she began to smile and cry at the same time.

The rest of her siblings, two sisters and two brothers, greeted her in turn, while her mother gathered a meal. She smiled for them, but she hadn't really missed them. It was as though she was visiting someone else's family. She knew them, but they seemed different.

"I've been keeping candles burning for you in the shrine," her mother said as she broke off a piece of flat bread. "Where were you? And why were you naked?" She put a hand to her mouth and widened her eyes.

Faylin had practiced many accounts during the journey home, but she wasn't sure which of the stories she was actually going to tell. Though they'd sounded clear in her mind, she fumbled for anything coherent to say. "No, I wasn't, I mean, I, I." Gol-damn it, she hadn't prepared an excuse for being nude.

Her mother relaxed and caressed Faylin's face. "You look exhausted. Tell me the whole story in the morning. I'm just glad you're home and safe."

Faylin let go of the breath she hadn't realized she was holding. She attacked the food as if she hadn't eaten in days, which of course she hadn't. When the lights went out, she lay on her bed. Half the night remained, so there was plenty of time to contrive a reasonable story.

She was asleep in two breaths.

The morning brought the welcome scent of breakfast. Faylin snapped open her eyes. She dressed in a hurry and tried to slip from the house. In a one-room house, though, it was an impossible task.

"Faylin, come eat and tell me what happened to you." Her mother waited amid a pile of food. She'd prepared steaming cornbread, fresh-picked berries, and a cold squash soup. Next to her mother, Shari sat smiling as she plucked a plump blueberry from the serving platter.

"I'm glad you're home," Shari said. She smiled with such genuine concern that Faylin forgot the many slights she'd endured at Shari's hands, and leaned in to hug her. "I have to go," Faylin said. "I promised Master Ganji I'd bring him a load of charcoal."

"Absolutely not!" Her mother's face shifted to alarm in an instant.

"I stayed too late last time." She nodded to the open door. "Nothing will happen in daylight. I'll be back before midday." She didn't wait for an answer.

"No." Her mother stood and put her hand on her hips.

"I'll go with you," Shari said. "Let me get my bow."

That seemed to mollify her mother, but she eyed the two girls with suspicion. "Master Ganji will go with you too. If he wants the charcoal so bad, then he can help bring it back."

Faylin peered back at the breakfast her mother had prepared, knowing she must have woken before dawn to make it. She told Shari to wait for her by the road and sat down next to her mother.

"What happened to you?" Her mother brushed the hair from her daughter's face.

Faylin popped a blueberry in her mouth. "I was attacked by a wolf." Her mother poured her a bowl of the soup and offered it to her. "I killed it."

Her mother's eyes went wide, but she remained silent.

"I don't know what happened. I was scared and ran away. I should have come home right away, but I was..."

Her mother embraced her. "You're here now, and that's what's important."

Faylin heard Shari calling from outside. She sipped the soup, then upended the bowl, letting it all flow into her mouth. Smacking her lips, she gave an appreciative sigh. She grabbed the flatbread as she stood.

"I'm going with you."

"Mother, there's nothing to worry about. I'll be with Shari and Master Ganji. We'll be back before lunch." She backed toward the door.

"If you're not—"

"I will be." Faylin walked out the door. She cut behind her house and bypassed Master Ganji's forge. She was on the eastern road when she heard footsteps running up to her.

"I thought we were supposed to get Master Ganji." Shari had an unstrung bow in one hand and a sack in the other. She had to jog to keep up with Faylin's brisk gait.

"You don't need to come. I can handle this by myself."

"I know." She caught up with Faylin. "Are we in a hurry?"

Faylin slowed to a walk, though it felt like a crawl to her. "You really don't need to come. Honestly."

"I want to come." Shari paused to catch her breath. "I was worried about you. Everyone thought you were dead."

"I doubt many people cared."

"I did. A lot of people did. Half the village was out looking for you."

Faylin stopped. "Really?" Shari nodded earnestly. "How long was I missing?"

Shari gave her a bewildered look. "You were gone for a week."

Now it was Faylin's turn to be shocked. She'd thought it might have been two days, maybe three, but not a week. Little wonder she was so hungry. She absently took a bite of the bread in her hand, then started walking again, still digesting the revelation. "Can I tell you something?"

"Of course."

"Can you keep it secret?"

Shari nodded and looked around, but they were alone. Faylin noticed for the first time that she'd left home without her moccasins. The packed dirt road was still cold and kissed with morning dew.

She took a deep breath and savored the cool air. Faylin exhaled again, unsure how to start. She spied the cart in the distance. "I see the mound." She broke into a run, putting the village and the conversation behind her.

The mound was intact. She smashed the walls and pulled out blackened logs of charcoal. They broke into smaller shards as she tossed them into the cart.

Shari ran up, out of breath again. She strung her bow, nocked an arrow, and placed them in easy reach. Then she grabbed a log, albeit one of the smaller ones. In short order, the charcoal was in the cart and the girls were covered in black soot. Shari tried to brush it off her skin and clothes, but Faylin knew better. "That just spreads it around more."

They loaded the tools, and Faylin pulled the cart. Her muscles strained to get the cart into motion over the uneven terrain. Shari pushed it from behind, but it was still like pulling a full-grown tree. They reached the road and stopped to rest.

"Was there something you wanted to tell me?" Shari asked.

Faylin grimaced. She needed to skirt the topic and get a sense of how Shari might react. If it didn't feel right, then she could back off the topic.

"I'm a skinwalker now." *Well, that was indirect.* She braced herself.

Shari's mouth opened and her jaw dropped. She stared at Faylin, and mouthed the word without speaking.

Faylin was committed now. "Don't be afraid." She stripped her clothes off, with only a slight sense of embarrassment. She reached for the wolf within herself, and her fayden responded. The newly familiar sensation rolled over her, and in a blink, she was on her four paws.

Shari jumped backward and fell on her hind end. She scrambled away from the road.

Faylin sat and put her face low to the ground in what she hoped was a docile stance. Shari stood slowly and locked her gaze on Faylin. She walked up hesitantly and extended a hand to ruffle the fur on Faylin's head. It felt surprisingly good.

She let the wolf go and put her clothes back on. The clothes felt restricting and wrong.

"You're a skinwalker." Shari sounded fascinated, scared, and exuberant all at the same time.

"That wolf I killed... it changed me. Are you afraid of me?"

"It was pretty scary to see you transform."

"I may look like a wolf, but I'm still me." Faylin said it convincingly, but she wasn't sure if it was true. She felt different now, whether she was in her wolf form or not.

"Being close to a wolf is frightening, but I realized it was you, and then I wasn't scared anymore." Shari reached out and touched Faylin's face. "What's it like?"

"Strange at first, but then you get used to it."

"Have you told anyone else?"

Faylin shook her head. The fourpriest, her mother, everyone had taught her to fear faydens. They were heretics, denying the gods, so now she was a heretic. They were horrid abominations, incapable of civilized behavior, so now *she* was an abomination.

"We should get back," Faylin said. "Master Ganji has been waiting for days."

They pushed the cart into motion. It moved much easier on the well-packed road. They made good time, and before noon, they were unloading the sooty lumps into a pile in front of the forge. Master Ganji helped them, and handed Faylin a string of beads. She saw silver and copper, but didn't bother to count them. It was more than enough to support her family for a week.

Faylin headed back toward her home with Shari walking next to her. The awkward silence lasted until they reached home. Shari cleared her throat, and Faylin braced herself for a polite rebuke. "I was thinking," Shari said, putting a finger to her mouth. "If you're a fayden– " She looked around and continued in lower voice. "If you're a fayden, then maybe you should talk to another fayden for advice. Meda must know something helpful."

Faylin smiled at Shari. She felt badly for assuming her childhood friend would disown her, when she was really thinking about how to help her. Faylin had felt a mixture of distaste and envy of her for the past few years, but now Shari seemed different.

"That's a fantastic idea. I don't know why I didn't think of it."

Faylin faced to the north and took two steps, then turned back and stared at Shari.

"I won't tell anyone," Shari pledged. "I promise."

Faylin nodded her thanks and walked away. It felt good to have someone else who knew her secret. Perhaps her fear was only in her mind. Perhaps her friends would accept her as a fayden, and she could stay in Walla.

Meda's small home was nestled between three grand oak trees, keeping it in near-perpetual shade. All the windows were open to let in the breeze, and she heard a conversation inside. Despite that, she walked to the door and rapped on it several times.

"Be coming in, Faylin," Meda said, opening the door, as though she'd been standing next to it waiting for her. She wore a short cotton dress that was far too short to be out in public.

"How did you know it was me?"

"I'm a seer. I am having the sight, after all."

Faylin stepped into the simple home. Like most homes, it consisted of a single room with a hearth. Another woman sat cross-legged on the floor next to a low table. She wasn't from Walla, and that was unusual. Not many people came to a place like Walla.

"Don't let her fool you, deary," the woman said. "She got up to get a drink and saw you coming through the window."

Meda scowled at the older woman. "This is betweening me and my flock, Akwane." *Betweening?* Faylin wasn't sure which was stranger: that Meda was making up new words or that she thought of the town as her flock. The townsfolk certainly didn't think of her as their shepherd.

The two women stared at each other in an odd contest of wills.

"Was I interrupting something?" Faylin said, uncomfortable at the silence. "I can come back later." She backed toward the door.

"Yes, interrupting," Meda said, not breaking her focus or turning to look. She walked backwards and reached for the door to shut it. Faylin couldn't get out of her way, so she ended up pushing Faylin's chest instead.

Meda jerked her head to face Faylin. Her hand, still outstretched, hovered in front of Faylin. Her eyes grew wide and a ridiculously large grin spread across her face. "When are you becoming a fayden?"

Akwane got up to her feet and walked to them. She put her hand out as well. "Fayden Form. Skinwalker. Greetings."

Meda took Faylin by the arm and pulled her toward the table. Meda placed a cup in front of each woman and a kettle on the table. Akwane reached into her blouse and pulled out a red gemstone. The pyricite was cut in a circular shape with a hole in the middle. She dangled the gemstone from a length of green string tied through the hole. The two younger women stared at the boiler stone.

Every home had a stone like this, but they were usually small, uncut, and none of them had strings attached to them. You dropped it in a pot and waited for it to heat the water.

Akwane twirled the stone a few times and then lowered it into the kettle with a quick hissing sound. She kept swirling the stone inside the kettle, and after only half a dozen circles of her wrist, quick wisps of steam seeped up from the water. She used her free hand to drop in twigs of scored sassafras root, followed by a ladle of honey. By the time the last strings of honey fell into the kettle, it boiled furiously. Akwane withdrew the gem and let the wetness burn off before putting it in a small pouch.

"It's wonderful," Faylin said. "How can you carry it? Isn't it hot?" The smaller crystals they had at home remained hot for quite some time.

Akwane held out the pouch for her to examine. Faylin marveled at the tightly woven green thread. She touched the pouch, expecting it to be hot, but it was cool. "It's made of wanis," Akwane explained.

"Where are you getting this from?" Meda asked. "Is worth more than my entire home." She waved a sarcastic hand.

Faylin agreed with Meda's assessment. The heater stone itself was expensive, but if the lanyard and pouch were made of wanis, then they were at least as valuable as the crystal itself. Only alchemists could make wanis. Somehow they transformed the vines of the sagia trees into a cord as strong as iron, but as flexible as rope. She couldn't even venture a guess at how much it had cost, and Akwane was using it to heat a pot of tea.

"Akwane is a Fayden Touch," Meda said, patting the healer lightly on the shoulder. "She is traveling from Galen Ferry. Healing our sick."

"I'm leaving tomorrow," Akwane said. "Meda is coming with me."

"You are leaving too," Meda said, giving Faylin a stern look.

"I'm not leaving," Faylin declared. "This is my home."

"You can't stay here," Meda said, shaking her head vigorously. "They won't allow a skinwalker to live here."

"I've already told one person and she accepted me. The rest will too. I won't hurt anyone."

"Meda is right, deary. They tolerate some faydens, *if* we have useful skills and don't pose a threat. Skinwalkers are not among those they will bear."

Meda waved her hands. "Even if they are tolerating you, you are still leaving. Danger approaching. A visitor is telling me of it. We must leave."

"She claims she met a Fayden Fate, and he told her tribulations were coming to Walla. I don't know if I believe her," said Akwane.

Meda scowled at her as though they'd been arguing about this before.

"What's a Fayden Fate?" Faylin asked. She'd heard about many of the Faydens, but never one called by that name.

Akwane leaned toward Faylin. "I've never met one myself. They're called mystics, and supposedly they walk in time."

"I am talking with one last week. He is telling me of danger and asking a favor. If I am not doing this favor, I am risking our future."

"Sure you are, deary." Akwane didn't mask her doubt in any way. She turned a sorrowful gaze to Faylin. "Regardless, you can't stay here. I know this is hard, but you have to accept your new place in life. You're a skinwalker, and *civilized* society won't accept you. It shouldn't be like that, but it is."

"I won't accept that. I'll make them understand."

Akwane's expression darkened. "This is hardest on your kind. You live so long without knowing you have a fayden. It's like some cruel master simply flips a switch and nothing is ever the same again."

Faylin got to her feet. "I thought it would be helpful to talk with another fayden, but I was wrong." She walked to the door. "Meda, if you know of a danger to Walla, you need to warn us. What's going to happen?"

"Death and destruction."

Faylin turned back to the women. "Why have you not warned anyone? You're supposed to help us. Do you have any details?"

"Calming yourself down," Meda said. "The visitor is only speaking of danger and favors."

"What favors?" Faylin asked.

"Little things, nothing really. He is warning me and telling me not to tell anyone else."

"That's not a small favor, Meda. If this danger is as bad as you think it is, he was asking you to let us all suffer. Tell me something I can tell the council, something that will let us know how to prepare."

"There is no preparing. This will happen, must happen, has already happened."

Faylin gritted her teeth. Meda was infuriating. She made no sense, and maybe that was all there was to it. Meda had had a mad vision, and now she was rambling about something that might have happened years ago—or perhaps only in her imagination, since not everything she predicted came true. Either way, there was nothing to learn here. She opened the door, trying to calm herself and ignore Meda's continued banter.

"The other favor was so odd," Meda said. Apparently, she'd kept talking, despite the fact that Faylin had walked out on her. "Convincing the council to reopen the forge."

Faylin froze. Meda had convinced the council to reopen the forge, causing master Ganji to ask her for charcoal, which put Faylin outside Walla, where she encountered the wolf. *A string of coincidences? I think not. That man caused me to become a fayden!*

Chapter Ten

Faylin turned and strode back into the house. "Where is this mystic? Why did he ask you to get the forge reopened? I need to talk with him."

Meda shrugged her shoulders and clicked her tongue. "Not knowing."

"You don't find a mystic, deary," Akwane said. "They find you."

"I thought you didn't believe in them," Faylin said.

"Oh, I believe in them," Akwane said. She nodded at Meda. "I'm just not sure I believe that she talked with one."

Faylin frowned at both of them.

"Is not mattering anyway," Meda said, putting her hands on her hips. "The council already was considering asking Master Ganji. I am making no difference." She sneered openly at the older woman.

"It *does* matter," Faylin said, more forcefully than she'd intended. "Master Ganji asked me to make charcoal for him, and while I was doing that, I was attacked by a wolf, and..."

"You learned of your fayden," Akwane finished in a kindly voice. She took Faylin by the arm and steered her outside. Meda remained in the house muttering to herself. The healer patted Faylin's arm as they walked. "We faydens must help each other. Fay knows no one else will."

"Does Fay exist?" Fay was the heretical god of the faydens. Everything she knew about Fay came from the fourpriest and her mother, neither of whom had anything but enmity for Fay.

"Do the Four exist?"

Faylin nodded. She was as certain of the four gods as she was of anything.

"Have you ever seen one of them? Have they ever spoken to you?"

"The fourpriest says he speaks to the gods and they send him signs in response." She pointed to Akwane's breast. "The boiler stone is proof of the Red."

The healer took a breath to speak, but paused. Her expression shifted to one of compassion. "Fair enough, but if a boiler stone is proof of the Red, then isn't the fact you can turn into a wolf proof of Fay?"

Faylin considered the words. The implications overwhelmed her. Everything she knew felt suddenly fragile, like thin ice over a pond. The cracks of doubt spread out in myriad directions, and fear gripped her just as solidly as if she was standing in the middle of a lake, listening to the creaking of the ice under her feet.

Akwane must have sensed her discomfort. "You should come with us. We will do what we can to help you."

Faylin only faintly heard what she'd said, and she couldn't formulate a response. She focused on the real sensation of Akwane's hand, which had shifted to her back. The gentle stroking comforted Faylin, but she still said nothing.

"I have seen this before. No matter what you may think, you cannot remain here. I know this is your home and it's unsettling to think about leaving, but you must."

"I'm staying here," Faylin said in a whisper. "This is my home. If there is danger coming, then maybe I can help protect Walla."

"You must find your way, Faylin. I suspect your path is out there," she said, pointing away from the village. She turned her hand toward Walla. "I fear only pain remains for you here."

"Meda lives here. You live in a town. Why can't I?"

"You're a skinwalker, and that makes all the difference. As I said, the ignorant people of these lands tolerate faydens, but only if they have useful abilities."

Faylin looked to the ground. "Like healing or seeing."

"Our abilities are seen as helpful; yours are not. They will see you as a threat. Perhaps not today, but soon." She spread her arms. "There are others like you out there. You should seek them. They can help you more than I can."

"It's not fair."

"No, it is not."

"Can you heal me of this affliction?"

Akwane gave her a sharp glare. "This is no affliction. You have a gift, not a curse."

"It doesn't feel like that."

The healer sighed, and her expression returned to a maternal state. "Regardless, my ability doesn't work like that. I don't heal, in fact." She chuckled softly to herself. "I can see into a person's health and I just know what remedies they require. Sometimes I see into them and know there is nothing that can be done. I diagnose and prescribe, but I don't heal."

"I'm going to stay here."

"I know. We will be leaving tomorrow, if you change your mind."

"How did you know I would stay? Are you a seer too, or can you see into my intentions with your ability?"

"No, I'm simply an old woman." She patted Faylin's back. "I've seen many stubborn girls in my time."

"I am that," she admitted. She gave Akwane an awkward hug and left her standing near the road. Her fayden sent emotions and visions to her that made it clear it believed the two faydens, and that Faylin should leave Walla. She ignored the thoughts and pressed on toward the shrine.

She hoped her mother would be there, and Faylin resolved to tell her as soon as she saw her. *She will accept me.* Streaks of doubt crossed her soul, but she kept moving.

When she reached the village green, she saw her mother walking with the fourpriest. He had his hands clasped behind his back. Her mother spoke with wild gestures. She'd always spoken more with her hands than her voice. Faylin didn't remember her and the Fourpriest being so familiar, but they walked very close together.

"Mother." The pair turned to regard her. Faylin took a deep breath and grasped for anything to say. They looked at her, expectantly at first, and then with annoyance.

"What is it, Faylin?" her mother asked.

"I was talking to Meda and she said something very bad was about to happen." She wanted to smack herself for losing the nerve to say what was really on her mind.

"Why were you talking to that abomination?" the fourpriest asked. Gasho was new to Walla, have only arrived before the spring equinox festival. The previous fourpriest had succumbed to illness during the winter after he refused any type of help from a fayden. It made sense to Faylin at the time, but now seemed plain foolish. *Am I being foolish too by ignoring their counsel?*

Gasho wore spring reds. The many long strips of dyed cloth gave his form an ambiguous character, making it hard to know if he was thin or plump. She judged by his full face that he was plump.

Her mother looked at her with equal concern. "You should never talk to her." She turned apologetically to the priest. "I've always told her not to associate with such creatures."

"She's just a fayden," Faylin said. They both returned open-mouth stares at her, as though she'd just hurled slurs at them. "I mean, there's nothing dangerous about her. She has a gift, and we should harness it."

They all stared at each other for a long moment. Faylin felt a rush of sweat flash across her body. Her gaze fixed on her mother, who seemed to grow in stature. Her mother's eyes bulged, and her mouth opened wide enough to swallow a pumpkin whole. Stepping back, Faylin felt the weight of dozens of horrified stares, and looked down to see paws protruding from her torn dress.

The tattered clothes restricted her movements. Her heart thumped furiously as she bit and tore the dress. Only when she was free of the garments did she realize she must have looked like a rabid animal as she wrested herself free of the clothes. The townsfolk had recovered from the initial shock and were mustering in her direction.

"Heretic!" Gasho shouted. He pointed a crooked finger at her.

Faylin looked to her mother, but she too was pointing. She mouthed the same word, but nothing audible came out.

Faylin broke into a sprint. She raced through the town, ignoring the surprised looks she garnered around every corner. Reaching home, she circled to the shed behind the house. She'd often hidden there when she was young. Webs and dust filled the corners. They used it to store wood for the winter, but since they hadn't started to stockpile yet, it was largely empty.

She settled to the ground and slowed her breathing. After a time, she was able to change back to her human form. As soon as she did, she started to cry.

"Faylin?" Shari poked her head into the shed. She stepped in and closed the door behind her. "Are you all right?" She carried a small sack, but put it down as she rushed to Faylin's side. She put a tentative hand around Faylin's shoulder. Only then did Faylin realize she was naked.

"It was awful, I couldn't control it! I turned into a wolf in front of everyone!"

"I know. I was there too."

"You were?" Faylin turned a hopeful glance at her. "Did you explain to them? Did you tell them I'm not a threat?"

Shari looked away. "No. I'm sorry. There was no talking to them. Gasho was organizing a party to hunt you."

"Mother?"

"She was crying, but she agreed. She said her daughter was dead now and replaced by a fayden."

"I have to think of a way to make them understand."

Shari reached for the sack and held it out to Faylin. "This is all the food I could find." She looked up at the shed around them. "When you weren't at home, I thought you might be here."

"Our old hiding place. Safe from the world." Faylin sniffled, but the tears were gone now. "I have to go, don't I?"

Shari nodded. "You can't reason with them."

Faylin took the sack and stood. "Stay here. I don't want them to see you with me." She walked to the door and opened it a crack. Though she heard shouting in the distance, no one was nearby.

"Here, take this." Shari stripped her dress off and offered it to her.

Faylin looked self-consciously at herself, and then at Shari. She saw plainly why the men of Walla were so interested in her friend.

"Take it," Shari insisted. "I live right next door. I think I can run that distance without being seen."

"Thank you." Faylin took the garments and put them on as fast as she could manage.

"Where will you go?"

Faylin shrugged. "South, I guess. Along the road and past the farms."

"Then what?"

Faylin sighed and shook her head. "I'll think of something."

"I'll try to get out there and bring you more food," Shari promised.

Faylin almost cried again in gratitude. She turned back to Shari and hugged her gently. "You don't need to help me."

"I want to help."

"You don't need to, but if you do, wait a few days before you venture out."

Shari nodded, and Faylin crept out into the daylight. She darted across the vacant street and past another line of houses. Behind them she found the shelter of the thick grove of trees that made up the western part of the village.

The distant shouts behind her faded as her ever-increasing pace put more trees between Faylin and her pursuers. Beyond the trees, she ran through the low rows of maize, casting frequent glances backwards. She made a long arc that brought her to the southern road.

Few families lived to the south. After the last farm home, she looked for shelter. Just west of the road, she saw a small rise covered in thick brambles and a smattering of tall trees.

She dropped her weary bones next to the trunk of an elderly oak. The thick tree was solid and comforting. She ate half the food in rapid bites; Shari had given her nuts, berries, and a few unripened squash. It was filling, but Faylin yearned for meat.

She spent the next day gathering fallen branches to make a shelter. She wished she'd thought to bring a hatchet or knife with her. By sunset, she had a crude roof to keep the rain off. She sat down and listened to her stomach's groaning protests.

She'd eaten the last of her food at lunch, and after spending the day dragging heavy branches, she was ravenous. The night brought a cool breeze that was refreshing—at first. When she started to shiver, she pulled her knees up to her chest and nestled against the oak trunk. *I should have brought a blanket too.*

She'd spent half the night trying to sleep before she realized she didn't need a blanket. She reached for her fayden and turned into her wolf form. The cold vanished immediately and she curled into a comfortable circle, resting her muzzle on her forelegs.

Faylin awoke the next day to rumblings from her belly. Sniffing the air, she picked up the scent of prey nearby. She stalked out of her den, keeping low to the ground. They were rabbits, though she wasn't sure how she knew that with such certainty.

She saw three rabbits munching on broad-leaf grasses. There were two males and a female. The males had the small antler buds that signaled they were both juveniles. When they reached adulthood, they'd have a full rack of pointy antlers to help them fend off predators.

They stopped eating and sniffed the air. Sensing they were about to bolt, Faylin burst forward into a full sprint. The rabbits scattered, but Faylin kept her eyes locked on the smaller male. He was the weakest.

The rabbit tried to make a quick turn to the right and get away, but Faylin reached out a paw and sank her claws into its hindquarters. Her momentum carried her past her prey, but her blow sent it sprawling. She shifted direction and got her paws on it before it could regain its footing. The rabbit struggled futilely. Faylin felt the hunger, and the need to clamp her teeth on its throat. She hesitated, loosening her hold on her prey. It wriggled its way free and shot across the field. She sat back on her haunches, thinking dully, *I'm not even a very good wolf.*

Faylin padded back to her den and listened to the protests of her stomach for the rest of the day. Despite the hunger, she refused to hunt again.

She sensed the images and feelings of her fayden like a second self in her mind. They weren't wild or aggressive visions. It sent her thoughts of peace and comfort. She tried to talk with it, but wasn't sure if it understood what she was saying. Regardless, it was trying to communicate with her. She didn't find it as disturbing as she had anticipated. Alone there in her den, it provided constant companionship.

They communicated like two people who could only trade drawings and facial expressions. After another day of hunger and communion with her fayden, she found a place of peace. The communication with her fayden became easier, and she could understand more of what it told her.

Her fayden also felt unfamiliar with the communication. It had slumbered within her for all her life, only awakening when she killed the wolf. The fayden wasn't a wolf spirit itself, but it had absorbed the spirit of the wolf. It would have done the same if she had killed a different beast.

She'd been around other animals being slaughtered for festivals. Why hadn't this happened sooner? Her fayden sent her a single idea: *gravitas*. Somehow, she understood. It had to be a beast of enough power to awaken the fayden. Killing a chicken or a rabbit wasn't enough.

By the next morning, she found clarity unlike anything she'd ever known. Her fayden wasn't a heretic, and neither was she. The fact she had a fayden wasn't good or bad, it simply *was*. Much of what she'd once known as right and wrong was really neither. She sat in the early morning sun and took a deep breath of moist air.

She caught a scent that disturbed her reverie. Once again, Faylin stalked out in a hunting stance. The grass wasn't high here, but it would be enough. The scent was familiar, and a lone figure walked along the road. Her tail wagging, Faylin walked back to her den and took her human form. She put on the dress and waved to Shari.

Shari carried a pair of satchels, one slung over each shoulder. Though she was glad to see Shari, Faylin didn't feel as excited as she expected to after such solitude. A quick image from her fayden reminded her that she wasn't really alone. It was somehow deeply reassuring to know she would never be alone again.

Shari dropped the satchels and embraced Faylin. "I'm sorry I couldn't get here before now."

"I'm just glad you're here now. How are things in Walla?" She dreaded the answer, but nonetheless waited with a sense of hopefulness.

"Not good. You've been declared a heretic. If you go back, they'll probably kill you. Maybe if you wait a few weeks, things will change."

It was what she'd expected, though a tiny part of her clung to the hope that she could return. She knew it was false hope. She could never go back, and that was neither good nor bad. It just was. "No, I can never go back. They told me this is how it would be, but I didn't want to believe them."

"Who?" Shari picked up and offered her one of the satchels.

"Meda and Akwane." Faylin reached inside and felt dried meat. She wasn't sure what kind of meat it was, and she didn't care. Gnawing off a bite, Faylin savored the flavor despite an overwhelming desire to stuff the whole thing in her mouth.

"I don't know Akwane, but Meda left two days ago. She didn't tell anyone."

"I should have gone with them."

"Where?" Shari asked.

"It doesn't matter," Faylin said, as she tore off another bite.

"I brought you a few things to help." Shari presented the second bag. "A few things that no one will miss."

"Thank you." Faylin swallowed another chunk of meat, which she now recognized as bison. "I'm sorry for the way I've been over the past few years."

Shari paused before saying, "I figured you were different and didn't want to be friends anymore." She shrugged good-naturedly.

"I guess I thought the same of you. You've helped me, and I'm thankful. You might be my only friend in the world now. Everyone in Walla must hate me."

Shari shook her head, but she didn't deny it. "They only see a skinwalker. They're afraid of you." She looked toward the village. "I should be getting back before I'm missed."

"Yes. Thank you again for everything you've done, but don't come back here. I'm leaving tomorrow."

"Where are you going?"

Faylin pointed to the open plains. "Somewhere out there. I need to find my way, and it isn't here." She sighed, knowing it was true.

"I won't see you again, will I?"

Faylin shook her head, a growing weight squeezing her chest. She stepped forward and embraced Shari. She whispered in her ear, "My fayden's blessing be upon you." The words weren't hers. Her fayden spoke directly through her.

Shari tried to hide her discomfort at the blessing. She stepped back and offered a quick smile. "I hope you find a place where you belong."

Faylin watched her walk away. Shari looked back several times, but kept fading into the distance. When she disappeared over a hill, Faylin took the bags and returned to her den.

She drew a hand-axe from the second satchel and hefted the handle. *Well balanced.* She would put it to good use. Though she liked her den, she'd spied better ground farther from the road. It was on higher ground and offered a better view of the surrounding plains. It would also lessen the chances of anyone spotting her.

She spent the day felling small trees and cutting branches. The entire sack of food was empty before noon, and by dusk, her stomach grumbled as she sat inside her new den. A few more days and she'd have it how she wanted it.

She changed into her wolf form and sniffed the warm evening breeze. She scented prey. Slinking out of her new den, she tracked the scent and found a husk of hares feeding by a stream. She studied them in quick succession, picking out the weakest.

The wind blew in her face, carrying their scent to her. That same breeze would keep them from smelling her, so she crept closer. Faylin took in the entire scene, noting every movement of the grass and the minuscule shifts in the wind.

One of the hares cast a glance in her direction, and though it hadn't spotted her, it still triggered a response. Faylin lunged forward into a full sprint, her eyes locked on her prey. The other hares shot off in every direction, but her focus was absolute.

The short chase ended with Faylin pinning the hare to the ground. This time there was no hesitation. Her powerful jaws locked on the hare's throat, and this time, she ate.

Chapter Eleven

Lord Darwan rode along the trampled remnants of a dirt road, now scarred and cut from the iron-rimmed wagon wheels slicing the ground. More men had walked this road in the last day than in the century before it.

Margella had slept much of the day away. When they finally got moving, she refused to push her horse above a walk. Darwan had to send Zane and the messengers ahead to join the warband while he kept pace with her.

She looked over her shoulder at him and smiled. Divided skirts of silvery cotton lifted high enough to reveal her knees. A tight silver tunic clung to her curves in a very intentional way. As before, a black veil covered most of her face.

They'd passed the burnt remnants of farms, and were nearing the village. "Shall we camp here for the night?" she asked.

Darwan looked at her and then to the village ahead. His confusion gave way to desire as her innuendo dawned on him... but the king would have his head, or other parts of his anatomy. Despite those concerns, he felt himself falling under her charms and considering her offer. He yearned for the pyrus, for the Red. It gave him strength, and he needed it now.

Zane approached them on a horse, to Darwan's relief and annoyance. Zane's horse was no warhorse like Darwan's mount. It was a simple traveling breed, well kept, but small and old. "We've secured the town ahead," he reported.

"I'm glad to see we can still secure a town of farmers," said Darwan.

"We're well on our way to making sure we leave nothing behind." Zane glanced toward a shrill scream coming from the village. "Well, almost nothing."

"Seeing to the needs of the locals?"

Zane laughed. "They won't soon forget this day."

"Soon they'll be our people to protect."

Zane looked up to the sky with a reflective expression. It didn't fit him or his diminutive mind.

"Rogan?" Darwan asked, pushing his horse into motion.

"Rogan is busy being Rogan," Zane said, shaking his head. "He's sweeping the town for recruits. He's mustered a few boys, but they're more suited to a game of lakros than being in an army."

"Rogan swears he can train them on the march," Darwan said doubtfully. Had the man never seen a game of lakros played at the Tekahtaman? The stakes for that *game* were grave, and the competitors played it like their lives depended on it, which it did. The winning team earned the right to sacrifice the losers to the gods. In the borderlands, stories said, the winners ate the losers.

Zane rode quietly next to him, waiting for Darwan to speak. It was pointless to ask the dullard his opinion, but he did anyway. "What do you think of his recruits?"

"I guess it's better to have him killing them than our own men. If there's a battle, he intends for them to lead. They can stop a few arrows, and the enemy will waste energy hacking them down."

"I'm not so sure of their value. Soon there may be more of them than us." Darwan pondered his own words, but Zane didn't seem to grasp any danger. Rogan called them recruits, but they were little more than a rabble. He did scantly more than torture them, though he called it training.

"Not a drop of beer in the entire town." Zane shook his head. "We'll have to drink more of that nasty field beer tonight."

"Lady Margella, perhaps you should camp outside the town tonight," Darwan said. "The screams can make it difficult to sleep."

She never looked at either of them, but she laughed softly. "I will stay in this town tonight. I find the lamentations of these people pleasing to my ears."

Darwan traded disgusted glances with Zane. He'd need the pyrus tonight to dull the screams, and she'd sleep like the dead, or maybe she'd stay up to listen. Either way, she was as ugly on the inside as she was beautiful on the outside. *Not unlike myself.*

"Have the men in formation at first light." Darwan nodded to Zane, dismissing him.

Zane remained by Darwan's side. "Sir. There was an... incident." Zane looked at him apprehensively, but then continued. "Rogan recruited some young boys. One of our men was *interested* in one boy in particular, and he asked Rogan for him."

"This does not end well, does it?"

Zane shook his head, looking at the ground. "Rogan told him he'd have to take the boy. Apparently, he thought Rogan was joking with him."

"Rogan has no sense of humor."

"Exactly. Rogan cut him down." Zane shrugged.

"One less Sarasin among us," Darwan sighed. "We're already the smallest warband in the army. Any other good news to share?"

"Your quarters are ready. I placed your standard by the door."

Darwan shifted his reins, and his horse moved into the small village. It looked different from last night. He dismounted and threw his reins to a warrior by the stable. There were only a handful of horses today.

Walking to the green, he puzzled at the stand of pikes topped by a mix of blood and ichor. They were low to the ground, so he assumed the king had mounted heads on them. *That is his style.* In the first village they'd sacked, Arta Nakis had impaled dozens of hapless souls. Those pikes were much taller, and the king stuck the entire bodies up there before he burned them. That was the reward he gave to oath-breakers.

Darwan was alone on the green, the villagers hidden behind closed doors and shuttered windows. He heard a sharp banging. His men were forcing their way into a house. He'd given them free rein to take whatever remained here, though he doubted there was much left.

His banner fluttered in front of a small house. Darwan passed the red-and-black flag and opened the door. His cot and desk were already placed exactly according to his preferences. He fell onto the cot, staring at the thatched roof. He slept fitfully until a knock at his door awoke him.

"Lord Darwan," a voice inquired from outside the door.

Zane again. He was a gambler, and had killed Darwan's previous steward in a fight over a game of dice. Under the rules of Tekahta, the Sarasin customs of succession, Zane became his new steward. Darwan knew Zane didn't like being a steward, but someone needed to play the role.

"Enter."

"The Lady Margella has asked for you." Zane said.

"Who does she think she is? Who's the lord and who's the king's ..." Darwan looked for the right word, but knowing how the drinking loosened Zane's lips, he held his anger and thought of a less dangerous word. "Adviser." Zane was clearly disappointed with his choice. "Inform her I'll be along as soon as my duties allow."

Zane smiled and backed out of the house with a slight bow. Darwan thought of her; it was hard not to think of her.

He rolled up and reached for the tin tucked away in his pocket. He took one cube of pyrus and held it up. It was warm, inviting, and he only waited a moment before plunging it into his mouth. It disintegrated into that luscious liquid, oozing down his throat. Warmth enveloped him. It was like eating iron shavings, but he was developing a fondness for iron. He let the Red take him.

Darwan stepped out into the evening feeling stronger, quicker, even taller. The Red was within him, making everything before him seem like ripe fruit to be plucked. He strode toward Margella's quarters, his senses sizzling. He threw open the door to the small home and walked right in. In the darkened room, he had to wait for his eyes to adjust. She reclined on several furs stacked in one corner of the room, unconcerned about his forceful entry.

His eyes focused on her form faster than normal, and he knew it was the Red. She was more vibrant than she should have been with almost no light, and he sensed a faint scent of jasmine about her. He hadn't noticed it before. She wore little more than a simple frock. It covered less than the long black hair draped over her chest. Her body was lithe, but curved in the right places, and she plainly enjoyed tempting men with it. She was never without her veil, wearing it even here in the privacy of her house.

"Darwan, you *pleasure* me," she purred, her voice like silk, "with your presence."

"You asked for me." He studied her clinically, without emotion or desire.

She sat up and threw her hair back, baring her chest, which was easily visible through the transparent fabric of her frock. He still felt nothing, and she seemed to know it. *It bothers her.* He felt a sudden surge of the Red starting in his belly and radiating outward, and as it did, she shimmered like a mirage.

Margella crooked her head and studied him. Her words came slow. "You are influenced. By what?" She sniffed the air and bent her head the other way. "You have the stink of the Red on you. What have you been doing?"

"What I do is not your concern. You asked for me, so what's your business?" he demanded. *How does she know about the Red?*

She stood up, letting her frock fall to the floor, while she scrutinized his reaction. He felt something now, but not what he expected. His hand shifted to the hilt of his sword. The Red wanted to slay her, but the urge was almost playful, if that was even possible. The pulsating senses echoed in his head, and he felt sweat bead on his hands and face. Again she shimmered, abruptly looking much older. Her arms grew sun spots, varicose veins formed on her legs, and her face withered. The surge of pyrus subsided as suddenly as it had come, and she was perfect again.

"Pyrus," she declared, stepping backwards. "Leave me. Come back when you're less filthy."

"As you wish, Lady Margella," he said, bowing and backing out of the house. He mused over how she had known of the pyrus, and why he'd felt the urge to kill her. It was his job to protect her. Given how young and beautiful Margella was, he'd assumed the king had simply been using her for his pleasures. Now he suspected Margella was using the king. Arta Nakis was firmly under her spell, so warning him might just as easily end with Darwan's own death instead of hers.

He perceived someone walking toward him, but he didn't need to look. The Red had sharpened his senses so much that from the quick pace and the smooth movement, he knew it was Rogan.

"My lord," Rogan said with a slight bow. "I hope your meeting went well."

"It was interesting," Darwan said without looking up. It was rude, but he was a lord and still deep in thought.

"The men are settled, as you ordered."

After a moment, Darwan looked at Rogan, reading his face. "You have something else to tell me." The pyrus surged again, and he could sense something about Rogan. Darwan's hand shifted to his sword. The Red wanted Rogan dead. The feeling was different from what he'd felt with Margella, but yes, the Red wanted him dead.

"My lord, the king's rayth has been walking around wearing almost nothing," Rogan said, taking a step backwards, his eyes shifting to Darwan's sword. "If you wish her to remain safe, you should warn her against the habit."

"I'll hold you responsible for her safety," Darwan said, his hands shaking. The Red was bubbling with worry and blind hatred of Rogan.

Rogan shrugged, unconcerned about his charge. He backed away, but kept an eye on Darwan until he was well away from him.

Once Rogan was gone, the Red allowed Darwan to relax, and he inhaled the night air, which was thick with smoke from a nearby fire. The Red reveled in the burning air, though it made Darwan's eyes water.

Rogan had called Margella "the king's rayth." Darwan had thought the term simple derision, but perhaps he knew more than he spoke. Rayths were humans touched by the Black magic flows, and the term was a common curse for men and women accused of evildoing. And perhaps Rogan himself was more than he appeared. *Or maybe all of this is the delusional work of the pyrus.*

The stench of warm beer filled his nostrils. He drank wine, as a proper lord should, but the men consumed beer as if it was sweet nectar from the gods. He let his feet follow the aroma and found whom he expected.

Zane stood over a cask of beer, thick foam frothing down the side. He was a legend for both his ability to consume beer, and not coincidentally, his ability to urinate for longer than it takes most men to eat their dinners. Zane offered the mug in his hand and looked genuinely disappointed when Darwan took it. The disappointment vanished as Zane took another mug. This one was bigger than the last, and he tilted the cask to fill it.

"A rare pleasure to drink with the lord," Zane announced unconvincingly, raising his mug in a toast.

Darwan raised his own mug in response, and despite himself, he took a long drink. He hated the rancid beer the men drank. It was horribly bitter, but he choked it down. Zane shifted his weight from leg to leg, his head swiveling around. Darwan wanted to walk away, but the Red was staying. The Red loved the beer, Zane's discomfort, and, most of all, Darwan's own discomfort.

Zane was waiting for him to leave, and the feeling grew as the moments stuttered past. Grudgingly Zane motioned to a set of logs surrounding a campfire. Darwan followed him and sat. He took a long swig of the vile swill, his nose revolting at the stink of hops, but still he let out a loud sigh of satisfaction.

"The ass end of the army," Darwan said. "That's our role. We follow behind the others and terrorize farmers."

"We're also guarding the King's ... adviser," Zane said with a snort.

"We're just keeping her out of sight of the queen. She'd crush the royal balls if she found the Lady Margella."

"I don't understand," Zane said. "We were in the van, at the head of the whole army before the last battle, and we held against the weight of the whole blasted Crotan army."

Darwan nodded. "And that was our undoing. We failed to follow the king's battle plan, and allowed part of the Crotan army to escape."

Zane stared at him blankly. "How did we do that? We held the blasted line. We lost three out of every four men. What more could he ask of us?"

"To die." Darwan looked at Zane squarely, so he would know the truth of it. "That was the king's plan, and we didn't die. That's why he put us at the front, at the base of that wretched hill." Zane's face twisted in confusion. Darwan wanted to stop talking, but the Red explained, "He knew the Crotans were advancing, knew they'd appear at the top of the ridge and see their advantage. He wanted them to attack down that hill and sweep right over us."

"We were bait."

"Yes. He wanted to draw the enemy in, to make them commit all their forces, and then crush them in one decisive battle." Darwan smashed his hands together. "He didn't tell me of the plan, lest our retreat appear insincere, or too quick. He was furious that we didn't retreat according to his plan, even though we didn't know about it."

"And here we are."

Darwan drained the beer, chewing the sludge that oozed out at the full tilt. He handed it to Zane for a refill. More than anything, Darwan wanted to stop talking to Zane. It was all true, but complaining about the king was dangerous. As his steward, Zane accompanied him to the king's war councils. If Zane reported such a conversation to the king, it could earn him some regard and Darwan a shallow grave. Though Zane had been a passable steward, it was time for a change. The Red liked the thought as it passed through Darwan's mind.

Zane returned with more beer. Somehow, it was warmer than the last serving, and more pungent. The Red kept him there for half the night, ruining the enjoyment of the men as they gathered around the fire. He hung around like a ripened carcass that no one could ignore or acknowledge. Darwan felt the discomfort of the men, and the Red basked in the flavor of unspoken irritation. Even

Darwan didn't want to be there, but a thick paste of surreal sedation kept him from leaving. The haze only lifted when a hand settled on his shoulder.

"Who dares touch me?" Darwan shot up, wheeling to face the man behind him. Rogan stood like a statue facing him, neither apologetic nor scared.

"Lord Darwan. I called to you three times. You didn't answer."

The Red was distant now, giving Darwan a measure of control again. He hadn't heard Rogan calling, but he said, "I answer when I please, and you will wait until I am done here."

"It's important, my lord. Something you must see."

"I will see it when I am through." Darwan sat, facing away from Rogan. He wanted to leave immediately, but he didn't want to bend to Rogan's request so readily.

"The men visited the king's rayth," Rogan whispered, his face uncomfortably near Darwan's ear.

"Did she enjoy them?" Darwan asked just loud enough for Rogan to hear. He smiled despite Zane's watchful eyes.

"Apparently."

The word hung strangely in the air, smearing the smile from Darwan's face. "Show me."

Three hulking men dressed in dirty tunics sat back to back in a triangle in front of Margella's quarters. They sat in a pool of blood, blackened by the night. Darwan saw the source of the blood at each man's crotch. Their manhoods had been cut off and stuffed in their mouths. Deep gouges raked their faces where their eyes should have been.

Darwan forced back bile and beer, barely keeping himself from vomiting. He didn't want to show Rogan any hint of weakness. Deep in his gut, the Red was amused. It was a repulsive sight, and by morning it would be an equally repulsive stench.

"We should bury them, before the rest of the men see." Rogan said.

"No," Darwan said. "Let them see. That should put an end to any other plans they have for Margella."

Darwan studied Rogan. He was a cold killer, and this could just as easily be his handiwork. Or perhaps the villagers had sought retribution. Unlikely, as most were women or old men. Any way you cut it, these men hadn't done this to themselves.

Amidst the prospect of impending battle, now they had a murderer among them. The Red mused at the irony of warriors worried about a murderer in their company.

Interlude

Black Rock

Tak shrugged off the last bits of restless sleep, noting the steady patter of rain on his thatched roof. He rolled off the bed of straw and grabbed at the one possession he'd need this night: his dagger. He stared longingly at the flute lying next to it. In better days, he had prized his flute above all his belongings. Now he left it on the floor, not caring if it would still be there if he returned.

He'd rented this hovel outside the walls of Black Rock because it was cheap and he had no beads to spare. The thatched roof was supposed to keep the rain out, but the muddy floor said otherwise. It didn't matter.

Tak put on his cloak, oiled to keep off the rain, and secured the dagger at his waist. He walked out into a cold drizzle, his high-topped moccasins caked in mud after two steps. The road through the small huts was dotted with puddles, but with his moccasins already muddy, Tak didn't bother to avoid them.

It was late evening and most of the peddlers had gone, the last few lingering to sell small skewers of indeterminate meat. Tak tossed two iron beads at one of them and then grabbed what he thought was a mouse and a crust of bread.

The meat was overcooked, cold, and wet. It tasted like he expected. Not much of a feast for what might be his last meal.

He walked through vacant streets to the main gate, a pair of high wooden posterns reinforced with great iron bands and spikes. He'd never seen them closed. People passed through them at all times of the night under the occasional glance of the town watch. When he'd first arrived, he'd thought their expressions were aloof, but now he knew they just didn't care. Black Rock was nothing like his village.

Inside the walls, the smells were pleasant, the people better dressed, and he was decidedly unwelcome. From the gate to the docks, it was a straight walk. He knew better than to linger on side streets. The only thing the town watch actually seemed to watch for was outsiders who strayed off the main road. The residents separated themselves by income, but the greatest difference was simply those who lived within the walls and those who lived outside them.

Tak walked to the docks, knowing the looming mass of stone was there in the darkness. He'd been impressed with it when he'd first arrived, but now it was just part of the landscape.

He turned left toward the north docks. They expected three ships tonight, and he was glad to see they were dispersed, so there would be fewer witnesses. He was working the *Running Bear* tonight, and that was perfect. The *Running Bear* was a typical pyreship. The ancient ships sailed up and down the Skykom River trading goods and delivering passengers, as they had done for hundreds of years. Crews changed, captains changed, owners changed, but the pyreships remained the same.

From the darkness, a man stumbled toward him. Tak didn't see him until it was too late and they collided. The man dropped to his knees and raised his hands. "Forgive me, kind sir. I'm only seeking pittances for the sake of Ahn."

Ahn, the god of the White, saw to the welfare of all, and in his name beggars solicited beads. Tak was a farmer at heart, and following Ahn's ideal of charity was an important tenet. With so many beggars in Black Rock, he'd become immune to the calls. *If this is my last night, then perhaps I should seek Ahn's favor.*

Tak tossed a short cord of beads. The man caught the cord in midair and lowered his head. "Thank you. May you always walk in the White and Ahn bless your endeavors."

Tak snorted to himself at the irony. Ahn would bestow no favors on his endeavors this night. He shook his head and walked past the man. As he did, distant torchlight caught the man's face for an instant, and the beggar's eyes flickered from blue to brown. Tak took two more steps and stopped. He'd never seen a beggar this far into the city. The city watch kept them well outside Black Rock.

Tak whirled to find no one. Where the man had stood, he only saw the cord of beads. A quick search of the misty streets and alleys revealed no one. He reached out to take the beads. His hand stopped short and hovered over the beads for a long moment, and then he stood up straight. He left them on the ground, turning back to the docks.

The *Running Bear* was at the northernmost dock, and Tak recognized the load foreman standing on the dock. He turned to Tak, his usual scowl etched on his weathered face. "You're late. Get to work." Without another word, he walked away.

Tak looked up at the deck of the pyreship, the rain gathering in his eyes. A crane swung over the dock and lowered an urn to the ground. He reached out to settle it and untied the rope. It was full of wine or oil. It didn't matter. His job was to lug it to the south dock or to a warehouse. That didn't matter either. He struggled to get it moving, rolling it around its base to the head of the dock.

"Over here," called the foreman from under a makeshift shelter. He took one look at the urn and said, "Wine. Warehouse Five."

Warehouse Five was close, but that just meant he'd be back for another urn sooner. This was life when you worked the docks in Black Rock. Each night, traders came in and dropped off their goods. Black Rock was the end of the line for both northern and southern traffic, so every ship would be completely emptied and most filled right back up with new goods.

The Skykom River forked at Black Rock. The towering rock itself seemed to split the river in two. Half the river flowed to the north and the other half to the south. Crossing from one branch of the Skykom to the other meant crossing the treacherous rapids between. No one ever made the crossing; it was easier to have laborers shift the cargo than risk a pyreship, though Tak, being one of those laborers, didn't think of it as easy.

They toiled throughout the night to empty and fill each ship. The pay was a pittance, and most workers drank away their beads before the next night. The work was hard on the back, but it was honest work.

Tak carried five more urns to the warehouse before he saw his mark. The ship's crew usually stayed aboard, retrieving and storing the crates and urns in the ship's hold. Once they'd emptied the hold, they'd help move the goods through the dockyard. They weren't being helpful to the dockworkers; they just wanted to be done sooner.

Gad was a thick man with powerful arms. He swung himself over the side and climbed down the netting to the dock. He looked around and then strode toward the end of the dock. Tak reached for his dagger.

Gad was a well-known deckhand. "Gad" was short for something, but no one knew his real name. His pyreship docked here every couple of weeks. Tak had followed the man on his last few visits. All he ever did was drink and fight. He liked the taverns outside the walls, beyond the concerns of the town watch.

The splattering rain and creaking planks of the old dock covered the noise of both men walking. Gad never looked back once. He stopped at the end of the dock and reached into his long leather jacket. He sheltered a pipe from the rain with his hands and puffed a steady cloud of smoke. "If you're going to do it, then you'd better finish it," Gad said, still not turning back.

Tak froze in place. The dagger was out now, but it shook unsteadily.

"Was it a woman?" Gad asked. "Tell me this isn't about a woman."

"You killed my brother," Tak said, with much less emotion than he'd expected. He'd practiced this moment hundreds of time. He had always imagined yelling those words, but here in the rain and near the man himself, it was barely a whisper.

"I don't remember most of the people I kill. Too drunk, usually."

Gad had a reputation for fighting and killing. That scared away some men, but drew others to challenge him. Tak had seen it once, and it ended with the challenger slumped on the floor in a pool of blood. He laid there most of the night. Eventually, the owner paid someone to get rid of the body.

"It was here in Black Rock, almost a year ago. He came here to—"

"I don't care what your brother's story is. I don't care why he came here, or who he was." Gad still hadn't looked back at Tak. "You think I killed him, and Dyn knows I've killed my fair share of men, so I probably *did* kill him. The question is, what are you going to do about it?"

Tak imagined himself jumping forward and thrusting the dagger into Gad's back, then shoving him off the dock; but in reality, he just stood there.

"I saw you, kid. Saw you watching me. Saw you the last time we were here, too. Figured I'd give you the chance to finish this." Gad was still smoking his pipe as though it was the most mundane moment in the world. "Dyn knows I'm a killer. I've done Dyn's work many times, but are *you* ready to become the hand of Dyn?"

Dyn was the god of death, the source of the Black. Dyn was evil. Tak was a farmer and only paid homage to Dyn to keep him away. Tak followed Gia, the Green, and Ahn, like most farmers. Ahn opposed Dyn.

Gad was right. If he killed him here, then he'd be marked for Dyn. He'd known this moment would come, though, and he knew what it meant. He'd told himself he was not doing it for evil ends. This was righting a wrong. The gods knew the difference.

His brother had traveled here to make his fortune, though Tak suspected he really wanted to escape from the family farm and his arranged marriage. He'd left with another boy from their village of Weaverol. The other boy returned with nothing but the story, and Tak had vowed vengeance on Gad.

Tak had fought other boys back in Weaverol, and he'd dueled with sticks, but he'd never tried to kill anyone. Gad was a killer. Tak was more likely to be the one tossed in the Skykom with a dagger in his side. There was no turning back, and yet his feet wouldn't carry him forward.

"What's it going to be, kid? I ain't got all night."

Tak hated himself as much as he hated Gad, but he wasn't a killer. He put the dagger away and stepped back, not taking his eyes off Gad. "That's what I thought, kid." Gad was still puffing on his pipe, still unconcerned, still looking across the Skykom. "Go home to mama."

Tak glumly shuffled back down the dock.

"Where are you going?" the foreman called after him.

"I'm done for tonight."

"Come back here. No one leaves until the job is done. We haven't even started to load yet."

Tak shut his eyes, still walking toward the warehouses.

"If you don't turn around, you're fired!"

"I quit." Tak didn't say it loudly. He wasn't sure if the foreman had heard him, and he didn't care. Walking through the empty streets of Black Rock, the night seemed darker, the rain colder, and the weight of his shame heavier. He'd pledged retribution to everyone back in Weaverol, but at the moment of truth, he was a failure. There was no reason to stay here, but he didn't want to go home, not like this. What would he tell them? Perhaps that he never found Gad. Perhaps that he was already dead.

Anything but the truth.

Tak picked up his discarded cord of beads and returned to his shack, finding his flute in a small puddle. Picking it up, he blew a quick melody, smiling for the first time in weeks. He pulled out the dagger, placing it in the puddle where he'd found his flute. He left the shack feeling lighter.

He stayed the night near the stables, soaking up rain into his clothes and playing low tunes. The rain muffled his songs well enough so that none of the slumbering townsfolk needed to fling a dung pie at him. Near dawn, he found two caravans leaving from the stables; one was going to Weaverol, so he paid his few remaining beads for passage and road rations.

After a night spent near Nali, it took three days before familiar farms came into view. The farmhouses were shattered, the fields stripped, and the livestock missing. Thin plumes of black smoke rose into the sky. The tension grew among the men of the caravan as they neared the village center. The guards readied bows and swords, and Tak felt a longing for the dagger he'd left behind.

Chapter Twelve

Sir Burke rode atop his warhorse, both man and beast clad in brilliant white scale armor. The armor gathered the light of the sun and reflected it back, making them a moving torch of light. With each stride, hundreds of interlocking metal scales tinkled together in a sound like a metal rain. He rode up to the top of a low hill, the setting sun to his back. Ahead, Lord Palus sat on his mount, identically armored. He looked to the south, without regard for Burke.

Burke stopped short and waited several moments, then said, "Commander."

Palus didn't break his gaze. In the distance, a town squatted along the banks of Skykom River. Most of the town was obscured by the wooden post wall, but many small huts and dusty paths scrolled along outside the meager protection of the walls. At the far end of the town, along the riverbank, a black monolith soared into the sky, making the town itself look like an afterthought.

"First Sword," Lord Palus said finally.

First Sword was an honorary title, not a rank; earned, not given. It had taken Burke twenty-five years to rise to be First Sword of the King's Armored Fist, but he cared little for that anymore. "It looks peaceful enough down there," Burke said. "No sign of Sarasins."

Palus looked at him, then back to the horizon without a word.

"Perhaps we are on a fool's quest," Burke said. "We've traveled all this way and seen nothing."

"You forget yourself," Palus said, shooting him a sharp glance. "The king is no fool. Were the men here to witness your words, I would have you dragged behind your horse."

"I meant no disrespect to King Alarak and did not mean to suggest him a fool," Burke said, hiding his irritation. Palus was a distant relative to the king, and eager to gain favor in the court. He was therefore dangerous. Burke needed to guard his tongue more closely with the new commander.

"We've had enough reports of a Sarasin incursion to know they're here somewhere," Palus said.

"The road leads west from here. Do you want to proceed?"

"We will stay in Black Rock."

"I thought we were to find the Sarasins," Burke said, motioning toward the town. "And they're not here."

"We also need to reassure the citizens of Black Rock that they are still protected by the king's army. And remind them of their loyalties."

Burke wrenched himself around to look down the hill. Ten horsemen, outfitted with the same white armor, waited at the bottom of the hill. "We only have ten men. Not exactly an army."

"There are twelve of us," Palus said. "You and I know we are alone, but they," he said, pointing at Black Rock, "do not. And will not. Why do you think King Alarak sent us, the men of his Armored Fist, on a simple *scouting* mission?"

"Because all the men in his light cavalry are dead now." Burke tried not to put his emotions into his words, but failed, and the words bit into the air, hanging like a rotting carcass. He fought back the emotions, cornering them in the distant reaches of his mind. The words were true, but his harsh tone belied his feelings. He waited for Palus to chide him again, though he cared less than he had a moment ago.

Palus glared at him. His glare turned to casual pity. "I will ignore what you said, given your situation." He cleared his throat. "What is your assessment of Black Rock?"

Burke moved his horse next to Palus' and scrutinized the town. "The town won't hold long against an assault." He pointed to the wooden post wall and the swarm of ramshackle houses surrounding it. "A quarter of the town isn't even within the walls, and the walls are just wooden logs. This town will either fall or burn, but either way, it won't take long."

"I do not care for your pessimism. Have the men unfurl the banners. Let us make our entrance a grand one."

Burke neither spoke nor nodded. He turned his horse back down the hill and rode away.

The men of the Fist were a glorious sight, drawing crowds everywhere they went. The full complement of the Fist was two hundred and fifty horsemen, along with hundreds of squires and attendants. Twelve men with no retinue was still a grand show, albeit a short one. The people of Black Rock lived at the fringe of the kingdom. It was a relatively peaceful region now, and they probably hadn't seen a regular military unit in years.

The people of Black Rock poured from their houses, the inns and taverns disgorging their patrons into the streets. The sound of the soft rain of their armor became a torrent with a dozen men and horses jostling simultaneously. Burke had always loved the sound of the march and the adulation of the people, but today it was odd. The stares were cold, though perhaps it wasn't the people who were different; perhaps it was him.

His peered through changed eyes clouded by a father's loss and longing. Burke's hands tightened around the reins. He fought back the tears and anger, pushing them back again to a well-used corner of his mind.

On his left, he saw rundown houses, complete with a decrepit stable and a squat inn. To the right was a makeshift scourge of shacks, some thatched, some shingled, and all on the verge of collapse. The roads on that side were dirt stains. The outer city was kindling for the Sarasins. He rode up to another man and asked, "Jaks, you're from Black Rock."

Jaks turned to regard Burke. "Yes, First Sword. My family still lives here."

"You should visit them. Is this how you remember the town?"

Jaks shook his head, as he brought his horse to a walk in time with the other men. "This is not my Black Rock. None of this outer town existed when I last visited." There was disdain in his voice. "I don't care for the new smells, either."

Burke noted the stink for the first time. He smelled the patchwork of sweat-stained laundry hanging to dry. Among the usual odor of stews and meat, he smelled warm urine and wet mold. "Is the town guard competent?"

Jaks laughed. "If you're asking if they can defend Black Rock against the Sarasins, the answer is no. They can barely manage to keep out the beggars."

Burke examined defenses as they passed through the gates. The high wooden platforms atop the wall held no lookouts, and the shacks of the outer town sat right against the wall. One could practically climb up on the shacks and jump the wall, though he suspected they'd collapse first. He shook his head. Up close, the town was more vulnerable than it had seemed from a distance. The gate looked as if it hadn't been shut in decades.

Past the gates, the dirt road met a cobbled plaza with sturdier buildings overlooking the streets. The largest was an inn, judging by the signs hanging near the door. Farther along the street, he saw other large buildings that looked like public meeting halls. It smelled distinctly better within the walls, with more food and less urine. He even thought he could smell spices and perfumes.

Lord Palus stopped his horse and waited. Burke continued until he was next to the commander. "I will arrange a meeting with the local council immediately," Palus said, frowning. "Have the men settle in at Lord Bayton's residence."

"Yes, commander. Who rules over Black Rock now that Lord Bayton is dead?"

"I suppose his son succeeded him as lord."

Burke shook his head. "His two sons were with him at the last battle. They died with him."

Palus shot him an annoyed look and rode off. "Follow your orders, First Sword. Settle the men and get to the hall."

Burke looked to Jaks. "Take the men to Lord Bayton's home. See to the horses first, then resupply."

"Yes, First Sword."

Burke turned his gaze and then his horse toward the looming black monolith. Though large from a distance, it was massive now. He had to see it up close. There were no crowds as he rode between the warehouses of the docks, nor did he see a single worker. He rode right up to the black rock, guiding his horse so he could touch the landmark that gave the town its name. Removing his gauntlets, he pressed bare skin against the cold surface. It felt like any ordinary rock, though it was as smooth as a river stone.

Looking skyward, he saw etchings high up on the rock. The script was old and meaningless. He knew the sigils, though he could not read them. These were the words of the great builders, the Gaitan. They'd departed these lands long ago to live in the lands of the north with the Tainted races, no longer interested in the matters of men.

He turned and saw two other black rocks. Smaller than the gargantuan one before him, they had a concave curve to them and stood in the water deflecting the raging waters of the great Skykom River. The snow-covered peaks of the Crescent Mountains fed the river, and it flowed unimpeded to this very spot. Here these great rocks split the mighty river, bending it to the mysterious design of the great builders. The monolith was as impressive as the town surrounding it was unimpressive. He rode back to the center of town, speculating on why the great builders had built such a thing.

The town hall was stuffed like a granary after a good harvest. The people parted for Burke. Lord Palus, seated on a raised platform so he overlooked the main floor, had already started the meeting. The men arrayed around the room were a mix of old and young. Burke wondered why so many able-bodied men were not in the army. A hush followed Burke as he passed through the room. Palus gave him the familiar scowl before turning back to an old man standing in front of the platform.

"As I was saying," Palus said. "King Alarak wishes you all to know the realm is safe. He assures you that he will easily repel this minor Sarasin incursion." The crowd seemed unconvinced.

Burke walked to the back of the room and focused on the conversation. The old man before Palus was a poor farmer. He wore rags, frayed and torn, and his sunbaked skin told of years spent in the fields. His bare feet were caked in mud, and he certainly wasn't one of the town council. "My lord, I live in Weaverol," the old farmer said. "The Sarasin army came with no warning. They killed my wife and took my granddaughters." The man's voice cracked and streams flowed down his cheeks, streaking the dirt on his face. "They took everything. Burning, looting, killing."

Palus looked past the farmer and addressed the rest of the room. "And yet you're alive." Palus apparently expected the crowd to laugh, but he badly misjudged the mood of the room.

The farmer stood speechless, his mouth open, eyes wide. After a moment, he spoke quietly. "When the Sarasins left, I came here."

Palus turned his gaze to the farmer. "How many men were in this Sarasin raiding party?"

"No party. It was an army. Thousands. Tens of thousands."

A heavy chatter spread out across the room, despite Palus yelling for quiet.

"My good man, you are mistaken. This Sarasin raiding party is just a few hundred men at most, but I could see how you might misjudge them given what you have been through." The petty attempt at empathy didn't work with the farmer or the crowd.

The farmer's face flushed and his hands curled into fists. He shifted and stumbled, a younger man rushing up to support him. The younger man also looked like a farmer. His tunic extended to his knees, with a cheap rope tied at his waist. The tunic was white, but bore streaks of rusty blood. He wore high-top moccasins, also caked in mud. The boy bore a striking resemblance to Burke's son, and he inhaled sharply, thinking just for a moment that it *was* Kern. He focused on the boy, his surprise fading to disappointment. The similarities disappeared on further examination. *Not my son, not even close, just fooling myself.*

"He speaks the truth," the young man said.

Palus sighed for all to hear. "And who are you?"

"Tak. I come from Weaverol too." The old man was steady now, and Tak stepped away from him, but still faced Palus. "This man is a village elder, and has always spoken the truth."

"And you were there to witness the Sarasin incursion?" Palus asked. Tak didn't answer; he only cocked his head. "The attack, boy, the attack."

"I arrived just after the attack."

"So you saw nothing. How can you know what this man says is fact, and not imagination?"

"I didn't imagine burying half the village in pit graves." Tak lowered his jaw toward Palus. "I didn't imagine burying my whole family."

Palus spoke without a hint of compassion. "Yes, but you were not there for the attack. You have no idea how many Sarasins there were."

"Who cares how many there were?" Tak shouted.

"My boy, that is the whole point of this discussion." Palus shook a long finger at Tak. "And I would remind you that I am a lord and commander of the Armored Fist of the King. Keep your tone under control, or I will control it for you."

Tak's words started out at an even volume, but quickly rose to a shout. "I know what I saw. I was there. Where was the king's army and your precious Fist? You left the people of Weaverol to die like cattle!"

"How dare you speak to me like that!" Palus leapt to his feet, his face contorted with anger. "I will have your tongue for your words against the king!"

Burke felt the mood in the room shift. The crowd turned against Palus, who had no idea what was happening. He never paid heed to anyone he thought to be his inferior, and in this room, that was everyone.

Palus looked to Burke. "Seize this dog and carry out the king's justice immediately." He turned his snarl at Tak and said, "You speak of dead cattle. I will see that your body is fed to them."

Tak stood there, mouth open. Faceless voices in the crowd questioned Palus. Where *was* the rest of the king's army? What had this man done wrong?

"I didn't mean to insult the king," Tak said, shaking his head.

"Get the men," Burke said to Jaks. "Bring the horses to the back door." When he turned back to the room, all eyes were on him. He looked to Palus, trying to signal him to tread lightly. "Lord Palus, I'm sure—"

"I did not ask you to speak! Take the boy and execute him." His eyes grew larger with each passing moment. "If you are afraid of a boy, then *I* will do what must be done." Palus drew his long sword, a brilliant white blade that made most of the crowd raise their hands to shield their eyes. They hesitated, but Burke could hear the grumbling and felt the building bravado. The initial surprise from seeing the blade waned, and the weight of numbers emboldened them.

Tak turned to the crowd, hands up in front of him. "No. This isn't what I meant to happen. The *Sarasins* are the enemy."

The crowd surged forward, clubs and knives flashing out from tunics in a blur. Burke cursed his instincts for not warning him sooner. They hadn't come for a meeting; this was an ambush. He raced to Palus, grabbing him by the back of his armor and jerking him toward the back of the building. Not everyone in the crowd was armed, and the bystanders were plentiful enough to impede their attackers. Palus tried to turn himself back toward the fray, but Burke propelled him through a half-open door, careful to avoid the bright blade.

"The Fist does not run from a fight!" Palus said. "I will slay them all!"

Burke grabbed him again and pushed him toward the horses.

"What are you doing?"

"Saving your life."

"From those thugs? I'll kill them all!"

Palus was surprisingly easy to handle, despite his anger. The mob spilled out the back door, growing like a gathering storm.

"You will all fall to my sword!" Palus screamed at them.

'All fall to my sword? What a pinhole. Burke chuckled at the sheer arrogance. But those words were enough for the mob. They surged forward.

Reaching the walled entrance to Lord Bayton's house, Burke looked to Jaks. He raised his open hand, fingers spread. Then he jerked his hand back to his chest in a fist. Jaks would understand. Burke turned to the crowd, knowing five of his men were rushing to his side.

The crowd stopped momentarily, as the hulking form of Burke whirled toward them, his armor giving off a quick jingle from the scales. The tall estate walls secured his flanks, and he heard his men running to support him. He put all of his strength behind his voice, and in a guttural tone shouted, "Stop!" It was simple, short, and effective. They actually stopped. "We're leaving now. I have no wish to butcher any of you." He had chosen his words well. The word 'butcher' had shaken them. Some still wanted a fight, but most unconsciously shifted their weight back on their heels. He had to give them an exit.

Tak came rushing through the crowd, and stepped between them and Burke. He raised his arms and addressed the mob. "This is my fault. I did not mean for this. The Sarasins are the enemy. We should kill *them*, not these men."

The crowd muttered angrily, and someone threw a club at Tak. A second club struck him in the head and he fell limply to the ground. The crowd flowed right over him.

Palus regained his composure and strode forward to address the crowd. "I will see this entire town burned to the last hovel, and all of you raised on pikes!"

The mob yelled a tapestry of oaths against Palus, but only a handful of men came forward. Burke stepped toward them and drew his sword. His blade was as white as the armor he wore, drawing light from the late afternoon sun. The sight of the star-like sword blazing caused all but one of the men to stop. Just one, Burke thought; it was a calculated risk. It might push the entire mob into blood lust.

The rioter charged, rusty daggers in each hand. Burke brought the sword down in a sweeping arc that sank into the man's right shoulder and sliced right through him. His lower body thudded to the ground, while his upper torso tumbled to a rest behind Burke. He didn't look. The man's eyes would still be moving.

"No one else needs to die!" he shouted. "We're leaving. We will not burn the town."

"I am the commander and I will give the orders!" Palus screamed. "The town burns!"

The crowd looked back and forth between Palus and Burke. Slowly, the mob receded.

"Mount up," Burke said. "Let's ride before they change their minds."

"The mighty Fist," Palus said, mockingly, "running from a mob of dogs!"

Burke turned on Palus, sword still drawn and dripping blood. "We'd have to kill them all."

"That was the general plan."

"They're farmers and fishermen, not soldiers."

"They're rioters. Rioting against the king. Enemies." Palus looked at the men of the Fist for support, but found none.

"I come from Black Rock," Jaks said. "I know some of those men. They're good people."

"I thought we came to reassure the citizens, not kill them." Burke said calmly, wiping his blade with a rag. "Quelling riots is a job for the town watch."

"Your *job* is to follow my commands, and if I say to kill rioters, then you kill rioters." Palus looked again to the men. He had even less support now. He swore an oath and stormed away to his horse. "We return to Barons Lodge."

The men looked to Burke. Most of what remained of King Alarak's army camped around Barons Lodge, waiting for the expected Sarasin invasion from the east. When they returned, Palus would have Burke charged with disobedience, and his head would roll. Burke worried Palus would also seek retribution on the other men. He had to ensure the ire of Palus was directed solely at him.

"We can return to Barons Lodge, but *he* doesn't have to make it with us."

Burke scanned the men to see who had spoken. The men were absently nodding, pondering the simplicity of the solution.

"We'll have none of that." Burke said it firm and final, looking from man to man to confirm that his intent was clear.

He glanced back at the crowd, now gathered a safe distance away. Tak lay motionless, with two men hovering over him. One was pulling off his moccasins and the other was untying his bead belt. The way the mob was eying Tak, Burke thought they'd soon bury a hatchet in his back. *I couldn't save my sons, but I can save him.*

Burke strode to Tak, the two men scattering like carrion birds. Looking at Tak, he imagined his son lying there instead. He knelt next to Tak and hoisted him up on his shoulders. Burke kept his head down, feigning a heavy burden, to hide his tears.

He took a horse from Lord Bayton's stable and secured Tak to the saddle. Taking the reins, he led the horse to his own mount. They rode from Black Rock with every eye in the town upon them. The hostile stares burned his back like a hot sun.

They still hadn't found the Sarasins, and he wanted to ride west to track them, to confirm the stories. West would also take them farther from Barons Lodge and the king's justice that awaited him there.

Lord Palus assumed the lead and turned north, but no one moved to follow him. Burke let out an exasperated sigh and turned to the men. "Lord Palus, we haven't accomplished our mission yet," Burke pointed out. He pointed to the west. "The Sarasins are out there somewhere, and in large numbers. We need to find out where and how many."

"So *you* decide when our mission is complete?" Palus sneered.

Burke neither spoke, nor moved.

"So what do you intend?" Palus asked.

"Nali is to the west," he said. "We'll arrive well before midnight." He looked up into the twilight sky. "We need to make the most of the light we have left."

Palus turned his horse around and motioned to the west. "And then what?"

"We ride to Weaverol. We'll get an assessment of their numbers."

Palus nodded to Burke to take the lead, a disturbing look of acceptance on his face.

"You don't need to come with us," Burke said. "You can be in Rivermar in three days." He hoped Palus would go, but he doubted the commander was up to traveling three days alone with no one to make his fire or pitch his tent.

Palus shook his head. "I will not abandon my command." He took the lead and put his horse into a gallop.

Burke and the Fist followed suit, but at a slower pace. The horses weren't properly rested and he didn't want to wear them out. He also didn't want to be near Palus.

How long can I avoid my fate?

Chapter Thirteen

Darwan woke, the shuttered windows still dark. Had he even slept? Throwing his legs out from the bed, he stumbled to his feet. As he picked up his padded underarmor, he heard the rustling of the pyrus. He took the tin from the hidden pocket. *I don't need it, I want it.* There's a difference. He was in control, not the pyrus.

Darwan should be checking the men, but instead he sat back on the bed holding the tin. He opened it and relief rushed over him. The pyrus was there, but not enough of it. He'd need to find more, but where? Where in this backwater would he ever find an alchemist?

Even if he found a city, how would he find an alchemist? He couldn't send Zane to find one; his steward knew too much about him already, and sharing this secret would be dangerous. His own movements were hardly discreet. He'd need to find a way, but that was a concern for another day. With great reluctance, he closed the tin and put it back in its hiding place.

Stepping out into the morning mist, he fixed the last of his armor over his chest. Rogan was standing outside his door and Darwan took an instinctive step back, losing his balance. He threw out an arm to steady himself against the wall of the house. Rogan had an annoying habit of sneaking up on him.

"Lord Darwan," Rogan said, nodding slightly. "It's a good time of day."

Darwan stepped from the porch and right in front of Rogan. "You were involved in a duel yesterday," he said, hoping to put his First Sword off balance.

"No, a duel involves two sides."

"We have precious few men left in our warband. You can kill all the Crotans you want, but our own men are too few." He stepped into the road, walking toward the grassy field. Rogan said nothing, falling into step with Darwan. "Why didn't you give him the boy?"

"He was a sick bastard," Rogan said with no hint of emotion. "I cured him."

"You yourself have killed several of the recruits already. Why protect this one?" Darwan tried to read Rogan's reaction, but he betrayed nothing of his feelings, if he had any.

"I cull the weak ones." Rogan took a deep breath of the morning air. "Besides, I wasn't protecting anyone. I've been meaning to kill that bastard for weeks. This was just the excuse. We're better off now."

"But the men will—"

"The men will do as I tell them. You give the orders and let me worry about how they get carried out."

Darwan turned away from Rogan, looking into the purple sky, a wisp of orange glowing on the horizon. "Call the men into formation. We march. Maybe we can catch up before this war is over."

Darwan made his way to the stable, unhappy to find Margella there waiting for him. "Quite a spectacle you left outside my door last night," she said, amusement in her voice.

"So you deny any knowledge of it?" he asked, hoisting himself up on his horse.

"Knowledge of what?" she asked, overacting the part of a naive girl.

"The dead men outside your door."

"I am but a weak woman," she protested. "I could never overpower four big men like that."

"There were only three."

"Ah, so there were," she said, a sick smile spreading across her perfect face. She said no more, urging her horse onto the road. "You smell better today," Margella said without looking at him.

He looked her up and down. "You look exquisite today." She didn't really, but he still felt desire for her, despite what he suspected she'd done to his men.

"The pyrus clouds your mind." She smiled, probably happy he was again falling under her spell. "I have known many who were used by the pyrus, and it never ended well for them. It will consume you."

"It doesn't consume *me*, I consume *it*." He was pleased with his clever reply, but then realized he'd confirmed his use of the pyrus. She had a measure of power over him with that knowledge.

They rode to the north edge of the town, along the shore of a small lake. He looked out over the water, seeing wrecked boats along the shore. This dismal village might soon disappear. Fields ravaged, boats sunk, men gone, and soon many of the women would be with child. He wondered how long they had lived here in relative peace. Exhaling, he forced the thoughts away and turned to see his men formed in a line of march, the wagons at the rear pulled by the new recruits. Rogan screamed at his sorry little band. They could barely manage to form a line. Would they really be of any use in battle? Darwan doubted it, but it kept Rogan occupied, and gave them a pool of workers.

Margella rode to rear of the line, garnering lustful stares from the men. Darwan shook his head. She was tempting them, daring them with her body.

He rode to Rogan, who stopped yelling at the recruits. He gave Darwan an annoyed look. "Did you dispose of the three bodies?" Darwan asked.

Rogan pointed to a small pyre burning just outside the village.

"Good. Are all the men accounted for?" Darwan asked.

"We're missing one."

"You searched?"

Rogan nodded.

"Did you search the lady's quarters?" he said.

"The rayth? That wouldn't be proper, now would it?"

"Search them," Darwan said.

Rogan shrugged and walked away. Darwan rode over to Zane, who was taking a short sip on his flask. He held up the flask to Darwan and grinned. Zane was amazing in his own way. He could stay up all night drinking, and still manage that stupid smile of his.

Darwan remembered their conversation the previous night, certain now that Zane had outlived his utility. That was the problem with stewards. Good ones got to know their lord well, which inevitably made them dangerous. Zane wasn't a good steward, though. It had taken him over three years to get to this point. Still, Darwan would look for opportunities to rid himself of his steward. "Get the men moving," he said roughly.

"Shouldn't we wait for the First Sword?" Zane asked.

"He'll catch up. He always does." Darwan looked at the remnant of his warband, just over two hundred warriors in four sections. They were moving alone, so he ordered the first section to send out flankers. They were following just a day behind the main army, so ambush was unlikely, but Darwan was cautious in foreign lands.

The second section got on the road, marching five abreast. Rogan's sorry troop of recruits came next: three score of miserable young boys, barely able to march in a straight line. Getting them in formation and on the road was like herding goats—very slow, very scared goats. The final two sections of warriors sandwiched the wagon train. The stronger recruits struggled to get the wagons moving, the warriors making no effort to help them.

He surveyed the fields, stripped and trampled by thousands of warriors. They searched the first few farmhouses, finding little more than carcasses. *These will soon be our lands, but who will tend the fields if we kill them all?*

"You were right," Rogan said, patting Darwan's horse on the rump.

Darwan restrained his surprise and anger. Rogan had snuck up on him again. "You found something?"

"There were human... bits in her quarters."

"Bits?" Darwan looked back at Rogan, who wore an expressionless stare.

"Pieces. Remnants. It was a mess."

"Our missing man?"

"Possibly." Rogan shrugged. "I'm not even sure if it was just one."

Darwan sighed and rubbed his face. How could this be? Margella seemed as dainty as a flower. "You call her a rayth. Is she?"

Rogan's face gained a momentary look of revulsion. "Seems like it."

"What makes you say that?" Darwan asked.

Rogan shook his head. "Just seems like it." *Rayth* was a slang term commonly hurled at women, but it was seldom meant literally. Rogan meant it.

Rogan walked up to him, his eyes on another farmhouse. "Lord Darwan, I see someone on the porch there."

Darwan looked for himself. The rising sun behind the house left the porch in gray shadows, so he saw nothing, but Rogan had uncanny sight. Darwan turned his horse toward the house. "Have the rest of the men continue. We'll take five men with us to investigate."

He slowed his horse to a crawl, knowing Rogan would take the lead. Rogan trotted ahead of everyone, his sword already out, though Darwan hadn't heard him unsheathe it. Now he could finally see what Rogan saw: a crumpled figure sprawled on the uneven porch. Rogan crept up, silent as a predator, and put his sword on the figure's cheek. The sleeper sprang up at the touch and backed into a wall.

"He looks healthy. He'll do fine for a recruit," Rogan announced. Behind him, the man's head moved from side to side. He moved fast for someone just awakened, grabbing a sword and lunging at Rogan's back.

Darwan had seen this before. Rogan turned his back on danger almost as a taunt; and just as with all the other times, Rogan spun just before the sword met his shoulder. Rogan only needed to nudge his attacker to send him to the ground. He hit the soil hard, his sword falling away from him with the rasp of his lungs emptying.

Rogan smiled broadly, hulking over the boy and shaking his head. "Is that all you've got?"

Apparently, it wasn't. The boy got his hands under him, but Rogan sent a foot into his side, putting him on his back this time. "Lord Darwan, he's a big one. Could be trouble. Do you want him dead?" Rogan kicked him several more times.

"I'm sure you can handle him."

Rogan smiled and kicked again; but to everyone's surprise, the boy deflected his foot with a powerful sweep of his hand, and this time it was Rogan who lost his balance. Darwan had never seen that happen before. Rogan hopped to the side to keep from falling.

"Oh, my. I'll enjoy breaking him."

The boy bounded up, throwing a fist at Rogan. He missed, of course. Rogan was around the boy in an instant, locking his arm and shoving him face-first into the ground.

"I would speak with your new recruit," Margella said suddenly.

Darwan turned around, unaware that she'd been right behind him. He turned back to Rogan, motioning for him to free the boy.

The boy rose to his feet and dusted himself off. Darwan studied him. He was taller than Rogan, much taller, and strongly built. His eyes burned with a hatred that made Darwan consider killing him now, particularly if Margella had an interest in him, but he motioned for Margella to ride forward despite his concerns. *Rogan will most likely kill him before the day is out anyway.*

Chapter Fourteen

Cayne stared up at the woman on the horse, her black veil shrouding her eyes. His gaze slid down her body, and though he felt embarrassed, his eyes refused to shift back up to her face. The flimsy frock covering her body flaunted everything, while exposing nothing.

"What's your name?" she asked, staring at him impatiently.

"C-Cayne," he stammered after far too long, his words getting lost somewhere between his brain and his mouth, most likely in his eyes. He watched her mouth, the thin red lines moving delicately. While her face was obscured, the rest of her was perfect—though he'd seen more of her than any other woman, so he had little to compare her with.

She grabbed his chin with unexpected strength. She shifted his face left then right, examining him like a ripe pumpkin. Her touch was cool and stirred feelings deep within him, feelings somewhere between flaming desire and total revulsion. He sensed danger behind him, and turned to face the warrior who'd soundly beaten him. He felt both sorry and glad to break away from her touch.

"This yours?" the warrior asked, thrusting out Cayne's satchel.

"Yes."

"Consider it a professional courtesy. I only respect those who can defend themselves without embarrassment. You did all right." There was a fleeting hint of respect in his face. He handed him the sword he had dropped as well.

"Thank you," Cayne said instinctively, taking the satchel and putting it on. He didn't want to be so polite, but his mother had drilled manners into him. His raw face and sore ribs didn't make it seem like he'd done a good job. Cayne thought to draw his sword, but he had no idea who these strange people were. They must be Sarasins given their harsh accent, but he didn't know for sure. *Father always says—said—I act too quickly.*

"Now get in line," the soldier said. He looking up at the woman on the horse and added, "When you're done talking with the Lady Margella, of course." He walked away, calling out over his shoulder, "I enjoy killing, but I truly savor it when I can kill someone I respect." There was no humor in his voice.

"If you kill Rogan," Margella said, motioning to the retreating figure, "I might find a suitable reward for you."

Cayne had no response. *That man wants to kill me, and this woman wants me to kill him.*

He heard fire crackling and faced his home, which was engulfed in flames. Now everything was gone. He looked up to the woman, expecting a comforting gesture, but instead she was smiling at him. "I'm done with you," she said. "Run along now. You're nothing important."

Fuming, Cayne shuffled toward the men lined up along the road, looking back at the burning house every few steps, breathing in the acrid air. He followed Rogan until they caught up with a long line of warriors. "You look strong," Rogan said, pointing to a train of wagons. "Get working."

The line of carts moved along the dirt road under a constant barrage of jeers from the warriors behind them. The last wagon had ground to a halt, as the young boys pulling it toiled in vain to get it up a shallow incline. The warriors shouted angry curses as they had to stop and wait for the wagon to start moving, but they made no effort to help.

They shouted at Cayne as he stepped toward the wagon. Instead of taking up the pull bars at the front of the wagon, he took up a position at the rear of the wagon. The taunting abruptly ended as Cayne let out a grunt and shoved the wagon so hard the wheels left the ground. Despite the incline, he found the wheeled wagon moved easier than the plow he regularly pulled through the fields.

Once they reached the top of the incline, he circled to the front. Two wooden shafts extended from the wagon. They had leather loops tied at intervals, and at each, a grim-faced boy stared at him. The boys wore a kaleidoscope of familiar clothes: leather britches, ragged tunics, and moccasins.

One boy's expression turned into a smile. Through the dirt-covered face, Cayne recognized his friend. "Cayne, I'm glad to see you," Tarken said. "I'm not glad they have you too, but I'm glad to see you."

"What's happening?" Cayne asked, his thoughts too tangled to ask anything more insightful. He grabbed the strap next to Tarken.

"We just joined the Sarasin army. They grabbed me yesterday and threw me in a house with the rest of us," he said, gesturing to the boys around them.

Cayne recognized them, one by one. The feet in front of him belonged to little Moki, the fisherboy. He saw Tamo, eyes fixed on the road, without his usual smile. In all, he saw six boys from Dahl Haven, eight counting Tarken and himself. He saw the twins Bale and Boon, Chesu, and Etu, whose eyes were swollen shut.

"He wouldn't stop crying, so they kept slapping him until he stopped," Tarken said, nodding to Etu. "Pretty stupid. Slap a kid to make him *stop* crying?"

Cayne and Tarken were the oldest. Moki was just eleven years old, and Cayne wondered, what use could the Sarasins have for warchildren? At least Cayne could wield a sword, but Moki would need both hands just to raise one. He'd fall if he tried to swing it.

"Sarasins," Cayne said. "Well, I guess if I want to kill Sarasins, I'm in the right place."

"A-are you crazy?" Tarken stammered, looking around to see if anyone was listening to them. "These are warriors. You'll just get yourself killed!"

"I have two in mind already." Cayne looked back at Rogan, who was leading the group behind them.

"Rogan? He's the worst of them. The guards were talking about him last night, and even they're afraid of him. They say he's a Fayden Blade."

The last two words made Cayne's skin itch. Fayden Blades were legendary for their prowess in combat. They were mad. They were outlaws. However, they weren't soldiers, at least not in any story he'd heard about them.

"Don't do it," Tarken continued. "He'll cut you down. We have to get away. We're waiting for a chance."

Ahead of them were seven other wagons drawn by boys he didn't know. Even Tarken was taller than average in this group. They marched on in silence, but the presence of Tarken and the other boys comforted Cayne. It was good to be among friends, even if they were veritable prisoners.

"Who's the other one?" asked Tarken casually, but then shot a quick glance over each shoulder.

"Other what?"

"You said there were *two* Sarasins you wanted to kill. Who's the second one?"

Cayne thought back on his words. His desire to kill Rogan was rash, born more from his recent thrashing than of any real bloodlust. His anger had subsided, and though he still hated the man, he didn't want to kill him anymore, but he had said *two*.

"Arta Nakis." He said it simply. Arta Nakis had killed his father and brothers. Cayne had known anger before; he was angry with Rogan, and so spoke an oath against him, but his feeling toward the Sarasin king was different, deeper, more searing than any anger he'd ever felt. He didn't just want the Sarasin king dead, he wanted to be the one to plunge a blade in his chest and twist it; to hear his screams, and smell his last breath, even if it was the very last act of his own life.

Tarken didn't ask more questions. He didn't even tell him how crazy the idea was. Tarken just nodded, silent for once.

In mid-afternoon, they saw the first escape attempt. The column of wagons passed a line of lanboe trees, and a boy bolted. Half of the boys stopped to watch, and the rest tried to keep moving to mask his departure.

Lanboe trees grew in clumps, their straight, nearly leafless trunks sprouting up like giant clusters of grass. They made the best arrow shafts, but exceptionally poor cover. The boy ran straight past the clumps, but he was visible the entire time. The narrow trunks did little to conceal him.

Cayne turned to see Rogan loosing an arrow from a short bow. It weaved its way through the trees and hit the running boy in the leg, sending him sprawling to the ground, howling in agony. Cayne had hunted animals before, but this was the first time he'd seen an arrow used on a person, a taste of bile reaching the back of his throat at the thought of it. Rogan strolled to the helpless boy, a broad smile adorning his face the whole way. The rest of the line turned to watch with horrid fascination.

"Leave him be," Cayne yelled, but no one paid him any attention.

Rogan reached down and, with a twist of his arm and an audible snap, he pulled up half the arrow. The boy screamed louder, and Cayne knew Rogan was smiling, though he had his back to him. Rogan drew the bow again, standing right over the boy, and sent another arrow down. The scream was louder this time, but then lowered into a sob.

Rogan looked back at them. *Making sure his audience is paying attention.* Then fired more arrows, in such rapid succession Cayne couldn't tell how many he'd shot. The boy was quiet now, and Cayne hoped he was dead. He saw the feather fletching of the arrows moving slowly, then not at all.

"Anyone else care to run?" Rogan asked as he strode to the line of boys standing in front of the wagons. "I have more arrows." He looked among the faces, then nocked an arrow, pointing it at them, as he shifted his aim from face to face. "Now, someone retrieve my arrows."

No one moved. He trained his bow on a boy in the middle of the line and nodded. The boy ran, almost tripping over his own feet. Rogan kept his bow up and watched the boy run. Then, with his head still turned away from the boys, he loosed the arrow, hitting another boy in the face. The boy's lifeless body dropped into the ditch alongside the dirt road, without even a whimper.

"Every time one of you tries to escape, I kill them, and then I kill another of you."

A horse rode up to Rogan, and he regarded the rider. "Lord Darwan. Just a small incident."

Darwan looked from the dead boy in the trees to the one in the ditch. "Rogan, why is it that whenever you're involved in an *incident*, we have fewer men at the conclusion?"

"Just keeping good order."

"Our numbers are low enough already," said Darwan, frowning. "At least you chose to cull the Crotan herd this time, and not our own men."

"Not much action here at the back of the army," said Rogan, sounding unhappy at the idea of missing combat. It was the first emotion Cayne had heard in the warrior. "We're just looting, raping, and killing our way across this land. Nice, though. If we were doing this in our own, we'd have our heads chopped off."

Darwan's expression suggested annoyance with Rogan, and he turned his horse back to the front of the column, shouting back, "Just get them moving again."

They trudged along the road for the rest of the day, and no one else tried to escape. They stopped mid-afternoon, and Rogan assigned the recruits tasks, while the Sarasins rested and ranted. The smaller boys collected firewood, Tarken set up the tents, and Cayne helped the brew master, Frant.

"Edge them closer to the fire," Frant said.

Frant was a portly warrior with a beet-red face. He'd taken off his armor, and wore a simple and thoroughly filthy tunic and leather kilt. He said it helped cool off his stones, and Cayne could certainly see what he meant after watching him sit on a barrel.

Cayne had dragged a trio of cast iron cauldrons from the wagons and filled them with water. Then he poured malted barley into them. He smashed down the mixture with a paddle, and at semi-regular intervals, Frant told him to move the cauldrons closer to the fire. The cauldrons were heavy, laden with the barley mash mixture, and he understood why none of the younger boys got this task.

He managed the cauldrons at first, but as they got closer to the fire, they got hotter, and he had nothing but thin rags to buffer his hands from the hot metal. Frant sat on the barrel drinking until he was too drunk to balance. He settled to the ground and kept yelling at Cayne. "Closer!"

The fat warrior measured the time by the number of drinks he'd consumed. Finally, he got up and wobbled to the mash mixture, taking great breaths of the rising steam. "Pour in the hops," Frant ordered.

While Cayne lifted and poured the sacks of hops into the cauldrons, Frant opened several smaller sacks and dropped fistfuls of different herbs and spices into the cauldrons.

"Now put them right up to the fire and boil them," Frant said, crashing back down on the ground.

Cayne tried to move the cauldrons, but they were too hot to grip now. He looked to Frant for guidance, but the idiot just smiled at him. Cayne put his leather moccasins against his forearms and used them to twist the cauldrons up to the fire. Frant shrugged and made a silent toast before downing another drink. The mixture boiled for another two tankards of beer.

"Now, meet the most important life in this whole stinking warband," Frant said, reaching for a sealed pot. He opened the lid and took a deep breath before offering it to Cayne. It smelled of rising bread.

"It's too hot to add this now," Frant said. He stood next to the fire, lifted his kilt, and pissed on the fire. He had poor aim, with some of the piss landing on the cauldrons and some on his own legs. It didn't seem to bother him. He yawned, but kept peeing until the fire was out, putrid steam wafting in the air.

Frant drank two more tankards and then added the yeast. "My work's done now. Fill the casks." He crumpled down on the ground and started snoring as soon as his head hit the soil.

Cayne looked around. No one was around. He brought two of the empty casks and set them on the ground next to the cauldrons. Putting a foot on each one, he balanced himself atop them. He lowered his britches and relieved himself into the cauldrons. They hadn't been given much water during the day, but he reached deep for every drop he could produce. They hadn't fed them at all, or he would have made a more substantial contribution to the brew.

Cayne then filled a dozen casks, smiling the entire time. It was full night when he found his way back to the rest of the Dahl Haven boys. They slept at the center of the camp under the open sky. No tents for them, apparently. In the darkness, he took the banner from his satchel and wrapped it around his waist under his britches. It'd be safer there. The angelia fruits glowed dully in his satchel. He'd need to find a safe place for those as well.

Cayne was a talented sleeper, but he kept his eyes open this night. He saw Rogan floating silently among the rows of recruits at odd intervals. The fifth time he came by, he stopped over a recruit at the end of the row. Cayne strained to see him without moving his head.

Rogan put his hand over the recruit's mouth and motioned for silence. Then he and the boy disappeared into the night. Cayne tried to see where they went, but the darkness swallowed them. He looked over to Tarken, who had fallen into a restless sleep, and the other sleeping boys arrayed around them. Cayne desperately wanted to sleep, but he felt a stronger need to ensure Rogan didn't take any of them. He fought to stay awake for most of the night, but the need to remain still eventually lulled him to sleep.

In a blink it was morning, the light spilling into his eyes as a hand struck him on the cheek. Rogan stood over him, swinging his hand for a quick backhand to Cayne's other cheek with the armored side of his gauntlet, and it hurt twice as much. Cayne rolled to his right and tried to get to his feet, but Rogan reached out a hand and shoved him, dropping a knee into Cayne's back and putting his mouth next to Cayne's ear. The moisture from Rogan's breath warmed his skin.

"I heard you yesterday, boy. Don't ever question me. You don't ever tell me what to do, unless you think you can back your words with deeds." Rogan stood up, releasing Cayne. He waited expectantly.

The sun was low on the horizon, but the morning clouds and fog obscured any hint of where it was. The ground under him was damp, still wet from the morning dew. He drew wild breaths and stayed on the ground, trying to recover his wits. He held his tongue and his anger, despite his desire to settle things. Seeing how his inaction annoyed Rogan, he casually dusted himself off and sat up, but said nothing.

Rogan grunted and walked away, saying, "Maybe I was wrong. Maybe you just got lucky."

Cayne didn't feel very lucky.

"What was that about?" Tarken asked.

"Nothing I can't handle."

"It didn't look like you could handle Rogan." Tarken was shaking his head with a knowing smile of a friend trying to convince him of the truth.

"I'll find a way."

"Why do you want to kill him? I know he's evil and ruthless, but why bother? We need to get away from him, not kill him."

"It's not that I want to, or need to. I think he deserves it." Cayne looked at Rogan, now halfway across the camp, noting how the men, both veterans and recruits alike, parted from his path. Cayne realized that his first instincts about Rogan had been right. He really did want to kill him. He was evil, indiscriminate, and his breath made Cayne want to vomit.

Tarken stared at him, fear in his eyes. "What have you become?"

"I'm... " Cayne couldn't finish the thought. *What have I become? A murderer, plotting the deaths of others? A warchild?* With his family dead, was this army to be his new family? Other than Tarken and the boys, he wasn't sure if anyone he'd ever known was still alive. They were alone now, orphans forged by war. *Warphans.*

"I'm different," Cayne finally said. "Aren't you?"

Tarken nodded as his stare dropped to the ground. "But it makes me want to run away, not kill."

"These people are responsible," Cayne said, keeping his voice low. "They brought this. They killed our families. Shouldn't they pay?"

"Cayne, I don't know the answer. I'd rather just never see them again."

Cayne looked away. Tarken was right. It's what his father would have said to him.

Rogan was walking back now and yelling something incomprehensible, but since everyone was getting up, Cayne figured it was time to break camp. He didn't want to provoke Rogan, so he got up too. Rogan had a boy by the arm; it was the kid he'd taken during the night. The boy looked confused and scared. Cayne felt a sick sense of certainty as Rogan threw the boy down in the center of the recruits.

"Seems you boys don't listen," Rogan yelled. "I told you not to run. I told you I'd know and I'd find you." He looked around, making sure he had every ear. "This one tried to leave camp last night."

"I didn't—" the boy cried.

Rogan punched the boy full in the face with his mailed fist, and it made a sickening crack. The boy dropped, holding his hands to his head and moaning. Rogan continued, "He tried to leave, but I caught him. I'll catch any of you that try to leave."

Cayne pulled Tarken close to him. "I saw him take that kid last night. It's a lie."

"Shut up," Tarken said. "You'll get us killed."

"We have to do something."

"Like what?" Tarken demanded.

Cayne didn't know.

Rogan threw a boot into the boy's side. "Now, I told you boys what'd happen if one of you tried to leave, but I have an offer for you. If you take care of your own problem," he said, looking at the boy on the ground, "then I won't kill one of you."

The recruits passed unsure looks at each other, but no one moved.

"I've got a plan," Cayne told Tarken.

"I don't like your plan." Tarken's eyes were wide and fixed on Rogan.

Cayne didn't waste another moment. He stepped toward the boy, drawing his sword from the scabbard. "I'll take care of this," he announced to the crowd of relieved recruits.

Rogan gave him a wary look, his brows furrowing, but Cayne strode up confidently until he was standing over the boy with his sword held high. He fixed Rogan's location in his mind and then turned his back to him to focus on the helpless boy. His sword arced down, but he spun and cut right through the place where Rogan had stood.

Rogan had stepped back and drawn his sword without a sound. Off balance, Cayne expected to be struck, but Rogan just stood there with the strangest smile Cayne had ever seen. *Tarken was right. This plan was a summer dung heap.* It stank, but Cayne was committed.

He lunged at Rogan. Rogan sidestepped the sword point, but Cayne gave a sudden twist of the hilt and the blade swept toward Rogan again. Rogan parried the blow effortlessly. He could have killed Cayne at that moment, but Rogan hesitated again, his smile growing broader. *He's enjoying this.*

Cayne brought the sword back in a spinning motion. Rogan's blade was there again. This time the crash of the swords was so jarring, Cayne lost his grip and his sword fell to the ground. Rogan eyed the fallen sword, then Cayne. "Not bad, boy. At least you had the stones to try." He motioned to the boy on the ground. "Kill him now."

Cayne shook his head. He was ready to die.

Rogan looked amused. He pointed his sword at the nearest recruit. "If you don't, then I'll kill him. And I'll keep killing your fellow recruits until you do it."

Cayne wasn't ready for this. *Do nothing, people die; do something, people die.* There had to be another way.

Rogan gave him no time to think. He shrugged, then burst in a flash of motion toward the recruit standing closest to him. Cayne wasn't sure he'd moved far enough to touch the recruit until he saw the boy's head falling away from his collapsing body. Rogan looked very pleased. His gaze turned to the next recruit, who looked at Cayne, then ran toward the boy on the ground, a small blade flashing out. He fell on the helpless boy on the ground and stabbed him several times.

Rogan looked at the recruit stabbing wildly and then at Cayne. "Now kill *him*."

Cayne picked up his sword and prepared to attack Rogan again. With no hope of surprise, he'd try to use his strength and bludgeon Rogan.

"What is this?" Lord Darwan called from his horse. "Rogan, can you go even a single day without killing someone?"

"Just keeping good order— "

"Enough! I have had enough of your 'good order'," Darwan yelled, his patience clearly gone. "These are my men, not your personal flock of victims. No more, Rogan. No more!" Darwan paused momentarily. "The next man you kill will get you demoted to a job you can handle. I'll find someone who can maintain good order without killing everyone within reach."

Rogan bared daggers in his eyes. He gripped his sword and his whole body tensed. Then he exhaled and put his sword away, his expression back to blank. He nodded to Darwan, who promptly rode away.

Rogan walked to Cayne and spit on him. "Not over, boy." He turned and walked away, screaming orders.

Tarken walked up to Cayne, putting his hand on his shoulder. "Well, that went well."

"That was my chance, and I missed it." His hands were trembling now, and his legs quivered. He dropped to his knees.

"It wasn't a very good plan."

Cayne smiled, suddenly happy and surprised to be alive. "You're wrong, Tarken. I never had a plan."

Tarken looked sick, but Cayne felt alive for the first time in days. After several breaths, he could stand again. He helped the rest of the recruits pack up the entire camp, after taking the time to dig graves for the two dead recruits. Tarken and Cayne gathered the boys from Dahl Haven near them.

They marched through mid-afternoon, and that night they slept in a tight circle, with Cayne keeping a watchful eye on them. Tarken took the second watch. They were both glad to see little of Rogan. The next day they marched again as they had the day before. Life in the army was monotonous. Each day was just like the last.

In the late afternoon on the fourth day, a hateful presence loomed on the eastern horizon: Rayl Goth, a dead city of the Black. The black spires and towering mount spread dread among recruit and warrior alike. The city watched them, warning them to keep away. Cayne knew the village of Walla sat along this road, in the shadow of the old city. He wondered how anyone could live so close to such a place.

Other than the ominous presence, this place was familiar. He saw the same crops, the same thatched-roofed farmhouses, and smelled the same odor of the dirt in the air. But just like Dahl Haven, the crops were pillaged, the farmhouses burned out, and the stink of rotting meat, human or otherwise, mixed with the normal farm smells.

The line stuttered as men filtered off the road and into the ravaged fields to either side. Lord Darwan waited for the men to stop before he spoke. "The king's army passed through here two days ago, but they were unable to remain here and provide a proper experience for the local citizens. The king's orders remain the same."

Lusty conversations coursed along the troops as they closed on Walla. Rogan jogged to the head of the line of recruits. "In case you didn't understand the lord, we're staying the night here. We're to make the stay as unpleasant as possible for the survivors."

Ahead, the line surged into the village with a menacing cheer. Rogan yelled above the din, "Some of you boys can become men tonight. We'll find a suitable place for the rest of you. Either way, I'll be patrolling, so if you try to leave the village, you'll be leaving this world too."

Most of the recruits stayed in line. A few of the older ones fell out and ran into the village. Cayne grabbed Tarken. "Let's go."

"What are you talking about?" Tarken demanded, holding his ground. "I'm not doing that! We're not like them!"

"Face it. This is who we are now." Cayne raised his voice to the rest of the Dahl Haven boys around him. "Follow me!" he said, eyeing Rogan, who was watching him carefully. None of the boys had moved, so Cayne pushed them into motion.

Tarken moved with them, but he pulled at Cayne's arm. "Why are you doing this?"

"We're soldiers now. It's time we start acting like it." He gave Tarken's arm an unforgiving yank, dragging him along. The other boy watched Rogan, relieved that he didn't stop them, but clearly not sure he believed Cayne's words.

Tarken still dragged his steps, so Cayne said quietly, "Trust me. I have a plan."

"I don't like your plan."

Cayne gave him his best 'trust me' grin and yanked on him again.

Chapter Fifteen

Burke looked back over his shoulder at the horsemen trailing behind him. He switched his reins to his left hand and raised his right fist into the air. He made a swirling motion, then pulled his fist down to his shoulder.

The hoof beats quickened as his men rode up to flank him. Even the boy, Tak, made his way to the front. Only Lord Palus remained farther back. *Just as well.*

They'd been riding by scattered farms for most of the day, amid a building stench of burnt wood and death. Now, looking down the slope of the hill, he saw trampled fields and dead livestock spreading out to the horizon. This was the high water mark, then. The Sarasins had left the farms behind Burke unmolested, and everything in front of him desolate.

Burke looked at the ruined farms, and then at Tak. The boy had awakened during their trip to Nali. He'd adjusted well, and pledged to lead them to Weaverol. They'd stayed in Nali for the night, and found the people loyal and accommodating, despite their late arrival. Tak's standard smile fled, replaced by a despairing grimace.

"It's like this everywhere," Tak said somberly.

"They left no garrison?" Burke asked, scanning the horizon.

"No, they marched north and left nothing but suffering," Tak said, his voice breaking.

Burke looked away from Tak, doing him the honor of not noticing his tears. His men would do the same. He wished he, himself, could let down his own defenses and mourn for his lost sons.

A horse sidled up to him, and then a mailed fist settled on his shoulder. Yenevas was a grizzled warrior who normally commanded the men of this unit. The Fist was divided into two main groups of one hundred and twenty-five. It was further divided into fingers of twenty-five horsemen each. Yenevas commanded this finger, though it was well below standard size.

"Our people bleed across the land," Yenevas said. He too had lost sons in the last battle, but he had more sons at home. He displayed none of the despair that Burke felt.

Perhaps he's just stronger than me, or maybe he hides it better. Burke banished the thoughts of his sons and the threatening tears.

"You should stay here," Tak said. He rode a dun gelding. It was like a pony beside the massive warhorses of the Fist.

Burke turned a questioning gaze upon him.

"I'll ride into the village center." Tak waved at their shining armor. "You're not very stealthy."

"We have cloaks to mask our armor," he said, "but we accept your offer. If you see any sign of the Sarasins, return immediately."

Tak nodded and slapped his horse into motion. Burke felt a sense of loss as the boy rode down the hill. *Have I sent him to his death?* Yenevas looked to one of his men, and the man nodded, holding his position. The riders dismounted wordlessly.

The armor was light, but it wasn't comfortable. They sat, legs extended in a rough circle. "How much more do we need to see?" Yenevas asked. "It's clear the Sarasins were here, and in large numbers."

Lord Palus sat away from the rest of the circle. He was listening, but said nothing.

"I agree," Burke said. "We'll talk with the survivors here, and glean what we can from their accounts. Then we'll make haste for Rivermar." He looked to Palus, who was getting up and walking to them.

"The king will want our report," Palus said. "And he is in Barons Lodge, not Rivermar."

"We still haven't sighted the Sarasins ourselves," he said. "From here, they may have traveled north or west."

"What does it matter?" Palus snapped.

"We can be in Rivermar in four days," Burke said. "From there we can ride to Walla. If we find signs of the Sarasins, then we can report more precisely."

"And if they are not there," Palus said, pondering, "then we can assume they headed for the coast." He sighed. "I will admit your plan has merit, but I will still have my reckoning."

"First Sword," Yenevas said. "We'll need to let the horses rest. We've been riding them hard."

Burke swore an oath and kicked the ground with his armored boot. "With the fate of the whole kingdom dangling, we rest?"

"No choice."

He knew the words were true, but searched for a way around it. Their warhorses were irreplaceable. Paired as horse and rider, only death or maiming injury could part them. Yenevas was right. They'd ridden the horses non-stop for the past five days, and now they were looking at another week of forced riding. Much of his anger faced inward, as *he* should have been the one to point it out. He was the First Sword. His role was to know the men and horses. "We'll remain here for the night, and then head back to Nali. We can rest there."

Yenevas grunted in agreement and turned his attention to a tough loaf of field bread. It crunched loudly as he ground it between his teeth. It was more like dried bark and tasted no better, but it sustained them for long journeys between proper meals. Palus, meanwhile, seemed satisfied with the outcome of the conversation, and drifted away from the circle.

Yenevas watched Palus warily, waiting until he was out of earshot. "We can take care of our Palus problem on the road to Nali."

"He's the commander," Burke said flatly.

"He'll see our heads cleaved from our shoulders," Yenevas said. The other men were pushing in closer to listen. Yenevas looked to them. "None of us will say anything." The men nodded.

"I'm the one he wants to see truly punished. You'll likely only get a crack of the whip on your backs." Burke shook his head. "We will have no more of this talk. We are the Fist, and we have honor. I will not see us turn into a band of brigands."

The men grumbled, but they stopped talking about it. After sharing a quiet meal of field bread and dried bison meat, they tended the horses and waited. It wasn't long before the scout reported Tak's approach. Yenevas was the first to mount his horse. "He's alone."

Tak slowed his horse's pace and rode in front of the troop. His somber words came slowly. "It's the same as when I left. They still haven't buried all the bodies."

"Will we find support here?" Yenevas asked, no sense of caring in his voice.

Burke sensed Tak's anguish, a feeling he knew all too well. He wanted to take the boy aside and comfort him, but what would he say? He had no solace to offer. "How are your people?" Burke asked.

"Most of them have moved to the village proper," Tak said. He waved his hands at the farms around them. "There aren't any crops to tend, and most of the livestock were either slaughtered or driven off." He paused to take a deep breath. "Survivors from Liloot are here too. They've abandoned their village altogether."

"We'll rest here for a day before we head back north," Burke declared. "We'll talk with the survivors, and learn what we can about the Sarasin force." He looked to Tak. "And we will lend our backs to the task of burying your townsmen."

Tak made a nod of appreciation, and then turned his horse toward Weaverol. They made the ride in near-silence. The fields were cut, trampled, or burned. They fashioned litters and hitched them to the horses. As they saw rotting corpses, they loaded them onto the litters, and ultimately dragged two-score bodies into the village center.

The surviving citizens were disheveled, their faces downcast. People stopped to gaze at the line of shining horsemen, but only for moment; then they sank back down and continued whatever menial tasks they were performing. There was no sense of awe or anger. They seemed drained of any emotion at all.

The Fist dug a large ditch and piled the bodies into the mass grave while the villagers looked on. After the burial, they interviewed those who would speak to them. Many of the people were from Liloot, where rugged, independent-minded famers grew cotton along the banks of the Skykom River. Across the river, the endless expanse of the Hashok Grasslands was as large a barrier as an ocean. Only the river allowed regular passage across the grasslands to the distant Seebolan States. Immense herds of bison, horse, and mastodon grazed across the vast land, feeding on the tall grasses. The grazers, in turn, supported large packs of wolves and prides of sabercats that would eagerly make a meal of hapless travelers foolish enough to try a land crossing of the Hashok. The farms around Liloot were small hamlets in their own right. Family groups lived in these compounds, which allowed for the manpower needed to tend the labor-intensive cotton crop.

Though Burke led the questioning, Lord Palus joined them and even asked several surprisingly relevant questions of his own. He'd made it a point to introduce himself as the commander of the Fist, but with most of the questions coming from Burke, most of the villagers addressed their accounts to him.

After they finished asking their questions, Burke knew several truths. They were tracking the main Sarasin army, and King Arta Nakis was leading it. The slaughter and devastation at Liloot had been total. The scant survivors here in Weaverol were all that remained of a thriving town. Despite the carnage, the Sarasins had claimed that it wasn't authorized and had apparently executed some of their own men, though none of the survivors had actually seen the executions. Whether it was fact or propaganda, it wasn't the act of a raider. It was the act of an occupier. *The Sarasins are coming to stay,* Burke mused.

"That will be enough for tonight," he said to Tak. "Tell your people they have the king's gratitude for the information they shared."

Tak nodded, then left the meeting hall. The members of the Fist gathered around a long table in the now-vacant hall.

"A bridge?" Yenevas said. "It's not possible. How could they bridge the Skykom in so short a time?"

"Too many Lilooters told the same story for it not to be true," Burke said. "Regardless of how they did it, they crossed both the Hashok and the Skykom. Neither of those is a small feat."

"From what they said," Yenevas said, "it took several days to complete the crossing. You know what that means."

"Their force is substantial."

"Yes," Yenevas said, scowling, "but that's not what I meant. A bridge like they described would have blocked pyreships sailing in both directions."

The Lilooters had described a strange bridge floating on the river. Burke saw the implication. He spoke quietly. "Some of the pyreships would have returned to Black Rock."

"Exactly," Yenevas said. He pounded his fist on the table and pointed at Burke. "They knew over a fortnight ago and they failed to raise the alarm."

"Traitors," Lord Palus said from the distant end of the table. "Those were the people you protected." He stood up and walked smugly toward the rest of the men. "Just admit you were wrong, and I was right. We should have put the whole filthy place to the sword. Clearly they are in league with the Sarasin dogs."

Burke glanced at Jaks, who sat staring at the floor. He turned back to Palus. "We're still only a dozen men."

"A dozen warriors of the King's Armored Fist. We would have slain them all."

Burke wanted to laugh in his face. True, they were well armed, but sacking a city was different from charging an army on the field of battle. He'd served in the Fist longer than any other man had, and he knew their limits. This fool did not. *Perhaps he's right, though; maybe* I'm *the fool.*

"I tried to join the army," Tak said from the doorway. He walked closer and continued. "When I returned to Black Rock, I tried to enlist in the army, but they laughed in my face. They said they'd turned away hundreds of men flowing in from the villages."

"That explains why there were so many fighting-age men there," Burke said.

"Traitors," Palus muttered again.

Burke quieted, his doubts growing. Maybe they should have cut a bloody path through Black Rock. But they hadn't. *The web once woven won't be unwoven.*

"We need numbers, estimates," he said, trying to shift the conversation.

"The king will see to their betrayal," Palus said.

"We can't rely on any of the numbers these people gave us," Yenevas said.

Burke turned away from Palus and focused on Yenevas, thankful he'd taken the prompt. "Based on the scale of the destruction, it's no raiding party. It's the full army."

"But no horse," Yenevas said. "Strange."

Burke nodded. Though they had seen scattered mounted warriors, neither the people from Liloot nor Weaverol had seen any large groups of horsemen. "They risk disaster by invading without horsemen to scout for them."

"Perhaps none of these people saw the horsemen. Maybe they were scouting ahead, or killed everyone who saw them."

"Possibly. We need more information."

"We have enough," Palus said. "The king must know."

"Agreed," Burke said, not bothering to look at Palus. "We'll ride back to Rivermar as planned."

"Tomorrow?" Palus asked insistently.

"The day after. We must rest the horses."

"While the kingdom burns?"

Burke shook his head. "We won't get there faster if our horses collapse."

"I care nothing of the horses."

Burke pointed to the door. "Then by all means, Lord Palus, leave this night and travel alone."

Palus huffed and walked to the door. "I will see to my accommodations myself and be ready to ride in two days."

"Dawn," Burke said. "Don't be late. We'd hate to leave without you."

Palus didn't answer. He stormed out the door, grumbling to himself.

"What kind of horseman doesn't care about his horse?" Yenevas asked. "He's a dandy who knows nothing of our ways."

The king had appointed Palus to his position; the rest of the Fist had earned their positions through years of service. Horse and rider were bonded as strongly as brothers. While scouts regularly wore out horses, the warhorses of the Fist were armored and survived many years, and many saw retirement.

"He's the commander," Burke said simply. "We will not lose our honor."

Yenevas shook his head and got up, putting a hand on Burke's shoulder. "Your pyre, old friend." He walked out the door.

The rest of the men filtered out of the meeting hall, until Burke was alone with Jaks. Burke waited patiently for him to speak.

Jaks let out three great sighs before he uttered a word. "I won't raise my sword against Black Rock."

"They're your people. I'd expect no less from you."

"Perhaps I should leave the Fist," Jaks said, his eyes averted.

"I think you still have honorable service left in you." He moved to the seat across from Jaks, waiting until Jaks acknowledged his stare. "I will not ask you to make war on your own people. If it comes to that, you will not be expected to participate."

"I feel like I'd have to participate, but not on the side of the Fist." Jaks looked back at him, a mask of tortured indecision on his face.

"Let us hope the gods don't guide us to that outcome." Burke got up and left Jaks to his reflections.

They spent the next day walking out to farms and burying the dead right where they lay. Palus remained in the quarters he'd commandeered, only coming out to eat.

When they left for Nali, Tak was waiting for them. He wanted to fight, and Burke would not deny him the right to vengeance.

Chapter Sixteen

Cayne looked back at the gang of scared boys behind him, then forward to the village. Now that they were at the edge of the settlement, it didn't seem much like Dahl Haven. Walla looked as if it grew from the forest, with a canopy of old oaks spreading out above the village.

The houses here, though, were much like those at home: wooden, plank-sided boxes with thatched roofs. The shuttered windows reminded him of the time right before a big storm, only it was sunny out. Shutters should be open on a warm day like today.

At the first intersection, he saw a market ahead, surrounded by rows of houses. Thinking the Sarasins might cluster around the market to loot it, he turned in another direction, making sure he didn't lose any of the boys. Sarasin warriors broke into homes everywhere he looked. He heard screams echo out, and quickened his pace. The pit of his stomach twisted. *Which way to go? Which house?*

They passed one road clogged with Sarasins, and then took a left at the next side road. This section of Walla was deserted for now. He picked a house, thinking how random his decision was. He ran to the door and shoved.

Cayne expected the door to swing open easily, but something barred him from entering. He heard alarmed voices inside the house, and behind him he saw Sarasins passing by. *We have to get off the street.* He put his shoulder to the door and steadily pushed it open with a grinding sound, then motioned for the other boys. "Get in." He looked back to the street, expecting to see Rogan watching them. Seeing scores of looting Sarasins, but no Rogan, he slammed the door.

With the shutters drawn and but a single candle lighting the interior, he saw nothing inside at first; but after a moment, his eyes adjusted. This was a plain, single-room house. Other than a small hearth, there was little else. Three women stood over a makeshift bed far from the door. He stepped toward them and they cowered, pressing themselves into the wall. One was his age, another older, and the last was old. They jumped at the sound of a nearby scream, as did most of the boys.

"We're not here to hurt you," Cayne assured them, raising his hands. "We're from Dahl Haven. They forced us into their army. We're as scared as you."

The women exhaled and relaxed, but the middle-aged woman stepped forward and eyed Cayne and his young companions. She wore a long leather skirt that fell to her knees. The colorful frills tied to the hem draped to the floor, hiding the rest of her legs. She kept her hair in a tight knot at the back of her head. "You're just boys," she said, after looking them over. "What's happening? We thought they'd come and gone."

Cayne looked to Tarken, but he had his stare locked on the floor. Cayne thought about how to explain what was happening—as another scream shattered the silence.

"I understand," the woman said sourly. "When that army passed through, we considered ourselves fortunate they only took our things. We should have fled."

"I can't stop that," Cayne uttered slowly, motioning outside. "They think we're doing that in here, too."

"I am Valia; this is my husband's mother, Rinna," she said, motioning to the old woman. Rinna wore the same garb as Valia except that she kept her white hair short, almost spikey. Her rosy cheeks formed a tight smile, but she kept silent.

"I'm Shari," said the younger girl, stepping forward. The other two women put a hand out to stop her, but she was too fast. Shari wore a similar leather skirt, but with no frills. It exposed enough of her legs to make Cayne forget their situation for the briefest moment. She looked at Cayne and Tarken and beamed a broad smile at them. "Two boys." Her grin grew. "I've been hoping you would come."

Cayne and Tarken traded confused glances. He noticed that the two older women exchanged similar glances. Shari ignored them all and gave both boys a formal hug.

"My name is Cayne Falconstorm." He said it without thinking. He moved on, introducing the others, then barricaded the door with the large rock the women had put there to keep out intruders. It hadn't kept him out and it wouldn't keep anyone else out either, but it might buy a few moments.

"We'll rest here for a while," Cayne said to Shari. "We won't bother you."

She bobbed her head and said, "I'm so glad you're finally here."

He nodded to her, scratching his head, then turned away and walked over to Tarken. His friend was sitting cross-legged by the hearth, his head in his hands. He looked up at Cayne's approach. "Why didn't you tell me this was the plan?" Tarken asked, letting out a loud breath. "I thought you'd become one of them."

"Tarken, how long have you known me? I didn't tell you the plan because I didn't *have* a plan." He shifted uneasily at another scream in the distance. "I had to do something. I wasn't going to sleep in a barn and listen to this. We had to try to save someone."

"Why didn't we just run right through the town?" Tarken asked.

Cayne frowned. He hadn't thought of that. The streets were full of Sarasins now. He figured they'd be posting guards along the roads. Then there was Rogan... Cayne doubted he'd believed the ploy.

"What now?" Tarken asked, looking at the younger boys. "Stay here?"

"No. Once things quiet down, we're leaving."

"But Rogan will catch us!" Tarken said. "He caught that boy the other day! What chance do we have with a whole troop of us trying to sneak out?"

"He didn't 'catch' him. I told you, he picked him so he could set an example, and make the rest of us think he can catch us."

"It worked," Tarken admitted.

"No, this is a big village, and he can't be everywhere. As soon as it gets dark, we're leaving."

"Um... why did you call yourself Cayne Falconstorm?"

Cayne didn't have an answer for him. *Why* had *he used his real name?* He shrugged.

Tarken looked over to Shari. "She's pretty. Do you think she'd talk to me?"

"I hadn't noticed her much," Cayne lied. Tarken never talked to girls. He just talked about talking to girls. Still, it was the first time since they'd left Dahl Haven that he'd seen Tarken smile. "Wait here." Cayne strode over to Shari.

"What are you doing?" Tarken said under his breath.

Cayne knelt beside her and asked, "Are you all right?" Her bright smile lit up, and it was enough to make Cayne wonder at her mental state. Either she was driven to madness by her own ordeal, or she was just plain crazy. No one should be smiling at a time like this.

"I was afraid, but now that you're here, everything will be fine."

"Sure it will," he said slowly, trying to hide his sarcasm.

"It will." Her certainty was absolute.

"You act like you were expecting us."

She nodded. "The seer told me you would come and take us from here."

Cayne looked at her in surprise. His plan didn't include any of them. "Did the seer tell you anything else?"

"She was a bit cryptic about it."

"Typical. I talked to a seer a few days ago, but he didn't say anything about you."

Shari's expression soured at that, but quickly returned to its smiling state. "When are we leaving?"

"Later." His plan now included the women, though he wasn't sure how that would affect their chances.

"Can I do anything to help?" she said brightly.

He pointed to Tarken, who was frozen in place, eyes wide. Keeping his own sorrows to himself, Cayne told her of Tarken's ordeal. Her smile faded, replaced by a dull stare and watering eyes.

She stood to walk over to a very sick-looking Tarken Ware. Cayne thought she looked back at him, but perhaps it was just what he wanted to see.

Cayne shot to his feet, hearing two of the boys arguing loudly. He ran to them, making entirely too much noise of his own. It was the twins, Bale and Boon. They were arguing as though they were in the safety of their own home.

"Shut up! Do you want them to hear you?" he said in a low voice.

The boys quieted, but still glared at each other. Cayne wasn't sure which one was which. One of them said, "He won't share."

"Share what?" Cayne asked.

The boys looked at each other. Cayne noticed their clenched hands.

"What do you have?"

One, Cayne still wasn't sure which, opened his hand, revealing a dull copper bead, its surface weathered blue. The other boy shook his head and kept his hand closed.

"Show him, Boon," Bale said.

Boon sighed and opened his hand. He had a thick silver bead in his hand.

"Where did you get those?" Cayne asked. Boys their age seldom had any beads at all, and if they did, it was iron, not copper and certainly not silver.

"He's supposed to share," Bale said. "We agreed to switch beads each day."

"The day isn't over yet," Boon said triumphantly.

"Where did you get those?" Cayne repeated, a bit louder this time.

"Rann gave us this," Bale said, looking at the copper bead. "He asked us to steal something for him. I forget what."

The story sounded dubious to Cayne.

"The fat merchant gave us this," Boon said, holding up the silver bead. "All he asked us to do was look scared and keep our mouths shut."

"Both of those sound difficult for you two. We can't have you arguing. Either learn to share, or I'll take them both. How does that sound?"

They sneered at each other, but then switched beads.

"We'll be quiet from now on," Bale said.

"We're sorry, Cayne Falconstorm," Boon said wryly.

So they had heard. *Better not to let them know it bothers me, or they'll use it continuously.* He shook his head and walked away.

Tarken sat with Shari, but as soon as he saw Cayne walking toward the door, he hopped up and moved to intercept him. "Cayne, what do I say to her?"

Cayne kept walking to the door. "You've already been talking to her." Cayne opened the door a crack, glad to see daylight fading. "What have you been talking about?" he asked, thinking on the many times Tarken had droned on endlessly on the most arcane topics.

"The last book I read."

"Which was?"

"*Mating Habits of the Black-Horned Tankadon.*"

Cayne shut the door and turned to Tarken. "You didn't."

"Yes, I did. I need help."

"Look, just talk about something you like."

"I like *her*," Tarken said wistfully.

"I think that might actually be worse."

Tarken let out a sigh and shook his head. "Maybe you could talk to her for me."

"Why don't you ask her what she'd like to talk about?"

Tarken looked up to the roof, then nodded. "I can do that." He walked back to Shari.

Cayne heard a shuffling outside and then a loud knock. Cayne gripped the hilt of his sword, and put a hand the door as it stuttered open. *Need to sound confident.* He stepped into the opening and saw the commander's steward putting his shoulder to the door. Zane gave a start and stepped away.

"You're a recruit," Zane said incredulously. He gave a dismissive snort and shook his head. "Make way for a Sarasin warrior."

Though Zane moved forward, Cayne held his ground, tightening his grip on his sword hilt. He wouldn't allow to Zane pass, and it surprised both of them. "We got here first. You can wait."

Zane smiled and laughed in his face. His breath stank of stale beer. "You don't understand. I'm a Sarasin and you, your job is to catch arrows and spears." He stepped forward, but again, Cayne stood firm. "Stand aside, farm boy." This time Zane gripped his sword and took a menacing stance, but then relented. "Wait. You're the recruit that stood up to Rogan."

"I'm not letting you by," Cayne said, lowering his center of gravity. Remembering his expected purpose, he added, "until we're done here."

Zane laughed again, this time long and hearty. "It was good to see someone finally stand up to that bastard." He looked around Cayne. "You've got something good in there. I guess I'd defend it too, but you're already sharing it with a crowd."

Cayne looked back at the scared women in the corner of the house and the even more scared boys near them. He turned back to Zane, loosening his grip on his sword. "This is our first time doing this sort of thing. We could use a little privacy."

"All right, I'll yield to you, but that looks good enough to wait for." Zane stepped away from the door and sat on a broken barrel, taking out a small flask from a hidden pouch under his armor. He took a long swig, not bothering to wipe the dribble. "From the looks of you, this shouldn't take long. Run along now and try your best, but when this is gone," he said, shaking the flask in the air, "I'm coming in."

Cayne shut the door. His entire body shook so much that he had to steady himself against the wall. He'd gotten them into this and now he needed to get them out. He looked to the women and said, "I need you to yell and scream."

They understood and traded defiant words. Cayne hoped the words were muffled by the walls, because even he didn't believe them. Still, he hoped it would garner them a short respite.

"He's a big drinker," Tarken said. "It won't take him long."

Cayne turned to the women. "Do you have any spirits?"

"No, the soldiers took everything," Rinna blurted out. The old woman answered before Cayne had even finished his question. Valia turned to her mother-in-law, who scowled back at her. Rinna said to her spitefully, "You could probably use what that man would give you."

"Your son certainly never had much expertise," Valia shot back.

Before the two women could get at each other, Shari stepped in between them and regarded her grandmother with pleading eyes. "Gran, would you wish that on me as well?"

Rinna grimaced, but walked to the corner of the house and kicked the floor. Then, with a well-practiced shift of her foot, a plank popped up. She reached in and produced a glazed jug. Handing it to Cayne, she proudly said, "This is my son's finest spirit." She smiled weakly.

"Gran."

Rinna's smile faded, and she sighed. "Only for you, child." She reached into her shirt and pulled out a clay flask. She handed it to Cayne, but he had to pry it from her grip. "My personal stock. Too strong for my son."

Cayne took the top off and lifted it to his nose, but Rinna stretched out a warning hand. "I wouldn't sniff that."

"What if I drank it?" Cayne asked.

Rinna surveyed Cayne. "You might just go blind." She looked to Tarken and said, "Your friend would probably die." She chuckled at her own words.

"It's that strong?"

All three women nodded. Cayne recapped the flask and took it outside to Zane.

Zane was sipping his own flask and smoking a pipe, not even bothering to look at Cayne as he approached. "That was fast."

He's vulnerable. Cayne put a hand to his sword, but he didn't draw it. Saying you wanted to kill Sarasins was far easier than actually doing it. He released his grip on his sword and said, "We're not done, sir, but we found something." That got Zane's attention. He eyed the flask in Cayne's hands, sitting up and leaning forward. "We wanted you to have it, for being so patient."

"Patience," Zane snorted, shaking his head, "my new best trait." He snatched the flask from Cayne, taking off the top and sniffing lightly. His eyes nearly popped out of his head and his face turned away. "Now *that's* a drink." He took a quick slug from the flask, followed by a long inhale and quick exhale. Zane motioned for him to be on his way.

Backing away, Cayne glanced across the road. Rogan sat on a woodpile, drawing a whetstone across the blade of his sword, while he surveyed the darkening street. Cayne slipped back through the door and slammed it.

Tarken was waiting for him. "Did it work?"

"Well, he's drinking it, but that's not our biggest problem. Rogan is sitting across the street."

"Well, that ends it," Tarken declared. "We're not going anywhere now."

"You didn't give him the whole thing, did you?" Rinna cackled with a snort. "He'll most likely be dead if he drinks the whole thing. I told you not to drink too much of it."

"No, you didn't," Cayne said, his eyes turning to Tarken.

"Great," Tarken said, "We poisoned Lord Darwan's steward."

"Didn't I tell you that?" Rinna asked. "Well, I should have. It's a sipping juice."

"Sometimes we use Gran's juice to strip paint," Shari said with a shrug.

After a short time, Cayne cracked the door. Zane sat with his back against the wall, both hands dangling lifelessly at his side, but Cayne heard a gentle snoring.

He closed the door and said, "He's sleeping. Maybe we can go out the back." He and Tarken looked at the back wall. There wasn't a door or even a window. "Actually, I guess we're staying until we come up with a new plan," Cayne said, and Tarken nodded.

The boys settled in for the night. Cayne sat next to the door and peeked out intermittently. Rogan would disappear for a while, only to come back after a short time.

The two older women fussed over the smaller boys, and generally stayed away from each other. Shari milled about for some time, though Cayne caught her glancing at him occasionally. His mind was focused on their situation, and he tried to think of a plan to get them away, so he didn't notice her walking up to him until she spoke.

"Why are you fighting for the Sarasins?" she asked demurely as she sat next to him.

"We weren't given much choice."

"Why didn't you fight for King Alarak?"

"I wanted to, and so did Tarken." He recounted the events of the past few days, ending by saying, "I'm not sure if it makes any difference which side we fight for."

"I'm sorry for your family," she said, taking his hand gently.

Her touch was tender, and warmed him for the first time in many days. He looked to Tarken, reading the worried look on his face. "It's not your doing," he said. "It's this war. These Sarasins."

"What will you do?"

"I wish I knew. I'm not sure it matters. King Alarak orders us to fight, and we die. King Arta Nakis orders us to fight, and we die." He believed the truth in his owns words and sighed. "Kings call, we answer, and we die. All we can hope to do is survive. We end up the same no matter which call we answer."

"If you can't win, then maybe you shouldn't play."

Her words were simple, and he pondered whether there was a way to avoid this king's game. "You're right. We're just helmets in a long, bloody line." He slammed his fist into his hand. "We're *not* playing this game."

"How are you going to avoid it?" she asked, surprised at his sudden emotion. She pulled away from him like his mother had when she thought he was getting too violent.

"I have no idea," he said more softly. Tarken was glowering at him. "Do you like Tarken?"

"He's nice. A little chatty, but nice." She looked to Tarken too, and he turned his face away. She turned to Cayne. "You want me to talk to him again?"

Cayne enjoyed talking with her, but he said, "Yes."

She got up, saying, "I'll do this for you, but later you'll do something for me."

"What?" he asked.

"I'll let you know," she said, and walked toward Tarken.

Cayne watched Tarken's expression turn to joyful apprehension, then fear. Cayne scowled to hide his smile.

Looking over at the other boys, he saw that none rested easy. They talked in hushed tones with frequent checks of the door. They all expected to hear a knock at any moment, and so did Cayne. Rogan must have known what they were up to. Why hadn't he done anything?

Cayne had to get them away from this madness before the first battle. He could see the death of these boys, thrown unarmored with rusty weapons at their own countrymen. They might be able to surrender, if they had the chance, but how could they surrender to a volley of arrows or a line of spears? They had to get away tonight.

He checked the street again. Zane still slept, his snoring loud enough to mask a passing army. Rogan was nowhere in sight, and that concerned Cayne even more than having him across the street. Looking back to Zane, he considered extracting some revenge. He steeled himself, building his rage, and focusing on a single thought: vengeance. *I pledged to kill Sarasins, didn't I?*

Cayne stepped quietly into the night. He stood next to Zane, who was still as helpless as a baby. Killing a man in his sleep was Dyn's work, and the god of the Black would mark him forevermore. That's what Cayne's father would have said. He felt for his small knife. He hadn't touched it since cutting the dynabane, so it should still be covered in poison. Cayne sparked visions in his mind. Visions of his family resting in their grave. He wanted to scream... but he couldn't bring himself to kill Zane.

I've failed again. Empty promises of vengeance are all that I can offer. The pain of the memories made his chest tighten. He sucked in deep breaths of cool, humid air until he thought his chest might crack open, but when he let it go, the pain remained.

He walked back to the door, sighing as he opened it. *Father would have said I'd just won a battle against the Black.* It felt like a hollow victory.

He watched four Sarasins leave the house across the street and saunter to the next. They argued briefly with the warriors in that house, and then moved on to the next house. That house already contained Sarasins as well, and they turned toward Cayne. He doubted he could talk them out of whatever they had in mind.

He leaned into the house and yelled, "Everyone up! We're leaving! Now!"

"What's happening?" Shari asked.

"No time," he said. "Tarken, take everyone and run across the street. Keep running until you can't run anymore."

Tarken was up and running to the door. He asked, "What are you—"

"I'll distract them." Cayne looked for the rage inside him again. The men were within speaking range, but now he noticed that they wobbled with each step, using each other for balance. He stepped toward the men. His heart hammered away in his chest, while a flood of energy surged across his body.

"Run, Tarken," he growled in his lowest register. His steps turned to strides. The Sarasins fumbled for their swords, but he was on them before they could draw a single blade. He lowered his shoulder and bashed into the lead man.

Cayne's shoulder hit solid iron breastplate, but the soldier fell backward into two other men, and all three crashed to the ground with Cayne on top of them. The last of the four spun around, trying to draw his sword, but lost his footing and tumbled to the ground.

Tarken led the boys and women across the road, but they were maddeningly slow. Cayne leapt over the men and sauntered away from them, trying to draw them away from Tarken. He waited until the men saw him before taunting them. "Sarasin trash." *Follow me, Gol-damn you.* He smiled as they swore at him and got to their feet. He turned to run.

"You! Stop!"

Cayne recognized the shout and looked back. Tarken and the others were standing in the middle of the road. *No.*

Rogan emerged from the shadows, a sword in each hand. He moved toward the boys and shouted, "Sit!"

"Tarken, run!" Cayne shouted, but he could see the boys already falling to the ground as Rogan had ordered. He lost sight of the boys as two of the men stumbled angrily toward him. The first man threw a lazy punch and Cayne easily dodged the slow thrust. Cayne connected with a punch, cracking the man's jaw. The Sarasin collapsed and Cayne pushed the falling body to the side.

He turned toward the boys, but thick arms wrapped his waist. He thrashed and groped for the man grappling with him. Another Sarasin jumped on his back and Cayne fell over, all three slamming to the ground. The fourth man rushed up to kick Cayne in the gut.

He struggled amid the blows, but they held him fast. Rogan loomed over them and smiled down at him.

"I've been looking forward to this, boy."

Chapter Seventeen

Darwan sat atop his steed, watching a horse approach from across the green, the first streaks of light painting the rooftops. He'd spent the night in a pyrus-induced haze and hadn't slept at all. He remembered the entire night, though it was still like a distant dream, as if he were watching someone else live his life.

His concerns about the way the pyrus affected him were trivial when compared to the problem of his dwindling supply. He felt the last few cubes smoldering against his chest. It comforted him to know they were there. He needed to get to a city, and soon. There he might find alchemist who could sell him more of the precious drug. These blasted villages held nothing but grain and worthless textiles. They had smoking-weed, but none of them had pyrus.

He reached absently for the javelins secured to the saddle, caressing the cold iron. They were his weapons of choice when hunting. To his surprise, his hand drew one of them. The Red pulsated with annoyance.

Darwan sensed darkness surrounding the approaching rider despite the slow, nonthreatening pace. He forced the javelin back into its holder, but his fingers kept sliding up and down the rough metal.

The shapeless rider cohered into Margella, and he pasted a fake smile on his face. "Good morning, Lady Margella."

"Lady? So formal today." She wore a silver veil and a long fur that hid most of her body.

"You're dressed warmly."

She gave him an odd look and said, "It's cold."

Darwan noticed for the first time that the temperature had indeed dropped. He had to force his senses to feel the chill in the air. It didn't bother him at all.

"Are we marching today?" she asked.

"Yes, we march west."

"West? That's a shame. You saw the city to the east?"

"Rayl Goth? What interest do you have in a dead city?"

"Not dead," she corrected him, "just not occupied."

"Not occupied for five hundred years, not since the Tainted Ones abandoned it. I'd call that dead."

"You know of Rayl Goth?"

"I am no fool." He shifted in his saddle. *What is she after?*

"I'm just surprised you know of such things," she said, crooking her head and raising an eyebrow.

"Do you have a point to make?"

"It would be a shame to come this close to such a glorious city and not visit it. Think of the treasures we might find."

He snorted. "After this much time, I doubt anything of value remains there, but it's an empty discussion. Our orders are to march west."

"And you *always* follow your orders." She might have tried to spin the words as praise, but they rang with sarcasm.

Darwan thought of the last battle. The king had ordered him to hold an untenable position. He had followed his orders. They were bait then. *What are we this time?*

Margella turned to regard an approaching horseman. "Perhaps you might find what you seek there."

Darwan's mind snapped to the pyrus. She knew of it, and knew he was using it. She could ruin him by telling the king, but what would she gain from that? *Does she really know where to find it? Is that what she's saying?* Before he could ask her, the horseman was upon them. "Lord Darwan, a message from King Arta Nakis."

Darwan nodded to the messenger.

"King Arta Nakis orders you to prepare a war council. He will arrive this morning. All the lords are converging on this place."

"It will be done," Darwan told the messenger calmly. The messenger didn't wait for another word, galloping off with nothing but a vague salute. The king had already passed through this village with the army, and now he was returning. *The army is turning, but why?* He turned to Margella, who seemed to be doing her own thinking.

"I must go and prepare for the king," she said.

"He's coming for a war council."

"I think he'll want to consult with me as well," she said as she turned her horse away. "Your secret is safe with me."

It will be when you're dead. She'd need to meet some unfortunate end, her and Zane both. He'd need to look more earnestly for opportunities.

Darwan shrugged and turned his thoughts to the preparations for the council. While he wanted Zane gone, at the moment he needed him. He rode through the deserted streets, seeing just a few sentries patrolling. They moved crisply and he followed them. Something was afoot, and the Red was drawn to it.

He heard the murmurs of a crowd. Both warriors and villagers were gathered on a side street. Darwan wasn't surprised to find Rogan at the center of the commotion, sword drawn, with a number of recruits kneeling on the ground. *Could he not restrain himself for even a single day?* The Red boiled at the sight of Rogan. Darwan had never liked the man, but now he had an overwhelming need to antagonize him. It was the pyrus, the Red. It hated Rogan, and wanted to see him suffer.

The crowd parted for Darwan's horse, and all eyes turned to him. Beyond the circle of people, he saw Zane sitting on a barrel shaking his head, as though he'd just been hit with a barn. *Typical for him. Drunk.* Darwan looked at the boys kneeling in the ground. Only two looked old enough to fight; the others were children. Several warriors stood over the two older boys. Rogan stood a few steps away with three women, two hags and one fair maiden.

"When this is over," Rogan said to the boys, "should I show her my attentions?" He was holding the chin of the pretty girl.

The two boys bristled, but with the warriors holding their shoulders, they didn't rise to their feet. They looked defeated.

The Red pulsed again and Darwan sensed violence in the air. Rogan drew one of his daggers and held it to the girl's neck. She pulled back, but his other hand grabbed the back of her neck. "Rogan, what manner of ceremony is this?" Darwan demanded.

Rogan didn't turn his attention to Darwan. He smiled and said to the boys, "My attentions are fleeting." He leaned in close and whispered in the girl's ear. Then he drew his blade across her neck in a quick motion. He threw the girl toward the two hags and turned to face the two boys. They writhed to get at Rogan, but the warriors over them held them firm. The two women pulled the girl away from the scene.

"Deserters, Lord Darwan," Rogan said. "I was getting ready to show them what we do with deserters."

"Was *she* a deserter?" Darwan asked more loudly than he'd intended.

Rogan looked up to Darwan. "Collateral damage." He shrugged.

Darwan pointed at the older boys. "You two, what are your names?"

The big one said, "Cayne and Tarken."

"Did you desert?"

Before they could answer, Rogan spoke. "I caught them sneaking out like thieves. The punishment is clear."

"I'll decide that," Darwan said. The Red squealed in delight at the hostility on Rogan's face. "The gods will judge these recruits in the old ways. You two will fight for your honor. Rogan, choose your second."

"I need no second," Rogan scoffed, eying the boys.

"That doesn't hold to the rules of honor." An idea flickered in Darwan's mind. He had just created his own opportunity.

"If you're worried about fairness, then you should give a sword to all the recruits," Rogan yelled. The Sarasins in the crowd laughed uneasily.

Darwan's eyes locked on Zane, and the inkling of a hope emerged. "Zane, you will be the second." Zane stood up and almost fell over. As he stumbled to the center of the crowd, the soldiers instinctively backed away to give the combatants space.

Zane stood wobbling next to Rogan, who was balanced and composed. They stood in stark contrast, as did the two boys. Cayne was limbering up his sword arm, and the other boy was trying to sink into the ground, eager to be away from here.

"Zane," Darwan said. "Take the big one."

Zane squared his shoulders, then launched himself forward in a clumsy thrust. One thing Darwan had to say for Zane was that he was bold; not too bright, but bold. Cayne sidestepped and slashed. His sword met solid iron armor at Zane's shoulder. It bounced off with a clang.

Rogan burst around Zane and hit Tarken—not with his sword, but with his gauntlets. It was enough to knock the boy off balance. Tarken hadn't even gotten his sword unsheathed yet. Darwan was unsurprised to see Rogan wait for the boy to draw his sword. It wasn't out of any sense of honor; Rogan wanted to prolong the contest, like a sabercat cub playing with its dinner before eating it.

The other two were more evenly matched. Zane was good with a sword, but he was blind drunk. Cayne wielded the sword with ease, but Darwan doubted he had ever shed blood with one. The way he kept looking at the other fight, he seemed more concerned with the other boy's fate than his own. *I hope the boy has enough skill to kill Zane before Rogan kills them both.*

Rogan parried several pathetic sweeps of Tarken's sword, laughing at each one. Then he poked the boy in the arm with the point of his sword, and blood reddened Tarken's dirty tunic. Rogan shook his head, chuckling again.

Zane was oblivious to the other fight, but Cayne got more desperate at the sound of his friend screaming in pain. The Red sensed the rage welling up in the boy as he lashed out, bringing his sword down on Zane.

Zane raised his armored forearm to defect the blow, but the

force of it made his elbow buckle, and he grunted loudly. Cayne spun around and struck Zane with a low slash to the unarmored back of his knee. The boy spun again, this time driving the blade into the side of Zane's head, where his helmet would have been if he had worn it. Cayne wasted no time. He rushed at Rogan, who was still taunting Tarken, his back to the oncoming charge.

At the last moment, just as the blade was streaking toward his head, Rogan stepped away and parried the strike, forcing Cayne to the ground. The boy rolled easily, coming up in a fighting stance. "Not angry enough, boy," Rogan shouted, "not by far."

Cayne didn't take Rogan's bait. He shifted his weight, looking for an opening; though if Rogan left an opening, it was a lure. Rogan moved on Tarken, Cayne lurching forward to protect his friend. Rogan parried the strike, then spun, sinking his blade point-first into Tarken's stomach. He withdrew it, sending a spray of blood across the road.

Rogan got exactly what he wanted. Cayne flew into a blind rage and threw himself at Rogan, to no avail.

"Enough!" Darwan shouted with all the authority he could muster. "The matter is decided!"

"It is *not* decided!" Rogan protested.

Cayne glared at Rogan, and prepared another attack.

"Boy!" Darwan yelled. "The fight is over."

"My name is not boy! It's Cayne Falconstorm!"

"Whatever," Darwan said dismissively. "If you press this fight, then you will die and then your other friends will die. Is that what you want?" The Red liked Cayne, though Darwan himself was indifferent. The boy had gotten rid of Zane, but he was still just Crotan scum.

Cayne looked from Tarken to the other boys lined up along the road. He lowered his sword.

"The gods have given their judgment." Darwan pointed to Tarken, doubled over and clutching his stomach. "That one was guilty, as you suspected, Rogan. His reward has been bestowed upon him." He shifted his gaze to Cayne. "This one is not guilty."

"They're both guilty."

"Rogan, you cannot argue with the gods, or with me, for that matter. That one acted alone," he said, pointing at Tarken. "I have determined it so, and by the customs of Tekahta, Cayne is my new steward."

Rogan's eyes bulged. The Red quivered with joy at his outrage. Rogan shook his head and said, "The rules of Tekahta don't apply to Crotan trash!"

Rogan might have a point, but Darwan was not about to let him have it. The customs of Tekahta dictated proper mobility within the Sarasin hierarchy. It was rarely extended to foreigners, but there was precedent. He needed Rogan as his First Sword, and he didn't want him as his steward. By tradition, this boy would become his steward, having killed his current steward. It'd be odd to have a local boy in such a trusted role. Still, the boy had managed to solve his problem with Zane.

As his mind rolled over the idea of having Cayne as his steward, advantages emerged. He could use Cayne to help him find pyrus. No one would take the word of a Crotan boy over a Sarasin lord. Besides, Cayne was a simple country dolt. He wouldn't even know how to take advantage of such information. He'd make a poor steward, but that was secondary, a very distant second to the pyrus.

On the other hand, if he let Rogan kill Cayne, then Rogan would become his steward. The thought made his skin prickle. Darwan eyed Rogan, standing tensed, ready to strike, daggers lancing out of his eyes at Darwan. This was a test of Darwan's authority. "We have no time for this. The king is coming, and we must prepare."

Darwan's eyes darted across the crowd, and fell on an odd fellow standing just beyond. He wore an unremarkable brown cloak, but his eyes... *his eyes*. Even from this distance, his eyes glowed a kaleidoscope of colors. Their eyes locked before a voice boomed behind Darwan.

"The king is *here*." It was the unmistakable voice of King Arta Nakis. "That was an entertaining duel. I agree with Lord Darwan's determination."

The king had sneaked into the crowd without notice, but then, the king was without his normal entourage. Darwan's eyes glided back to the mysterious man, but he was gone.

Darwan got off his horse and took a knee in front of the king, the rest of his men following suit, even Rogan; Cayne alone stood staring at the king. The king was an impressive sight, sitting astride his massive warhorse. "Your Majesty, we did not expect you so soon," Darwan said.

"No matter. Ride with me." The king turned his horse, never doubting Darwan would follow.

Darwan mounted. He faced Rogan and Cayne, both eyeing each other warily. "Under the rules of honor this duel commenced, and under the rules of honor it ended. Rogan, what is the condition of the fallen?"

Rogan studied the two men on the ground. Zane had not moved or made a sound since Cayne had struck him. Tarken was balled up and whimpering, a pool of blood flowing out around him. "Zane's dead. The boy is dead too, but it may take some time for him to pass."

"Very well, then. Cayne, you killed my steward, and under the rules of Tekahta, you must take over his role."

"You—you can't," Rogan stammered.

"It's the will of the gods, and we must honor their decree."

"Then the gods must want you dead," said Rogan with a shrug. "I'll wager you'll soon have a blade in your back." He had a smile on his face, and Darwan wanted it gone.

"We need to prepare a war council. See to the arrangements, Rogan." That seemed to work, a familiar scowl forming on Rogan's face. Darwan turned to his new steward. "Cayne, bury the dead."

"He's not dead," Cayne said, looking to Tarken.

"By the time you dig his grave, he will be. Such a wound cannot be healed. Rogan would have been more merciful had he beheaded your friend." Darwan looked to Rogan, who just shrugged again, apparently pleased with his work. "You might do well to end his suffering yourself."

"I won't!" Cayne insisted.

"It matters not. Bury the dead and get to the war council. If you fail to arrive in a timely manner, I'll give one of those little boys to Rogan to torture. Perhaps you'll move more swiftly once you hear his screams."

Darwan turned toward the king. Soon they left the crowds behind, riding slowly down the street. The king waited until they were far from prying ears before he spoke. "Darwan, the old ways are for our people, not theirs."

"These *are* our people now. This land is ours."

The king pondered his point, amused. "Well spoken. You may be right, but Tekahta is a Sarasin code. The conquered have no right to it."

"It serves my current purposes, Your Majesty. I will dispose of the boy in time, just as we'll smash King Alarak's army."

"I like your confidence," Arta Nakis said approvingly.

"We gave them the advantage in the last battle. They charged down the heights on my men, yet we stood firm, and held them. Then we pressed them back, and they broke. They'll break again."

"Yes, they will," said Arta Nakis, nodding. "And this time there will be no retreat. If only we could draw them out..."

"You know of their positions, your majesty?"

"We have very good information," the king said, hinting at deeper knowledge. "The oath-breaker hides in battlements at Barons Lodge. We cut a path of devastation through his lands, and he hides behind walls."

"Are we still moving west toward his capital at Aconia?"

Arta Nakis grunted, giving no sense of what the noise meant. "My sons will be arriving soon. Ensure they make it to the war council, and nowhere else." The king was hinting at something, but Darwan didn't understand at first, which seemed to annoy Arta Nakis. "I'll be consulting with Margella until the council."

"I understand, Your Majesty."

Arta Nakis started to turn, but then he asked, "Do you really intend to bring that boy to the war council?"

"He is my steward now."

"Our plans might soon find their way to the oath-breaker." Both men shared a glance.

"There may be an opportunity here," said Darwan, pondering.

Arta Nakis grunted indeterminately again and rode away.

Chapter Eighteen

Cayne dragged the lifeless body to a clearing in the trees just beyond the houses of the village, letting Zane's feet drop with a thud. The soldiers had forced him to take Zane first. He needed to get back to Tarken while there was still time.

He raced back between the houses, and was glad to see only a few soldiers standing near Tarken. Cayne knelt next to his friend, smelling the rot of death. "I'm taking you to a spot I found in the trees," Cayne told him quietly.

Tarken smiled faintly, his teeth stained red. "It hurts to move."

"If I don't do this fast, the rest of them will get killed," Cayne said, raising his voice.

"You're right, Cayne. Do what you have to. Make it quick."

Cayne got close to Tarken and whispered, "I have a plan."

Tarken sputtered, coughing blood into his hands. "Your plans haven't worked out very well for me lately."

Cayne grabbed Tarken under his arm, pulling him up despite his moans. They walked to the trees, Tarken muttering curses under his breath the whole way. Cayne had never heard Tarken swear before, and was impressed with the range of curses he knew. Cayne himself didn't know the meaning of all of them, and he smiled ever so faintly. *This plan will work.*

Cayne settled Tarken in the clearing as gently as he could. Tarken was almost at the end, his breathing lowered to a light wheezing. Somehow, he built up a smile for Cayne and said, "It's all right, Cayne. Let me go now."

"You're not going anywhere," he said, reaching in his tunic.

"I'm ready to go. It doesn't hurt anymore." Tarken's eyes fluttered and closed.

"Shut up and eat this," Cayne said, drawing several angelia fruits from his tunic. The berries glowed in the scattered light under the canopy of the trees, and Cayne swore he heard bells ringing in the distance.

"You know, what you said makes no sense," Tarken said, opening a single eye. "How can I shut my mouth and eat —" His eye focused on the angelia fruit, and then his other eye opened. "What is that?"

Cayne popped a berry into Tarken's mouth. Then for good measure, he dropped in another few and held his hand over Tarken's mouth. Tarken's eyes flew open, a white glow surrounding them.

Cayne stepped back, eyes widening. The glow pulsated off Tarken like rain on a beating drum. A small geyser of white light sprayed from the site of his wound. Tarken exhaled as if he had never-ending breath. Cayne wasn't sure if the white light was pouring into him or from him, but it became more intense, reaching a crescendo. Then it trailed off to a dull hum.

Tarken moved his hands to his stomach and laughed. "How did you do that?"

Cayne rushed forward and put his hands on Tarken's mouth. "Quiet."

"What was that?" Tarken opened his mouth and spit, but nothing came out.

"Angelia fruit," Cayne said flatly.

Tarken gasped. "Where did you get it?" He seemed to have forgotten about his recent brush with death.

"Tarken, not now. Help me get this armor off him," he said, looking at Zane's body.

As they peeled off the armor, Tarken peppered him with questions about the angelia fruit, without waiting for answers. When they finished stripping the armor and placing it on Cayne, they dug a shallow grave, deposited the body, and hastily covered it with a thin layer of dirt. Cayne adjusted the armor, shifting the padded undershirt, tightening the wraps of the greaves, and pushing layered black and red iron bands around until he could move comfortably. He was well protected on the front, but there was little protection at his back.

Tarken looked up at him. "So you had no idea how the fruit worked," Tarken concluded. "How did you know it wouldn't kill me?"

"Well, to be honest I didn't, but you were dying. I figured it was worth a try."

Tarken pondered the point, and appeared satisfied with Cayne's logic. "Are we going now?"

Cayne shook his head. "The rest of the boys are still back there, and they'll be killed if I don't go back, but you're free. They think you're dead."

"They might be dead already. Maybe there's nothing you can do to save them." Tarken seemed offended by his own words. "You saved me, and you can save yourself now. You can't save everyone."

"If I don't go back and try, then I'll wish I was dead." Cayne looked at Tarken, seeing the conflict in his eyes. He didn't want to abandon the other boys, but he didn't want to go back either. "It's all right, Tarken," he said reassuringly. "It's better if you don't go back. Stay here until dark, then head south."

Tarken was relieved, but then his expression darkened. He was usually long on words, but he said nothing, though he opened his mouth several times. He kicked the dirt in front of him in frustration. "Back there," Cayne began, "the king on the horse. Was that who..."

"I didn't see him," Tarken admitted. "Only heard him. But, yes, that was the man who killed your father. I'll never forget his voice."

The rage came then, rippling over his body and quickening his pulse. The rage congealed into resolve. "I'll save the rest, and then I have a few matters to settle."

"Shari?" Tarken asked.

Cayne lowered his head. "I'll try to find her, but it's probably too late."

"Bastard." Tarken slammed a fist into the ground.

"I'll take care of him."

"Rogan is too good a swordsman."

"Let me worry about that," Cayne said slowly. "I'll kill that bastard Arta Nakis too."

Cayne saw the shock on Tarken's face, but didn't bother to wait for a response. He clasped Tarken's arm and was glad to feel some strength in the other boy's grip again. Cayne stood and backed away from Tarken, turning to the town.

Cayne crossed the road, noting that the number of Sarasin warriors had dwindled to just a handful, and they were preoccupied with looting. He opened the door to Shari's house and found Valia and Rinna hunched over a body. He steeled himself and walked over to them. All three women started at his approach. He froze a few steps away, shocked that Shari was alive. A thin line of red painted her neck, but other than that, she appeared fine.

"You're alive! I thought Rogan had killed you."

"Just a scratch," Shari said, as she rubbed her neck.

"You stay away from us," Rinna said, stepping in front of Cayne protectively. "You almost got my granddaughter killed."

Cayne held up his hands. "I only wanted to see if she was all right. I'll go." He backed to the door.

"Wait," Shari said, a desperate tone to her voice. "We have to leave. We can't stay here."

"Is there a choice?" Valia asked. "They won't let us leave!"

"No, but there might be another way," Cayne said.

The two older women looked at him doubtfully, but Shari stepped around them and said, "Yes. I'm leaving. What do we need to do?"

Cayne held Shari's torso while Rinna and Valia each held a leg. He'd wrapped his tunic around her neck. It was soaked with Tarken's blood, and he hoped it looked convincing enough. Two warriors eyed them as they left the house, but dismissed them as a burial party.

They kept up the charade until they reached the clearing. Tarken stepped out from behind a large oak. The sword in his hand quivered before he dropped it. He ran to them, ignoring Cayne and heading right to Shari. They put her down, and she got to her feet.

"You used the angelia on her too?" Tarken asked.

"No time to explain," Cayne said. He turned to Valia and asked, "How deep are these woods?"

"Perhaps two hundred paces to the south, much more to the west."

Cayne nodded to her. "Tarken, take them deeper that way." He pointed in the direction he hoped was west. "Wait until dark, and then head south. Keep parallel to the road until you're sure there are no sentries, and then take the road to Dahl Haven."

Tarken scratched his head. "How will we see the road in the dark? How will we know if there are sentries?"

"I don't know. Figure it out." He glanced back toward the village. "I have to go." He backed away, pointing deeper into the woods. "And so do you. Get going."

Cayne made for the main road, finding it clogged with lines of warriors streaming into Walla. He felt conspicuous in the Sarasin armor, but no one gave him a second glance. Still, he kept his head down and walked along the side of the road. He heard hoof beats nearby and turned in time to see a black horse bearing down on him. He moved quickly, but the horse clipped his leg and sent him to the ground.

The rider yelled an insult and continued on his way. Cayne picked himself up and looked at a second rider, slowing as the palomino reached him. Cayne thought he might get a boot in the chest from this one, but the rider was a young woman.

"Are you well, warrior?" She wore long purple riding skirts, and her hair bobbled back and forth in a thick braid. Her expression was one of extreme indifference.

"I'm fine," he said, unsure how to address her, "my lady." He bowed his head.

"My brother was in a hurry to attend an important meeting."

The rider on the black horse came thundering toward them, shoving right between them. Cayne felt a solid kick to his chest, the momentum of the horse helping to knock him on his back. Before he could regain his feet, the rider leapt from his horse, his sword drawn and pointing at Cayne.

"Pevane, stop this. He did nothing wrong." The woman jumped from her horse and planted herself between Cayne and Pevane.

"He spoke to you, Ayasha. I saw it."

Ayasha looked down at Cayne. "He's a foot soldier. So what if he speaks to me?"

Several warriors gathered behind Cayne, as he got to one knee. He stayed there, unsure of what was happening.

"Prince Pevane, is this one bothering you?" one of the warriors behind Cayne asked.

Pevane stepped toward Ayasha, but she stood her ground. He looked at her, then the warriors, before slapping her. She dropped to her knee, holding her face. She let out one loud whimper. He stood over her, his face a mask of rage.

Cayne began to stand, readying a fist, but Ayasha laid a hand on his shoulder. She seemed to know what he was thinking, her head shaking slowly.

"Get away," Pevane yelled at the surrounding warriors. He turned to his sister, and his expression softened. "Why did you make me do that? You can't defy me in front of others."

He offered his hand to her, but she swatted it away. She used Cayne's shoulder to steady herself as she rose to her feet.

Cayne stood up next to her. He was a head taller than Pevane and two taller than Ayasha. Pevane stepped back from him.

"I won't hurt you," Cayne said, smiling and acting like he was talking to a child in the market.

"I'm not afraid of you," Pevane said, looking over his shoulder at some passing warriors. They didn't notice him and kept marching. Turning back to Cayne, he squinted and said, "You don't look like a Sarasin."

"Don't you have a meeting to attend?" Ayasha asked her brother. She turned to Cayne. "Where were you going?"

Cayne mumbled incoherently before forming real words. "I, uh, a war council. I'm a steward."

Ayasha smiled at Pevane. "All this over a steward. Were you afraid I might marry a steward?"

"Your honor was at stake," Pevane said. "He sullied you just by looking at you."

Her smile grew, and she asked Cayne, "Would you help me onto my horse, good steward?" She kept her gaze locked on Pevane's bulging eyes as Cayne easily hoisted her into her saddle. He edged his way back, trying to get away from the situation.

"My saddle is large," Ayasha said, flashing her gaze to Cayne. "You may ride with me." She looked back at Pevane, smiling at his open-mouthed expression of astonishment.

Cayne took in a deep breath, knowing it was wiser to walk away... but he was jumping up to the saddle before his wits could plot a more prudent course of action. As soon as he was on the horse, Ayasha leaned forward and urged the palomino into a trot. Cayne looked back at Pevane, whose shock was gone, replaced by vengeful hatred. *That was definitely a bad decision.*

Cayne turned back to Ayasha and rested his hands on her sides. She shifted his arms around her and clasped his hands together, letting them settle onto her stomach. He felt embarrassed and excited. Cayne gave Pevane a mischievous smile and nodded to him. Ayasha noticed the gesture, but waited until they were beyond earshot before speaking.

"Are all men idiots?" she asked.

"As far as I know, we are," he admitted. "At least, that's what my mother always said." His own words stabbed at him. As usual, he'd spoken before thinking. He thought of his mother, and the emptiness filled his heart.

The ride was dreadfully short. The center of Walla was a hive of activity. Scores of horses were hobbled on the village green, and a crowd of soldiers surrounded a large building. Some wore the familiar black-and-red armor that Cayne himself now wore, but most others had wildly different colors schemes.

Ayasha brought the horse to a stop on the green, and Cayne vaulted down to hobble the horse with a tether around its front legs. Then he helped Ayasha down from her saddle. This time, he faced her as he moved her to the ground. She was younger than he'd thought at first, younger than him. Her face had a fine sheen, as though painted with delicate artwork. He stared at her, and they briefly gazed deeply into each other's eyes.

The moment passed, and Cayne lowered his eyes. "Thank you for bringing me here, my lady."

"I fear I may have placed you in danger," she said. "Bad things always befall men who look upon me. Worse things happen those who speak to me." She wrung her hands.

"It was worth it," he said, looking up to share another moment. She smiled at him, and then looked away, shuffling her feet.

"Your war council awaits," she noted, nodding to the building surrounded by warriors.

He gave her a regretful glance and turned toward the war council. Cayne didn't look back, though he wanted to see her one last time. He forced a measure of confidence in his stride, and made for the front entrance. "Where do you think you're going?" asked a burly man at the front door, as two other men closed in around him.

"I'm Lord Darwan's new steward, and he ordered me to come to this meeting."

The man let out a belly laugh—and he had plenty of belly for it. "Meeting? Meetings are for dandies. This is a war council." A spray of spit misted Cayne, reminding him of over-fermented hops and urine.

"He's with me," Ayasha said, as she approached them. "My escort."

The man bowed his head slightly. "Of course, princess. I didn't know."

"It's not your fault you're ignorant," she said as she strolled by the man.

Cayne turned to follow her, but the man put out a hand. "Not with that sword." He nodded to a long, neat line of swords leaning against the side of the building.

Cayne quickly undid the scabbard ties and handed it to the man, forcing a half-smile and a nod. The man sneered and dropped the sword to the ground. "Do it yourself. Do I look like your servant?"

Cayne grimaced at his own stupidity and picked up his sword. He found a space for it along the wall. The other swords were lavishly adorned. The jewel-encrusted scabbards had fancy silk tassels and ribbons, each one unique. His plain sword stood out, if only for its dreariness.

Ayasha waited for him. "I have to join my father. Thank you for the escort." She smiled briefly and then melted into the crowd.

The room was thick with warriors adorned with a dizzying array of color combinations. While Cayne's armor was covered in dirt and blood, the men in this room wore gleaming armor without a speck of dirt on it. He saw swirls among the crowd as some men passed with trailing eddies of attendants. He assumed they were lords. He searched for the black-and-red of Darwan's warband.

The floor at the center of the room had a map painted on it. The milling men avoided stepping on the map, keeping to the sides.

"Rogan will be disappointed," Lord Darwan yelled over the din of the crowd. "I didn't think you'd return. You have some stones, boy. I like that."

Cayne studied Lord Darwan. His armor was polished like that of the others in the room. He had a strong build to him, and he was much older than Cayne, perhaps thirty or forty years old. Cayne found it hard to judge ages much beyond his own.

Lord Darwan carried himself with an air of confidence and an odd smirk. His eyes were bloodshot, and Cayne met his gaze for a lingering moment. There was strangeness in his eyes. Cayne couldn't hold the stare for long enough to determine what it was.

"My friends are safe?" Cayne asked, breaking his gaze.

"I told Rogan he couldn't torture them unless I expressly allowed it." Darwan gave him a reconsidering shrug. "Well, any more than he normally does with you recruits."

The conversation in the room squelched like a torch thrown in a lake, and everyone took a knee. Cayne tried his best to follow suit. He found it awkward to kneel wearing the greaves, and he drove his knee hard into the floor, making a loud knock that garnered him several annoyed glances. The others, obviously more practiced, managed the movement with little more than muffled thuds.

A young herald scampered into the room and yelled, "The king of all Sarisa, from the Kiotan shores to the Bowl of the Gods, from the Wampan forests to the Toltan mesas. King Arta Nakis." Then the man took a knee as well.

King Arta Nakis advanced slowly into the hall. He wore banded iron armor like the others, but his was a solid dark purple. His hands and head were bare, but other than that, he was dressed for battle. Looking across the room, his eyes settled on the lords in the room. He looked right past the stewards as though they didn't exist, but as his gaze passed over Cayne, it stopped on him for a long moment—too long a moment—before finally moving past.

Cayne understood Tarken's fear of the king. He was a hulking man, not fat but thickly muscled, and stood two heads above Cayne—and Cayne himself was considered tall by most. Arta Nakis stepped into the center of the room, followed by three men.

The three were roughly the same age as Cayne. They too wore purple-banded armor, with a single white band at their chests. The first was as tall as Cayne, his cruel features sneering at the crowd. The second looked no kinder, but his expression was more calculating. The third and shortest by far was Pevane. *Great.*

Behind them were two women, the only women in the entire hall. One was regal, older, but with a youthful vigor in her eyes. The other was Ayasha. She had a completely different look on her face now. Where she'd smiled broadly before, she currently appeared disinterested, her gaze sliding randomly around the room. She looked right past Cayne with no hint of recognition. He turned his gaze back to Arta Nakis and thought the king had been watching him, but the king's eyes shifted to Lord Darwan, and there was a quick gesture between the two men.

Cayne found himself standing on the edge of the map, right next to Darwan. He had a perfect view of it, and easy access to the king. Though he had no sword, he still had his small knife. The dynabane sap was supposed to be poison, so just scratching the king should kill him. The king wore armor, but his hands were bare, and Cayne figured he'd use those to defend himself. Though the king was close, he'd only have a brief moment before the rest of the room reacted to stop him. He waited for his moment, sweat flowing freely down his back.

"The oath-breakers hide behind walls at Barons Lodge," Arta Nakis said, stamping his foot on the ground near a painted circle. The paint was still wet, and his boot splattered paint around, which distract him momentarily. He shook his foot, greaves clanking. "If they will not defend their lands, then we will *take* their lands."

The men in the room rumbled approval, and the king continued, "Lord Darwan's warband is here and will head to the east, to Rivermar. His warband will lead them to believe we are headed in that direction."

Arta Nakis walked over to the spot Cayne thought was Walla and put his foot on top of it with another spray of paint. "The rest of us will continue our march west, pillaging everything from the land until we reach the oath-breaker's capital." This time he pointed to a spot in the crowd. "If he cannot defend his capital, then his allies will abandon him."

Arta Nakis stepped closer, and Cayne reached under his armor, gripping the knife in his sweaty fingers. The king was so near... a single step closer was all it would take. Uncertainty seized him, his muscles tightening around the handle of the knife, but he didn't draw the blade. He tried to force his legs to step forward, but they were frozen in place.

What if he killed the king? What would the Sarasins do to the rest of the Dahl Haven boys? He'd get his revenge, but those boys would pay the price. Their deaths would be on his hands. *Kill Arta Nakis or save the boys.*

Cayne glanced at the princes. Two seemed bored, but Pevane stared directly at Cayne, his face twisted with malice. His eyes flicked to Ayasha and then back at Cayne. Ayasha's uncaring mask vanished for a moment. She locked eyes with Cayne, but quickly resumed her dull survey of other faces. Pevane had noticed the glance, though, and redoubled his hateful glare at Cayne.

Conflict and indecision racked his mind, and in the swirl, his chance faded. Arta Nakis turned and walked out of the room. His sons shadowed the king, followed by Ayasha and the older woman. *That was it?* No debates, no arguments, no discussions? It was more like a monologue than a council.

Darwan put his hand on Cayne's shoulders, and he almost drew the blade in his hand without thinking. "Cayne, it's time for you to learn your new job. Find Rogan. Tell him we march at dawn tomorrow. After that, find my quarters and wait there."

Cayne nodded and made his way through the murmuring crowd. He was the only one who left. The others lingered in the room as if waiting for something.

Cayne took his sword and shuffled across the street to the house he guessed was the one Lord Darwan had mentioned. He looked back at the town hall, but still no one had left the building. Rogan strode toward him, and Cayne instinctively grabbed his sword.

"I don't know why Lord Darwan would trust you," Rogan said, making no move to draw either of his swords. "I think he's a fool." Rogan stood in front of Cayne, his arms folded across his chest. "Maybe you'll kill him in his sleep. He'd be getting what he deserves." Cayne wasn't sure if he was trying to suggest something to him.

"I'm no murderer," Cayne protested, meeting Rogan's cold stare.

"Would you murder *me* in my sleep if you could?" He waited just a moment before saying, "That's what I thought, boy."

"Lord Darwan said the men need to be ready to march at dawn," Cayne said.

"I'll see to that," Rogan said, walking around Cayne. "I'll be watching you, boy. You'll do something, and I'll be there. I've got you measured, boy."

Cayne watched Rogan walk away, and wondered what he'd been measured for. A grave?

Chapter Nineteen

Darwan entered the small tavern and looked for Verak. He saw the other man's bald head shining in the firelight in a corner of the room. Darwan passed through clouds of smoking-weed and clumsy lords stumbling through the crowd. The Red filled his head, giving him the grace to weave an effortless path to Verak's table. The unlord sat alone, brooding over a tankard of wine. He didn't bother to ask Verak for permission to join him, and ignored the man's rolling eyes. The Red felt playful, and Darwan hated that. He knew himself as a serious man, so the mirth and affability of the Red grated on him. Darwan offered him a healthy smile. "Verak, you look like a sweating hog before the slaughter."

"Hogs don't sweat, you idiot."

"Well, I suppose that was a bad analogy," Darwan admitted, "but regardless, you look like a warm turd on a cold day."

"What does that even mean? You're horrible at analogies."

"Fair enough," Darwan said, "but I make up for it with other talents."

"What do you want?" Verak asked curtly, shaking his head.

"Why, the pleasure of your company."

"*What do you want?*" Verak leaned across the table, wafting his wine-soaked breath into Darwan's face. He stared intently at Darwan and waited.

"I may be leaving my current lordship for a new one."

Verak sat back and cocked an eyebrow. He swept his eyes around to see if anyone was listening. "How? What new lordship?" Then he nodded knowingly. "This stupid mission the king is sending you on."

"Like I said, I have many talents."

"Continue," Verak said, leaning in to listen.

"I have no real ties to your former lordship. When I leave it, I will recommend a successor to the king." Darwan nodded his head slightly and waited for acknowledgment.

Verak returned his nod, then sighed deeply. "Regain my lands without combat? Miss out on the chance to smash your face in? Pass."

Darwan leaned back in surprise. He'd expected Verak to jump at the opportunity and offer pledges of honor to him. The Red tickled his liver, or that's how it felt. It was laughing at him. He regained his composure, quelling the torrent of energy the pyrus injected into his blood. He was getting better at channeling and controlling the Red.

The Red laughed at that thought, too.

"Just days ago," Darwan said, "you said you were waiting for one of us bastards to die. You'd have taken a vacated lordship without a fight then."

"I'd hoped the king respected Tekahta enough to order a contest for the lordships." Verak tilted his head and smiled. His familiar scowl returned. "But that wouldn't happen, would it?"

Darwan pretended to ponder the question for a moment, then shook his head. The king was abandoning the old ways. He was trying to create a new path, a dynasty.

"No, I guess not," Verak said. "I'll be the king's appointment." He spat the last word. "But I won't be in your debt for my position." He locked eyes with Darwan.

"I'll still make a recommendation to the king," Darwan said, getting up from his seat. "It needn't be a positive one."

Rage flared on Verak's face, and Darwan moved his hand to his sword. The Red was ready for a fight. With it, he'd strike down Verak in mere moments. To his disappointment, Verak remained seated. "You think we don't know what Arta Nakis is doing?" Verak growled, his balled fists trembling on the table. "He seeks to make us all his servants and place his sons on his throne after him. It will not be! Tekahta won't be forgotten. Our people will know it long after we've forgotten the name of Arta Nakis."

"You forget your place, unlord," Darwan said calmly. He looked up at the rafters and then back at Verak. "Did you say *we*?"

Verak didn't acknowledge the question. He looked at his tankard of wine, shaking his head.

Darwan left the tavern and looked to the nearby campfire on the village green. He almost expected to see Zane there, drinking with the other stewards; then the faintest sense of regret crossed his mind, but the thrum of the Red muffled it to a whisper. He sighed and took a step toward his quarters. A hand on his arm pulled at him, and he turned, ready to strike until he saw the familiar purple-and-white of a kingsman.

The warrior leaned close. "The king requests your presence," he whispered. He turned to lead Darwan through the streets. Darwan watched the back of the boy's head. *Are warriors really this young now?*

They snaked through streets and between houses, arriving at a nondescript house at the edge of town. There were no guards or any other sign of the king. Darwan prepared himself for an ambush, but the boy went on, unconcerned. He walked to the door of the house and opened it slowly. He lowered his head and whispered, "King Arta Nakis, I've brought Lord Darwan."

"Why don't you just make a sign and post in on the door?" The king's unmistakable voice boomed. "Get in here."

Darwan relaxed and quickly entered the semi-dark room. It was an ordinary hovel. The main room was a box with a door. An alcove at the back corner created a relatively private area; the alcove held a raised bed, a table, and two chairs. Arta Nakis stood next to the table, and Darwan saw Margella lying in the darkness that shrouded the bed. The king motioned for Darwan to sit at the table. Darwan saw the young guard post himself by the door and asked, "Is it wise to have your guard on the inside?"

The king waved away Darwan's concern. "I choose the youngest boys for a reason. They're naive and ignorant. They don't know what to do with the information they overhear. And I change them out regularly."

Darwan sat and faced Arta Nakis. Even seated, the king was a head taller than Darwan. Margella made no effort to join the conversation, nor was she even turning to listen. "I wanted to make sure your task was clear," the king said. "It was too rushed before the war council."

Darwan nodded. "I'm to lead my warband east, then discharge our spy near the Crotan settlement. I foresee no issues."

"You've done well with your first task," the king said, motioning over his shoulder to Margella. "Done properly, this new task will draw the Crotan cowards out from behind their walls."

Darwan nodded in agreement, though he wasn't sure the king's plan would work. "The boy will find his way into Crotan hands," he said, careful not to promise anything more. Would he be held to account for the success of the overall plan, or just his part in it? The king was fickle.

The conversation seemed to be over, with Arta Nakis glancing over to Margella now. Darwan didn't want to mention his conversation with Verak, at least not until he'd had time to think about how he could benefit from the information. The Red had no such reservation, forcing the words from his mouth. "Your Majesty, I have heard whispers of a plot against you."

Arta Nakis stared at Darwan, lowering his jaw and cocking his head. He motioned for Darwan to continue. Darwan's legs shook. He had no idea what to say, no idea if what he'd already said was true. The Red gleefully fed words to his mouth. "The lords long for the Tekahtaman and distrust your reasons for not holding it. They may move against you." He had no proof of any of what he'd said. Sweat dribbled down his back.

Arta Nakis squinted at him, then leaned back in a hearty laugh. "Darwan, there isn't *a* plot against me. There are at least six, at last count. To be king is to be plotted against." His tone became that of a father to a foolish son. "I appreciate your information, but I have sources that far exceed anything you might have heard." He stopped his laughing and looked at Margella again. "Now go."

Darwan lowered his head. "Should I dismiss the guard?"

"Why?" Arta Nakis asked with a smile. "What will he learn from what he hears? That the king is a virile man. That it is good to be the king." He laughed again, waving Darwan away.

Darwan backed away, glancing at the lone guard at the door. The king was vulnerable. The young guard was no problem for Darwan, and Arta Nakis was preoccupied and unarmored. Darwan tried to think through the implications, though the Red clouded his ability to think clearly. Killing the king wouldn't put Darwan on the throne. The high lords would demand an immediate Tekahtaman to determine the new king.

He shook away the idea. Darwan was a junior lord, and with such a pent-up need for the contests, anything could happen. He might end up losing his lordship. Better to keep the king alive and have a chance at a High Lordship. He tried to turn away, but the Red kept his feet planted in place. The idea of complete chaos in the wake of an assassination amused the Red, but it relented.

"Do you wish to watch?" Margella said throatily from the darkened corner.

Darwan spun toward the door, smiling to the unsteady guard as he left. He walked to the house he'd claimed as his quarters. *I may look back at this missed opportunity with regret.*

He crossed the main road, noting the many-colored armor of the lines of men streaming into the town. The whole army was moving toward this place. It would swell the size and population of this village to that of a major city. They couldn't stay here for long. Their food supplies were low. He'd seen bison and mammoth herds on the march north, so they'd need to organize hunts. Darwan longed to be on the hunt, chasing game at a full gallop, javelin in his hand.

He looked for his new steward outside his quarters, but the useless boy was nowhere to be seen. Darwan snorted and went into his quarters: a plain, one-room house with nothing but his cot and desk. Seated at his desk, back turned to him, was Queen Tabila. "Darwan, where have you been?" she asked, sounding as though she knew exactly where he'd been.

Darwan looked around the room, expecting to see guards, but there were none. She was as vulnerable as the king was. He moved behind her, but she didn't seem concerned in the least. She lifted her nose and sniffed quietly once. She stood and waited for Darwan to pull the chair back. Darwan moved to her back, noting her perfumed scent, and drew the chair back. They were close, and she rose and turned to him without bothering to back up a respectable distance. Her movements were graceful—not like a dancer's, but like a puma's. She fixed him with a glare.

"This mission of yours. Delivering this boy. You go on a fool's errand." She kept her eyes on him, waiting for his response.

"It was the king's plan," Darwan said. The Red thumped in his veins. It was fading. He needed to take more.

"As I said: A fool's errand."

"Am I the fool?" Darwan asked, trying hard to keep his gaze on her, despite her intense scowl.

"One of them," she said. She walked slowly past Darwan, leaving a breeze of flowers in her wake. "If he had thought to consult with me, I'd have prevented this ridiculous farce."

Many lords speculated that Tabila was the one responsible for the assassinations that had brought Arta Nakis to power. The king was a mighty warrior, but overt. He openly challenged the other lords, but they died at such convenient times that it couldn't have been coincidence. Though assassinations were not the king's manner, the queen was another matter. "There's still time," Darwan said, leaning against the chair. He tried to calm his breathing, but Tabila irritated the Red and it made his skin itch.

"Not after he's made statements in front of all the lords. Better that he be seen as foolish than weak."

"I don't think anyone could see him as weak," Darwan said.

"What has he promised you?" she asked, turning back to Darwan. She again tried to read him.

"Why don't you ask the king?"

She lowered her head, giving him a stare that made him certain he didn't want her as an enemy. He sensed that she was more in control of the kingdom than Arta Nakis was, yet she didn't know of the king's bargain with him.

"I will get it out of Nakis if you prefer."

No one called the king by his given name alone. When he ascended the throne, he took the name Arta in front of Nakis. He said it meant 'conqueror' in an old tongue, and he tolerated no one who chose not to use it.

She slowly turned to the door, giving Darwan plenty of time to consider his options. She'd find out. Everyone feared the king, but the king feared Tabila; or perhaps the proper word was "respected." Either way, she'd soon know the details of their bargain, and Darwan would have gained nothing from it, except a potential enemy.

"A High Lordship," he said. He adjusted his armor unconsciously.

She raised her head and turned halfway back to him. "That's a large reward for such a small task."

"He said there were more tasks."

"And so there shall be," she said, turning away and leaving the house without a backward glance.

Darwan sighed heavily and settled on his cot. He reached into his armor, digging for the pocket that held the pyrus. The tin was lighter than he would have liked. He took a cube and put it in his mouth. The astringent liquid crawled down the back of his throat, coating and burning its way to his stomach. He laid his head back and closed his eyes.

Darwan mounted his horse in a fuzz the next morning. The previous night was a blur. He still felt he was getting better at controlling the Red, though it chuckled every time that thought went through his head. He'd spent most of the day in a pyrus-induced stupor. It was strange how some of the pyrus cubes were more potent than others. He struggled to stay in his saddle while the Red swirled around in his head, whispering plans to him.

They had marched the entire day with Rayl Goth shimmering over the fields to the southeast, yet Margella had not spoken a word about it. He was sure it had been her idea to send them toward the city. Today she rode at the end of the column of soldiers, and wore a purple veil; the king's color. It would be interesting if the queen found her wearing that color. Margella had been watching him for some time, but she waited until he was riding beside her before she spoke. "Beautiful city, isn't it?"

He looked at Rayl Goth. It was black, like a permanent shadow on the land, and even from this distance, it made him feel uneasy. "It's hideous, like a burned boar's head," he declared, watching closely for her reaction. If she was of the Black, then what he'd just said was an insult.

She took a quick half-breath. "You would do well to guard your words against Dyn so close to one of his cities."

"I didn't speak against the shadow god," he protested.

"His city."

"I thought this was the home of an uhkanuwa, not a god."

"Why do you goad me this way?" she asked, studying him.

"I didn't realize you were such a disciple of Dyn. I myself favor all the gods equally." He hid his joy at finally finding a way to unnerve her. "Was our selection for this duty your doing?"

"Your king gives you a chance to redeem yourself after your past failings, and you think it's my doing?"

He knew she was trying to burrow under his skin. He tried to hold back the anger, screwing his face into a tight ball to do it. Her growing smile irritated him even more.

"I'm surprised you're not going to this city the fates have put before you, Lord Darwan." She said his name too politely to be anything but mockery. "When the Tainted Ones abandoned the city, they left many treasures behind. Riches, artifacts, maybe even some pyrus for you."

She was manipulating him again, but the mere mention of the pyrus made his heart quicken and fired the hunger inside him. He was certain she was baiting him, but the thought that a cache of the drug might survive in the city was overwhelming. "If there were riches or treasure," he said, "then it was looted long ago."

"No men go there."

"Men will do anything for riches."

She'd played him like a stone on a crissage board, yet even though he knew it, he would go to Rayl Goth now, searching for something that wasn't there, scratching his way through a dead city just for the possibility of pyrus. Crissage was a game of skill and strategy he'd played as a boy. He sucked rocks at crissage. Even as he aged, effective movement of those infernal stones eluded his grasp. Thinking several moves in advance was difficult for him. He suspected Margella was thinking dozens of moves in advance.

Darwan rode to the front of the column and ordered his men to turn off the road and toward Rayl Goth. The men hesitated, and even he felt a strong need to ignore his own orders; but he chided them until they were walking across the open field headed right toward the dead city.

Chapter Twenty

Faylin surveyed Walla from the roof of the farmhouse. She'd climbed up there in her human form, and then turned into her wolf form after neatly folding her dress. Her vision was better as a wolf.

She had seen the approaching army from her den two days ago, yet there was little she could do but watch. The warriors had looted houses and pillaged the fields on their way into Walla, and everyone fled before them, including the inhabitants of this farmhouse. Faylin helped herself to a new den overlooking the village from a safe distance.

She watched as the army poured through Walla. Just as she thought the last of them had left, another warband descended on the village. That had been last night. Faylin kept vigil through the night, listening to wails and cries ringing out across the fields.

There was still nothing she could do. It was just her, and she was no match for a warband consisting of hundreds of soldiers. Her hopes that they would soon leave had been dashed earlier in the day as a steady stream of warriors flowed into the village from the west and north, their movement sending columns of dust high into the sky. They pitched tents along the edge of Walla, and set up a checkpoint south of the village. Even now she spied roving bands of soldiers patrolling through the barren fields. She took human form and dangled her legs over the side. She didn't bother to put on the dress.

"Meda." She spoke the name like a curse. The seer had known, but chose to save only herself instead of warning the others. She had left them to this fate.

Faylin heard a muffled scream from the fields. She stood and became her wolf to get a better view. Four people ran through a field: three women and a man. Three warriors pursued them, and would soon catch the stragglers. One of the women was older, and the man was helping her, but it was futile. She was too slow. Faylin though idly that he shouldn't be risking his life for hers. It was the way of things. The weak perished, while the strong survived, until they too, became the weak.

The lead woman was younger and familiar. Faylin drew in a panicked breath. It was Shari! Then Faylin recognized Valia and Rinna. A surge of fear and anger roiled within her. She morphed to her human form and jumped from the roof. As soon as her foot hit the ground, she was a wolf, barreling across a field of broken maize stalks.

She hurtled past Shari and Valia. The man helping Shari's gran drew a sword and faced an approaching warrior. Faylin zipped right past the man and leaped at the warrior. She hit him square in the chest, and her momentum knocked him to the ground. With her claws grasping at his armor, she rode him like a wagon as she tore a vicious hole in his neck. She felt a detached surprise at how slow men moved when she was in her wolf form.

Faylin rolled off the dying warrior and regained her balance. She jumped into a patch of maize. Moments later the other two warriors came running up, their weapons drawn and their attention on the boy. Though from a distance he appeared to be a man, she could see that he was very young. His sword shook nervously in his hand. The warriors ran past Faylin and forked to either side of the young man.

Faylin pounced on the nearest warrior. They wore armor that covered the front of their legs, but not the backs. She sunk two paws worth of claws into his legs just above the knee, then shredded her way down his calf. He screamed and fell backward. She let him fall and lunged, aiming for his neck, but she missed.

Her teeth sank deep into his mouth and nose. She tasted blood as her wild thrashing tore his face open. Her left paw found his neck, while her right scraped viciously at his eyes.

The last warrior whirled to attack her, but as soon as he turned, the boy attacked him. The warrior easily parried the strike and readied a counterstroke. With his arm drawn back to swing, it was like a gift to Faylin.

She jumped and locked onto the warrior's arm, letting her entire body weight drag the arm down. She wrenched his arm back and forth until his weapon fell away. The boy rained a flurry of strikes on the exposed warrior, and Faylin leaped away from the scene.

The boy kept chopping the warrior. She wasn't sure if he was angry, scared, or both. He wouldn't stop hacking at the corpse.

"Tarken!" Shari shouted, then said more gently, "You can stop now."

He slowed, then stopped amid his own sobbing. He was little more than a boy, but that boy pointed his blade at Faylin. It shook so unsteadily she thought it might fall from his hand at any moment.

Shari stepped to his side and put her arm on his until the sword pointed at the ground. "I know her."

"You know a *wolf?*" he asked incredulously.

Valia called to them from a distance. "We need to go. More will be coming."

"She's right," Faylin said.

Tarken hadn't seen her change back into a girl, and now his eyes bulged from their sockets. His jaw opened wide. He stared for a long moment before his eyes locked themselves on his own feet.

"Yes, I'm naked. You can look if you want. I'm not ashamed."

"Mother is right. We need to go," Shari said. Faylin cast a pensive glace back at the carnage she'd wrought. She'd never killed anyone before, nor even thought about it. In her wolf form, it was unnervingly easy. She shook off the pang of regret, knowing it was necessary, then went to retrieve her dress.

They ran farther from the road, and Faylin led them through the dark to her old den. It wasn't big enough to hold them all, but the spot afforded a good view. If anyone came along the road looking for them, Faylin would see them approaching from a good distance. They settled in a small circle. "We were hoping to leave after dark," Tarken explained, "but a patrol spotted us, so we had to make a run for it."

"I thought you were leaving, Faylin," Shari said, with a quick nod to the den.

"I didn't," Faylin stated matter-of-factly.

"Well, I'm glad she didn't," Tarken said. "They'd have caught us for sure."

"I'll drink to that," said Rinna, holding an imaginary cup in the air. "I wouldn't suppose you have a little drink somewhere in there?" She pointed hopefully at the den.

"I'm sorry, Gran," Faylin said. She knew Shari's Gran always had a sip of spirits handy. "I can find you some water."

"Bah." The old woman waved her hand dismissively. "My body doesn't need water."

"We're going to Dahl Haven," Shari said. "We'll come back after they've gone." She gave Faylin a meaningful look. "Will you come with us?"

She considered the idea for a moment, then answered. "No. They won't accept me there any more than they did in Walla. My path is out there on the plains."

"That's what you said last time," Shari pointed out.

"Do you know how my family is? It sounded very bad last night. I'm worried."

A long silence prevailed as Tarken shared troubled looks with Shari. Finally, Shari whispered, "We don't know."

Neither of them looked at Faylin. She took a deep breath and tried to tell herself it didn't matter. *It's neither good nor bad. It just is.* She repeated the thought several times in her head, but it rang false each time. It *did* matter, and it was decidedly bad, but knowing wouldn't change anything. Still, she was anxious to know.

"You should rest." Faylin told them. "I'll keep watch."

They obeyed her as though commanded, or perhaps they hadn't slept in a couple of days. She wolfed and made a circuit of the area. Though she sensed no danger, something was off about Tarken's scent. Faylin sniffed him from several directions as he slept. Her fayden thought he'd been touched by the White. A persistent but pleasant odor wafted from him. Still, she didn't care to be around him if she could help it.

He'd been brave. He stayed with Shari's gran even though he could have left her behind and saved himself. And when the warriors caught up to them, he had been willing to sacrifice himself to buy her time. Judging from the way he'd handled his sword, he probably would have died immediately.

Faylin sat a short distance from the slumbering forms, not feeling like she should be among them. She rested with her eyes open until first light. Taking human form, she woke them and led them to the road. "This is as far as I go," Faylin said. "Tarken, take care of them."

"I will." He didn't look at her when he spoke. He hadn't looked at her at all since they'd left her den. She sensed overwhelming modesty and respect in his attitude. She'd considered wearing the dress, but opted to keep herself ready to wolf instead. "Can I ask you a favor?" Tarken asked timidly.

"I was wondering when you'd ask. You've been mulling something over ever since you woke."

"My friend Cayne and a group of boys are back there in Walla. If there's a way you can help them, I'd appreciate it."

"I thought you were going to ask me to pose for you." If there was any doubt of Tarken's genuine modesty, it was gone now. He turned bright red, like a beet, and coughed several times. Faylin smiled at Shari, and the two of them shared a playful giggle. It felt good to laugh. She realized she hadn't laughed since she'd left home. When she was alone, there wasn't any reason to laugh, or anyone to laugh with.

"I don't think there's anything I can do. I've never met them, and the place is overrun with warriors. How would I even pick them out?"

Tarken held up his hands in defeat. "I could describe them, but that wouldn't work."

"How about this," Shari said, holding out a shirt. "It was Cayne's. Maybe you can track his scent."

Faylin took the shirt and gave it a quick sniff, knowing her nose would be more sensitive as a wolf. It reeked of sweat and blood, but was otherwise unremarkable. "I'll give it a try and do what I can. Tarken, even if I can track your friend, he's in an army. I can't just walk up to them without getting a face full of arrows." She tore off a piece of the shirt and gave the rest back to Shari.

"I thought it was worth asking, but I understand if there's nothing to be done. I feel bad for leaving them."

She decided she liked Tarken, despite the fact that he reeked of White magic. He was good-natured and spoke with genuine respect to her. He also had a good measure of fear of her, and that didn't hurt.

Faylin stopped walking and waved to them as they continued on. Shari stopped, waiting for the others to move farther away. Tarken ran back to them, but only close enough to yell, "I forgot. There's a Fayden Blade among the Sarasins! Be careful, he's dangerous. He almost killed me and Shari."

"He may not be a danger to me," Faylin speculated. Blades were indiscriminate killers, but there was a sense of respect among faydens. She'd felt it with Meda and Akwane. She wondered if that respect applied to all the variants of faydens. Her own fayden believed that it did.

Tarken kept his eyes lowered and nodded before running back to the older women. Shari pressed closer. "He didn't really try to kill me—the Fayden Blade, I mean. He did hold a knife to my throat, but then he whispered in my ear. He said I was lucky there was a fayden's blessing on me, or he would have killed me. Then he gave me this scratch across my neck." She touched the straight scab that marred her neck.

"The blessing I gave you?" she asked. "But they were just words. How could he sense that?"

Shari shrugged. "I don't know, but he did. It saved my life. Tarken was right, though. That man is dangerous."

"I'll be careful with him, but I don't think he'd attack another fayden."

Shari took a deep breath, but paused a moment before speaking. "I know Tarken asked you to help his friends," she said with apprehension, "but don't put yourself in danger for them."

"I won't."

Shari shook her head. "Yes you will."

Faylin smiled to her friend. "This is goodbye, then."

"It wasn't the last time you said that, and I hope it's not this time."

Faylin gave her a long hug and a playful push toward the others. "Tarken is nice. You two make a good couple."

Shari cupped her hand over her mouth in mock horror. "He's nice enough, but not in that way." She walked away a short distance and turned back to say, "We *will* see each other again."

Faylin waved to her. *I hope you're right.* She waited until they disappeared from view. Tucking the piece of cloth in her mouth, she took her wolf form and broke into a run. After walking with the others for much of the day, she hadn't realized how much she missed the speed of sprinting.

She raced up a gently sloping hill and spotted a group of grazing gazelles near a pond. She slowed to a crawl. Over a dozen of the small creatures stood eating the tall grass. She clung to the ground and stalked forward. There was so much open ground between them that there was no way for her to approach them unnoticed.

The bushes behind them rustled, and a tankadon ambled out toward the water. It was young, with dull nubs where one day it would have long, sharp horns. Only half the size of a man, it would be much slower than the gazelles... but what came out of the bushes next eradicated any thought about hunting the baby tankadon.

First one, then three full-grown tankadons emerged into the open. These were the size of houses and sported horns longer than Faylin. She froze.

Faylin backed slowly toward the road, not wanting to draw any attention. She was hungry, but not *that* hungry. It made sense to her. The gazelles were the early warning system, and the tankadons were the deterrent. Together they were safer and stronger. *There's something important about that strategy.*

She tucked the thought in her mind and padded back to her den. Exhaustion overtook her and, in a blink, day was full night. She sniffed the piece of cloth several times, committing the scent to memory, and set out to see if she could track this Cayne.

She had no intention of going anywhere near the army, but she was surprised to see she didn't have to. Despite the myriad scents crisscrossing the fields, she discerned his scent among the others. It was stale, though. She circled to Walla's eastern side, still far from the campfires. The scent got fresher, and she realized the freshest scent came from the east, away from the village. She was certain that most of the warriors were still in and around Walla, but a small group had traveled eastward, and Cayne was among them.

Not knowing how old the scent was, she set out immediately on the eastward road. She suddenly smelled a nasty odor, like the steam that billowed up from Master Ganji's tempering vat when he dropped red-hot iron into it. Her fayden knew the smell. It was the Red.

There was another scent, too. This one was putrid, like rotting corpses.

It was the Black.

Rayl Goth

Hakan cursed his companions as they turned back and left him on his own.

Six of them had made the trip from Rivermar without incident, but once they left the safety of the road and trekked toward Rayl Goth, everything changed. The distant foreboding that was always present whenever they could see the dead city became increasingly palpable.

They started to argue about little things: who was carrying the heaviest pack, who was walking the slowest, and who spoke too much. As they neared the city, the conversation stopped, replaced by the splitting headaches. They were so bad three of his so-called friends turned back, wishing them the best of luck.

They'd heard tales of mountains of gold within Rayl Goth. There were stories of fantastic artwork from the Tainted Age, and wondrous artifacts. They were all experienced enough to know stories were just that: stories. They were told by people who had never been there, or even knew people who had been there. Still, over the years, they'd talked about going, never actually intending to do it.

All that had changed had last year, when Chesu died. He'd been the heart of the seven friends. Together they'd traveled to ruined cities and abandoned mines, trekking as far north as the Hadara Swamps, trying to reach the underground city of Necha Mak. They'd actually reached one of the entrances and entered the cave system, but they'd gotten lost and abandoned the task before finding the city itself.

When Chesu died in a bar fight, stabbed by a sailor, the rest of them decided they should try to loot Rayl Goth. It was so close to home, and it would be a tribute to their fallen friend. At first, they all took credit for the idea. Now they all blamed each other for the stupid notion. Just the sight of the city gave most people the distinct feeling that evil still lingered there, and the closer one got, the more visceral the sensation.

Hakan had reached the breaking point. He was the only one left still putting his feet forward toward the city now. The other five cowards had abandoned him, though they'd probably wait and see what he brought back.

His feet shuffled onto a white powdery layer surrounding the city like a ring, and he instantly felt a shudder run through his spine. He still managed to step forward, despite the overwhelming sense of dread and fear radiating out from the city. The more the city repelled him, the more he thought about how few others could have withstood this mental onslaught. This terrible city might still hold its treasure, despite the passage of time. He kept his eyes on the ground, watching his feet, though he could sense the looming walls growing larger in his peripheral vision.

Hakan approached the city walls, crossing a field of crushed white something. He wasn't sure if he was stepping on white stone or old bone fragments. His vision blurred and his eyes watered like someone had sprayed onion juice in his face. He pushed on to the edge of the band of white, the high walls looking down on him with hate.

His moccasins trod on blackened ash now, and it was the worst yet. Dread and anxiety mixed with fear and disgust. Step after arduous step, Hakan pushed himself forward, visions of gold in his mind.

Then it just went away. All of it. No more headache, no blurred vision, no sense of dread. Rayl Goth lay ahead of him, surreal and inviting. The sun high was high, but strangely indistinct through the hazy sky. His footsteps sounded as if he was listening to them from a great distance.

Hakan spent a few moments wiping his eyes and gathering his senses. Then he turned his greedy eyes to the high city walls. The walls were concave, and looked like a wave of black stone was crashing toward him. They narrowed on either side of him into a wide causeway of crushed obsidian shards. The walls loomed over him on both sides, as if he was in a tunnel. He'd brought a grappling hook, but the city gate was wide open. The causeway expanded into a wide area with three distinct districts.

To his left, he saw neat rows of angular buildings made of black stone with green geometric highlights. On his right, he saw clusters of low huts, also made of black stone, but these had red stone highlights in a dizzying array of designs. In contrast to the ordered buildings, the huts were strewn across the space in a chaotic tangle of small and large structures. In front of him, a wide boulevard let to an irregular rocky mount, perhaps the only thing not made of black stone here.

He turned to the right, as he always did. When searching a place, it was important to be thorough, systematic. He would search the huts on his right, then the mount in the center, and finally the buildings to the left. He'd gather any goodies here in the central plaza. It would have been easier with his companions, but now it would all belong to him.

The huts in front of him weren't actually huts. Carved from black stone in roughly circular shapes with low, slanted roofs, they were more like stone tents. He marveled at the thin stone skin that covered the buildings. It was barely a thumb's width thick and had no apparent support structure. Inside the first one, he found nothing except a stairway descending into the ground. He peered into the darkness, but sensed only a cold breeze.

Hakan reached into his pack and pulled out a bronze tube. The outer tube had a slotted opening and rotated around an inner tube. He turned the outer tube until it aligned with the opening in the inner tube, exposing the floricite crystals inside. He put the tube light in front of him, and took a step into the darkness. The light shone a pale green, but it wasn't strong enough for him to see the bottom of the tunnel. He edged downward anyway.

The stairs and walls of the narrow shaft were made of smooth black stone, but thirty steps down they changed to roughhewn rock. The seam between the two was sharp, as though someone had placed the carved stone neatly onto the rock in a perfect fit. He ran his finger along the gap between the two. It ran all the way around the stairs in a straight line. He dismissed his admiration of the precision and pressed on into the darkness.

Hakan descended the steep stairway until it opened into a spacious room with several doorways, one large and several smaller. Then he waited until his eyes had completely adjusted to the dim green light. This main room was empty. The small doors led to a maze of tiny rooms, but they were empty too. Low ceilings kept him hunched over. He didn't like them. They felt like tombs.

Assured that this area was void of anything valuable, Hakan went through the larger doorway. It led to a wide corridor with worn murals on curved walls. The corridor inclined to his left and twisted downward in the other direction. He turned right, sensing the weight of the rock above him increasing with each step. He searched a dozen doorways, finding each empty. The corridor grew wider, then opened into a massive chamber with a ceiling that sprawled up at least thirty man-heights.

The apex of the ceiling held a lattice cage filled with glowing floricite crystals. It bathed the entire complex in green light. Eight other smaller cages surrounded the main light source. In all, they provided more than enough light for him to see, so he put his own light away.

He stood on a rise on a cobbled roadway. The road drifted downward toward the center. The scale of the chamber struck him as he tried to judge distance. Dozens of hive-like stone huts stood clustered haphazardly across the floor of the chamber. The largest of them rose three stories high, but most were just a single story. By rough count, he estimated there were five hundred buildings. Was this a town here under all this rock?

Hakan turned back to the glowing cages. Floricite would fetch a handsome price if he could reach them. He reached into his pack and pulled out his grappling hook. Looking up, he wondered if he could secure the hook in the latticework. He tried, but his hook didn't get halfway high enough to even touch the cage. It fell back to the ground, almost hitting him. He jumped back just in time. The hook clattered around, the echo reverberating several times.

Hakan waited for the silence to return before reaching to recover his hook. He heard a distant shuffling. Fear swelled over his greed as he remembered he was far under the dead city of Rayl Goth. He backed toward the tunnel entrance, fumbling for his light tube; he dropped it to the rocky floor and cursed reflexively. A screech answered him from somewhere in the green gloom. He didn't bother to check to see if it was man, beast, or something else; he just grabbed the light and ran.

Hakan raced through the tunnel, taking the first doorway he saw. He jumped up the stairs three steps at a time. This stairwell was longer than the one he'd descended. It snaked its way through the rock, switching back on itself three times before he saw daylight. He scrabbled his way up to the surface. Upon reaching the top, he ran out into the light, then dropped to one knee, breathing hard.

Hakan didn't like these caves, and he'd found nothing, but at least nothing had found him either. He was an idiot for going down there alone. But soon his fear subsided and his greed returned, emboldened by the reassuring light of day. He cursed himself for running away at the sound of a rat or whatever had made those sounds. There was nothing to fear. This place was devoid of life. Still, he wasn't going back down there.

He dusted himself off and returned to the central boulevard. Keeping his standard practice of moving right to left, he walked toward the rocky outcropping at the center of the city. The boulevard led to a wide plaza of cobblestone—black, of course.

Hakan crossed the grand plaza; on the far side stood the hulking stone mount. He circled it, but found no way into the structure, though high balconies above hinted at interior passages.

There must be some way inside, though he'd be damned before he went back underground to find an entrance. Maybe if his weak-willed friends were with him, he'd have gone back down, but not alone.

Back around the front of the mount, he spied a lower balcony that overlooked the plaza. The rock face was too smooth to climb. He drew his grappling hook.

Hakan twirled the hook and sent it flying up to the balcony. It took ten tries to get it into the opening above the balcony, but it failed to hook on anything, and came clattering back to the ground. Undaunted, he tried again and again. After landing it on the balcony seven times, it caught on something.

He tugged the rope and then hung his entire weight on it. He didn't want to fall here. There was no help for him. For the first time he considered turning back, in sudden realization that he was truly alone. Climbing the rope was foolish, and yet, now he had a way into the mount. He climbed.

The balcony provided a view of the entire city. It was a place a king might sit to look over his subjects. He checked the hook and found it lodged securely in a wide crack in the floor. He left it there, in case he had to make another hasty retreat, before moving cautiously into the passageway behind the balcony. It was wide enough for a dozen men to walk abreast, and tall enough for a giant. The passage turned, and the daylight disappeared. He opened the tube light and waited for his eyes to adjust.

The passage led to a huge chamber, where he found nothing at all. He cursed aloud, and his words echoed in the open space. Several openings suggested further passages. He turned to his right, taking a small passageway.

A faint glint caught his eye. His fingers probed a small crack in the floor; he felt something round and cold. His practiced hands knew he'd found something significant. Managing to get a pinch on it, he drew out a glittering coin. He looked in awe at the uhkanuwa head on the face, and his smile grew to epic proportions. Hakan laughed, not caring about the noise. He'd found gold! Where there was one coin, there were more. He strode into the passageway.

The tunnel sloped downward, and he braced himself against the low ceiling. A thin layer of dirt on the floor made his foot slip. He fell flat on his stomach. His fall knocked out his breath, and kicked up a cloud of dirt into his eyes and mouth.

He slid downward. Clawing at the floor, he tried to stop himself, but it was smooth, with nothing to catch hold of. He accelerated, whipping around two sharp turns before he felt the ground under him fall away. He felt weightless for several moments, and then he stopped very abruptly, to the sound of snapping bones. His pack had fallen off during the descent, and it and the tube light fell around him.

Hakan lay in a chamber lit by enormous floricite crystals mounted in the ceiling. There were three of them, and he figured they were at least as big as he was. They were worth a fortune.

He looked at his legs, knowing they were broken, and yet he felt no pain. He didn't feel them at all. Even his hands failed to respond to his attempts to move. Beyond his legs, he saw treasure beyond description. Ignoring his broken body, Hakan looked around the room. He saw stacks of minted coins, like in the stories of the ancient times, before the use of beads became widespread. He saw jewelry and uncut gemstones the size of his fist. In the center of the cavern a boulder of black metal glinted in the green light.

Hakan laughed out loud and couldn't stop himself, despite the metallic-tinged spittle he sprayed from his mouth. Louder and louder he laughed. No one would come for him. He couldn't leave. He was going to die here. But he was going to die rich, rich as any king!

His thoughts slowed, and he fell into unconsciousness.

He awoke to distant, guttural voices. He tried to raise his head, but it dropped back down with a *crack* against the stone. He drifted off again.

Hands on his face. He was awake, but only a single eye responded to his efforts. Figures around him. His so-called friends? Returned to save him?

"Alive," one of the figures said. Its voice was gritty and dispassionate.

"But broken," said another with a similar tone.

"Bring him," a third commanded, and walked away.

Hakan tried to stay awake, but he slipped back into blackness. Someone was dragging him. He awoke again, neither of his eyes opening this time. He heard rustling around him. Dozens of feet scraping on stone.

"He may die soon."

"Keep him alive. I like my dinner fresh."

Chapter Twenty-One

Darwan placed Rogan at the end of the column to make sure everyone left the road. He put Cayne at the head. He gave the boy the simple order to walk toward the dark city ahead of them. His new steward had proven to be inept at everything thus far; still, Darwan saw promise in him. Yes, this boy had brought him nothing but opportunities.

The men, normally talkative, grew silent as the city grew from a vile vision to an ominous presence, a low, hateful chanting seeming to rumble up from the ground. The men fixed their eyes to the road, not looking beyond their next few steps. Even Darwan himself began to falter under the thrum of the Black. With so many eyes averted, he used the opportunity to slip a cube of pyrus into his mouth. The Red surged into his mind and Darwan found he could look full on at the city as the forbidding chanting in his mind quieted. The Red didn't fear this place.

Otherwise, only Rogan and Margella were unaffected. Margella stared at the city like a long lost girl seeing her home again for the first time. Rogan was still Rogan. He watched for some enemy who might be on the horizon. *I doubt any warband is foolish enough to be this close to Rayl Goth,* Darwan thought. The Red chuckled at the irony. As they closed on the city, the green grass shrank from knee-high to ankle-high, and then gave way to bare ground. Then he saw bones, broken and powdered, covering the ground. The men slowed and stopped every few steps, and only through constant haranguing from both him and Rogan was he able to keep them moving. His own horse constantly pulled at him to turn around.

A hundred paces before the walls of the city, everything changed. The white powder gave way to black dust, but nothing grew in that space, and the men refused to step onto the dust, despite his orders.

Rogan tried to push the men forward, but finally declared, "This is the end, Lord Darwan. They'll go no farther."

Darwan dismounted and hobbled his horse, so it couldn't run away, but it immediately began to skitter away from the city despite the restrictive ropes. "Steward!" He grabbed Cayne by the arm and pulled him forward. "Where I go, you go." They both stepped onto the dust, Cayne putting his hands to his head immediately. Darwan felt the pain too, but it was bearable thanks to the pyrus.

Margella stepped next to them without hesitation, a refreshing smile on her face. *No doubt she is of the Black.* "Rogan should come as well," she said. "We might need a sword."

"Why would we need a sword in a dead city?"

Margella regarded him as though he were a schoolboy. She stepped off toward the city without a word.

Darwan second-guessed himself one last time. She was leading him toward something of her design. Though he knew he should turn back, his need for pyrus drove his feet forward. Rogan stepped onto the black ash as easily as Margella, though not with the same fervor. He didn't appear to like the place, but neither was he afraid of it... or at least he didn't let any fear show.

The four walked toward the city as the rest of the warband fell back from the city without orders. Darwan had to shove Cayne in the back to get him to move forward. The boy was so preoccupied with holding his head that he didn't resist the constant pushing.

The walls of the city stood four man-heights tall, and were made of seamless black stone. They weren't normal vertical walls. The profile was concave, like the surf of a stone sea. Once they reached the wall, the distant pain disappeared completely, much to Cayne's relief. They passed through an open gate of matching black stone and into a corridor bordered on each side by more walls, with black towers jutting into the hazy sky. The causeway between the walls was made of fist-sized black stone cobbles.

"There's nothing alive here," Cayne said. His hands no longer clutched his head. He shifted his gaze between the walls.

"It *is* a dead city," Darwan pointed out.

"I know, but there's nothing at all. I don't see anything, and I don't hear anything. Not even a bug or a fly."

Darwan looked around. No sound. No life. Not even the wind dared to enter the city. The walls bore no vines, the streets no grass, the air no insects. Even their moccasins only made muted scraping sounds on the cobblestones, as though they were far away.

They left the tunnel-like corridor behind and entered a long open space. They were in the city proper now, and smaller walls separated the city into districts. These walls were lower, and the curved sides pointed straight up into the sky instead of curling to any side. They ran in long arcs away from the central plaza.

To the left, intermixed cobbles of green and black stone, laid out in a complex pattern, led to a sprawl of structures. There were hundreds of low buildings of black stone arrayed in straight lines, with the buildings growing in height toward the center of the complex. The design seemed perfectly symmetrical.

To the right, the cobbles formed a seemingly random mix of blood-red and black stones. This avenue led to more black buildings, but these were squat, round huts. Though none was taller than a single story, there was a tremendous variety of sizes. Straight ahead, a rocky outcrop of jagged stone loomed over an expansive plaza. Beyond that, there was another cluster of buildings in a third section of the city. The stone mount was at the center of the city. He'd heard the stories of the uhkanuwa, but had never seen a lair before, never seen anything that might indicate the stories were actually true.

"That is one of the merchant quarters," Margella stated, pointing to the left. "You should search there for whatever may have been left behind. I will go to the shrine in the uhkanuwa quarter to make an offering to Dyn." She looked to Rogan, and asked him to accompany her for protection.

"Am I the offering?" he asked, without a hint of levity.

"Of course you are not the offering," she said with a rare laugh, and then she started toward the mount.

Rogan eyed her suspiciously, and then looked to Darwan for approval. There was strength in numbers, but the Red didn't like either of them, and given what Darwan was searching for, it was best if Rogan didn't see anything. He nodded. Rogan shrugged and stalked after Margella.

Darwan led Cayne to the neat rows of buildings. Crushed black rock edged the road. In every direction, he saw silent stone under a constant haze, the blue skies hidden, and he wondered if the sun ever shone directly on this place.

He instructed Cayne to search the first building. Margella had called this a merchant quarter, but nothing here looked right. No trading booths, no blacksmith. Cayne reappeared shortly, too shortly, and declared, "There's nothing in there."

"If she has lied to me," Darwan swore under his breath, "I will strangler her myself, king's advisor or not." He walked over to Cayne, pointing to the next house to the left. "Search that one. I'll check the next one over." He entered the second building and found it a perfect rectangle with not a piece of furniture or errant belonging, not even any dust. It was just a box with a few square-hewn windows. The black stone made it difficult to see until his eyes adjusted. He saw nothing, and no place for anything to be hidden. Angry, he stomped outside and found Cayne shaking his head with his hands open.

"It's all one piece of stone," Cayne said, running a hand over the smooth wall of the building.

It felt as though they were walking in a dream with no real sensations, save the remote scraping sound of their own steps. The buildings were all the same, like they were forged from a common mold. At an intersection, Darwan chose to turn back toward the uhkanuwa mount. The mount in the center of the city served as an ever-present landmark, comforting and unnerving at the same time.

Cayne spun suddenly and Darwan had his sword out, thinking the boy was attacking him, but he was peering back in the direction they had come. "Did you see something?" Darwan asked.

"I thought I saw something move," Cayne said, his eyes searching the street.

Darwan surveilled the streets. He saw nothing, but sensed something beyond, like the weight of eyes watching them. Still, he continued to walk, half turned, so his back wasn't to Cayne. "You know, my order still stands. Should any unfortunate accident befall me, whether your fault or not, your friends die."

"I know," Cayne said, nodding grimly, "and something may happen to you, but it won't be my doing. I'm no murderer." With that, the boy sped up, taking the lead. It made Darwan more comfortable to have him in front.

"You killed Zane."

"It was a duel," Cayne protested. "You ordered the duel, so *you* killed Zane."

"Would you have preferred I let Rogan slay all of you?" Darwan asked.

"Why didn't you?"

Darwan mused about telling him the truth, but as in most matters, the truth was seldom his friend. "It was proper that the gods be allowed to pass their judgment," he replied. Surprisingly, that satisfied the boy.

Darwan's thoughts turned back to the streets in front of him, and he felt a sudden surge of the Red, quickening his senses. The weight of the invisible eyes grew, but still he saw nothing. They walked in silence, the buildings growing taller toward the center of the grid, his unease growing with each one they passed.

The buildings grew to two stories on this wide street, and Darwan stopped in front of one. "Search this one. I'll take the next." Cayne nodded and stepped into the house.

Darwan felt hopelessness creep into his mind. The city was enormous. He probably wouldn't find anything of value, even if he had his entire warband searching. Deep in thought, he heard sounds behind him, but reacted slowly. He turned to see a hulking form lurching toward him. The Red came to him, but too late. Darwan's sword was in its sheath, and he wouldn't reach it in time.

Taller than any man, even the king, the figure had dark, almost leathery skin. The eyes were sentient, with emerald green irises inside a moonless midnight-black sclera, where normally there would be the whites of the eyes. Its arms rippled with muscles, and the right arm was drawn back, wielding a grisly sword, just now beginning its forward motion toward Darwan. Well-worn leather boots covered its feet and ran halfway to the knee, exposing thick calves. It wore leather half-pants dyed black. Over its massive chest it wore a sleeveless jerkin.

On a primal level, Darwan knew what his attacker was. One of his tutors was from the northlands, near the Black Hills, and she told horrid tales of the Tainted Ones, though he never believed them to be true. Still, everyone had an inherent fear of them. Magic coursed through them, changing them, but while a single magic flow touched the Pure, the Tainted Ones were touched by two magic flows, and that made all the difference.

Darwan thought it proper that a lord be killed by one such as this. It was more fitting to be slain by one belonging to such an ancient race.

This was one of the Drakken.

Interlude

Pryeship

Tali looked over his precious engine. He listened to the rumbling and hissing, confident that all was as it should be. He surveyed the tangle of pipes and chambers in awe. No matter how many times he saw his engine,ในnever failed to amaze him. Rows of floricite gemstones flooded the engine room in a green light. They absorbed green magic and turned it into a brilliant glow. Each crystal was unique, and the builders had customized each fixture to fit perfectly.

The engine was the heart of a pyreship, and Tali ran the whole contraption. His father had been the engineer on this pyreship, and had taught him all he knew. They lived on the ship, and when his father died, Tali took over as the engineer. No one even asked him. The captain just started giving Tali the wage his father had once earned.

"Dinner." A burly deckhand came into the engine room carrying a tray of food. Placing it on a table, he looked Tali over and shook his head.

Tali wore only a leather loincloth on his wire-thin frame. The engine room was sweltering despite the ventilation shafts that kept a constant breeze rushing through the room. He knew the look well, and it didn't bother him. He groped through his memories for the man's name, but he couldn't find it. He had no mind for names. He thanked him and nodded. As he was leaving, Tali remembered his name and said, "I thought we'd have reached Rivermar by now, Fad." Yes, his name was Fad. He was supposed to be some kind of tough guy.

"The name's Gad, not Fad." He turned back, briefly rolling his eyes. "We've been doing three-quarters speed for a while now. As the engineer, shouldn't you know that?" He smirked and turned to leave again.

"Why are we going slower?"

The deckhand snorted and shook his head. "It's the damn fog. Can't see anything out there."

Tali let the man go as he thought about the fog. There were signal lights set in the center of the Skykom River, but in the fog, they'd be hard to see. It was dangerous to move in fog, and usually ships anchored until the fog passed.

While he'd thought they were going too slow just moments ago, now he thought they were going too fast. He looked at his engine. There were four large boiling spheres, each with a pipe bringing fresh water to them from the front of the ship and another pipe carrying super-heated steam to the rear of the ship.

His father had taught him to make the work seem complicated, but it was simple. When one engine exhausted its water supply, he closed the outlet valve, and then opened the inlet valve to bring in new water to the boiling sphere. By alternating boiling spheres, he provided a steady stream of steam to the pyreship. The captain controlled how much of that steam went to the back of the ship to propel them, and how much was expelled up the main vent pipe.

Tali walked to one sphere and pulled a hefty lever. The iron outlet pipe hissed to life. He stepped to the next sphere and threw the same lever, but upwards this time, closing an outlet pipe. He opened the inlet valve and listened to the sphere fill with water, the pyricite crystals instantly vaporizing the first splash of water. The trick was knowing when to close the inlet valve. Too much water, and the pressure wouldn't get high enough. Too little, and it would steam out too fast. He closed the valve and stepped back to admire the engine.

This pyreship was over five hundred years old, and ran like it was new. The Gaitan had built these great ships. Iron Gaitan made the piping, Wood Gaitan crafted the hull and decks, and Stone Gaitan did most of the decorative work, including impregnating the wood and iron with stone to make them last. It was more art than ship.

Most people thought he could fix the engine, but the truth was that he had no idea how it was built. Tali didn't know how to repair even one thing on it. Luckily, it never broke. The iron never rusted, the wood never deteriorated, and the stone never cracked. It was magnificent.

Tali had some time before the next lever had to be thrown, so he decided to see the fog for himself. Navigating at night using only the dim green light of the signals in the center of the river was difficult under the best of conditions. As he reached for the door, the entire room shuddered, and Tali flew backward toward the bow. A powerful thud came from every direction. He landed on the deck, tumbling all the way to the front of the room.

Tali had a few scrapes, and his head hurt. He felt a wetness on his head. It was worse than blood; it was water. The pipes were spraying water! The engine was wounded! Steam whistled out of the outlet valves, and cold water gushed from the inlet valves. He needed to get out before he got steamed to death.

Putting his hands on the deck, he felt the odd motion of the ship. It wasn't moving forward; it was twirling sideways. He scrambled to his feet and wobbled to the door. When he got there, he felt like the ship was sailing backwards.

Tali struggled up the stairwell, opening the hatch to breathe misty air. All along the deck, men shouted. Some yelled commands, and others made confused reports. All the voices held a tight and growing concern. Tali ignored the chaos on the deck and wobbled to the stairwell leading to the next level.

The stairs here were slick with condensation from the fog. He slipped three times, but he kept his hands clamped on the handrails. Normally Tali admired the workmanship of the handrails each time he used them. Tonight, he simply admired their function as he put all of his weight against them. He made his way to the bridge and found the captain just outside on the main lookout deck.

"Put the sweep oars in the water," the captain yelled into the fog.

"What happened?" Tali asked.

"We hit a Gol-damned signal light!"

Tali's stomach dropped. The signal lights were in the center of the river. They were huge stone pillars inset with floricite crystals. Beacons to all mariners, the lights were visible from a great distance. Looking out at the fog enveloping the ship, Tali wasn't surprised they hadn't seen it. Of course, that was why no one sailed in heavy fog.

"Get the engines going," the captain demanded. "We need double the steam until we right ourselves."

"We're steaming out," Tali said. He didn't need to check the engines; he could hear the excess steam venting out through the main stack pipe rising from behind the bridge. "The pipes are ruptured. I'll have to wait until they steam out completely before I can go back in the engine room."

The captain gave him a sharp look, but then turned back to the deck. Their swirling course was accelerating. He looked back at Tali, but they just stared at each other.

A deckhand burst onto the deck. He ran up to the captain. "Get the sweeps into the water," the captain ordered.

"Captain, we've been trying the sweep oars ever since we started spinning."

The ship shuddered again, knocking all three men to the deck. The captain got to a knee and bellowed, "What in Dyn's name was that?"

The deckhand got to his feet. "The sweeps aren't working. The water is swirling too fast. We can't control the sweeps. We've snapped a dozen already."

The Captain looked down and then to Tali, before letting out a deep sigh. "Rapids," he muttered.

"The sweeps are useless," Tali said. "This isn't what they were meant for."

"I know that. They're as useless as you are right now."

Tali saw something swirling through the fog above the ship, and then it was gone, like a giant hand grasping at the ship. He saw another one. It was a tree branch.

The old ship groaned violently to a stop, and then all was quiet except the gentle gushing of the river around the ship.

"Grounded," said the captain. "Thank the gods. We'll hold here until the fog passes."

Tali knew they didn't have any choice but to wait, but he kept his comments to himself.

A throaty howl reverberated from the forest. Tali struggled to fix the direction of the howl. A creeping fear gripped him; the howl was close, and made his guts tremble. He'd traveled this river his whole life. He'd heard the howls every night, but never from so close. Tali looked at the captain, whose eyes were as wide as Tali imagined his own were. Another howl answered the first, followed by a ferocious chorus of outcries.

Traffic on the river traveled along the west bank, never crossing mid-river, for the far bank harbored more than just rocks and rapids. The forest on the far bank was an impenetrable tangle of thickets and trees. Massive sagia trees soared high above the forest canopy. Drinking up the Green magic flows, the sagias were the oldest and tallest things in the world, as far as Tali knew.

No one feared tall trees and darkness, but tokiri lived in the forest.

The howls of the tokiri were a constant reminder of why no one traveled along the eastern bank. They were scary enough from the other side of the river. Tali's tight fists were clammy, and he had to force air into his lungs. His head swiveled as a chorus of screeches came from every direction, and most frightening of all, from above.

Tali stumbled to the railing and looked down on a deckhand. The fog dissipated enough for him to recognize Gad. The fog above him swirled, and a tokiri burst out of the fog, swinging on a thick vine. It landed right behind Gad. He was a huge man, but the beast next to him made him look like a child. Covered in long, dark hair, it stood erect on two feet and held an enormous cudgel.

"Gad!" Tali screamed. "Look out!"

The tokiri let out a howl that shook the ship as it crushed Gad's head with the club. The monstrous beast let out a louder roar as Gad's lifeless body collapsed on the deck.

Tali saw more vines whisk across the deck, depositing half a dozen tokiri on the ship. Though they appeared insubstantial to his eyes, he felt the thump as each crashed down on the deck. Recognizing the threat, the crew screamed wildly, trying to organize. They grabbed whatever they could use to defend themselves.

Tali wanted to run, but his feet were stuck in place and his hands grasped the railing in a death grip. The beasts ran like men, though with much longer strides. Behind him he heard the captain scream, followed by a sickening thud. Tali turned his head, his hands still clenching the rail. A massive beast stood over the captain's body. It turned its gaze to a deckhand crawling on the floor. He was trying to sneak past the tokiri, but it grabbed him by the back of his vest. Its other hand smacked down on his neck. Then, with a step and a heave, it threw the crewman right over the railing like he was a doll. Now it turned to Tali.

The face was almost human, but larger and covered by long brown hair. The beast came forward to Tali, and even though he couldn't see its full expression beneath the hair, he sensed hatred from it. It took two quick steps toward him and then sent a hairy fist into Tali's face.

Tali's head snapped back, and his body smashed into the railing. Viselike hands squeezed his thigh. In a gust of fog, Tali hurtled through the damp air. He heard his spine crack as he smashed into the deck. Then, thankfully, he knew nothing more.

Interlude

Rivermar

Warrek had hoped to find some solitude in the early morning calm; the dawn was a smudge of blue over the Crescent Mountains to the east. He was at the end of the docks watching the pyreships put out to the Skykom River. It was far from quiet, with the jets of steam rushing from the pyreships, but at least he could be alone. The only problem was that he *wasn't* alone. "I just thought you could do something about this," the farmer behind him said pleadingly.

Warrek kept his back turned, thinking he might leave, but the man was persistent. Warrek gripped the warm mug of tea and lifted it to his mouth, pretending he was alone.

"They cut Jolun into pieces," the man said.

Warrek took a sip of the honey tea. It was as sweet as he could make it, and he savored the honey as it slid down his throat.

"They cut him into pieces and scattered him along the road." The man was near tears.

Warrek sighed, letting any hope of solitude go. He turned to the farmer. The middle-aged man wore a wide-brimmed hat and dirty pants.

"You name your livestock?" Warrek asked.

"I've had Jolun for twelve years. He's sired half my herd."

Warrek glanced at a warrior walking toward them and smiled.

"It's not the first goat you've lost?"

The old man shook his head and said, "It's like I told you. I've lost five head already. I'm not the only one either, but they do seem to be picking on my farm more than others."

"And you think it's a cult of Dyn?"

"Who else would be carving up our livestock? They're not even taking the meat. They're just killing them to kill them."

The warrior reached them but pulled up short, not getting close enough to join the conversation. He gave Warrek a nod and a smile.

"This sounds like a matter for the town watch," Warrek concluded. "I'm the garrison commander. I'm here to defend the city, not police it."

"They won't do anything," the farmer declared. "I've told them. We all have. They don't do anything about it."

"Very well, I'll come to your farm and look at the remains," Warrek said. His warband had taken over the defense of Rivermar a fortnight ago. Since then he'd had to deal with one crisis after another, none of which had anything to do with defending the city. His days were filled with petitions and logistics.

"They killed Jolun a month ago."

Warrek raised an eyebrow. "A month ago?"

"Yes, and we already, uh, ate him."

"You ate Jolun," Warrek said slowly.

The man shrugged. "Most of him. He was a goat, you know. It's what we do with them."

Warrek looked to the warrior, who had an annoying grin on his face. He looked back to farmer. "What exactly can I do for you, then?"

The man pointed to the setting moon. "It's a full moon tonight. That's when they do it. I'm certain they'll kill another one of my herd tonight."

Warrek took directions to the man's farm and promised to send some men that night. The farmer bowed deeply and back away. Once he was gone, the other man stepped forward. "Harlen, good to see you," Warrek said, extending an arm." Harlen was two years younger than Warrek, and would lead their clan if anything happened to him.

Harlen grasped his arm. "Cousin, I see you're well and suitably employed."

"I didn't know you were back."

"My company returned last night. I thought my report could wait until morning."

Warrek took a sip of his tea and turned to the pyreships steaming into the deep waters. He'd sent his cousin to Barons Lodge, where most of the Navataw camped among the rest of the Crotan army. Harlen stepped up beside him and put a hand on his shoulder.

"New orders from the new lord," Harlen said sarcastically. He waited for Warrek to give him a questioning glance, and continued. "Enigo is now the lord of Storm tribe. His father died a few days ago. The camps are too crowded, and disease is rampant."

Warrek let out a long, exasperated sigh. Enigo was too young and spoiled to wield such power. He needed at least another decade or two before he'd be ready to lead the whole tribe. Warrek led his clan, but he hadn't gained his status until he was past 40 years. He'd needed those years to wring out the foolishness of youth and learn the hard lessons of experience.

"He's not ready," Warren said, shaking his head. Harlen shrugged. There was nothing to be done. The father was dead, so the son inherited his titles. It was Navataw tradition. "Who's counseling him?"

"Lord Thrall has taken him under his wing."

Warrek stifled a groan. Lord Thrall ruled over the powerful Fire tribe from the grand city of Gotham. Fire tribe was mostly farmers and fishers, and was the largest of the five tribes. Their own Storm clan clustered around the city of Manteo amid the northern forestlands. All the Navataw clans had common cause with resisting the Crotan oppression at the current time, but absent that enemy, the openlanders of Fire clan were his traditional adversaries.

"Any orders from this lofty cabal you met with?" Warrek asked.

"We're to keep a watch for approaching Sarasins, but not force an engagement. They don't want us to shoot even one arrow against them."

"So, a plot then," Warrek ventured. It didn't matter to him. Whether they sided with the Sarasins or remained loyal to the Crotan king, they were both the same: not Navataw. "We'll need to get word to the outposts."

"And there's to be another war council," Harlen said. "Here in Rivermar. You're the host."

"Great. Any other good news?"

"Enigo wasn't pleased that you sent me to the council. He thought you were slighting him by sending someone as lowly as me."

Warrek didn't care for the concerns of the new lord. "I need to replace the western outpost. Are your men ready?"

"I'm sure they've tired of this place and are ready to be back among the trees."

"Good. You can make it before sunset."

"Good luck with the council, then," Harlen said. He slapped Warrek on the back and jogged away.

Warrek kept his watch over the river, enjoying his moment of solitude before heading back to his command post. There he found written guidance for the coming council, as well as directions for how to handle interactions with the Sarasins. He memorized what he read and burned the letters.

He dispatched details to each outpost, giving each the orders not to engage the Sarasins. He gave the orders personally to the commanders, to make sure there was no mistake. When he finished wading through the drivel of orders, decrees, and requisitions, his men dragged him to the Sleepy Gaitan Inn for a meal. It was a goat stew with somewhat crusty bread. It reminded him of his pledge to help the farmer.

After the meal, he ordered his men to rest and meet him at dusk. In his quarters, he drifted past more piles of work and took a nap. He awoke with the last rays of day fading through an open window. He gathered his men and ate a quick meal before they set out for the old man's farm, finding it easily in the twilight.

He had five stout men armed with short swords and bows. Warrek had his normal bow, but a quiver of special arrows. In place of broadheads, they had little sacks filled with sand. They wouldn't penetrate skin, but they'd knock a man down and leave massive welts and bruises.

They took up position in a small thicket of unkempt bushes near the pasture. The full moon rose, filling the darkness with a silvery light. They saw and heard nothing but goats—at first. Well after midnight, they saw a blur of movement along the road, and fuzzy figures materialized into hooded people clustered in a small group. They moved silently across the grass, and Warrek wondered if they were more than just cult members.

He counted nine of them, all clad in black robes. They communicated with hand signals and didn't utter a single word. He wanted them to get closer, close enough to capture most of them. With enough surprise, he might get them all.

He motioned to his men to prepare. They fanned out to the sides, as he had instructed them to do. One slipped in the darkness, but steadied himself before he fell.

The approaching mob stopped instantly at the noise. Warrek heard muffled whispers and a few shouts of confusion. He nocked an arrow and took aim at the nearest figure. They were farther away than he wanted, but when they turned to leave, he loosed his arrow.

The arrow tumbled to a stop short of the target. Warrek cursed and drew another. He hadn't compensated enough for the blunt point. He stood up and walked toward the faltering figures.

They shouted to each other and ran. Warrek let fly with a second arrow. This one found its mark, hitting one of them in the leg and knocking him to the ground.

Warrek's men let out a battle cry and ran forward in pursuit. They had little chance of catching them. His men wore light armor, but the cultists wore only robes. That, along with the head start, ensured they got away, except for the one Warrek had hit with the arrow. That man stumbled to his feet, but his run was more of a hobble. The warriors caught him easily. "Got a name, friend?" Warrek asked him in a bright tone.

He glared at Warrek.

Warrek shrugged. "Bring him."

They dragged the cultist to the rickety building that the town watch used for its headquarters. At this time of night, only a single watchman manned the desk. He shot to attention at the sight of the warriors dragging a man through the main entrance. Warrek recognized Lakta, the second in command of the watch. He was passably competent, for a town watchman. "Sir Warrek," Lakta said, looking at the man they deposited on the floor.

"We caught this man trying to kill livestock," Warrek said. "There were others."

Another man entered from outside. This man was meatier than Lakta, and decidedly incompetent. His name was Gann, and he was the leader of the town watch.

"What is this?" Gann asked. "You woke half the town dragging that man through the streets, including me."

"They said he was poaching livestock," Lakta said.

"Sacrificing them," Warrek said.

"Did you actually see him doing it?" Gann asked.

Warrek leveled his gaze at the Gann. "He had friends. I think with the proper persuasion, he'll be willing to reveal the rest of his group."

"Is he a cultist?" Gann asked.

Warrek nodded. "Most likely. Probably a follower of Dyn."

Gann leaned to the prostrate man. "Well, are you?" The two men traded looks, but the cultist was as defiant as he had been with Warrek. "Good enough for me." Gann drew a small blade and slit the man's throat before shoving him to the floor. "Join your god of death."

Warrek was as shocked as everyone else in the room.

Gann cleaned off his blade. "What? You don't think we have swift justice here? We're fine with the cultists going about their business as long as they don't step out of line. Killing a man's livestock is a crime." He turned to Lakta and said, "Clean up this mess." Then he turned to Warrek. "Anything else I can do for you?"

Warrek shook his head. He'd misjudged this man, badly misjudged him. In every other instance, Gann had been a sluggish excuse for a town watchman, never missing a chance to do nothing.

"Good. Then I'm going back to bed." Gann strolled away without a glance back at the dying man.

Warrek and his men shook off their surprise and helped Lakta drag the body outside the walls, to a plot of land used for burials. No one wanted to build a pyre for the man, and no one spoke any words for him. They dug a hole and buried him in it.

After dismissing his men, Warrek settled in to sleep. He awoke to a gentle knocking at his door. It was morning, and he swung open the door to find the same farmer, his hat in his hand. "Thank you, thank you, I knew you'd help me!"

"I don't think they'll bother you anymore."

"No, no they won't." He lifted a basket and handed it to Warrek. It was filled with bread, cheeses, and dried meat. "A gift for you."

Warrek took the basket and grabbed a piece of meat. He was hungry, and the meat looked good. It was tough and over-spiced. "Goat?"

The man nodded.

Warrek put the meat back in the basket and gave the man a sidelong glance. "Jolun?"

Chapter Twenty-Two

Burke rode north along the road to Rivermar, watching Lord Palus, who was well ahead of him. Palus had ridden off the road, stopping on the banks of the Skykom. He was now furiously signaling a pyreship. No doubt he wanted passage to Barons Lodge, and to be rid of their company. Burke was in no hurry to meet his fate. Whether he'd done the right thing or not, it was unlikely the king would tolerate open disobedience.

"I hope he gets on board," Jaks said as he brought his horse up next to Burke. "I'll be glad not to have him in camp."

"He's eager to find his justice, and I'm sure he's afraid for his life." Last night someone had left a dagger buried in the ground next to Palus' head, and Burke couldn't help but wish they had shoved it a few hands to the right, despite his orders to the contrary.

That's what this was all about: orders. Palus had given orders, and he'd failed to follow them. Why did he expect the men to follow his own orders? Once soldiers start ignoring orders, the core of an army falls apart.

Palus got the attention of the ship, and it was angling toward him. The Skykom was a big river, making the ship appear insignificant at its current distance. It had a wide bow, not meant for cutting through ocean waters, but well suited to the river. A great iron tube rose from the center of the ship, a steady plume of steam rising from it and trailing the vessel.

The ship neared the shore, growing in proportion, the tiny dots on the deck becoming full-size sailors. Sweep oars appeared like the legs of an insect preparing to land, guiding the ship right up to the riverside. Anchors dropped fore and aft as a great cloud of steam billowed into the sky. Burke was surprised such a large ship could maneuver so close to the riverbank.

Palus shouted at the men hanging on the deck rails, then signaled the Fist to come to him. Burke reluctantly led the men off the road and to the shore.

Reed-lined pools of standing water pockmarked the lowlands next to the river. Early morning mist still clung to the swampy ground, and the horses made loud sucking noises as they pulled each hoof out of the mire. The swamp stink increased as they neared the river's edge.

"The captain says he can have us in Barons Lodge in two days," Palus stated. "I want all the men on board immediately."

"I didn't know you meant all of you," the captain shouted down. He was a balding, red-faced man, and though only his face was visible over the side of the ship, it held enough folds to suggest he was of considerable girth.

"These are my men, and they will accompany me," Palus shouted back.

"We can't take the horses. We need a proper dock to load livestock."

He may as well have asked them to leave their arms. Horse and rider were a single entity among the Fist. None of the men would leave their mounts.

"We're not getting on that ship," Burke said. "We still have a job to do, and we can't do it from a ship."

"And what job might that be?" Palus asked. He injected more in power into his voice.

"We're looking for the Sarasin army."

"I would not have thought you were doing anything of the sort, given the leisurely pace you've set."

"We're going to Rivermar," Burke stated. "From there we'll head west."

Palus chuckled without any mirth. "The king sent us south, and I'm sure he sent others to the west." When no one made any move to dismount, he said, "Very well, then. I will go to Barons Lodge. Should I expect to see you there at any point, or will you be running from your judgment?"

Burke had considered this question himself and still had no answer.

Palus dismounted and climbed into a small boat that ferried him to the pyreship. After he was on the ship, he yelled back at Burke. "You *should* run, though be assured, I will have my justice when this matter with the Sarasins is resolved!"

Burke took up the reins of Palus' mount, wrapping them around the pommel of his saddle, and they trudged back to the road, not bothering to wait for the ship to get underway. The men were waiting for him to speak, but he had no words for them. He struggled to sort the thoughts in his mind: abandon the army, or finish the mission. "You've followed my orders, and I fear I have brought you all to ruin," he said at last.

The faces staring back at him were pensive, but not hostile. He'd thought they should be. After all, he'd let them down. "We should have stuck a dagger in his throat," Jaks said flatly.

Burke let out a great sigh. He hadn't been able to do what needed to be done. His honor had won out over his sense of self-preservation, and now these men and their mounts would pay the price for his virtue. He wasn't the leader these men needed. As First Sword, he was good at carrying out orders, but actually giving orders wasn't coming easily to him.

"I will ask no man to continue with me," he announced. "You may take flight as Lord Palus suggested. He probably doesn't know any of you by name, so you should be safe." He looked back at the river. The pyreship was building up a head of steam. "I will continue to Rivermar and then turn west."

"Are you still trying to finish the mission?" Jaks asked.

"The king tasked us with finding the Sarasins, and we've not done that yet. If we don't find their signs by the time we reach Walla, then we'll know they moved to the coast."

"What if we find them?" asked Yenevas. "Do we return with the information, so they can cut our heads off?"

"I don't know," Burke said. He had no plan in mind. These men deserved a leader who could lead. "I don't think King Alarak will have much sympathy for our crime."

"You think what we did was a crime?" Jaks asked. "I think we did the right thing. The real crime would have been following the commands of that fool Palus."

The men supported his actions more than he had thought. He'd thought they had disobeyed Palus solely because of his orders. Still, this mire was of his making.

They'd passed through Rivermar on their journey south, not even staying long enough to have a drink. This time he hoped to enjoy a good night's rest at one of the inns and share a drink in a tavern. He remembered several of each establishment on the town green, and looked forward to a night in a bed, maybe even a hot bath.

Their arrival at Rivermar wasn't what he expected. An unmanned tower stood on the western side of the road and ran north along the road, joining the main wall that circled most of the city. On the eastern side of the road there were no defenses at all, just a crowded mass of houses. It looked like they'd run out of gold while they were building the wall, and never finished it. Near the river, workers dragging up clay from the riverside paused in their labors, but their stares looked worried. The Fist rode between the lonely wall and the squat worker houses. There wasn't even a gate. The Sarasins would have no problem taking this city.

They rode along the streets of Rivermar proper, but instead of townspeople lining the streets, he saw nothing but shuttered windows with occasional frightened glances from the few who scurried along the streets. On the green they found soldiers, perhaps two hundred, and not the local militia: these men were fully armored. They held an assortment of bows, spears, and short swords. A tall man barked orders while he watched the Fist approach. Next to him, standing smugly, was Lord Palus.

Burke led the Fist to the green, but stayed far enough back that they would have room to maneuver. A glance backwards showed more men covering the street from which they had emerged. All the exits from the green were suddenly flooded with warriors. *This will be settled here.*

"I am Sir Warrek," the tall man next to Palus said, "and I'm the commander of the garrison here. Lord Palus has accused you of willful disobedience of the king's orders." Warrek looked like he'd rather be anywhere but here.

"What are your intentions?" Burke asked. "Do you wish a fight?"

Warrek hesitated. "We don't want a fight, but you're accused of high crimes. Lord Palus has judged you," he said, looking to Palus with a grimace. "You are to be beheaded. Your men will be lashed, but then returned to service."

Burke found the offer acceptable. His men had suffered greater hardships. He studied their indignant stares and knew they were ready to fight. He raised a hand and dismounted. "I yield."

The first row of soldiers moved toward Burke. The shrill sound of swords gliding out of their scabbards froze the advancing soldiers. "This will not be," Yenevas roared. Spears shot up, arrows readied, and more swords appeared. "You will not behead him before you've killed all of us."

"Yenevas, let this be. The punishment is mine to bear."

Yenevas stared back, his glare not relenting. "You chose to do what was right, and not what was ordered. We choose the same."

Burke felt both frustration and gratitude. Still, he didn't want this to end in bloodshed over his fate. The tension grew, swords swayed in ready hands, and bows strained, holding back arrows. A single misstep, and the whole situation would become uncontrollable. Warrek raised a hand and motioned for Burke to meet him in between the two groups. Palus was right behind him. Warrek gave Palus an annoyed glance.

As Burke walked, he assessed the men in front of him. They were northern men, Navataw by their look. They had conical helmets, a mixture of leather and banded iron armor, and the occasional wooden buckler reinforced with iron. All of them wore deep green undergarments visible in the gaps of their armor. Their banners showed silver lightning crashing down around a wolf on a field of green.

The Navataw had only come under Crotan rule in the last fifteen years. The initial subjugation was brutal, as were the subsequent four rebellions. He'd seen action in each engagement, and he knew these people were rugged and defiant. He looked at the grizzled faces arrayed around him. If there was to be a fight, it would be hard-fought. He estimated at least three hundred men. The Fist would kill many Navataw, but there were only eleven of them, and the confines of the town would work against them. The Fist was an open-field weapon.

"I don't wish a fight today," Warrek said, "but, if it can't be avoided, I will oblige." Warrek studied the men of the Fist. "The Fist's reputation in battle is known, but you are few in number."

"We've been outnumbered before," Jaks warned him.

Burke glanced back and saw Tak standing with the Fist. His horse wore no armor, but he'd found a sword somewhere. Tak's face was as determined as the rest of the Fist's. He'd be the first to die.

Warrek seemed surprised that Jaks had heard him, but he nodded respectfully to Jaks. Turning to Burke, he said more quietly, "You have few options. You can surrender yourself, and only you will die. If you fight, then you'll still die. But so will the rest of your men, and many of my men as well."

Burke considered the options and knew it was better for one to die than many. "The first option is preferable," he said, "but my men won't allow it. They'll fight. Perhaps there are no options at all, then."

"Too many will die for your sake." Warrek's eyes darted around to his men. Burke didn't know if he was searching for another option or considering battle tactics. He walked back toward his men with Palus close behind him, but then stopped so abruptly that Palus ran into him.

Warrek almost pushed Palus out of his way, but restrained himself. He looked from Palus to Burke several times. "Lord Palus, you accuse this man of high crimes." He turned to Burke. "Your men contend you are the righteous one." He raised his voice for everyone to hear. "I can make no determination of who is right in this matter."

Palus' face was painted with shock and confusion. "No one asked you to make a determination. I have determined him guilty."

"One of you is a lord and Commander of the Fist. The other is the First Sword of the Fist. This matter can only be decided under the eyes of the Four. No unjust man can prevail over a just man under the watchful gaze of the gods."

Burke understood what Warrek was saying long before recognition dawned on Palus. Warrek was Navataw, and they had strong customs of honor. An accused man could fight for his honor. It was the right solution. Only one man need die. "I accept," Burke said, drawing his sword. The sword shone like the sun itself under the midday sun, and he heard an audible gasp from the assembled crowd.

He stared at Palus and waited. Everyone stared at Palus and waited. Sweat seemed to spray from the lord's face as Palus looked around, dumbfounded. "What is this?"

"We will settle this by the judgment of the Four," Warrek told him. "Single combat."

Palus uttered several words, but none of them formed anything coherent. Finally, he said, "If that is what must be done, then so be it. I will deal with you next, Warrek."

Warrek looked to Burke and then to Palus. "I doubt it," he said, walking away from the two men.

Palus drew his sword, anger growing in his eyes. His sword was the same brilliant white as Burke's blade. He stalked slowly, taking a stance often used for training. As a noble born, he'd have had many of the finest swordsmen for teachers. Burke's father was a landed man, but his father was the only teacher he'd ever known. He'd learned most of his skill while in the Fist, on the field of battle.

Burke swung his sword in a large arc, cutting the air in between them. The blade felt light in his hand. He could see the anger in Palus, and waited for him to strike first. He didn't wait long. Palus stepped quickly forward and reached with his sword in an exploratory strike. It was just a weak feint, and Burke easily knocked it away. The blades met with an unexpected tinkling sound. Iron swords made a satisfying clang, but apparently, ahnril swords made just a tiny sound when struck together. Ahnril blades were so sharp the Fist never used them for sparring, and Burke had never heard the sound before.

Palus spun around in a pretty but foolish move. It was the type of movement that looked good in practice and helped develop balance, but it wasn't meant for combat. His sword came around, but Burke parried it again.

Palus pulled back, and Burke saw his opening. He flung his sword out in a feint, but when Palus parried, Burke's sword wasn't there anymore. He had shifted his weight and his hold just before the swords crossed, and his blade struck Palus in the thigh. Ahnril sword met ahnril armor. Nothing happened. Ahnril didn't cut through ahnril.

Though he wore the armor, Burke hadn't fought against it. The lightweight sword made for a strike that was hardly noticeable, unlike an iron sword, which would have bruised Palus' thigh. To the onlookers, it must have seemed like they were playing with toys.

Palus jumped back, throwing his right hand out as he leaped. A fine powder sprayed out from his hand and into Burke's face. He closed his eyes and staggered backward, but it was too late; the blinding power burned and brought an instant stream of tears. The world morphed into fuzzy shapes, and he struggled to find the blob that was Palus. He'd be following up the powder with a quick attack to keep Burke from clearing his eyes.

He couldn't see Palus, but his gleaming sword stood out from the rest of the blurry world. It was high in the air, and Burke guessed it was an overhead chop, and he threw up his own sword to block the move. He felt the swords cross. Taking a second guess, he assumed Palus had used a two handed attack and kicked the air. He connected with a body. It wasn't a full hit, but it was enough.

He threw off his helmet and instinctively brought his left hand to his eye. He wiped. It got worse. He'd only managed to get more powder in his eye. Squinting with his one good eye, he blinked the other furiously.

He didn't see the next attack coming. He felt the light sword strike him across the shoulder, close to his unprotected head. Knowing that meant Palus was to his side, Burke stumbled forward. He was lucky his head was still attached. Turning, he scanned for the sword.

A bright blur slid across his vision, but he couldn't tell how far away it was. He put his sword up to parry. Nothing. He forced his good eye open. It burned, but he kept it open. Palus was close and readying a lunging attack. With his poor vision and lack of depth perception, Burke had no way to parry a strike like that.

Palus began his forward movement, and Burke threw his sword at him. Palus batted it away, but it was only a distraction. Either this attack worked, or Burke was dead.

He rushed forward into Palus, grabbing for his helmet. He twisted it, knowing the eye slits would be out of alignment. Then he pulled up. Burke drew a dagger and jammed it where the helmet met the collar. The point hit the ahnril, and he slid it down until it inserted into flesh.

Palus gasped as Burke shoved the dagger in to the hilt and pulled. Palus gurgled and collapsed. Burke stepped back, his arms outstretched, trying to sense anyone around him.

"He's dead," Yenevas shouted. "I have water."

Burke felt a bottle being placed in his hand. He leaned his head back and poured the water into his eyes. When he was done, his vision was still blurry, but he could see people again. Warrek stepped toward Burke. "The gods have judged you." He looked to Palus' body. "Few men in my land would accuse another, unless he knew he could beat that man in combat." He handed Burke a cloth.

Burke took the cloth and wiped his face. "We already have his horse, but we will want his armor and sword as well." He recovered and sheathed his sword before seizing the other sword lying on the ground. He glanced casually around the green. The Navataw had sheathed their swords and were unlimbering their bows. Most of the men appeared relaxed.

"What are your plans?" Warrek asked.

"We've been in the field for some time. I'd like to stay the night here and rest our horses."

"We'll find rooms for your men."

Burke walked back toward the Fist. "Yenevas, see to the horses."

Warrek led Burke toward a large building. "I've never seen an ahnril sword before. Armor, yes, but not a sword."

"The king has an alchemist of great skill. Most ahnril can only be forged in small pieces," he said, flipping up an armor scale. "The king's alchemist can make swords."

"It didn't look very effective at dealing with armor."

"It has its advantages. We'll head west tomorrow and try to find the Sarasins."

"I have a contingent of Navataw stationed along the road. Could you bring them supplies?"

"It will slow us to take wagons, but we'll oblige." Burke noted that Warrek still thought of himself as Navataw, not Crotan.

"Good. Now I think you owe me a drink," Warrek said, laughing. "That Lord Palus seemed quite the pinhole."

"He got most of Black Rock angry enough to riot."

"The news from the traders is that Black Rock is in open revolt. We heard they asked the Sarasins for protection. Yes, quite the pinhole."

Burke assessed Warrek and went with his gut. He felt a clear sense of honor and trust from Warrek. He was someone to fight next to, not against. Looking up, he saw the sign for a tavern in front of them, but he stopped, waiting for Warrek to turn back toward him. Warrek looked back questioningly, until Burke thrust out the ahnril sword, hilt first. "Take it."

Warrek looked confused, but then took the sword gingerly. He drew the blade, his eyes wide. The gleaming metal gathered the light, making strange shadows on his face. He sheathed it and regarded Burke.

"There is something you need to know." Burke looked around, making sure there were no curious ears about. "I mentioned that they were flexible enough not to shatter, but they also slice."

Warrek looked back with a stare that said, *Of course it slices, it's a sword,* but he said nothing.

"This sword will slice through iron as though it was bean curd." To illustrate his point, he grabbed an iron nail from the ground. Standing next to Warrek, he partially drew the blade. He put the nail on the blade without any force, yet the edge slid right through the nail, half of it falling to the ground.

"I see the value now. Will it do the same to a man's armor?"

Burke nodded, then added, "And the man."

Warrek put the blade back in the scabbard and motioned to the tavern. "Perhaps I owe *you* a drink now."

"You can buy the second round," Burke said.

Chapter Twenty-Three

Cayne crept up the stone stairwell like a thief. He expected to see someone around every corner, but the second floor of this strange house was as vacant as the first. Light spilled in through open windows, illuminating the jade-green stone walls.

Walking to a window, he peered down at Lord Darwan in the street below. A large, dark figure silently stalked Darwan. Whether man or beast, it was like nothing Cayne had ever seen before. Fear tied his tongue.

His feet worked well enough, though. Sprinting down the stairs, he saw the figure skulk past the doorway. Cayne rounded the doorway, and drew his sword with a muffled scraping sound. The creature hefted a great sword above Lord Darwan's back. It was at least two full heads taller than Cayne.

Cayne grunted an incoherent battle cry. His sword cleaved into the beast's back, just above the shoulder blade. Though it wore hide armor, the blade cut through leather, muscle, and bone. The creature let out an oddly distant wail, and spun to face Cayne. With his sword lodged in bone, the sudden shift pulled Cayne off balance.

Lord Darwan's sword flashed into the beast's thigh. Dark blood spurted out. It twisted back to Darwan, and Cayne got his sword free. Darwan struck it again, this time under the left armpit, almost cleaving the arm off completely.

Cayne struck the creature at the back of the knee, and it slammed to the ground with another muffled scream.

Darwan landed a killing blow to its head, and it screamed no more.

Darwan and Cayne shared a glance, but no words. They turned, back to back, searching the street for assailants.

"What was that?" Cayne asked.

"It was a drak."

Draks were one of the four Tainted races that had once held dominion over all of Anavarza. They lived in the far north now, and in mythic legend. They weren't something you saw in the street, though this was no ordinary street. In the stories, they were taller than a building, ate people, and never died.

Looking upon the face of the drak, Cayne felt an instinctive fear of these former oppressors, awe of a magical being, and sorrow for the role he'd played in killing it. In myth, there was a price to be paid for defying the Drakken.

Cayne spied movement. It was another drak, and a dozen other creatures. They looked like ants, if ants were the size of sheep. Their dark brown bodies had three segments, and they walked on the four rear legs of six. The center segment had a pair of grabbing claws, and the face held mandibles on either side of their mouths.

"We have more visitors," Cayne said.

Darwan snapped around and sized up the approaching force. "The other way is clear."

Cayne was running before Lord Darwan finished his sentence. He was glad to see the creatures weren't fast. The two men raced down the street and came to an intersection. A quick glance to the left showed more of the big ant things marching ten abreast toward them, so they turned to the right.

"What are those?" Cayne asked.

"We have to find Rogan and Margella!"

"This city is supposed to be abandoned!"

"Obviously it's not," Darwan panted, exasperated.

They ran, houses on their right and a field of crushed rock to the left. A high wall and massive tower lay beyond the open space. Cayne saw an opening where the outer city wall met an inner wall in the shadow of the uhkanuwa mount. He pointed at the opening, and they both ran across the gravel.

The drak and his ants slowed even further in the uneven open space, but they continued their pursuit. Cayne saw another wall meeting at the same opening, and strange complexes of buildings in yet another walled area of the city. To his right he saw the uhkanuwa mount and a wide plaza. The sprawling space was large enough to fit Dahl Haven into twice over and still have room to spare.

Near the center of the space, Rogan fought a horde of the ant creatures, while two draks held Margella.

Rogan's sword was a blur, in constant motion. Pieces of ant flew as he smashed them, but they continued to swarm him. Darwan took the lead; he had surprising speed for someone in full armor. Cayne struggled to keep up. The clunky armor changed the way he had to run, and his muscles hadn't adjusted to the new pattern of movement yet.

Behind Margella, more of the ant-things streamed toward Rogan, like real ants milling toward overripe fruit. More draks converged on the melee from all directions, seemingly in no hurry. Darwan and Cayne covered the ground quickly, careful to make eye contact with Rogan, so he wouldn't mistake them for ants.

Ichor covered Rogan's face, except his savage eyes. Around him, the carcasses of ants lay knee-high for thirty paces. Rogan kicked broken bodies out his way as he carved a path to Margella. Dying ant pincers ripped anything they could reach, which was mostly other ant bodies.

Cayne crunched over dismembered exoskeletons scattered on the ground. It stank like aged bile mixed with fresh dung. An ant turned from Rogan and snapped at Cayne; Cayne slashed at the ant's thick midsection. His blade cracked the exoskeleton and continued clean through the beast, slicing it in two in a spray of ichor and organs. As fast as that, Cayne was covered in blood. The gunk in his nose tasted like the fetid mess he smelled. He gagged as he swung at another ant. Lord Darwan chopped ants just to his left, and he too wore their entrails over his armor.

"They have Margella!" Darwan yelled to Rogan.

Rogan shot him a withering glare. "Hold them here." He didn't wait for either of them to acknowledge his order as he jumped over several carcasses, kicking grasping claws, and ran at Margella. He slashed two ants in a single swing of his sword, and then the blade was returning to pierce another. Cayne and Darwan tried to keep up with him, but he moved too fast.

An ant came around his right side and tried to grab Rogan, but Cayne chopped away two of its legs. It skittered to the ground and then reached for Cayne. A quick kick to its midsection delayed it long enough to land a killing blow.

Rogan had two ants left near him, and they fell in pieces as his sword cleaved them. The two draks backed away from Margella.

Unexpectedly, Rogan spun around and thrust his sword point-first into Margella's chest, all the way to the hilt. She shuddered, loosing a piercing scream. Rogan's subsequent twist and yank threw her frail form backward off his sword, her scream silenced as she hit the ground.

Silence ruled for a moment. Even the ants paused momentarily. The draks drew huge, black swords, but didn't advance. Darwan's mouth hung open. "Rogan! What have you done?"

"This was *her* doing!" Rogan shouted to him.

Margella looked at Rogan and gave him a strained smile. She coughed up bright blood. "Fayden trash," she croaked. Then her head fell back, and she screamed in agony.

The draks let out a grating battle cry and surged forward. Rogan stepped back to prepare for their assault, but they stopped short and called strange commands. The ants responded immediately, and as one, they converged on Rogan. They moved twice as fast as they had before. The three men gathered in a circle. "Which direction?" Darwan demanded.

Rogan looked at both men, telling them to follow him with a glance. They sprinted toward the uhkanuwa mount. There were ants gathering around them in every other direction.

At the base of the mount, a thin line of the ant-creatures waited for them. Rogan slowed as he reached them, waiting, so they all hit the line at the same time. Cayne swung his sword at the first ant and made contact right at the center of its midsection, but there was no spray of blood, just a dull clank of iron on some type of armor. These ants were larger than the others, and their exoskeletons were much darker. They didn't just wait in line to die; they surged forward, grabbing with their clawed arms and lunging with their mandibles.

Cayne felt the claws and pincers grabbing at his legs and arms. His lungs struggled for air as the ants closed in on them, but he reached for the rage and found it. With thoughts of his father and mother dying, these ants were the culprits in his mind, culprits that Cayne didn't want to escape anymore; he just wanted to kill them.

"Go for the joints," Rogan screamed. He stood a short distance away, surrounded by ants.

The fury in Cayne's mind rolled down his arms and erupted in his sword. He swung it with a single hand, using his free hand to punch at the ants. He hacked a leg off a nearby ant, but it recovered quickly. Did Rogan mean the joints of the appendages, or the joints between sections?

Cayne swung at the joint between the head and the midsection. The head came off, but the rest of the body kept fighting. It grabbed another ant by the leg and dragged it away from Cayne. He swirled and harmlessly struck an ant, missing the joint. He kept his sword in constant motion, using every bit of energy he had. He tempered his rage with focus, and his strikes became more precise. He ignored the claws, even as they scratched at his armor and clung to his arms and legs. His movements slowed, encumbered by the ants attached to him. Their claws sawed at the padded under-armor, tearing the fabric and slicing into skin.

He focused on the ants attached to him, hacking them to pieces with his sword. Grabbing their arms, he twisted them off. He used the dismembered arms like clubs. The joint between the head and the midsection was the weakest point. The lower body had the four legs, but cutting that off left the upper two sections to continue to grab and pinch, though with no mobility. Cutting off the head left the claws of the midsection to clutch aimlessly, and more often than not, they grabbed another ant.

Rogan and Darwan moved steadily through the ants, but Cayne made no progress. He didn't want to escape. He hacked at ants, moving to avoid the reach of the immobilized ones. He wanted them to *die*. "Cayne, this way!" called Darwan from the base of the mount.

Cayne cleaved the last ant around him. There was no place to go. Backs to the mount itself, ants closed in on them from every direction. Darwan held a rope in his hand and offered it to Rogan. The rope disappeared into a large opening in the side of the mount. Rogan climbed the rope with the speed of a spider.

"We don't know what's up there," Cayne said.

"True," Darwan replied, "but we know what's down here." He looked to the ants. "I doubt the rope can support three of us. Be a good steward and cover our ascent." Then he leapt up onto the rope.

Cayne swore his best oath at Darwan, and then spun to meet the oncoming hoard of ants. *No chance that this ends well,* he thought.

The ants were stalking ever closer, but Cayne found his rage again. He sneered and screamed, "Falconstorm!" It was common to yell your family name in battle, but he'd never done it before. It seemed right, and he charged forward. The ants stopped as he charged a gang of four of them.

He chopped down on the first one. The exoskeleton of the head was hard, but he cleaved off one of its antennae and sliced into a bulbous eye. It shuddered and let out a high-pitched screech that made the other three back off. Cayne swept his sword low, and cut out its two front legs. The ant fell forward, reaching for him with its grabbing arms.

"Get up here, you fool!"

Cayne recognized Rogan's voice, but didn't look. *Easy for him to say.* Cayne jumped back, but the three ants surged forward. The fallen ant grabbed one of them and held it firm. Cayne swept low again and heard the satisfying snap of legs. He smiled, realizing he didn't need to kill the ants; he only needed to immobilize them.

Cayne ran back to the rope, sheathing his sword as he ran. He reached up and pulled himself off the ground. Lord Darwan still struggled to reach the top, and the rope shuddered with each movement he made. Cayne hoped he'd get off the rope soon.

The ants approached the rope, and he wondered if they climbed up walls like their diminutive cousins. He climbed faster.

Below him, the rope jerked from side to side. The ants were clawing at it and trying to shake him off. Looking up, he saw Darwan scramble up onto the ledge. Then he saw Rogan lean out over the side and aim an arrow right at him.

The arrow whistled by Cayne's ear. It landed in the eye of an ant pulling at the rope. It crumpled. The other ants pulled its carcass away like it was trash. Cayne's arms strained as he pulled himself higher. Another arrow zipped by and bit into an ant. Another perfect eye shot.

Cayne's hands were sweating. It was getting harder to keep his grip. He twirled the rope around his arm, dried his free palm, and then did the same with the other hand. Taking a deep breath, he pulled himself up. He timed his breath with his pulling, not taking another rest until he felt hands yanking him up onto the ledge.

Cayne lay on his back, panting, while Darwan struggled to pull up the rope.

Rogan stood out over the ledge and fired three arrows in rapid succession. Cayne watched as he drew more arrows from his quiver. Rogan shot arrows in a way Cayne had never seen before. He grabbed the arrows by the fletching, three at a time between different fingers. He brought the one between his first and second fingers to the bowstring and nocked the arrow on the right side of the bow. Cayne had learned to nock on the left, and "sight" the shot down the arrow shaft. Rogan didn't even aim. He released the first arrow and nocked the second before the first was even fully away. The third followed immediately. It was the fastest he'd ever seen anyone shoot. Rogan grabbed three more arrows, and loosed them in another rapid volley.

"Lucky they can't climb," Darwan said.

"They might not have to," Rogan said, pointing to the back of the ledge. A tunnel led into inky blackness. It was wide and smooth, with enough room for ten men to march side-by-side.

Rogan counted his arrows and looked to the other two men. Darwan was the lord and didn't carry any arrows. They didn't trust Cayne enough to give him a bow. Rogan nodded sharply and stowed his bow over his shoulder.

"We can't make a stand here," Darwan said, shaking his head. "Too wide. Maybe we can find a choke point farther in."

Rogan motioned toward the darkness. "After you."

"I'd rather stay here and see them coming," Cayne said.

"For once the boy speaks sense," Rogan said. "Hopefully they're as dumb as they look, and don't find another way in."

"They don't need to find a way in," Cayne said. "They just need to wait."

"What are they doing?" Darwan said as he squinted across the plaza. "They're taking her."

Two draks held Margella's wailing body high over their heads. They were taking her toward the section of the city with the low huts. She was still alive and squirming in agony. Her screams phased in and out, as if she was getting closer and farther away at the same time.

"Are they going to eat her?" Cayne asked.

Darwan pointed his sword at Rogan. "What were you thinking?" he demanded. "How can I explain this to the king?"

"Tell him the truth. She was a rayth." Rogan's voice had no sympathy.

"The truth is, you killed her," Darwan stated. "The king may want both of our heads."

"Let him try," Rogan said. "It was her or us."

"The king would have preferred it be *us*."

"Perhaps it was your steward who killed her," Rogan said, looking at Cayne.

"Perhaps he did," Darwan said. "That might save *your* skin. But I was the one who allowed him to be my steward in the first place, so I allowed him access to her."

"Then it was them," Rogan said, pointing at the swarm of ants milling across the plaza.

"Yes, I can imagine how that conversation would go," Darwan said. "Your majesty, the Lady Margella was killed by draks and giant ants." He shook his head.

"Not ants," Rogan said. "They were ghants. Ants long corrupted by the Black."

"Another name from myth," Darwan said.

"They didn't feel like myth," Cayne said, rubbing the cuts on his face. Both men regarded him as an unwanted stranger in the conversation. He disregarded them and kept talking. "Is that the best name they could think of for them? Giant ants—ghants? Not very original."

"I didn't name them," Rogan said.

They watched the draks drag Margella into a hut. The remaining draks shouted commands, and the ghants formed orderly lines, leaving their dead behind. They marched single-file into the huts and were gone. Silence settled over the city.

Darwan shrugged and ordered Cayne to descend first. He touched down on the black stone with a muted thud and drew his sword. He walked into the center of the plaza; they were alone. Darwan and Rogan joined him, and they jogged to the entrance of the city.

Piercing the edge of the city was easy this time, since he was running away. It seemed Rayl Goth itself was pushing him away. He saw Darwan and Rogan ahead. Finally out of danger, Cayne wanted to collapse, and to vomit, and to scream. But he remained on his feet, fought back the bile, and let out a battle cry. The two men regarded him with amusement.

"Thanks for killing those ghants with your bow," Cayne said with mixed feelings. He hated him, but Rogan had helped him fight off the ghants.

Rogan snorted. "I was more likely to live with there being three of us. If it would have increased my odds of survival, I'd have fed you to them a piece at a time, starting with your privates."

"They probably would have been full after that." It was an old quip, often used among the boys in Dahl Haven, and it came to his lips without thought. Darwan shook his head and walked away, but Rogan just squinted at Cayne.

The warband camped by the road. The three men entered camp, still covered in ichor and reeking of death. They answered none of the questioning glances.

Darwan gave Cayne his armor to clean and ordered him to clean his own, telling him his steward's dress reflected on him. Cayne cleaned well into the night, the dried ghant ichor and drak blood resisting his efforts. After scrubbing until his fingers became numb, he allowed himself to think of sleep. He found the boys sleeping in a circle and took his place at the center. He waved in the air, sure Rogan was watching from somewhere, and then put his head down. Dreams marred by ghants and the Drakken, he awoke more tired than he had been the night before.

The camp was in full motion, readying for another day of marching. He'd learned something about the Sarasins in the few days he'd spent as Lord Darwan's steward. They were not, as he originally thought, one people. The warband was composed of a multitude of different nationalities. By day, they wore the same armor and looked homogeneous, but at night they separated by tribal groups. Few of the men were actually Sarasin—mostly just the ones in charge. The rest of the men were from tribes subjugated by the Sarasins. These men regarded him with some measure of respect. *They're probably like me. Trapped in an army they hate, fighting someone else's war.*

He'd met Kiotan, Unamook, Wampan, Natn, Puccan, and Ravahnan warriors—people representing nearly all the Sarasin conquests. The only people not in the warband were men from the Toltan tribes. Cayne learned there had been a recent revolt among the Toltan, and those warriors had deserted the army as it quelled the unrest.

Lord Darwan sent a steady stream of orders for Cayne as the army broke camp. The road curved north, away from Rayl Goth, before turning east again. Throughout the march, the dead city watched him, making his skin itch. The long plains turned into rolling hills crossed with small streams. Sparse stands of trees turned into groves, and then a full forest north of the road. The gentle breeze carried with it the smell of damp wood in the heat of the day. To the south, an expansive herd of grass-eaters watched them warily.

Cayne looked at the bison, gazelles, mastodons, and tankadons grazing on the tall grasses. He saw meat. The army subsisted on beer, small amounts of dried meat, and bread made from whatever roots they could find. He expected the bread to be tasteless, but unfortunately it wasn't. A fresh kill would bring a welcome change in menu. Between the nasty food and constant marching, the boys were losing weight, and meat would help them get their strength back.

He suggested a hunt to Lord Darwan. Cayne had heard him talk of hunting, but Darwan dismissed the idea and lectured him on the dangers of a herd of charging tankadons. As a lord, he ate well each night on private stocks of dried meat and cheese. He didn't have the yearning Cayne and the rest of the men felt for something more substantial.

In mid-afternoon, Darwan ordered Cayne to stop the warband and set the camp for the night. Cayne assigned the regular tasks before returning to Darwan. "Can you ride a horse?" Darwan asked. After Cayne nodded, he continued. "Take Margella's horse. I trust you can find it. I want you to scout up ahead on this road."

"Me?"

"You are my steward, and I have no intention of scouting for myself. Now, if you have no other stupid questions, get on with it. Ride a good measure up the road and then return before dark. Report what you find." Darwan turned away from him.

Cayne left in a stupor. *Does he trust me to return? Or does he want me to escape?*

He found the horse and saddled it. From the saddle, he saw the Dahl Haven boys staring at him. He rode up to them, but Rogan was there to intercept him.

"Where are you going?" Rogan demanded.

"Lord Darwan ordered me to scout ahead."

Rogan scoffed at him. He stared hard at Cayne, then relented. "I told him you'd put a knife in his back, but maybe his foolish trust will just cost him a horse."

Cayne wanted to speak with the boys, but not with Rogan there. He turned his eyes to the east and slapped the reins. Looking back, he saw their wide-eyed faces begging him not to leave them alone.

"One thing to keep in mind, Cayne," Rogan said. "If you don't come back, these boys will pay for the horse. In blood."

Chapter Twenty-Four

Faylin kept her head low to the ground. They were coming out of the dead city, and she didn't intend for them to spot her.

She had easily tracked the warband as it plodded away from Walla. At first, they seemed to be heading for Rivermar, but then they surprised her by marching off the main road toward Rayl Goth. No one went there, not ever.

She'd lived her life in the shadow of the dreadful place. It was how you knew which way was east. Even in the dark, you could sense the malice radiating from Rayl Goth. Her fayden, however, did not fear its magic.

While the warband slowed as it neared the city, she felt none of the apprehension she once had when moving closer to it. They eventually came to a stop on the outskirts. Most retreated, but four people entered.

Faylin watched them from a distance, and opted to wait for them to return. She sensed that sources of both the Red and the Black were among the group. She also sensed an opportunity—Tarken's friend was with them—so she hid along what she hoped would be their line of retreat from the city.

She waited north of the city amid the short grasses. Though four entered, only three emerged from Rayl Goth. Her hiding spot was almost too well chosen, and they passed within a few strides of her. Luckily, they were agitated and couldn't maintain proper situational awareness of their surroundings.

She scented them, despite the wretched odor of the Black emanating from Rayl Goth. She smelled Cayne and the Red, but not the scent of the Black. Interesting.

She kept pace with them, staying beyond the range of their hearing. One stopped suddenly and cast his eyes back in her direction; she froze and settled into the grass. She couldn't see him, but knew he was a fayden, a Fayden Blade. Though her fayden didn't fear the man, her human mind was panicky; Fayden Blades were ruthless killers. Tarken had warned her, but she still felt a cold wave of terror creep over her.

They moved off toward the road, and Faylin was content to let them go. Her fayden urged her to continue her pursuit, but she decided to give them a wide berth, keeping well away from them. They rejoined the warband, and Faylin kept her distance.

The warband struck out early the next morning. They kept up a horribly slow pace, and Faylin found time to hunt small game without fear of losing them. A large herd of grazers watched her warily, but she didn't think the risk was worth the reward.

When they made camp for the night, she found a safe place among a stand of thorny bushes along the bank of a muddy pond. Midway through the night, the constant chirping of insects gave way to the grunts and low notes of large animals. She looked through a break in the bushes around her, and saw a herd of gazelles and bison drinking from the pond. They were close, but hadn't detected her yet. In the darkness, she had an advantage. Her only fear was getting trampled in the confusion she was likely to create.

She crept forward, sighting a gazelle a few paces away. Its tail wagged from side to side. Bringing its head up every few moments, it looked around carefully. Her muscles tensed as she readied herself for a quick strike.

The grunts of the herd quickened. They stopped drinking. Every one of them looked alert. *Did they sense me? No, they aren't running away.*

Howls and menacing growls echoed from a short distance away, and the herd stampeded. Faylin saw her chance as the gazelle bounded toward her. She leaped forward, pouncing on the surprised animal. She locked her jaws on its throat and settled back into the thorn bushes. Around her, the herd thundered away amid a chorus of canine yelping. She waited patiently for the life to drain from her prey. Killing it was neither good nor bad, just necessary. It was simply dinner, though she wished it would stop struggling so much.

The cacophony of stamping hoofs faded into the distance, and the melody of insects returned. When the little gazelle stopped moving, she used her sharp teeth to tear into it. After only two bites, she sensed danger closing in on her. Grabbing the gazelle, she dragged it back toward the road. She wasn't sure what the danger was, and wasn't interested in finding out.

The threat was closing fast. She dropped her meal and spun to face her pursuers. Six pairs of hungry eyes glistened in the darkness. As they approached her, they took the shape of wolves. Her fayden had no sense of skinwalkers among them. They fanned out to either side of her. Faylin bared her teeth and growled. The large wolf in front of her kept its eyes locked on her, but the others glanced at it for cues. *The leader.*

Faylin stepped back from her kill to gauge their reaction. They moved in, the largest taking the lead. They sniffed the carcass in turn, but then fanned back out around Faylin.

It must be about territory, then. She was trespassing on their turf. Shari's words flashed in her mind: *It wasn't worth risking her life to help people she didn't know.* There was little she could do to help them anyway. Faylin resolved to give her kill to these wolves and Tarken's friends to the Sarasins. She would walk away from both... and do what? She continued to back away from the pack, but they kept coming toward her.

Two wolves tried to get around behind her while others lunged in and nipped at her hindquarters. Her fear faded, replaced with anger at the painful swipes and bites. Still, she thought better of acting on her emotions. She turned and ran.

They were fast, but she was faster and had more stamina. The big one stayed on her heels, but the others fell farther and farther back. Faylin thought she could outlast the wolf, but to her surprise and his, she wheeled on him with a violent burst of speed.

The big beast tried to lurch to its right, but Faylin was on it before it could dodge her. The first strike was hers, and she took advantage of it. It lowered its head, protecting its neck, so she locked her fangs on its right leg. It let out a satisfying yelp as she pulled the leg out from under it. She had thought the men she fought were slow and expected the wolf to be much faster, but it moved in like a turtle. It tumbled to the ground, trying to scramble away from her. She knew the fight was over and it was yielding to her, but she maintained her grip on it.

Faylin rolled it over, noting it was a male. Her paw smacked down hard between his legs, but she didn't extend her claws. Still he shrieked in pain, and she let him go. He limped away as his pack arrived. They looked from Faylin to their leader and chose to keep a respectable distance away. She saw a brief opportunity and barreled forward. They scattered, and several lowered their heads to the ground in submission. She chased the ones who stayed upright until they too submitted.

Faylin sniffed the air and gave a rough bark. She trod into the darkness and the wolves followed, even the large male. *So I'm a pack leader. Now what?*

She rested until the painting of the sky signaled the coming of the sun. The murky light and damp ground were perfect for a hunt. She followed the scent of a herd. Alone, she always targeted the weakest, but with half a dozen wolves with her, she felt bold.

Her plan was simple: Drive the herd and wait to see who fell behind. She had no way of telling her pack what the plan was, though. She tried motioning with her muzzle and clawing at the ground with her paw, but nothing worked. Then she sent images of what she wanted through her head and tried to project it to them. Nothing.

The sun peeked over the horizon before she got the wolves fanned out around her. Four were females, ranging from adolescents to adults. She had one young male and the older one she'd fought. Gray patches covered the old male, and she guessed he was the oldest. The others accepted her leadership with no qualms, but the mottled gray male hesitated and growled with each command she gave.

When she had them spread out enough, she moved forward, but her pack stayed where they were. Finally, after several tries, she got them moving the way she wanted. They moved on the herd, jogging abreast of each other, and when she yipped, they joined her.

The herd reacted as she expected. Panic sent them into a wild stampede away from the wolves. She accelerated, feeling the wind in her face and exhilaration pulsing through her body. A small mastodon fell behind of the main herd. She quickened her strides and passed it, driving the herd farther away. Then she turned on the lone beast as her pack converged. Her pulse flared in the crescendo of the attack.

The beast was larger than the wolves, but far smaller than a full-grown mastodon. It circled to keep the wolves in front of it, but they surrounded it. The young beast wailed and swung its tail, but missed them.

Faylin saw her chance and zipped in at its neck. She bit into thick hide. Thrashing and tearing brought a trickle of blood, but not the torrent she expected. The panicked mastodon called again in desperation.

Wolves lanced in, nipping the beast. When it raised a meaty leg, a wolf latched on to it. A frenzied kick sent the wolf flying into the dirt. Others closed in to harry the other side. This time two wolves grabbed a leg and pulled it violently out from under the mastodon. When it kicked, it lost its balance and fell over with a massive thud. A cloud of dirt flew up and obscured everything. Faylin kept her grip throughout. Now the wolves, her wolves, swarmed the beast. The big male joined Faylin at the neck, but it tore mercilessly through the hide, digging and biting until it found an artery.

Cool torrents of blood spurted out, coating them from muzzle to tail. The mastodon struggled against the weight of the wolves, but the movements became slower and the cries weaker. Faylin disengaged from the neck and walked a short distance away. The wolves tore into the flesh and ate, even as the mastodon continued to struggle. With the rush of the hunt subsiding, Faylin felt sick in her gut, though her fayden saw nothing wrong with hunting.

She thought of a chant she'd recited many times. It gave her comfort now.

Red transforms us
White heals us
Green shapes us
Black equalizes us
And the circle of magic goes round and round.

This was not the circle of magic, but of life. It was neither good nor bad; it was life on the plains. The grazers ate the grasses. The hunters ate the grazers, and eventually they all fed the grasses with their carcasses. One big circle leading nowhere.

She waited until the beast was dead and moved in to take her share of the kill. She knew on an intuitive level that she both gained and lost respect with the wolves by doing this. The hunt was wildly successful. She doubted they'd eaten so well in months. Still, the fact that she ate last made them doubt her strength.

Is this my place? Among cold hunters on the plains?

Both Faylin and her fayden knew the answer. This was *not* her place in the world. She recalled the laughter, the conversation, and yes, the tears she'd shed among fellow humans. She couldn't be among humans anymore, and she didn't want to remain among the wolves, but what alternative remained? Solitude?

After they ate, they spread out around the kill and rested. Smaller hunters and scavengers ventured into to steal what they could, but the wolves protected their prize. The buzzing of flies grew like a chorus at festival. Faylin had no interest in eating any more of the meat, but the other wolves ate once more before they departed at midday.

On a whim, she decided to try something. She stopped the pack and padded a short distance away from them. She took a deep breath and then shifted into her human form. The wolves jumped back, traded looks, and then growled. She wolfed quickly, and again the wolves backed away in confusion. After several moments, all but the former pack leader had once again accepted her.

Faylin growled and he too yielded to her, but she sensed resistance in him. That had been stupid, but she had learned two valuable facts. First, she could never be in her human form among the pack. Second, they weren't following her, they were following the wolf skin she wore. Her outward appearance was all that mattered to them, not the person inside. The thoughts filled her with remorse and dread.

Faylin led her pack along the road, heading east. The wolves eyed her with suspicion, but they obeyed her for now.

The successful kill emboldened her to try to help Tarken's friends again. She felt stronger with the pack around her, though she wasn't sure what they could do against a warband. Still, helping people seemed more important than hunting.

They'd lost much ground, and she wasn't sure how far the warband had traveled. She scented Cayne at an abandoned camp. Judging by the cold embers of the fire pits, she guessed they were at least a day behind the warriors. With darkness setting in, she indicated they were stopping for the night. She found herself inexplicably stepping in a circle before settling down to sleep.

Akwane's words haunted her. Perhaps she had no place in the world. She sighed heavily and shut her eyes.

Faylin slept so deeply, she didn't wake despite the violation of her space. She flickered awake to find the big male on top of her. He wasn't attacking; he was trying to mount her. Faylin scrambled, but found his weight upon her, restricting her movements. She broke free and faced him. The rest of the pack watched passively, satisfied to wait and see who won the match.

She raged at the thought of what he'd tried to do to her, but she kept her distance. They circled each other. He made the first move. He flanked her, then darted in behind her. Faylin let him, but when he tried to mount her, she rolled and came up biting.

Her bite tore away a nice patch of gray fur from his chest. Though she'd hoped to hear a pained yelp, he only growled louder. She restrained a growing fear, instead feeding her anger with thoughts of her recent life. Her whole life was ruined. All that she knew and loved was gone… and he was going to pay the price for all of it.

They paced around, leaving a good distance between them. She sensed his attack even before he moved. He took two long steps and leaped into the air at her. Faylin ran forward and leaped to meet his attack with one of her own.

Chapter Twenty-Five

Cayne saw little but small game scurrying about and birds arcing overhead. After being in the Sarasin warband, he'd grown accustomed to being with other men. He hadn't realized the comfort that provided, but now he felt very alone. At the same time, he felt free. Still, he would be returning; he wouldn't let those boys pay for his freedom.

He saw a pack of wolves stalking him, but ignored them. They couldn't catch him on the horse, and he would be safely in the camp by nightfall. It was disturbing that he should think of the Sarasin camp as a place of safety. *Perhaps I'm becoming a soldier after all.*

Ahead, the road plunged into a dark forest, and he felt a forbidding presence in those trees. Cayne saw nothing in the shadows, but in his mind, he saw ghants and draks. He rode right up to the tree line and stopped, studying the trees, but saw nothing.

"Where are you heading?" asked a voice.

Cayne nearly fell off his horse. He spun to see a warrior holding his horse by the reins. He wore green-brown leather armor and a conical cap, swept backwards. While his right hand held the horse, his left held a short sword at the ready. He studied Cayne.

"I said, where are you headed?" His voice was calm, but firm.

"West," said Cayne, looking around, as twenty men filtered out of the trees. They wore the same green-brown armor. More men appeared all around him. Clearly, he wasn't a very good scout.

"Strange. You ride all this way, and then just turn around. Where are you from?" He stepped closer. He smelled of damp bark.

"I'm from Dahl Haven." The grizzled warrior's expression didn't change, so he added, "It's just to the south of Walla."

"You're a long way from home."

"Who are you?" Cayne asked, as innocently as he could.

"We'll ask the questions." There were more men now, maybe sixty, all gathering around Cayne. "What's your name?"

"My name is Cayne Falconstorm." He spoke before his mother's words of warning could change his last name to the one he had grown up with. He regretted it immediately.

A murmur went up among the warriors surrounding him, and even the man in front of him was taken aback. *Mother warned me.* These men recognized his name, and she had said men would kill him for it.

"Falconstorm," the old warrior repeated. "I've not heard that name in years, not since the last of them was murdered." The rumbles among the other men became angrier. "Who was your father?"

"Nate."

"Nataniel Falconstorm had a son named Cayne. Both of them are dead, so either you're lying, or they weren't murdered after all." He examined Cayne's face for a time. "Get off your horse. We have questions that you will answer."

"I have to return before dark."

"There's no place you can reach before dark, so why don't you tell me what you're really doing here, and who you really are." The men crowded around him, making it impossible for him to dismount, even if he wanted to comply.

He took a chance and told them everything. It would either gain their trust, or lead to his death... and the death of the Dahl Haven boys. He recounted his mother's words, as best he could remember them, and the events following the arrival of the Sarasin army.

They listened, whispering among themselves. When his story was complete, their leader returned his attention to Cayne. "Three hills over. A warband of Sarasins. The whole Sarasin army near Walla and heading west."

Cayne nodded, not sure if any of them believed him.

"You look right," the man stated. "And you know the right things. If you are who you say you are, this changes things."

"You're Navataw too," Cayne said, hoping he was right.

The warrior nodded. "I'm Sir Harlen. We're forestmen from Manteo, between the rivers."

"How many of you are there?" Cayne asked, looking around the trees.

"We have enough to handle those Sarasins, if it comes to that."

"Good. If I'm right, then you owe me some loyalty," Cayne said. He tried to keep it from sounding like a question. He spoke a silent prayer that these were some of the shieldmen his father had mentioned. "I am who I say I am, and I have a plan."

"It's nice that *you* have a plan," Harlen said. "What makes you think it's going to be *our* plan?" He reached for Cayne's sword and untied it from his waist. He took the sword and examined it, paying close attention to the scrollwork on the blade. "Splendid sword."

"It was my father's."

"I know," Harlen said, handing the sword back. "I gave it to him."

"You knew my father?"

Harlen nodded and offered his hand to help Cayne dismount. He waved his men away, and they faded back into the trees. Harlen walked along the tree line. Cayne kept pace and waited.

"My father was a shieldman to your family. Your father and I were both wards of Lord Niatha. When I was old enough, I swore an oath to the Falconstorm banner." He thumped his chest with a fist. "I thought you were all dead."

"And now?" Cayne prompted.

"I don't know," Harlen admitted. "Your name is still revered among some of our tribe, but your family has been absent for many years. Things have changed. Power has adjusted."

"Would I be welcomed back?" Cayne asked.

Harlen shook his head and took a deep breath. "You're a threat. Those who took power won't risk you trying to reclaim your titles."

"They'd kill me." Cayne said. "Then you're taking a risk by not—"

"I swore an oath to your banner. My word means more than my life."

"I'm just one person. How am I a threat? I don't even own any land."

"It's the name," Harlen said, turning on Cayne and standing in front of him. "Falconstorm. The lord of Manteo had been a Falconstorm for generations. Even today, some would rally to your call without hesitation." Harlen looked troubled and uncertain. "I swore an oath to the Bearstorm banner, but only because I believed all the Falconstorms were dead." He paused for several moments. Then he grasped Cayne's arm in a tight hold. "My oath to the Bearstorm clan is secondary. Now that a Falconstorm is here, I will follow you, Lord Cayne."

Cayne waited for Harlen to laugh or tell him it was a joke, but he just stood there smiling. "This changes things," Harlen declared. "Your family was the last to resist the Crotan scum when they took our lands. Will we be resisting once again?"

"I don't know," Cayne said. "I need to think on this."

"Your grandfather was a thinker, too. He never made rash decisions. He always wanted to know his options."

Cayne resisted the urge to correct Harlen, to tell him that rash decisions were his hallmark. Harlen and his men were looking to him for leadership. *He's sowing his hopes in the wrong ground.* And yet, Cayne wanted to lead.

"Who are these Bearstorms?" he asked.

Harlen spat on the ground. "They were shieldmen to your family. They became the leaders of Storm tribe with your family's demise. I've always suspected they had a role in that."

"The trap where they killed my grandfather?"

"My father was there too. He died defending your grandfather." Harlen rounded back toward the road. "The Bearstorms seized control of Manteo with the support of the Crotan scum. Lord Enigo Bearstorm rules over our tribe now."

"My grandfather was lucky to have men like your father by his side." It seemed the right thing to say, though he knew nothing about Harlen's father. He'd died alongside Cayne's grandfather, though, and that was enough.

Harlen nodded his whole body in agreement. "How much do you know of our lands and our history?"

"My father never spoke of it," Cayne said.

"Your father was a good swordsman," Harlen said. "Did he at least teach you that?"

"Some," Cayne said. "Not that much, really. He was hurt in a battle and it was difficult for him."

"Show me," Harlen said, pointing to the ground a few paces ahead.

Cayne walked to the spot he'd pointed to and drew his sword, though he wasn't sure what to do. Harlen hadn't drawn his sword, so this didn't seem like a sparring match.

"Forms. Did he teach you forms?"

Cayne's father had taught him the basic fighting forms, but it had been a while since he'd practiced them. He stepped back and took his sword in two hands. Then he executed a series of slashes and jumps. When he was done, he looked to Harlen.

"That was awful," Harlen said. "You'll get yourself killed. It's a good thing you're so big. You can power your way through most fights, but if you meet a real swordsman you'll be in serious trouble." Harlen drew his sword and took a fighting stance.

They went through five basic forms until Cayne got them done fairly well. The setting sun drew long shadows on the hillside. "I need to return," he said.

"To the Sarasin camp?" Harlen asked. "Why do that?"

"I need to help my friends escape."

"An honorable cause, but we could just storm their camp."

"They're camped on a hill with long views," Cayne said. "We couldn't approach without being detected." Cayne pointed to the road. "We'll be heading this way in the morning, and I have a plan."

"You mean *we* have a plan, Lord Cayne." Harlen walked Cayne to his horse while he listened to the plan. "Good luck, Lord Cayne. After we take care of these Sarasins, we'll talk again. There is much about history and politics that you need to learn—and we have to work on your sword forms."

Cayne rode to the top of the hill and waved back at Harlen. He raced the slivering sun back to the Sarasin camp, arriving with scant time to spare. He made it a point to ride past Rogan on his way to Lord Darwan's tent.

Cayne announced himself before entering the tent. It was dark inside, with just a single candle casting a shifting light. Darwan stood and stared at Cayne for a long time.

"You're back," Darwan said, showing more than a little disappointment.

"No choice. Rogan said he'd take it out on my friends if I didn't return."

Even in the dim light, Cayne could read the annoyance in Darwan's grimace. "Rogan. Of course. I'll have a talk with him. You can go."

"Did you want my scouting report?"

"Did you find anything?"

"No."

"Then get out."

He found the boys serving meals. He helped them finish their tasks and then settled in the center of the sleeping circle. They slept, but he lay there worrying about the multitude of ways his plan could fail. A misting rain came and went before dawn, leaving them shivering and huddled together.

Rogan woke them the next morning. "You had a talk with the lord," Rogan said, standing over the group of boys. "He's bent on letting you all go, but he won't say it. You're to scout out again when we set camp tonight. You can take these recruits with you."

Cayne rubbed his eyes and processed the words. He could take *all* the Dahl Haven boys and leave the warband? All he had to do was get through one more day. *The Navataw. My plan.*

"Well, I don't like this," Rogan said. He spit on the ground, though some splattered on Cayne's feet. "His lordship had me cut the men off from roca leaves too. He doesn't know what he's doing. These men will be ready to kill each other by the end of the day. " When Cayne still didn't say anything, he turned and stalked away.

The Sarasin tactic for the recruits was clear. When they formed for battle, the recruits went at the front. Pinched between the Sarasin swords behind them and the arrows and spears in front of them, they blunted the impact of the initial clash. Cayne's plan might still work if the Sarasins didn't get the chance to deploy. In line of march, the recruits were farther back and could escape during the confusion. Rogan marched in the last group, with the recruits in front of him. That way he could keep his eyes on the entire warband. Ahead of the recruits were three more groups of regular Sarasins, with Lord Darwan normally riding with the second group.

Cayne ate breakfast. He had stale bread made from roots and grains foraged from the land around the camp, and warm soup that tasted like it was made from the same roots. He thought of mother's breakfasts. She always sent them to the fields with something hot and delicious in their bellies. He longed for those days. He had to make it through this one day, even if it was his last.

They broke camp and formed the five marching groups, but it wasn't the same as the other days. Cayne rode near the recruits, but none of the other lines started marching.

Rogan walked up to the recruits and ordered them to take the lead, fear putting a spring in their step. Cayne rode over to Rogan and asked, "What is this?"

"Something the matter, boy?" Rogan said, smirking. "We're close to the enemy now. I'd like to make sure I get some use out of these recruits in case we run into anyone or anything, today." Rogan walked off with a low laugh.

Cayne bit his lip in frustration, cursing Rogan's knack for anticipating almost everything. *Did he know?* Cayne was an awful planner, and he cursed himself. He'd set a trap for the Sarasins, and now it would be sprung on the very boys he was trying to free. Thanks to him, they might all die now.

They marched down the road, and the Sarasins fell in behind them. Cayne put his horse to a gallop, heading for the front of the line, an idea forming in his mind. He told the recruits to slow their march up the first hill, and then faded back to see if Lord Darwan had any orders for him.

Darwan was strange this morning. His orders were random. First, he ordered Rogan to march in the rear line, then he ordered him to march beside him in the second line. It annoyed Rogan, which amused Cayne, but it was out of character for Lord Darwan, at least from what little Cayne had observed.

They crested the first hill and naturally picked up the pace going downhill, but as they climbed the second hill, Cayne rode forward and had the recruits slow their pace even more than last time. He could hear the grumbling from the other lines, and he hoped someone would order another group to take the lead and set a faster pace. He needed the boys to be at the rear of the formation, not the front.

Lord Darwan was oblivious. He fidgeted endlessly in his saddle and swiveled his eyes across the rolling hills. Cayne had asked for permission to scout ahead, but Darwan didn't even acknowledge his question with a glance. He was lost in thought, his focus off in the distance.

They started down the second hill, and he saw the final hill forming in front of them. After that, they would meet the forest, and his time was up. He slowed the recruits again, this time to an agonizingly slow pace. He still had no real plan. He simply needed more time.

The grumbling in the other lines grew, and finally a voice cried out. "What's wrong with these recruits?" Darwan demanded of Rogan. He was alert and focused for the first time. "Can they walk no faster than a cow?"

Rogan was at the rear of the formation, but he sprinted up to Lord Darwan. "I'll move them along at a run for the rest of the day." Rogan moved forward, but Darwan raised a hand to stop him.

Cayne rode up beside Darwan. "Lord Darwan, I can shift the recruits back to their normal position in the warband."

"No." Darwan looked at Cayne, a flash of red in his eyes. Not bloodshot, but glowing red. "I've had it with these recruits. They eat our scarce supplies and they can't even march properly. This experiment is over."

"I can train them," Rogan said. "They can at least be useful to stop arrows."

"I am tired of hearing about these arrows from you. Are they useful today, right now?"

"They will —"

"I said now!" Darwan yelled. "Are they useful to me *right now?*"

Rogan gave a slow shake of his head.

"Honestly, Rogan, I think you just keep them for your own private torture troupe." Darwan chuckled at his own quip, but he was the only one. His expression turned to stone. "Get rid of them. We'll move faster and they won't eat any more of our supplies."

Rogan shrugged casually. He turned to the men of the second line and ordered, "Kill the recruits."

Chapter Twenty-Six

The second rank of Sarasins lurched toward the boys of the first line, who stood frozen by a complete lack of understanding. The Sarasins had their swords out, and hammered on the back row of recruits.

"Tagan," Lord Darwan yelled. "That isn't what I —"

Cayne saw his latest plan end worse than he could have imagined. He let out his family battle cry and drew his sword. He swung it at Lord Darwan. He couldn't miss at this range, but somehow he did. Darwan slipped of the way. His horse was not as fortunate.

Cayne's blade struck Darwan's horse on the neck. He hit the thick leather cowl. It wasn't a seriously injury, but the horse didn't know that. It reared up, sending Darwan tumbling. Cayne was riding away before Darwan hit the ground. He rode at the line of Sarasins killing the recruits, trampling two Sarasins on his way.

"Run!" Cayne commanded the recruits, but many were too scared to do anything but stare; and staring, they died. Thankfully, half the recruits ran over the rise and down the far side of the hill. The Sarasins moved through the remaining recruits with no resistance. Some of the recruits dropped their arms and pleaded, but the Sarasins laughed and hacked at them with bloodstained swords.

The Dahl Haven boys were among those running away, but there were no more than twenty recruits altogether in that group. The others were dead or dying, and their screams burned Cayne's ears. Their deaths were on his hands as surely as if he had killed them himself. This was his doing, his actions, but these boys bore the consequences. He rode ahead of the recruits as they sped down the hill toward the forest. He studied the trees, but saw nothing. Were they running away from a massacre and right into the trap he set?

Riding up to the tree line, Cayne still saw no sign of the Navataw. He turned back and saw the pitiful band of boys running from the horde of Sarasins. The boys had long since dropped their weapons and anything else they carried. The Sarasins were taller and stronger, with strides twice that of the boys, and they closed on the boys. Four of the faster Sarasins were nearly upon three of the young stragglers.

Cayne slapped his horse, riding to the left of the road, and then angling back toward the road and the four Sarasins. He urged his horse into a charge and readied his sword. The Sarasins didn't react until the last moment, but they were ready for him.

The horse slammed into one of the Sarasins, knocking him to the ground. Cayne's sword came down on the breast of another with a loud clang. The vibration of metal on metal almost caused him to lose his grip on the sword. The man stepped back, stunned but not badly hurt. Cayne continued past the Sarasins, noting that six more running toward him. He turned his horse for another pass, but he hadn't ridden far enough. The two unhurt Sarasins were right beside Cayne, swinging swords at him.

Both Sarasin swords struck flesh, breaking bones and severing arteries. Cayne felt the horse falling, unable to stand on just two legs, and he leapt away. He fell in a heap. His horse make a sickening death whinny and thrashed on the ground. Digging for the rage, he hauled himself to his feet and wheeled to meet the two attackers. Instead of two, there were eight now, and more were coming. He turned and ran.

Cayne had lost his horse, but had bought time for the boys. The first of them had reached the tree line, and they kept running into the darkness of the forest. He was glad the Navataw had not followed his plan, but where were they?

He ran. He wore the same armor as the Sarasins, but was still not used to running in it. Despite the weight of the armor, he caught up to the last of the fleeing boys. They were well short of the tree line. Looking backward, he saw two Sarasins hot on his heels, and scores more behind them. He was out of options. He couldn't pass the boys, or they'd be cut down. If he didn't pass them, *he* would be cut down. Just before reaching the boys, he spun around and attacked the two pursuing warriors.

He swung his sword in a wide arc at the man on his right, still running toward him, surprising him with the sudden attack. The blade buried itself in the warrior's neck. Blood erupted from the gash, and he fell to the ground.

The second Sarasin barreled down on him. Instead of a sword, Cayne took a shoulder to the chest. Cayne felt as though a raging bison had just stampeded into him, and he went flying backward. He tumbled, his head spinning. His eyes opened to the sun riding high in the sky. The Sarasin stood over him, sword in hand and sadistic smile on his face. Two more Sarasins pulled up next to him, others running past to pursue the boys.

A wooden wind whistled over him. The banded iron armor was primarily a defense for melee combat, but it also deflected arrows, if the angle was oblique or the distance was great. Unfortunately for the three Sarasins standing over him, neither of those conditions were true. In the blink of his eyes, arrows seemed to spring from the warriors, though he knew it was illusion. They fell backward to the ground.

More arrows sailed over him and into the mass of Sarasins running down the hill. Just off the road, Navataw warriors rose from tall grass. Cayne hadn't even noticed the grass. The Navataw numbered about fifty, and now each was hurling a tomahawk. They let out a war whoop, and then charged the surprised Sarasins.

Cayne rolled to his stomach and looked at the tree line. The boys were still running, but the Sarasins that had been chasing them were sedentary lumps on the road with arrows sticking out of them. More Navataw filtered out from the trees. They too let out a battle cry, and issued forth into the sunlight.

Swords crossed with iron clangs and men screamed. Navataw warriors trampled past him and up the hill.

"Up with you," Sir Harlen said. Cayne rolled over and took his hand. He pulled Cayne to his feet and looked him over. "You look no worse for the wear, but you can't go into battle wearing that armor." He looked to the battle raging on the hillside. "Wait here. Armor will be available soon." A contingent of Harlen's guards surrounded them. They all seemed eager to join the battle.

The din of crossed swords filled Cayne's ears, masking most of the screaming. Near the crest of the hill, a troop of Sarasins massed in a semi-orderly line. They let out a battle cry of their own and rolled down the hill to join the fray. Rogan walked casually behind them as though he was out for a leisurely stroll. At the very top of the hill Lord Darwan, remounted on his horse, watched the battle below, but made no move to join the combat. The Sarasin line slammed into the mass of Navataw, pushing the battle down the hill.

Harlen motioned to one of his men, who promptly sounded a horn. Several score of Navataw jumped up from the grasses on the exposed Sarasin right flank. They threw a volley of tomahawks and then charged into battle. Harlen turned to the warriors around him. "With me!" He raised his sword, and they charged into the battle, leaving Cayne alone to watch.

Two men carried a third to Cayne, lowering him to the ground. One of them looked to Cayne. "Sir Harlen sends his regards. Don the armor and join your kin in battle." They were both running back into the fighting before the words hit Cayne's ears.

The Navataw warrior on the ground was in his mid-twenties, but he'd age no more. Cayne wanted to know more of him, and he felt guilty for taking his armor, but he started doffing his Sarasin armor just the same.

With the battle raging paces away, Cayne swore at the armor. He tugged and yanked at the straps, but the ties were different from the Sarasin armor. He kept the Sarasin padded undergarment, as that would be hidden. Everything else he changed for the green-and-brown enameled Navataw armor. It was a tight fit, too short in the legs and narrow in the chest, but he was glad to be rid of the Sarasin garb.

By the time he fastened the last straps, the battle was nearly over. There were small pockets of fighting left. Most of the men from both sides lay on the ground. The moans of the dying were constant now, with the occasional sound of swordplay. It had happened so fast.

Cayne saw a single Navataw fighting two Sarasins, and he ran to help. He caught the Sarasins by surprise, his sword cracking one man's skull. The other Sarasin pushed his blade between the Navataw's bands of armor and shoved it deep in the warrior, who let out a guttural cry. To Cayne's astonishment, the Navataw pulled the sword deeper into himself, lunging at the Sarasin with his hands and biting his nose off. Cayne hit the Sarasin behind the knee, where there was no armor. Then he chopped the man in the neck, like a piece of wood. The Navataw gripped the Sarasin and the two men fell to the ground in a death embrace.

Sir Harlen kicked a staggering warrior, pulling his sword from the dying Sarasin. Harlen looked around, his eyes locking on Cayne with a nod, and then he turned to the remaining Sarasins. Only two of his guards remained.

A small group of Navataw remained fighting halfway up the hill. The Sarasins were reforming in two groups to pinch the Navataw between them. A dozen Navataw against thirty Sarasins.

Harlen waved for Cayne to follow, and started walking toward the last of his men. Two Sarasins stood in his way. The closest was barely standing, his arm hanging limply, the rest of him covered in blood. Harlen's guards attacked him from two sides. He never got his sword up to block the blows that killed him.

The second Sarasin walked easily toward Harlen, two swords at the ready, a broad smile on his face. *Rogan.* Harlen's guards ran out in front of him to engage Rogan.

Cayne hopped over the bodies strewn across the road, ignoring the fetid smell of blood, feces, and urine. Two men in front of him lay dying on the ground. They were still trying to kill one another. The Sarasin had gouged out the other's eyes, while the Navataw tightened his choking grip Sarasin's throat. Cayne tasted vomit, but kept it down. He was too far from Harlen, so he yelled his warning as loud as he could: "Sir Harlen, he's a Fayden Blade!"

Harlen looked back at Cayne and raised his sword. Cayne ran forward, hoping Harlen would wait for him, but the man turned toward Rogan.

Harlen's guards approached Rogan from two sides. He waited for them to attack, and then leaped to the side, dodging both attacks. His two swords flashed and struck one guard several times, blood casting off with each slash. He flung one man into the other and then pressed his attack. Cayne slipped on a patch of bloody dirt. He steadied himself right away, but when he looked back at the combat, both guards were falling amid a flurry of precise strikes.

Harlen ran at Rogan and swung his sword at Rogan's head. Rogan knocked the blow away and his two swords became a blur of violence. They struck Harlen in the legs, arms, and gut in fluid motion. Harlen grunted, but recovered to take another futile swing. Rogan landed a myriad of blows at Harlen's arm and shoulder, cleaving his right arm completely off.

Harlen screamed loud enough to cover the other sounds of suffering for a moment, but just for a moment. With no sword, Harlen tried to back away, but Rogan kicked him in the chest, sending him backwards, the arterial spray from his arm shooting like a fountain as he spun to the ground. Rogan looked past Harlen and right at Cayne. He smiled.

He stuck downward with his two swords into Harlen's chest, taking his time to ease the tips between the iron bands. Cayne was too late. The last of the Navataw had fallen to the Sarasins, and there were about twenty Sarasins left. They walked slowly down the hill toward him. Lord Darwan had finally left the safety of the hilltop, and his horse was trotting toward them as well.

"I knew it would end this way," Rogan said. He stepped over bodies and closed on Cayne. "Since you're the last, I can take my time and really enjoy the moment."

"Unless I kill you," Cayne said.

Rogan gave a hearty laugh.

"You've got a lot of blood on your hands."

"More than you know, boy." He stepped closer, twirling his swords.

"Do you think you're the hand of Dyn?" Cayne asked.

Rogan spit on the ground. "Piss on Dyn, your false god. All of your gods are frauds."

"Not wise to tempt the gods right before a fight." Cayne stepped toward him. It had to be now. Once the rest of the Sarasins reached him, he had no chance. *Why fool myself? I have no chance either way.*

"Any chance you'd bring my body back to Dahl Haven?" Cayne asked.

"No, I'll leave it here for the wolves and maggots."

Cayne took a deep breath and sprang forward. He put all of his strength and rage into the blow, but Rogan deflected it away, as if dismissing a child. Cayne gripped the sword tighter. His sweat-soaked hands made the leather wrap feel slippery. Rogan hadn't countered with anything except an infuriating smile.

"Come on, boy. You can do better."

Cayne swung upward, hoping to surprise him with the odd angle, but a quick turn of Rogan's sword sent Cayne and his sword off to his right side in disarray.

"Try again, boy."

"My name is *Cayne!*" he yelled, trying to assault Rogan with the sound of his voice. He turned and brought the sword back. He cut through nothing but air. This time Rogan answered Cayne's strike with a counter blow to his left shoulder.

Cayne's armor stopped the blade, but the force of the impact sent waves of pain across his back, causing him to drop to one knee. Rogan planted a boot in his side and shoved him to the ground. The concussion was enough to knock Cayne's sword from his hands. Cayne rolled onto his back and stared up at Rogan's smug face. "Just do it, then."

"Now, that's not fair. Get your sword and die like a man."

Cayne groped for his sword, never taking his eyes from Rogan. He took the sword and rolled to a knee, getting ready to spring up with a final attack. Rogan prepared to block the strike before Cayne even moved. His cocky smile disappeared in an instant, though, and confusion crossed his face. Rogan looked uncertain for the first time since Cayne had met him. He half-turned as a javelin slammed into his back, spitting blood from his chest as it popped through his breastplate.

Cayne wasted no time, surging up, putting his legs into the strike. He brought the sword up and connected with the protruding javelin head, wrenching it upward. Rogan groaned in agony and dropped both his swords. He looked to Cayne in utter hatred. His stare turned back to Darwan on his horse, another javelin in his hand.

Cayne considered Rogan dangerous whether he had a sword or not. He spun around and chopped into his neck. Rogan went face-forward to the ground. Just to be sure, Cayne found a seam in Rogan's armor and shoved his sword into his back. Rogan didn't move again.

Cayne looked up at Darwan. The Sarasin lord opened his mouth to speak, but then his whole body jolted upright and his stare went distant. Cayne backed away, but still Darwan paid him no mind. The other Sarasins, however, were splitting up into two groups and riding around Darwan's horse toward Cayne. They seemed confused about what their lord had just done, but they didn't let that stop them from pursuing the last Navataw standing.

Cayne hobbled back toward the trees. He had a short lead on them, but he didn't think it would last long. His eyes fixed on the road where it entered the forest, and he ran toward it. The darkness of the forest canopy obscured the road after only a short distance, but he swore it got lighter farther into the woods.

He heard the hoofs of approaching horses and the sound of peculiar metal rain; then the dark road became a fountain of light as a band of gleaming horsemen came charging out of the forest. They rode around Cayne on either side without slowing. He turned to watch them overrun the now-fleeing Sarasins. Cayne didn't know who they were, and he didn't care.

In the distance, Lord Darwan retreated beyond the crest of the hill while his men died. Cayne stumbled back up the hill, looking at the bodies. The gravity of his surroundings struck him, and he fell to his knees. He saw the scene as if through a remote lens, none of it feeling real. Hundreds of men lay around him, some still moaning, but most still and quiet. Insects and carrion birds were already flying to the feast. This morning these men had been alive, and now they were dead, Navataw and Sarasin alike.

"What happened here?" a voice above him demanded.

"A battle," Cayne said. He turned to see half a score of horsemen clad in shining white scale armor. "This was my fault."

The man talking to him gave Cayne a knowing nod and jumped off his horse. He put his hand on Cayne's shoulder, luckily the one that didn't hurt. "You're Navataw, judging by your armor."

"No. I mean, yes. It's a long story."

The gleaming horseman turned away and addressed his men. "Jaks, take two men and scout the road. The rest of you prepare a funeral pyre, a big one." He turned back to Cayne. "Now, why don't you tell me that story?"

Cayne told him a shortened version; not knowing this armored horseman, he left out many of the sensitive details. He stated the main points, as he remembered them, but his thoughts were jumbled and he had to change the order several times. The horseman listened intently to the whole story. After Cayne finished speaking, he pondered silently for a time, until the three men returned and reported. They had only seen a lone rider, too far ahead to catch, but no other Sarasins.

They men called him 'First Sword,' and Cayne decided to use that title as well. "First Sword, everything I've told you is true," he insisted.

"I don't doubt you, son. The boys we found gave us the same general story, but without the details you had."

"They're all right?"

The First Sword nodded. "We told them to wait in the trees. We'll camp here tonight and return to Rivermar tomorrow. From there, I'll take you to King Alarak. He'll want to talk with you about what you've seen."

Cayne's mind swooned: another king. Mother had said King Alarak had slaughtered most of his family; King Arta Nakis had seen to finishing the job. He didn't feel the same hatred for Alarak as he did for Arta Nakis. Perhaps the Sarasin's atrocity, being more recent and against people he knew and loved, made it more worthy of his rage. Still, he felt he *should* hate Alarak.

The boys came out of the forest. He counted thirteen in all, but only four Dahl Haven boys were among them. He found the bodies of Bale and Boon at the top of the hill. They must have died in the first moments of the massacre.

He occupied his hands gathering dry brush with the other boys. The horsemen dragged dozens of fallen trees out into the grassy expanse at the base of the hill. They piled the bodies on them, not bothering to strip them of any belongings.

The Sarasins were thorough killers, having left none of the Navataw alive. Two score Sarasins still struggled for life; half died before the pyres were completed, and none would survive the night.

He carried Bale and Boon to the pyre, but set them down short of it. He knelt next to them and opened their fists. They each clutched a metal bead: one silver, one copper. Cayne shook his head and took the beads. He looked up to see the First Sword standing over him. He wore a dark cloak that covered most of his armor. In spots, the armor was visible, and it glittered in the firelight.

"You had a difficult day," the First Sword said. "But you saved those boys today."

"Not all of them." Cayne turned back to the two small bodies.

"You did what you could." The First Sword put a fatherly hand on Cayne's shoulder. "You can't hold yourself responsible for the rest. The Sarasins were responsible."

"It was *my* plan."

"You acted to save them," the First Sword said.

Cayne ignored his words and opened his hand, showing him the beads. "These two fought over these beads from the moment we left Dahl Haven. They'd probably want to be burned with them."

"Who gets the silver?"

"It doesn't matter," Cayne said. "I could never tell them apart." He tried to laugh, but it came out as a more of a whimper.

The First Sword dug into a small sack he wore on his waist and pulled out a string of beads. He untied the knot and handed Cayne a silver bead.

Cayne began to object, but settled on a simple nod of thanks. He put a silver bead each into the right hands of the two boys and closed their fists. Then he carried them to an unlit pyre.

Cayne watched as Jaks lit the pyre. The brush caught quickly, and soon an inferno of flames danced high into the twilight sky. The pleasant smell of burning wood filled the air, but was soon overwhelmed by the smells of burning flesh and hair. *More smells I will never forget.* "What will happen to us now?" he asked aloud.

"We'll make arrangements for the boys to sail to Black Rock," the First Sword said. "From there, they'll have to make their way home as best they can."

"They're just boys," Cayne said. "How can they make it home alone?"

"There is much suffering in our kingdom. At least they have a chance to find their way home." When Cayne kept shaking his head, the First Sword added, "I'll see what I can do to get them an escort."

"What about me?" Cayne asked.

"We need swords."

"Then I am to fight?"

Burke nodded to him.

"I'll get the chance to kill Sarasins?"

The First Sword nodded again.

"Good."

Chapter Twenty-Seven

Darwan pushed his horse ever faster. After so many days of walking at the pace of marching soldiers, his horse was eager to gallop. As sunlight faded, the low clouds conspired to block the starlight and rising moon. He had to slow the horse to a walk.

He still felt the Red coursing through his veins. It gave him incredible prowess, but he was a slave to its whims. It had goaded him to release the recruits, though mostly to antagonize Rogan. Even the Red was shocked when Rogan had ordered them executed. True, they were just peasants, but Darwan had enough blood on his conscience.

Today's atrocity belonged to Rogan, and no other. Perhaps it was Cayne's fault too. Darwan might have stopped the carnage if the boy hadn't knocked him from his horse. In any case, Rogan got his just reward.

I killed my own First Sword. No—the Red was responsible for that. It wasn't me. The Red had hated Rogan. But even then, he'd only lanced him with the javelins. Cayne had administered the killing blow.

But he had to do it. The king had ordered him to deliver Cayne to the enemy, and he couldn't do that if Rogan killed the boy. So once again, it wasn't Darwan's fault; Arta Nakis was to blame. It was the king's ridiculous plan, and Rogan had to die to accomplish it. The Red marveled disapprovingly at Darwan's ability to shirk responsibility for his actions.

His horse tensed, and he sensed the same danger. Darwan smelled the bestial breath before he saw them.

A pack of wolves stalked toward him. Darwan let a dark smile form on his face. The Red would enjoy this, however it turned out. He wondered if the wolves would feel the effects of the pyrus if they fed on his body.

He checked his sword and his javelins. He'd left one impaled in Rogan, so only two remained on the right side of his saddle. The left side held three more. He took them, two in his left hand and one in his right. They felt like bolts of ice in his hands.

He urged his horse to a trot, the wolves coming into clear view. There were seven wolves. He veered to the right, closing on the nearest one. The javelin pierced the wolf and drove into the ground, fixing the dead beast in its spot. The others sensed the danger and leaped forward. He tasted their surprise, but they lacked fear. *They should be afraid.*

Despite the darkness, despite the speed of the wolves, and despite being on a wavering horse, the Red surged, and Darwan's iron darts flew true. Another wolf died with a whimper, and then another. Three javelins and three dead wolves. The final four faltered. While they hesitated, Darwan jumped from his horse, sword in hand, eyes burning.

On his own feet, he felt free from the awkward movements of the horse. He almost laughed at the foolish lunge of the first beast. His sword beat it aside, slicing open its belly. The Red pulsed through Darwan, but there seemed to be something else there, something he'd not felt before with the pyrus. Perhaps it was bloodlust.

And lust he had. He ran at a pair of wolves. The smaller bounded to the attack and died. The larger one held back, circling Darwan. It had mottled gray fur that made it look old. Darwan lowered his sword, and it jumped to the attack. Darwan breezed aside from the attack and his blade halved, then quartered the beast.

The last wolf was the largest, and it stood its ground, growling at Darwan. This wolf was different from the others. It was more aware, more confident, more deadly. *This is not a wolf,* he realized. Darwan had never seen a skinwalker before, yet he knew with absolute certainty that this *was* one. In his spirit, he felt the truth of it. There was no doubt. It was a Fayden Form, a human able to take the form of a beast.

They stared at each other, but neither moved. Darwan felt a struggle between the Red and another burning feeling in his gut, a desire to let this fayden live. The skinwalker, too, seemed less inclined to fight, its teeth no longer bared. He lowered his sword, and the beast sat, eyes still locked on Darwan.

After a long moment, it turned away, loping back into the darkness. The Red hated him for not killing the beast. "You'll have to find a new pack," Darwan called out.

He recovered his javelins and looked for his horse. It was gone; Darwan saw no trace of it in the darkness. Though he had no visible landmarks, he could feel the presence of Rayl Goth to the south, so he turned west on the road. Darwan sheathed his sword and kept a javelin in each hand, tossing the others aside.

Running through the night, Darwan paused only to drink from the infrequent steams and ponds near the road. The Red drained away after midnight, and he had to slow his pace to a jog. He resisted the urge to take a cube of pyrus, and decided to rest until daybreak.

He awoke while it was still night. The clouds had retreated, and the shimmering moon silvered the land. A hulking form ambled toward him. The ground shook as it neared, the horns of a tankadon glinting in the moonlight. It smelled of strong oil, and Darwan knew it was in musth. They normally traveled in herds, but males in musth were too aggressive to stay in a herd. Darwan rose to his feet, gripping the two javelins. Not even a perfect strike would do any good against the thick hide of a tankadon. He had to hit the eye, and even then, the angle needed to be perfect to penetrate to its small brain. He needed the pyrus, but there was no time for it.

The bull charged and Darwan leaped out of the way, throwing a javelin. He heard it deflect off the bony frill and saw a flash of light as it fell to the ground. The bull charged fast in a straight line, but it struggled to turn around. Darwan ran to keep himself behind the beast, and away from those long horns. He got too close, and the flailing tail lashed out at him. He sensed the blow coming, but without the Red he wasn't fast enough to avoid it.

It felt like being hit with a mountain, knocking every bit of breath from his lungs. Darwan flew through the air and skidded across the ground. He lost sight of the tankadon, his vision obscured by bright, spinning stars. The ground shook as the tankadon tramped toward him.

A nimble wolf ran at him from the other direction. It leaped right over him and bounded toward the tankadon. The wolf let out a menacing growl, and the tankadon answered with a trumpet blast. Neither call signaled fear.

Darwan cleared his head and rose to a knee. His chest heaved. His armor had a dent where the tankadon's tail had struck it. He felt for his last javelin, finding it a few steps away.

His sight returned, and he staggered toward the melee. The tankadon was turning in circles, trying to get at the wolf on its back. It seemed unconcerned with Darwan now. It would pay for its indifference. The wolf rode the beast, its claws gripping the hard skin, its teeth sunk into the shoulder behind the frill. The tankadon seemed to sense the futility of trying to reach the wolf, even as it failed to realize that it was in little danger from the wolf's relatively small teeth and claws.

Darwan gripped the javelin and ran up to the bull from the side, careful to avoid the horns and the tail. He stayed glued to the bull's right side as it turned. It stopped for a moment, and Darwan seized the opportunity. He swung the javelin like a dagger, gripping the leather wrap as tight as he could. Darwan saw the eye and aimed for it. The javelin pierced the eye easily, with a faint sloshing noise, and then struck solid bone. The beast trumpeted so loudly Darwan's ears must have started bleeding. He left the javelin embedded in the eye and tried to stay with the thrashing beast. It turned and stamped on the ground, trying to get at Darwan now. He stayed to the side of the beast, just behind the armored frill.

He drew his sword and plunged it into the soft neck behind the frill. The bull thundered out another trumpet call. Darwan gave another hard shove on the sword hilt, and the blade slid farther into the neck. Then he shoved up on the hilt, pushing it vertically inside the neck. Blood gushed from the wound, and the bull tankadon stumbled to the ground, one leg buckling under the strain.

Darwan put all of his weight on the hilt, driving it down this time. The tankadon collapsed with a weak trumpet blast. Darwan worked the sword deeper, twisting and angling it around, and then pulled it out. Without the sword to hinder the flow, the wound bled like a river.

Darwan withdrew to a safe distance. The wolf still rode on the back of the tankadon, growling and tearing with its teeth. The bull made faint rumblings between labored breaths that became softer and less frequent. It let out one last, rumbling breath and was quiet.

Darwan stood, breathing heavily. He'd lost sight of the wolf and was searching the night for it when a soft voice said from the darkness, "It was good hunting with you."

Darwan turned to the voice and saw the outline of a woman. *I know her.* It was the skinwalker he'd encountered earlier. He wasn't sure how he knew that, but he did. He kept his sword ready, though he felt no danger. Other than the glistening layer of blood, she wore nothing. Darwan had no clothing to offer her.

"I need no clothes," she said firmly. "I only took this form to talk."

"You're a skinwalker," Darwan stated.

"And you have a keen grasp of the obvious," she said. "You killed my pack."

"Are you seeking revenge? Why save me, then?"

She didn't answer.

"Were you following me?" Darwan asked, "Or were you hunting me?"

"I'm not sure. My pack attacked you, and you defended yourself. It is the way of things."

Darwan discerned little about her in the dim light. Her voice sounded young, but defiant. She was shorter than he expected. Despite being covered in blood, he perused her naked form. "One of my pack tried to mount me," she said in a knowing voice. "He was the big wolf. The one with mottled gray patches on his stomach and only one testicle."

Well, that broke Darwan's mood. He thought of more practical matters. The horns of the tankadon were valuable; he should take those. He would have liked to get a meal from the kill, but he had no fire.

"I never dreamed to take down such a creature, not even with my whole pack to help me," the woman continued.

Darwan edged over to the lifeless carcass and hacked off the horns with his sword. Then he tried his best to separate a leg, but the armored skin was like seasoned leather. As he labored, he saw a light. The bloodied woman had made a campfire from sticks.

He cut away a piece of leg muscle and brought it to the fire. She stuck the meat on a stick and put it near the growing fire.

"I haven't had cooked meat like this in a long time," she said. "My father and I used to eat like this when we were out making charcoal."

"You're good with fire," Darwan said. "I'm sure you could have made a fire to cook your meat."

"My pack liked their meat raw. They also didn't like me in this form."

"I can't imagine why." He was purposely ambiguous in his tone. Darwan mapped her body in the light, noting that she was pretty in a rustic kind of way, though she had several nasty scars on her back and legs. He guessed she was of marrying age, and his thoughts turned more amorous again. Then he thought about her changing back to a wolf and biting off treasured parts of his anatomy, and the carnal thoughts dissipated.

"Where are you going?" she asked.

"Walla."

"I was born there. I can take you there, if you like."

"This road doesn't go anywhere except Walla."

"I wasn't offering to lead you, I was offering you a ride."

He thought of riding a wolf, and it seemed ridiculous. Her wolf form was big, but not that big. He dismissed the thought, and she said nothing more about it.

They ate tankadon meat until they could stomach no more. As the morning sun crept up over the horizon, they walked together to the road. Carrion birds and small animals were homing in on the tankadon carcass.

"So, do you want to mount me?" she asked, without the slightest hint of innuendo.

"I've never seen a man ride a wolf."

"I didn't mean mount me as a wolf," she said.

Darwan stopped and tried to assess her intention. She wasn't flirting.

"Stupid men," she said, reading his thoughts again and rolling her eyes. "How can you not know about skinwalkers? I was with the tankadon when it died a violent death."

Darwan still didn't understand what she was alluding to, so he shrugged and waited.

"Skinwalkers can take the forms of those that they kill. And I thought *I* was the most ignorant fayden around."

Her body exploded—or at least, that was the best description Darwan could come up with. Her legs shrank and puffed out. She doubled over on all fours, and her bulk expanded like a dry sponge in water. In a moment, he was standing next to a full-grown tankadon. He stepped back instinctively. The beast waited and motioned with its head.

Darwan shrugged and climbed onto the tankadon. It was far from comfortable, but he sat, legs spread wide, and held onto the frill like the horn of a saddle. She took several pensive steps forward, swaying to one side before stopping. The second effort was smoother, and after a few more tries, she managed a steady gait. It wasn't the full gallop of a horse, or even a trot, but it was faster than he could jog.

She kept the pace for short intervals, stopping occasionally to graze on tall grasses by the roadside. By midmorning, Walla was on the horizon. She stopped and motioned for him to dismount. Darwan jumped off, straightened his clothes, and turned to see the same naked woman, this time covered in dust instead of blood.

"This is as far as I go," she said.

"You were born here. Surely they would remember you."

She shook her head. "Oh, they remember me all right. I went back right after I discovered I had a fayden. I had little control at that time. I turned into a wolf in the middle of the town green," she said, a look of longing on her face. "They chased me away."

"Very well, then," he said with a strange regret. "You never told me your name. Mine is Darwan." It was probably the first time he'd left off his title when introducing himself.

"My name is Faylin, but I have your scent now. You won't see me again." She turned and became a wolf. She sped off with remarkable speed and disappeared into the high grass.

Darwan turned to the village, wondering how to explain all this to the king. In the span of a week he'd lost his entire warband, and gotten the king's favorite consort killed by one of his own men. The only thing that went right was delivering that boy to the Crotans. He looked back toward the open field. *I should have gone with her.*

Chapter Twenty-Eight

Cayne stared out the second-story window of the Sleeping Gaitan Inn. He'd never stayed at an inn before, but the First Sword had insisted they stay there with him and his men. The other boys were crammed into a single room, but Cayne got a private room.

He poked at the strange material in the window. It was glass, and he could see right through it. He'd heard of such windows, but he'd never actually seen one. All the windows in Dahl Haven were just holes in the walls with shutters around them. There was something unsettling and constricting about these windows.

He hoped Tarken had made it home, though he wanted to talk with him more than anything. Tarken was the closest thing to family Cayne had now.

Turning to the bed, Cayne tried to remember how long it had been since he'd any real sleep. He walked halfway to the bed but paused, feeling a sudden twitch. He turned back to the window and then jumped back to the bed. Markas stood an arm's reach away.

"Apologies. It's sometimes quite hard not to have that effect on people. My name is Markas."

"I know," Cayne said. "We've met."

"I'm never sure who's met me."

"You warned me. You knew what was going to happen to my family!" Cayne found himself shouting as his nails dug into his palms. "Why didn't you tell me? I could have stopped it. I could have changed everything!" Instead of sending fists at Markas, Cayne felt tears in his eyes. "Why?"

Markas' own eyes were full of tears. "I cannot change what has already happened."

"It hadn't happened yet! You knew."

"It's hard to explain," Markas said, wringing his hands.

Cayne's tears faded, and he felt the rage return. He stepped away from the bed toward Markas, getting right in his face. "Try."

"I don't know what I told you."

"What?"

"I haven't said it yet."

Cayne stepped back from Markas, confused. He wanted to ask a question, but he couldn't form one.

"Do you know what a Fayden is?" Markas asked.

Cayne took another step backwards, looking for a handy weapon, but the room was bare. His sword leaned by the door, and Markas was in between him and it. Cayne said, "I've known two Faydens. One was crazy, and the other was... crazy. A Fayden Sight and a Fayden Blade."

"A Blade," Markas said, shaking his head. "They aren't very well behaved yet, are they?"

Cayne shook his head, still looking for a useful weapon. "What are you?"

"I'm a mystic, a Fayden Fate."

Cayne shrugged.

"Not familiar with my kind? Few know of us. Have you heard of a Fayden Step?"

"Travelers? Yes, they can travel great distances in an instant."

"A mystic is much like that, but we travel in time, not space."

Cayne sat on the bed, his mind spinning.

"I'm like the Fayden Sight," Markas said. "But while they see visions of the future, I know it as fact, for it's my history."

"You knew exactly what would happen to my family."

"I cannot change what has already happened in my past. My fayden would not allow it."

"Then what's the point?" Cayne asked. He struggled to keep up with the conversation. *Gods, I need Tarken now.* "Why are you here, if you can't change anything?"

"I'm not here to change history. I'm here to ensure it."

"That makes no sense," Cayne said, shaking his head. "You should talk with my friend Tarken. He might understand."

"I have," Markas said, sitting on the bed next to Cayne.

"You mean you *will*?" Cayne said, a happy connection forming in his mind.

"From your perspective, yes."

"I get it. Your past is my future," Cayne said, smiling. "That means Tarken made it back to Dahl Haven."

Markas nodded. "I met him long ago. He's a very wise man."

"Yes, he is," Cayne said. "How did you get in my room?"

"I rented this room after you departed and then I did what mystics do."

Cayne shook his head again and laughed lightly. "Are you really here, or am I imagining you?"

Markas turned to Cayne and slapped him on the cheek. "Was that real enough for you?" Cayne jerked his head back and stared in surprise at Markas, who was chuckling. Cayne stated to laugh himself in spite of his stinging face.

"Sorry about that," Markas said, though he didn't seem very sorry. "I did have your permission to do that, though."

"Yeah, that sounds like me. We're friends, then?"

"I count you as my friend, and mystics have few friends. I cannot change what has happened and what will happen, however." He patted his chest. "Faydens live within us and control us to some degree. My fayden would not allow me to say something that might change what must happen."

"It's alive?"

"In a manner of speaking, yes. It's like two souls living in a single body."

Cayne wondered what it would be like to have another voice yelling in his head. He let out a breath. "If you can't change anything, then why bother trying?"

"You misunderstand. There are points in time where the true path may deviate, when people have choices. My history tells what choices you've made, but that doesn't mean you'll make that choice. That is our job. We make sure that you, and others like you, make the right choices, proceed down the right paths, keep history on its true course."

"Sounds like a crappy job."

"Sometimes." Markas looked at his feet. "My time is short. I sense the movement coming." Markas reached out for Cayne's arm, clasping it at the forearm. "Mind your words. Dangerous men abound."

Cayne returned the clasp, felt the squeeze on his arm, and then—nothing. Markas was gone, as though he'd never been there. Cayne felt his cheek, still sore from the slap.

He put on his sword and his weathered satchel. Making his way through the dimly lit hallway, he headed for the noise in the main room. He looked across the many tables and patrons until he saw the First Sword drinking with several men.

The First Sword stood. "Cayne. We were just talking about you. Sit." He grabbed a chair from another table and motioned to the barkeeper for a drink. Cayne sat, glancing around the table. Two of the men wore the same white armor as the First Sword, but the other two wore Navataw armor. The barkeeper reached over Cayne's shoulder and set down a tankard of beer with froth running down the sides.

"I was telling your story," the First Sword said.

"We were very interested," the older Navataw said gravely. "I sent Sir Harlen along the road with very specific orders. He didn't follow them."

Cayne fidgeted in his seat. He took a short sip of beer, and was glad to discover it was *real* beer, not the Sarasins' field brew swill. "What are your questions?"

The younger Navataw leaned forward. "Is that how you address your betters? Remember your place, farmer." Though younger than the other, he was at least ten years older than Cayne.

Cayne lowered his eyes and said, "Forgive me, sir, I meant no disrespect." He turned to the older man. "Sir, what questions can I answer?"

The younger man blew out a snort. "Address your answers to me. I am Lord Enigo of Manteo." He gestured to the older man. "Sir Warrek is one of my shieldmen. He asks his questions on my behalf."

Cayne avoided eye contact with everyone at the table. The informal mood of the previous night was gone. Everything felt tense and proper.

Warrek cleared his throat and said, "Sir Harlen had explicit orders *not* to force an engagement, and to report any contact with the Sarasins. He did neither of those. Why?"

Cayne struggled to remember what he'd told the First Sword. Had he told him about his meeting with Sir Harlen? Apparently, Harlen hadn't sent any messages about it. These Navataw were exactly the men his mother and Markas had warned him about.

"Do you have an answer?" Enigo demanded.

"I don't know," Cayne said, still not making eye contact.

"All those warriors. And only you survived," Warrek said. "You were with the Sarasins, and yet you wear Navataw armor."

Cayne sensed there was a question, but Sir Warrek had a way of talking that made it hard to tell if he was asking a question or stating a fact. Cayne shifted in his chair and took a long sip of beer, hoping someone else would start talking.

"Boy, can you explain yourself?" Enigo asked. "Why do you wear Navataw armor?"

"I switched during the battle, my lord. I didn't want to be mistaken for a Sarasin."

Lord Enigo stood up, his leg knocking the table and spilling the drinks. "I've heard enough. While my men were dying, you decide to strip the armor off a dead Navataw warrior. Despicable!" He looked around the room. It was silent and all eyes turned to him. "Take it off!"

Cayne unfastened the straps. He felt like everyone in the room was laughing at him, but it was utterly quiet and every expression was solemn. The only sound was the clank of armor as he dropped pieces to the floor.

Lord Enigo stood watching, fidgeting as though Cayne wasn't going fast enough for him. "The tunic, too."

Cayne took off the tunic and was left with nothing but his breeches. His thickly muscled body was on display for the entire room, but he felt ashamed and weak.

Lord Enigo turned to Sir Warrek. "Collect the armor. I'll waste no more time on this dolt. If I ever see him wearing Navataw armor again, I'll kill him myself." He didn't give Cayne a further glance as he exited the inn.

The patrons turned back to their drinks, and the low murmur returned. Cayne turned to walk away, but Sir Warrek's hand shot out and grabbed him by the forearm. "Sit," Warrek said, his tone firm.

Cayne pulled his arm away, then remembered that this was a table full of titled men. He sat, his eyes on the floor.

"Sir Harlen was kin to me," Warrek said. "I would know more of his last battle."

"The Sarasins were killing all the children. Sir Harlen's men surprised them." They listened intently as Cayne spoke. "I fell from my horse. I would have died, if not for Sir Harlen. He was the one who told me to take off the Sarasin armor and put on the Navataw armor, so they wouldn't mistake me for a Sarasin."

"No," Warrek said. "Harlen sees the Sarasins killing children and then saves one of the Sarasins? It makes no sense."

"I'm from Dahl Haven. I was scouting the night before, and Sir Harlen's men captured me. I told him about the Sarasins. We planned the trap."

"You didn't mention that detail to me," the First Sword commented, his expression turning suspicious. "What else did you leave out?"

Cayne shouted out in his mind. It was hard to remember what he'd told the First Sword and what he hadn't. "I was confused after the battle. I didn't mean to forget things, but my thoughts were muddled."

The First Sword gave him the same skeptical look his father would have if he were here. The look was so much like his father that Cayne paused in introspection.

"Perhaps if you'd mentioned that Sir Harlen told you to don the Navataw Armor," the First Sword said, "Lord Enigo would not have been so harsh."

"Lord Enigo is not his father," Warrek said, shaking his head. "He's new to his lordship. His father died recently. One of the sicknesses sweeping the camp."

"Sicknesses?" asked the First Sword.

Warrek nodded grimly. "There are many. We were glad to get this post. The camp is crowded and supplies are running short."

Cayne watched the men exchange knowing looks and waited for them to look back at him. He took a deep breath and continued, "I talked with Sir Harlen, and he said his men could handle the Sarasins, so we planned a trap for them. It didn't go as we planned."

"It seldom does in war," the First Sword said.

"That's the part I don't understand," Warrek said, rubbing his chin. "Harlen knew his orders. He should have sent a messenger to me and pulled back to Rivermar. I can't understand why he did the complete opposite."

"Perhaps he thought he needed every sword for the coming battle," the First Sword offered. "As it turned out, he did."

"Maybe he didn't want to send word until he had confirmed the information," Jaks said, leaning into the conversation for the first time.

"Perhaps," Warrek said. "Perhaps he was unwilling to take the word of a farm boy." He seemed slightly satisfied, but still suspicious. "Did you see him fall?"

Cayne nodded. "He was the last to fall. He was killed by a Fayden Blade."

In unison, the men around the table sat back in their chairs. They glanced at each other, and then back at Cayne.

"A Fayden Blade?" the First Sword asked. "Another detail you forgot."

"Harlen was a good swordsman," Warrek said. "It will comfort his family to know it took a Blade to lay him low."

"The Sarasins had a Blade in their army," Jaks said. "Surprising. I didn't think they could get along with anyone, let alone conform to army life."

"How exactly did you survive combat with a Blade?" Warrek asked, his eyes narrowing on Cayne.

Cayne shifted in his seat. "He would have killed me too, but Lord Darwan hit him with a javelin."

"A Sarasin lord killed his own warrior to save you?" Warrek asked incredulously.

"I thought he was trying to let me escape their army. Or it may have been because I saved his life." The men looked at him with increasingly disbelieving scowls. "A drak ambushed Lord Darwan, but I attacked before it could strike him."

The silence and stares traveled out from the table. The entire room went quiet, and all eyes turned to him. Low, worried mumbles radiated around the room. The First Sword alone was unsurprised. Apparently, he hadn't shared Cayne's story with anyone else.

"Did you say *drak*?" Jaksasked.

"He's lying," the third man of the Fist said. Cayne remembered his name as Yenevas. "The Drakken haven't been seen this far south in centuries."

"My lands are close to the Black Hills," Warrek said. "And I've never seen a drak. The Tushko people talk about raids by the Drakken, but they don't venture any farther south."

"He's heard too many fables," Yenevas scoffed. "He's making all this up. Maybe he got hit in the head."

"I'd never seen one of the Drakken," Cayne said. "But that was what they called it. I don't really know if it was one or not."

"The Sarasins had a drak in their army?" Yenevas asked. The First Sword put his arms behind his head and smiled, waiting for Cayne to clarify.

"No, we found them in Rayl Goth."

Again the room went silent, the fear replaced by disbelief. Snorts rang across the room, and most of the onlookers waved hands at him in dismissal. Their discussion regained a sense of privacy as the patrons went back to their own conversations.

"And now he went to the Rayl Goth," Yenevas said. "No one goes there."

Cayne described the city as he remembered it: the arcing black city walls, the deathly quiet, the neatly laid out section of the city, and the uhkanuwa mount. He looked around, trying to see if anyone believed him. They didn't. He told them of the ghants, and even how Rogan had killed the Lady Margella.

"You can't believe him," Yenevas said. "He's a Sarasin spy sent to give us false information and start rumors."

"He could just be delusional," Jaks said.

"I think you're right," the First Sword said to Yenevas. "But I don't think he was witting of it." He turned to Cayne. "Tell me again how you became the steward for this Sarasin lord."

Cayne recounted their failed escape and the duel with Zane and Rogan. Then he told them of the war council and Arta Nakis.

"The gods watch over you," Warrek said with a hint of sarcasm. "Saved in battle twice, a lone survivor, and matched in a duel with a drunken soldier. If you'd drawn the Fayden Blade in the duel, you'd be dead instead of your friend."

"Tarken is better now. I used some angelia berries on him and they healed his wounds."

"I've had enough of this," Yenevas said, getting up from his chair. "You can waste your time listening to this fable. I have better things to do."

The other men drew back from the table.

"I'm telling you the truth."

"I want to believe you," the First Sword said, "but listen to your story. Drakken, Rayl Goth, ghants, Fayden Blades, and angelia fruit."

"It's like something out of a bard's tale," Jaks said.

"And we have nothing but your word," Warrek said.

"Convenient," Yenevas said. "There isn't anyone who can confirm your story."

Cayne bit his lip. He looked at them and tried to stare them into believing him. Reaching for his satchel, he fumbled with the contents, until he felt the bundle of cloth. He pulled it out and set it on the table. Cayne stared at them again, but this time with a look of daring.

The First Sword reached out and grabbed an end of the cloth, and gingerly lifted it. He uncovered several white Angelia fruits. Yenevas fell back into his seat. The First Sword put the cloth back over the fruits, then scanned the room to see if anyone else had seen it.

"Are those what I think they are?" Warrek asked. "I've never seen one."

"I may not have ever seen the streets of Rayl Goth," the First Sword said. "But I've seen an angelia fruit before—just one." He turned to Cayne, a new respect in his expression. "So let's say everything you've said is true. I still think they used you to pass faulty information. You were never in the Sarasin army. You were a prisoner."

Jaks reached into the cloth and fondled one of the small berries with his fingers. "Surely the Sarasins searched you. Where did you manage to hide these?"

"You really don't want to know," Cayne said dryly.

Jaks abruptly let go of the fruit and wiped his hands on the table.

"Some information is certain," the First Sword said. "The Sarasins were in Walla less than a week ago. Whatever direction they're moving doesn't matter. They're behind us and we must move to meet them, wherever they are."

Two Navataw warriors burst into the room and searched until they saw Sir Warrek. He stood as they approached. Both men bowed their heads and pounded their right hands on their chests.

"Sir Warrek, Lord Enigo requires your presence."

Warrek nodded to them. "I'll be along directly." The two warriors bowed their heads again and rushed out the door. "Cayne, I wish to speak with you further about Harlen. I think there may be more to your story, but for now, I have duties." He turned to Jaks and took his arm. "Sir Jaks." He exchanged regards with Yenevas and then took the First Sword's arm. "Sir Burke."

Hearing his brother's name shocked Cayne. His thoughts turned inward. He relived that awful day half a dozen times in a matter of moments. When he looked up, Warrek was gone.

Burke turned to Jaks. "You'll escort the boys to Black Rock and use your contacts there to arrange for their safe passage home."

"Me? Mind a bunch of children?" Jaks protested.

"Yes. You'll need to leave your armor. It would not be well received in Black Rock. We'll keep it safe until your return."

Jaks was still shaking his head.

"These are our people, our children," Burke said. "It's important, and I'm not choosing you because you are the least of us, but because you're the best of us."

After a few moments, Jaks nodded, and a look of determination settled on his face. "I will do this and then return to the Fist at Barons Lodge. I'll see to the arrangements immediately." They exchanged arm clasps, and then Jaks left.

Burke got up and nodded to Yenevas, who had resumed his brooding disposition. He nodded back at Burke, but just stared at Cayne. Burke pointed to the door. "You. Cayne. Walk with me."

Cayne put the angelia fruits back in his satchel under Yenevas's sour gaze. He followed Burke out of the inn. Torches lit the town green with a mellow orange glow, but Burke gleamed with a pure white light from his armor. He threw on a cloak, but pockets of light still twinkled from the gaps and folds. "You should get some sleep," Burke said.

"Your name is Burke."

"You should call me First Sword, or Sir Burke."

"My brother's name was Burke."

"The one who died?"

"One of the two murdered by Arta Nakis," Cayne corrected.

Burke nodded solemnly. "How old was your brother?"

"Fifteen."

"Burke is a common Crotan name, but you have the Navataw look to you. Was your brother named after someone?"

"A friend of my father's, but I never met him. They said he lived far away."

"Your family came from elsewhere," Burke said, turning to Cayne with new interest. He studied him again, deep suspicion returning to his gaze. "Where? Navataw lands? What was your father's name?"

Cayne felt cornered and alone. Sir Burke's questions had a sense of urgency to them. Sweat trickled down Cayne's back. He wanted to stop the conversation, but Sir Burke showed no signs of relenting. Cayne sighed and muttered, "Nataniel."

Burke stepped back, his eyes darting. Cayne could almost see the thoughts rushing through his head, but Burke's expression was unreadable. "Your mother was Silya," Burke stated, and Cayne nodded. Now Burke let out the sigh. "Somehow, I always knew this day would come."

"Did you know my parents?" Cayne said, in the most innocent voice he could manage.

"In a manner of speaking. I was the one who killed them."

Chapter Twenty-Nine

With entrenched sentry posts on the main road and a veritable city of tents covering the fields, Darwan knew the full army was camped around Walla. He passed the guards along the road and made his way to the town hall. The guards had told him the king was holding another war council. They'd given him odd looks for both his dress and the burden he carried over his shoulders.

Arta Nakis and his three sons sat at a long table surrounded by their lords. Despite making a quiet entry, Darwan drew every eye in the room. Though he'd hoped to make his report in a less public way, they had seen him now. They wore polished armor, and he wished he'd taken the time to clean himself off, but it was too late for that too. His armor was covered in streaks of blood and caked in dirt. He couldn't imagine what his face looked like. Shrugging, Darwan strode forward and tossed his burden onto the floor in front of the king. The three horns clattered in a jumble. He bowed to the king and said, "With my compliments. I ran across a tankadon last night."

The king raised a questioning eyebrow, and Darwan took it as an invitation.

"My warband marched east and was ambushed by Navataw, judging by the dress." That surprised Arta Nakis, and he made no effort to disguise it. "We were outnumbered, but my men fought well. In the end, I was the last man standing." No one seemed as impressed as Darwan thought they should be. "I spared the life of our oblivious spy, so he might deliver what he knows to King Alarak, as Your Majesty ordered."

"Why did the Navataw attack you?" Prince Varthan asked from his seat to the right of Arta Nakis. "Or did you attack *them*?"

"Prince Varthan, they gave no reason, and I left none alive to tell me." Varthan was the king's firstborn. Just now reaching manhood, he was a brute.

Arta Nakis treated his boys like a team. Keeping the throne was Varthan's job. Any Sarasin lord could challenge the king to single combat; that was how Arta Nakis rose to the throne in the first place. Varthan had trained in combat ever since he could hold a stick, and now, as a man, he beat his sparring partners with merciless abandon. He was the power behind the trio, the enforcer.

Next to Varthan was Kaan, the second son. Arta Nakis had groomed him to lead the armies, teaching him the maxims of war, including the importance of supplies, logistics, and communications. Last was Pevane. In him, Arta Nakis had put the prosperity of the kingdom, sending him to neighboring kingdoms and faraway lands to learn the arts of economics and trade.

Unfortunately for Arta Nakis, his sons utterly detested one another, and vied for power in endless plots and contests. They didn't challenge each other directly, instead using subterfuge and indirect attacks to undercut each other. Wise lords gave them a wide berth, and Darwan considered himself one of those lords.

"This does not seem right," Queen Tabila said. She was the only woman in the room. "Why would the Navataw attack us?"

"Darwan, matters have changed since you left," Arta Nakis said. "Our disposition is much improved. The matter of the little spy is of no consequence now."

Darwan snorted aloud, though he tried to stop himself. He was confused at most of the conversation, but the idea that his entire mission was inconsequential offended him. Luckily, the king had not noticed his emotion. The queen scowled at Darwan, though, so he knew the king would hear of it soon.

"Darwan," the king said, "what are we to do with you? You've completed what you started in our last battle. You've lost your entire command." The king said it in amusement, and the other lords laughed along with him. Darwan saw no humor in it.

"I am at your command, Your Majesty, as I have always been." He wanted to tell the king it was his orders that had cost him his command, but he choked back the words.

"Of course you are," Arta Nakis said with a grin. "At the moment, I need you to deliver a message for me. You will ride east to Rivermar and give this to Lord Enigo, and only to him." Arta Nakis put a sealed leather tube on the table and pushed it toward Darwan.

"The Crotans control Rivermar," Darwan stated.

"King Alarak has left the defense of Rivermar to the Navataw, and I have reached an accommodation with them." Arta Nakis seemed pleased with himself. The lords weren't listening to the conversation, so Darwan figured they already knew of the king's plans. "My army is concentrated here," said Arta Nakis. "We will march to Rivermar tomorrow, and should be there in seven days. I expect you to be there well ahead of us to prepare the way." The king motioned to a servant and said, "Show Lord Darwan to suitable quarters."

Darwan skulked after the servant. They walked a short distance past the market and to an inn. Darwan ignored the servant as he showed him to a small room at the back of the inn. This was what he had become? When this army had left Sarasin lands, he was the first lord in the line of march. He led the vanguard, absorbed the charge of the Crotans down that bloody hill, and even pushed them back. For his efforts, Arta Nakis relegated him to the rear guard, to pick up stragglers and discomfort the locals. Then the king made him a delivery boy, to bring that boy to the Crotans. Now his entire command was destroyed, and he was just a messenger—a lowly, common messenger. The war council continued with the other lords in attendance, and he was sitting in this tiny room alone.

The room was probably the smallest in the entire inn. It had a small table and a wooden chair. On the table was a single candle, melted almost to the base. The only other appointment to the room was a small bed. He settled into the chair and fumed, fingering his last cube of pyrus. For the first time in a long while, his anger outweighed his desire for the pyrus. He wondered how much farther he could fall.

His door opened without a knock or announcement. Darwan jumped to his feet, thinking it might be an assassin entering his room. Arta Nakis breezed into the room and slammed the door. It was a tight fit for both of them. "Have you seen Margella?" Arta Nakis tried to mask his urgency, but it was plain in his voice.

Darwan paused to consider the question, but knowing any silence might be interpreted as an answer, he parroted, "Margella?"

"Yes, Margella. I told her to stay in that house while I gathered the army. Her quarters were empty when I returned."

Darwan hid his surprise. He'd assumed that the king had sent Margella with him on his mission, but clearly he hadn't. With Darwan's entire warband dead, the king need never know her fate, and especially Darwan's role in her demise. "I don't know where she is," Darwan said. Technically, it was the truth, but that wouldn't keep his head on his shoulders if the king ever found out the rest of the story.

Arta Nakis was quiet, pondering with an annoyed grimace, and Darwan wondered what else he knew. The king always had more information than he shared.

"I fear she may have gone to that infernal city by herself," the king said. "She was obsessed with it. If she went there alone..." His voice trailed off, and he looked to Darwan.

Darwan offered no signals to him, not a nod or a shake. He just stared back intensely, hiding his joy behind a look of concern. "You could send—"

"Send what?" Arta Nakis demanded. "Send a warband? And tell them what? Who would I tell them to find?"

Darwan understood his predicament. The lords chattered like little girls, spreading rumors and speculations. Everyone would know about Margella in a matter of days. Then again, almost everyone already suspected something of the sort.

"You're headed east, Darwan. It will be a short detour. Check Rayl Goth for any sign of her."

Arta Nakis had no idea how hard it was to get there. The barrier was strong. One didn't just walk up to Rayl Goth. Things were easier when you were telling someone else to do it. In any case, Darwan didn't need to go there. She was dead. "I'll do my best to find her," he promised.

Arta Nakis seemed about to thank Darwan, but then turned to leave. He paused at the door, said nothing, and left. Kings didn't thank people.

Darwan exhaled, and the bare walls amplified the sound. He collapsed into the chair and stared at the lightly glowing cube on the table. Sweat sprang from his entire body. He didn't remember leaving the pyrus on the table. Had the king seen it? He gave no indication, and he was distraught over Margella, but if he *had* seen it, then Darwan was ruined. How could the king have missed a glowing cube in a dark room? Darwan swore at himself for being so stupid.

He scooped up the pyrus, placed it back in the tin, and secured it close to his chest. Standing, he looked at his armor. Covered in mud and blood, it was as hideous as this town. There was no one to clean and polish it for him now.

The common room was small, but seemed spacious after spending time in his diminutive room. There was a large hearth with a roaring fire, despite the warm night. He supposed the room was normally filled with farmers and travelers, but with the Sarasin army in town, lords populated the chairs and tables.

They were his peers, and many were below him in stature, but on this night, he felt below them all. They wore well-polished armor, and he felt the weight of the stares on his battered, filthy armor. "Wine," he said to the bartender.

"I'm sorry," the bartender said meekly. "We're low on wine, but I have beer."

Darwan looked around and saw many lords carrying goblets, and he was sure he smelled wine. He added it to the list of insults he'd endured, and nodded to the bartender.

He took his beer to a small table near the fire. In the already stifling room, no one wanted to be close to the fire. He sweated alone. The beer was better than the swill his men made on the march, but still left a bitter taste in his mouth. Darwan signaled for a second mug. When no one came, he had to walk to the bar to get it. He downed it at the bar and settled back to his table with a mug in each hand.

Darwan sensed shadows hovering over him, but kept his head over his beer. Whoever was standing there should go somewhere else. He heard a clearing throat, but still didn't look up until an unctuous voice said, "You look much the worse for wear."

Darwan looked up then. Prince Pevane stood there, scratching his fuzzy attempt at a goatee. Pevane wore a smugness that made Darwan want to check his belt to see if he'd lost any gold beads as he pulled out a chair for his sister and then seated himself.

"Prince Pevane, Princess Ayasha. I'm honored by your presence," Darwan said. Looking down at his shoddy attire, he said, "I am not dressed well enough to properly address you."

"We're not here socially," Pevane said, rolling his eyes. "My father ordered you to ride to Rivermar. I have a request."

Darwan looked around the room. The lords were watching, but they were too good at the game to let him see them watching. He looked to Ayasha, but she'd mastered the stare that looked right through him, yet never made eye contact.

"What might I do for you?" Darwan waited. *This is trouble.*

"I have a simple, yet discreet petition to discuss." Pevane glanced around to indicate the matter was not for prying ears. "You will be traveling east to Rivermar. I have... suggested to Prince Kaan that you should have an escort. I have made... arrangements to ensure the men selected are loyal to me."

By that, Darwan presumed Pevane meant that he had paid these men. With them along, he couldn't make a discreet detour to Rayl-Goth, as the king had ordered. Then again, he had no intention of going there, but now there would be witnesses to that fact.

"You will be assuming control of Rivermar," Pevane told him. "You will have... authority over many matters." He took a folded piece of paper and, with well-practiced sleight of hand, dropped it into Darwan's lap so no one saw it. "I have secured... a warehouse. The address is written on that parchment."

He hated the way the prince paused before saying what he thought were important things. Darwan looked at Ayasha, but her eyes remained aloof. The Prince must trust her enough to say these things in front of her, but it seemed unwise to discuss such matters in front of a woman.

"My warehouse is currently... empty. I would hope that you could use my warehouse to store such objects that might be of... interest to a prince. My men will guard the warehouse until I arrive and can make... arrangements for the goods."

"The king instructed me to accomplish some other objectives along the road, and it would be... complicated with your men along." Darwan threw in the dramatic pause to mock the prince, but Pevane seemed happy about it. "Does the king know of your... enterprise?"

Pevane kept his composure, but his eyes sent a clear warning. "I have been in the full council and in the private council, and no such orders exist for you. You're either lying, or—what were those orders?"

Darwan regretted his hasty words. Now the boy-prince smelled intrigue. "The matter was between the king and me alone. Either you or I could talk with him and see if he would consent to your knowing such things."

Pevane drew back, his eyes darting as though he was reading an unseen book on the table. He looked to Ayasha, but she gave him no more of a look than she did anyone else. The silence continued while Pevane considered the point. "No need to bother my father," he said after a pregnant pause. "I can assure you of the discretion of my men."

Darwan disliked being stuck in the middle of these royal maneuvers. "I should check with the king on this matter," Darwan said.

"I have influence," Pevane said, drawing close. His voice was as menacing as a young boy could muster. The pauses vanished from his speech. "What were the taxes on your lands last year? They might go up this year. They might double."

Darwan pulled back to make his own considerations of his predicament. He wasn't actually going to Rayl Goth, so Pevane's men wouldn't witness anything.

"I think I understand your instructions," Darwan said. "Your men will escort me to Rivermar, and they will gather whatever valuables we can find there."

Pevane smiled, but just for an instant. "Excellent." He got up and helped Ayasha to her feet. "If you will excuse us, I must escort my sister to her room."

Darwan was glad to watch them leave. He should have stayed in his own room. He gulped both his beers, and then stumbled back to his quarters. He opened the door... and there at the table was Queen Tabila. She wore royal robes of purple silk, her hair tied tightly in a ball at the top of her head. And he'd thought the night couldn't get any worse. Darwan took a knee before his queen.

"Can we dispense with the ceremony?" the queen said, sighing. "Sit."

"What may I do for you, Your Majesty?"

She sighed again. "Do you know how I got to be queen?"

There was no right answer to *that* question. Darwan cleared his throat to stall. He looked at her, and saw she was waiting for an answer. This was more dangerous than talking to the king or the princes.

She was still waiting.

"The gods have judged you and King Arta Nakis —"

Tabila let out a snort much louder than he'd thought possible. "Really, Lord Darwan, I expected more from you. You spoke with the king, here in your room. What did you tell him?"

Darwan reached for words, but found nothing but a stupid expression.

"I know what he came here for," she said. "He came about his filthy little rayth." She gave him a disappointed look. "It is my business to know something about everyone, and everything about some."

Darwan was glad to sit and listen, sensing the sharp mind lecturing him. The less he said, the better. "I know all about Margella," she said. "To be honest, I'm glad to have her around. When she's near, it keeps the king's testicles off me." She hinted at a laugh, but then drew close to Darwan, speaking slowly. "What did you tell the king about her?"

Darwan took a deep breath. She was so close he smelled her hair. It smelled like lightly scented rainwater. He tried to ignore it. "I will tell you exactly what I told the king. I don't know where the Lady Margella is."

The queen crooked her head and squinted at him. "She's missing? That explains much of his recent behavior." She laughed. Tabila stared hard into his eyes for longer than was comfortable for Darwan, which at this point was anything longer than the blink of an eye. "You speak the truth. I would—" Her eyes snapped back to his. She looked at him as though she were seeing him for the first time. "Strange," she said, raising her hand toward him. "But no." She let her hand fall, though her confused stare remained.

She stood up, reached into her robe, and tossed him a small parcel. She muttered something indecipherable to herself as she left the room. He heard a single word: *fayden*.

Darwan grasped the parcel. It was only three fingers wide and felt good in his hand. Neatly tied with twine, the parcel was made of rolled fabric, finely woven and clearly expensive. It felt smooth to his touch, as he rubbed it with his thumb. It radiated warmth.

He salivated and tore off the twine.

Pyrus.

He didn't even attempt to resist its grasp. Grabbing a cube between his thumb and forefinger, he tossed it into his mouth. Darwan closed his eyes and let the Red wash over him. *So many plans, and I must play a part in all of them. The Red will sort them out.* He stood up and walked to his bed to lie down in his reverie. *It will guide my steps to the path that leads through these machinations.* Closing his eyes, he gave himself over to the Red. All these schemes, the war, the lordship and High Lordship; they were insignificant compared to the Red. He'd worry about them tomorrow.

Chapter Thirty

Fayin dangled her legs over the side of the precipice. She dropped a rock and counted as the stone fell to the bottom. She made it to seven before she heard it smack a boulder. There were no mountains or rocky outcroppings in the plains, but she had found a rough ravine where a stream had cut a deep chasm.

Faylin had looked for her place, as Akwane had told her, but there was no place for her. Her fayden ensured she'd never be alone, but also that she'd never belong anywhere either. Humans didn't accept her, and she had no desire to live among wolves, or the tankadons for that matter. She wasn't a wild animal. She could be one for a time, but at her core she was human. If her only option was to live apart from the world, then she wasn't sure she wanted to continue. Her fayden understood, and though it didn't desire death, it wouldn't restrain her.

She sensed a presence, but knew it was her imagination. She'd scented the area before she sat, and there was no one nearby.

The only bright spot was using her ability to save Shari and Darwan. It felt good. She'd made a difference in their lives. Though she'd tried to help Tarken's friends, that hadn't gone as well. Still, she'd tried, and that felt good, too.

Again, Faylin sensed the presence. She twisted around to see a stooped figure standing a dozen strides away. He held up his hands non-threateningly. The old man wore a tattered brown cloak, and her eyes were drawn to his as she realized they were glittering in the sunlight. Faylin tensed and rose to her feet. It was one thing to throw yourself off a ledge, and quite another to be pushed. Stepping away from the precipice, she readied herself to shift into another form, but her fayden indicated no sense of danger. In fact, it welcomed the stranger.

"May I join you?" he asked.

Faylin motioned for him to come forward. He walked past her, and to her surprise, sat with his feet hanging over the edge. He was also a fayden, she realized.

Patting the ground with his hand, he said, "Faylin, please sit with me."

She hesitated, considering the man. A quick look around told her that no one else was in sight. Of course, she'd thought that before the stranger appeared, too.

"Who are you, and how do you know my name?"

The old man peered up at her. "I forget sometimes. The last meeting is the hardest." When she didn't move, he continued, "My name is Markas, and as you already know, I have a fayden." He patted the ground again. "Please sit. My fayden wouldn't allow me to harm you even if I wanted to, and I don't."

"What kind of fayden are you?" she asked, cautiously taking a seat near Markas.

"I'm a Fayden Fate. The most accursed of all faydens."

Meda's account flooded back to her, a mixture of intrigue and anger rolling over her. "You spoke to Meda. You're responsible for me being a fayden." She spit the words out with pent-up fury and almost shifted to her wolf form.

"No. You've always been a fayden, you just never knew it."

"I'd rather have remained ignorant than be like this."

He turned to her and fixed her with a stare. His eyes mesmerized her, flickering with multi-color flashes. Though she was naked, his eyes never wavered from hers. "Don't talk to *me* about affliction." His words were hard and full of anguish. "We all have our parts to play, and so we play them."

"I don't want to play a part. I want to be normal again."

"You and I both want that, but it will never be."

"What's so bad about your fayden? They said you walk in time. How is that an affliction? It seems like a blessing."

"I walk, but always backwards." Markas took a deep breath and continued. "I was much like you. My fayden didn't manifest until I was in my twenties. I had a wife and a daughter." He paused to wipe his eyes. "My wife was named Dena and my daughter was..." His voice trailed off into a sigh.

"What happened to them?" she asked.

"I don't know. I'll *never* know. You see, my curse is that I only travel backwards in time." He saw her question before she asked it. "Oh, I'm here now traveling with you forward in time, for a little while; but when I shift next, it will be back before I appeared here. I can never be in the same time as a past me, or a future me."

Faylin nodded, but then shook her head slowly. "I don't understand. You're from the future?"

"I'm from one future, but there are many, and that is my function. There are points in time where the fates may fall in many directions, only one being along the main path. My job is to ensure they fall in the right direction."

"How can you... how..." Her mind spun in confusion. None of this made sense, yet her fayden believed him.

Markas thumped his chest. "My fayden knows what must be done. It guides my actions."

Realization filled Faylin. He was truly alone, in a way unlike anyone else in the world, even her. He could never have a relationship, not even with a wolf.

"Can you ever return to your family?"

"No one I know has even been born yet. My first shift in time threw me back before my parents were born. I'll never see any of them again."

"How do you go on?" she asked.

Markas glanced at her with those eyes. His voice took on a steely resolve. "I play my part. I keep the timeline moving in the direction it should. It's the only thing I can do for my daughter, and I will do it until I die, if it means giving her a chance to live."

Faylin shot him a questioning glance.

"I know it's hard to understand temporal discussions. I've had the benefit of years of contemplation. If the timeline strays from my future, then the people I loved may never be born."

Markas stood up and dusted off his cloak. He closed his eyes and took a long breath. She saw him now as a frail old man, fighting for his daughter's future, and couldn't begrudge him. "You do this for her?"

He nodded without looking at her.

"Even though she'll never know what you've done."

"I think that's why my fayden waited so long to awaken. It needed me to be invested in my time, so I'd have a reason to carry out my tasks. Otherwise I might cast myself into a hole." He motioned to the chasm before them.

"I wasn't going to jump," Faylin said.

"Of course you weren't," he said ambiguously. "Anyway, my fayden scoffs at the notion, but I still think it's true."

"You talk to your fayden too?"

"We all do." Markas kicked a stone into the ravine. "Have you found your way?"

"Why does everyone think I need to find a way?" Faylin was tiring of the question.

He lowered his eyes and raised one eyebrow.

"I don't belong anywhere," she declared. "Why can't all faydens live among people without fear of being lynched?"

Markas pursed his lips and nodded to her. "Well, that's a noble ideal. Why *can't* it be like that?"

She tossed up her arms in frustration. "I don't know." She thought for a moment and then asked, "Is it like this for faydens in your time? Or was it? Or will it be? I'm sorry, I'm not sure how to ask that."

"No."

Faylin reeled back from him, letting the idea sink in. In his time, the future, faydens wouldn't be ostracized. A glimmer of hope rose in her for an instant, but vanished as she speculated how far in the future that would be. It could be lifetimes from now.

"I'll be leaving soon," Markas said.

"Why can't you stay?" Faylin didn't want to be alone again. When he didn't answer, she looked back into the ravine.

"Did I tell you about my daughter?"

"Yes."

"My daughter's name is Faylin."

"She has the same name as me." Faylin felt an odd sensation gathering around Markas, and stood to face him.

"That is no coincidence. We named her after you. Many girls share her name in my time. Now step away from the edge, and play your part."

Markas vanished before her eyes. One moment he was standing in front of her, and then he wasn't. Faylin didn't look for him. She knew he'd gone into the past, maybe to see Meda next.

She looked into the chasm one last time, and then stepped away. With a new sense of purpose, she stalked out onto the plains. She didn't know what her part was, or how to find it, but it was important. She was either going to find it, or forge it herself.

Chapter Thirty-One

Cayne tried to fathom Sir Burke's statement, but it sloshed around in his mind like incoherent goo. He'd said that he had killed Cayne's parents, but that was impossible.

"Let us not speak of this here," Burke said, putting his hand on Cayne's shoulder.

Cayne pulled back from his touch. "What are you saying? I'm not going anywhere with you."

"I'll explain it," Burke said. "But not here." He walked off the green and down a main street.

Cayne stared after him. It could be a trap, but he ran to catch Burke. As they walked, the crowds thinned, and he saw the Skykom River in front of them. In the growing darkness, the dockworkers unloaded crates and barrels from pyreships. Burke led him to a deserted dock and walked to the end.

Cayne kept his distance from the First Sword, his hand on the hilt of his weapon.

"I should explain before you do something stupid with the sword," Burke said. "It was so long ago, and yet it seems like only a fortnight past. King Alarak was new to his throne and eager to expand his dominion, so he looked north to the Navataw lands." Burke looked out over the slow waters of the Skykom, as though he were somewhere else. "The southern territories fell quickly after we took Gotham, but the north was stubborn and the land difficult. The king shifted from force to subterfuge. King Alarak made a pact with the lesser clans of the Navataw to bring them to power in the north. In exchange, they plotted against the Lord of Manteo, your grandfather."

"Lesser clans? Lord Enigo?"

"His father."

Cayne considered adding Lord Enigo to his list of retribution. He already hated the man for humiliating him, but now he had a true vendetta against him. He already had two kings on his list; what was another lord?

A season past and he'd have been in awe of anyone with a title, but now it seemed to him that the higher people rose in power, the more he hated them.

"King Alarak proposed a truce with your grandfather, and they met under the protection of the lesser clans."

"They betrayed him."

Burke nodded. "And many of his loyal shieldmen. Some of your kin didn't attend. King Alarak decreed that they all be hunted down and killed."

Cayne stared at him, mouth agape. He couldn't believe what he was hearing. Here was a firsthand account of the treachery that had destroyed his clan. With his parents gone, he'd thought he'd never know the story. Though he'd never met any of his distant kin, he wanted to avenge them.

"I captured your parents. Your mother was pregnant, and your father stood to defend her and a small child. I can only assume that was you. Obviously, I didn't kill them. I stowed them in a cart and escorted them far enough away that they could escape."

"They named my brother after you," Cayne said.

"So it would seem."

"Why did you say that you killed them?"

"Because those were the king's orders. Bodies weren't hard to find in those days, and I acquired some that passed inspection. As far as the king is concerned, I killed Nataniel Falconstorm and his family. If they knew of you, then my lie would be exposed."

"Are you going to kill me?"

Burke squinted at him quizzically, then burst out laughing. It was a deep, hearty laugh. Hearing it comforted Cayne. "No, but you can't tell anyone of this story, and for the sake of the gods, don't use the Falconstorm name. You're all supposed to be dead."

"What now?" Cayne asked.

"We do exactly as planned. We go to Barons Lodge and inform the king of the Sarasin disposition."

"You mean the king who murdered my kin?" Cayne said, with more enmity than he expected.

"Cayne, don't do anything foolish."

"You sound like my father."

"Apparently foolishness is one of your vices, then. It's not a good trait for a soldier. It gets men killed."

"Now you *really* sound like my father."

"Cayne," Burke said, waiting for Cayne to give his full attention. "I mean it. This is not a game. You could get us both killed."

Cayne thought carefully, understanding that his actions would impact Sir Burke, a man who had saved his entire family. He didn't want to disappoint him. "I'll guard my actions and my words, sir."

"See that you do."

They stood on the end of the dock looking over the steady, uncaring flow of the Skykom. They stayed for a time, not speaking at all. Cayne placed his satchel and sword safely away from the ends of the dock and sat, dangling his legs over the side.

"Why didn't you kill us?" Cayne asked. "I thought the Fist did whatever the king ordered."

"If the king wanted a murderer of women and children, then he should have sent assassins, not men of honor. It's a hard thing to choose between personal honor and duty. I was reminded of my honor just before I captured them. If I hadn't been... well, let's just say the decision was a close one."

"Thank you," Cayne said. "You know, for not killing us."

Burke flashed him an odd look and shook his head. "You remind me of my son."

"I'll take that as a compliment. Where's your son? Is he with the army?"

Burke looked sharply away and said nothing. Cayne sensed his misstep. "I'm sorry." Burke didn't look back for an uncomfortable length of time.

From the distant side of the river, savage howling rippled through the silence. An instinctive fear seize Cayne. He searched the darkness across the river. "What was that?"

"Tokiri," Burke said nonchalantly. "You get used to it after a while."

Tokiri were more stories from Cayne's childhood. He'd believed in them all when he was young, but as he grew older he saw them for what they were: fables to scare children and make them fear the night. Now he was seeing them again.

"Are there any myths that aren't actually true?" he asked.

"Most have at least a kernel of truth in them. Many have more than that. I'm sure some are exaggerated, though."

"I've heard the Skykom is so powerful that it pushes you right out if you try to step in it." Cayne pointed to the pyreships. "That's how those stone ships float."

"Do you have any rivers back home?" Burke asked.

"Just small streams, but Lake Haven is large."

"Have you ever floated in Lake Haven?"

"No, I sink to the bottom if I don't swim."

"You can swim, then?" Burke asked.

"Sure, I —"

Burke shoved him in the back, and he fell into the darkness. He smacked into the river, panic overtaking him.

Cayne poked his head above the water and heard rollicking laughter. A rope hit him on the head and he reached up to grab it. He hauled himself up to the dock and lay on his back. Burke was still laughing.

"Did you float?" Burke asked. "I guess you can call that myth debunked!" He was almost in tears.

"Next time you can just *tell* me."

"Can you use this?" Burke asked, picking up Cayne's sword. His serious tone returned, and Cayne considered jumping back into the river to bring back the laughter.

"I thought I was a good swordsman, but apparently I'm not," Cayne admitted.

Burke held a hand and pulled him to his feet. "We'll have to remedy that. There's a battle brewing." He looked Cayne up and down. "And for the sake of the gods, let's get you some decent clothes to wear."

"I think I look pretty good wet."

Burke rolled his eyes. "Come on. Let's get to a shop." Off the main road, they found the market. It was on a dirt path winding through shacks and tents. Most of the merchants were eating or sitting around the common fires drinking. They found a shop selling garments, but it was unoccupied—though as soon as they lingered to look at a tunic, a merchant appeared from the shadows. He had a line of grease dribbling from his jowls. He wiped his hands on his shirt and proceeded to sell them a plain red tunic.

After they exited the place, Cayne's steps were light. He felt a smile creeping across his face for the first time since he'd left Dahl Haven. Despite the coming meeting with King Alarak and the sense of battle on the horizon, he was free of the Sarasin yoke.

They made their way back to the green and walked toward the inn. Cayne tugged on his new tunic. "I look good in red, don't I?"

Burke gave him a pinched expression, but then he smiled broadly.

"First Sword," a young man yelled, as he ran up to them. "I heard you were back in town. Are we going to join the army now?"

Cayne tensed at first, but relaxed when he saw Burke raise a welcoming hand.

"Cayne, this is Tak from Weaverol. He'll be coming with us to Barons Lodge."

"You're joining the army too?" Cayne asked, as he extended his arm for a greeting.

Tak grabbed his arm and nodded. "The name's Rowtak, but everyone calls me Tak. I want some revenge on the Sarasins."

Cayne saw the eagerness and naivety in Tak. *That was me half a moon past.* He didn't feel like he'd grown up in that short time, but he didn't feel the same either.

"Cayne was in a battle with the Sarasins just yesterday," Burke said.

"Did you kill any of them?" Tak asked.

Cayne looked to Burke, but he gave him no hint at what to say.

"I killed a few," he said, fumbling for more substantial words.

"What was it like?"

"It was... unpleasant."

Tak's attitude faltered, and he squared his shoulders. "They killed my whole family," he said to Cayne. "I'm glad you killed them."

"I don't regret it," Cayne said, "but it wasn't enjoyable. It wasn't what I thought it would be."

"I want them to pay," Tak said.

"They killed my family too," Cayne said, looking him dead in the eye. The rage bubbled in Cayne, his momentary introspection dissolving to a distant inkling of doubt about the lives he'd taken. Then he envisioned the remains of his family in the grave, and all doubt was gone. Though he thought the Sarasins deserved to die for bringing this war, he said, "It doesn't matter how many I kill, it won't bring my family back. Or yours."

Tak nodded solemnly. "Is it worth it then?"

"I don't know," Cayne said, resolve growing in his voice. "I'll let you know after I've killed a few hundred more. They need to suffer. Whether it makes a difference or not... well, I guess it does to me."

Not all the men in the Sarasin army were evil. Some wanted to leave as much as he had, but they were all complicit. They'd cast their lot with the beastly king Arta Nakis, and they would bear the consequences. King Alarak was no better, and that knowledge rankled. Alarak was every bit the murderer Arta Nakis was. The idea of following a "just" king was folly. *Mother was right about that. Fools on a fool's errand for fools.*

Looking at the two men in front of him, he realized that it felt right to fight alongside such comrades. Sir Burke was a man of honor, and Tak sought the same vengeance that Cayne himself hoped to extract. If a battle was brewing, then so be it. He'd take as many of the Sarasins as he could before they struck him down. There was nothing else left for him but revenge. No family, no home, no life.

Burke put a fatherly hand both of their shoulders. "I'll caution you both. If you live only for revenge, you'll find it a hollow reward. There's nothing to it. No relief, no joy, and no end." He held their attention for a moment. "Get some rest. We travel tomorrow." He dismissed them both with a slap on the back.

Cayne gave them a mirthless grin and left. He found his room, but he hated the quiet and solitude of the wooden walls. He knocked on the door next to his and tried to push his way inside. The boys had blockaded the door with the bed, and were sleeping on the floor. He crawled into the dark room and took his place in the center for the last time.

He slept like a corpse until he heard a heavy knocking next door and recognized the voice of Sir Burke. He moved the makeshift fortification away from the door and peered into the hallway.

Burke raised an eyebrow. "I should have known you'd be there," Burke said. He waved his arm and turned to leave.

Cayne followed him to the green. It was still dark, but the sun was working its way up into the sky. Tak was already there, looking every bit as groggy as Cayne.

Burke handed them each a heavy iron rod and showed them several sequences of sword movements. Then he left them to practice.

Soon the rest of the Fist assembled to join them. After a time, even Sir Burke rejoined them to practice. For a while they sparred at half-speed, and Cayne found every one of them a vastly superior swordsman to himself. The only one he could beat was Tak.

Burke explained that they always trained when they were in camp. When Cayne told them that he'd not seen the Sarasins train even once, they laughed.

When the sun was full in the sky, Burke dismissed them to prepare for the coming journey. Cayne was glad to put down the iron bar. It weighed more than a sword, and it got heavier with each swing. But to Cayne's dismay, Sir Burke instructed him to carry the rod at all times. Doing so, Cayne gathered his meager belongings and roused the boys. They brimmed with excitement at the prospect of traveling on a pyreship.

Jaks was on the pyreship waiting for them. He wore his shining armor, and was arguing with a man on the deck. Cayne gave each of the Dahl Haven boys an arm grasp. Even the boys who weren't from Dahl Haven lined up to give him their thanks. Moments later, Jaks disappeared below the deck and reemerged without his armor. He handed the gleaming armor to Burke, telling the First Sword that he had wanted to wear it one last time. Jak spledged to rejoin them in Barons Lodge, but both men acted like it was improbable.

Cayne marveled at the pyreship in the full light of day. The hull was made of stone, and stood there like a sculpted mountain. If not for the gentle bobbing, he'd have thought it was connected to the bedrock like an ordinary pile of stone. The small fishing boats on Lake Haven were wooden. It made sense for them to float. Wood floated; stone sank.

The steam flowing from the tall pipes hissed louder, and the ship began to move. The boys stood on the deck, and he watched them move away down the river until they were unrecognizable specks. A part of him wanted to go with them, but there was nothing for him in Dahl Haven. A cold and rapidly expanding part of him was glad to be free of the responsibility he felt for their welfare. Now he could focus on his only remaining desire.

Somewhere out there, the Sarasin army lurked. He'd squandered his chance to kill Arta Nakis, but if the chance ever presented itself again, he wouldn't hesitate. Short of that opportunity, he'd exact whatever price in flesh he could render.

He walked toward another pyreship, where the Fist was busy loading their horses. Tak stood on the deck, practicing with his long iron bar. The fascination Cayne had felt for the pyreships just moments ago vanished. They were transport to bring him closer to his revenge. The training, too, was simply something to help him kill more Sarasins. The Fist, Tak, Sir Burke, and the whole Crotan army were nothing but a supporting cast to enable his vengeance.

Epilogue

Pain.

Ten thousand invisible needles pricked every patch of skin. Muscles shuddered, refusing to cooperate. Eyes burned despite being closed. It was *wonderful*.

Margella tore her eyes open, blinking the crud away. They ached like they were filled with sand.

She rolled to her side and shoved her legs over the side of the stone alter. The wound in her chest had crusted over with a thick layer of tough scar tissue.

The dark room had no decorations, and was unfurnished save for the altar in the center. Two dark figures stood on either side of the door. The first was large, too large to fit through the doorway without hunching over. The other was short, in a burly way. She couldn't see them clearly, but she knew they were both watching her intently.

Margella looked at her hands, barely visible in the greenish light cast into the room from the hallway. They were her hands, but they felt foreign, as though they belonged to someone else. She felt no pulse, heard no rushing of blood in her ears or anywhere else. Margella shrieked with laughter. She'd done it, succeeded where all others had failed!

Margella was no longer a rayth, no longer simply touched by the Black. She was *one* with it. The Black had fused with her. It guided her, acting through her.

The figures by the door waited in silence. Taking an awkward step, she stumbled. They made no move to help. She would have killed them if they had.

She walked between them and out into a wide hallway. It was a tunnel hewn from the stone. Rough floricite crystals speckled the ceiling, casting a green glow over everything.

The two figures stepped out of the room. On her left stood a drak, tall, with angular features and a poised stature. Its eyes were a sea of black with a disk of green, a telltale sign of its bastard heritage. Endowed by the Black, but cursed by the Green. At her other side a wark fidgeted, its black eyes marred by red irises that glowed faintly in the dim light.

The Tainted Ones sickened her.

Three mortals issued forth from a dark side chamber. She'd sensed them before they moved; they were rayths, two men and a woman. The Black knew them well, and in the recesses of her mind she remembered them. They'd been her peers.

"You've done it."

"Yes, Shada," Margella said, the name coming to her effortlessly from the Black instead of her own memory. The two males were Deezil and Wakiza. All three stared at her with reverence—and a hint of both suspicion and envy. She wanted to reach out and strike them down, but they were part of the Black, and she needed servants to carry out her will.

"I watched it," Wakiza said. "It could not have happened better for you."

Margella noted his use of *you* and not *us*. "I thought it would be Darwan that I would push to kill me. His pyrus habit made it easy to twist him to my will." She gave them a painful smile. "But being slain by a Fayden Blade was beyond my hopes."

"The Black Council awaits," Shada said. "They say the Black guided them here."

"I know," Margella said flatly. *Who does this rayth imagine herself to be? Who is she to tell me what the Black has done? I am* the *Black.* She shook her head and strode past them. The Black sensed the Council through the thick stone of this subterranean catacomb.

Every step sent stabbing pain up her legs. Her right foot felt like she was running over a field of broken glass. Her left felt like she was walking on hot coals. She savored the anguish of each step.

The wide hallway opened ever larger until the ceiling sprawled up to dizzying heights. Gigantic floricite crystals shone down like distant green suns. A complex of stairs and buildings stretched out beyond sight. This was an ancient Warkken city.

She wove her way up a dozen flights of uneven stairs worn smooth by millions of feet. She found a crowd gathered on a great balcony overlooking the vast abandoned dwellings below.

The Black knew them. The leaders of the nine great tribes of the Drakken. None could stand the company of the other; it was a testament to the dominion of the Black that they had not killed each other yet. The Warkkan stood in two scattered groups, the seven northern clans distancing themselves from the five southern clans. The north-south division kept the normal inter-clan hatreds at bay, their hatred of their immediate neighbors replaced by distrust of their distant cousins and the presence of the Drakken.

The Drakken stood tall and aloof, keeping serenely to themselves, but with a wary eye on their smaller counterparts. Though they appeared calm, the Black knew they were deeply distrustful of the Warkkan, and dreaded being this far underground. They were an outdoor people, living in the forests and rugged terrain of the north.

The Warkkan were stocky and boisterous, but just as distrustful. For them, enemies were a matter of perspective. They watched the Drakken with animosity, their distant kin with loathing, their neighbors with venom, and even their clan members with hostility. The world was a constant maelstrom of enmity for them.

It would take an iron grip to keep these races in line and working together. Margella would emphasize their scraps of unity. They were all touched by the Black, and that would be enough. She would replace their scorn for each other with a more repugnant and ancient enemy. The Dahla and the Traghs were out there. Also touched by magic, they were horribly afflicted by the White, a circumstance only curable by their destruction. The mere thought of those vile creatures made her want to retch. It was an affront to the Black that they still walked this world.

With each pained step, she drew closer to the gathered leaders. They watched her, but made no moves of deference or acknowledgment. She expected no respect until she earned it. "This is it?" one of the warks called out. "We've trekked all this way to see a human touched by the Black?" He spit on the ground in front of her. Warks could spit long distances, a particularly useless but often-used talent.

Margella smiled to herself. This was what she needed. "If you think me unworthy of your devotion, then kill me." She headed right for the wark, who still had a line of spittle running down his chin.

Foolishly unafraid, the wark drew a curved short sword. He raised it and shifted into a combat stance. The warks around him backed off to watch the spectacle.

"Come," she said. The wark stayed in his stance. She turned her back on him, knowing it would trigger a response. "We have no time for this."

She heard him move, but more distinctly the Black felt him draw on its magic flow. The Tainted Ones harnessed two flows. In the case of the warks, it was the Black and the Red. Magic powered their bodily systems: digestive, muscular, and the like. It made them powerful, but it also created a dependency.

She cut him off from the Black.

She reveled in his instant agony as half of the systems in his body shut down in the span of a heartbeat. The exact systems varied from individual to individual, but losing the support of half of your body was debilitating no matter which ones they were.

His torment was pure pleasure, and she drank in the moment, turning to watch his struggles. He sprayed black bile from his mouth, and his arms convulsed uncontrollably. The crowd watched indifferently until he stopped moving. *That was too quick.*

"It would appear one of the Warkkan clans is in need of a new leader," she said. "Hopefully, one with more guile than the last wretch." She put her bare foot on the dead wark's face. It was warm and slick, and she pushed it to one side with a contemptuous kick.

"Know this," she said. "You are of the Black, I *was* of the Black, and now I *am* the Black. I have joined with it. Everything the Black senses, I sense. I know all of you." She swept her gaze across the stony faces of the assembled leaders. "Resist me, and you resist the Black. Resist the Black and..." she nodded to the dead wark.

"But to know a thing is not the same as to experience a thing," she growled. She cut every one of them off from the Black. They filled the vast empty void of the chamber with tortured screams as every wark, drak, and rayth collapsed to the stone floor. She held it a moment, basking in the collective misery, and then let the Black flow back to them. *They will remember that.*

She turned to the rayths behind her. "What of the humans?"

Wakiza tried to stand, but fell to his knees. He gasped, "They march about, looking for battle."

"Excellent. Precisely as I intended," she said. "They sap their strength on each other. We will roll down from the northern forests and boil up from the ground itself. The pathetic human kingdoms will fall under our heel—and we will settle our accounts with the Dahla and the Traghs."

One of the draks raised a dark fist. "We have no need of subterfuge. We will crush them whether they are many or few."

There was a tone of respect and fear in the drak's voice. Margella didn't care about gaining their respect. "No. We should savor this time and enjoy the suffering we bring.

"How often do we get a chance to restore the hateful rule of the Black?"

Afterword & Further Reading

Warphan is the first tome in the Anavarza Archive set on the world of Anavarza. Look for other titles that continue the story as it expands out to the far reaches of the world.

If you liked *Warphan*, please leave a review or tell a friend. Authors live by word of mouth and reviews.

Want to read more about the world of Anavarza? Click on over to JDMulcey.com and check out the blog. In addition to lore about the world, you can follow the story of Lyssa and Nodin after they departed the main storyline. But wait, Nodin is dead, isn't he? Hmm, not quite.

I hope you enjoyed reading *Warphan*.

J.D. Mulcey is the author of the Anavarza Archive series of fantasy tomes. He lives in the thin air of Colorado with his wife & family.

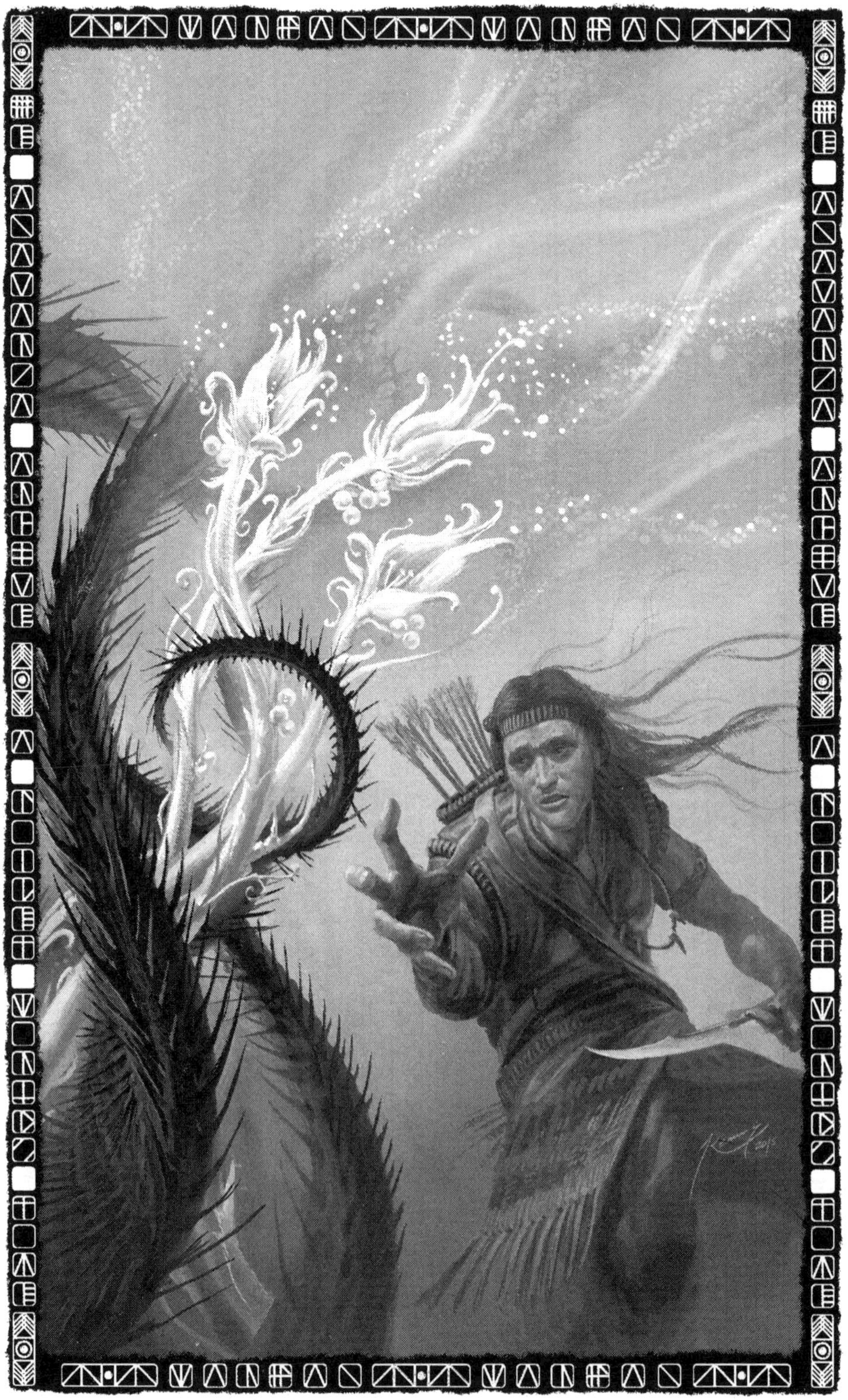

Made in the USA
Charleston, SC
27 November 2015